Lillelord

By the same author

The Red Mist

Lillelord

A NOVEL BY JOHAN BORGEN

Edited with an Introduction by Ronald E. Peterson

Translated by Elizabeth Brown Moen
and Ronald E. Peterson

JOHN CALDER
LONDON

First published in Great Britain 1982
by John Calder (Publishers) Ltd
18 Brewer Street, London W1R 4AS

This English-language edition is published
by arrangement with Gyldendal Norsk Forlag, Oslo

Assistance for the production of this volume
was given by the Norsk Kulturråd, Oslo,
whose support is gratefully acknowledged

British Library Cataloguing in Publication Data

Borgen, Johan
Lillelord.
I. Title
839.8'2374[F] PT8950.B713

ISBN 0-7145-3692-X

Typeset in 10 point Baskerville
Printed & bound by Murray Printing Company, Westford, Massachusetts, U.S.A.

JOHAN BORGEN'S *LILLELORD*

Johan Borgen (1902–1979), one of the major figures in modern Norwegian and indeed Scandinavian literature, is only now beginning to receive the wider recognition his work merits. *Lillelord* is the first of his books to appear in the United States and only the second to be published in England.

Borgen was, in many ways, the complete man of letters. During the twenties and thirties he worked as a journalist for two Oslo newspapers, *Morgenbladet* and, especially, *Dagbladet*. His literary debut came in 1925 with a volume of short stories, *Mot mørket* (*Towards Darkness*). He excelled in this genre, received national and international prizes, and published several collections. Borgen was also well known for his satirical and humorous essays written under the whimsical pseudonym *Mumle Gåsegg*—the first sizable gathering of these, *Seksti Mumle Gåsegg* (*Sixty Mumble Goose Eggs*), appearing in 1936. In addition, his first important play, *Mens vi venter* (*While We're Waiting*), based on motifs from Luigi Pirandello, was staged in 1938.

Borgen's first novel, *Nar alt kommer til alt* (*When All is Said and Done*), was published in 1934, but despite his early successes it was not until the Second World War that he moved to the front ranks of Norwegian literature. Because of his political views, he had been forced to spend part of the war in an internment camp after the Nazis occupied Norway. He drew on this experience for his *Dager på Grini* (*Days at Grini,* 1945) and for one of the earliest significant novels dealing with the German occupation of his country—*Ingen sommer* (*No Summer*), brought out first in Sweden (1944) where he spent the final years of the war.

The centerpiece of Borgen's literary career, however, is undoubtedly his Lillelord trilogy: *Lillelord,* 1955; *De mørke kilder* (*The Dark Springs*), 1956; and *Vi har ham nå* (*We've Got Him Now*), 1957. These three books brought him international recognition, especially the first volume, which has been translated into other languages. The trilogy focuses on the childhood and adult life of Wilfred Sagen from the period just before the Great War to the end of World War II, a time of vast cultural change for Norway, and depicts the main character's gradual moral and physical degeneration. In addition to describing the social conflicts which confront the hero, the author gives a strikingly vivid picture of the psychological forces that rage within Wilfred and ultimately cause his destruction.

Although not autobiographical, *Lillelord* reflects much of the life Borgen himself knew as a child growing up in Oslo (then called Kristiania) before the First World War—a time when life seemed simpler and more innocent than during the following decades of the twentieth century. Borgen was the youngest of four children in a well-to-do family; he lived on the "better west side" of the city, attended private schools, was accustomed to being waited on by servants, and spent long, joyful summers at his family's summer house on an island in the Oslofjord. His sheltered world included a good deal of music, art appreciation, and the reading of books and newspapers in foreign languages, particularly German and English. But as he matured during the second decade of this century, Norway was being drawn into a more active role in European political and cultural life by the war and by technological and other advances.

Lillelord carries the hero from his over-protected childhood as a kind of Little Lord Fauntleroy (hence the title), through an increasing awareness of "grown-up" activity and the disturbing aspects of his father's life and mysterious death to the point where he can no longer be called Lillelord and has to start a more adult life as Wilfred Sagen. The hero's loss of innocence is echoed by the intrusion of world events into Norway's peaceful life. Actual happenings such as the sinking of the Titanic and the appearance of the first fire truck and airplanes in Oslo are woven into the narrative, the most important innovation being the displacement of gas and kerosene lighting by electricity, heralding a new era, one where imperfections and criminal acts are exposed to a brighter, harsher glare.

The realistic details in the novel, however, only supplement the central ethical and moral questions posed by Borgen. Wilfred must come to grips with the consequences of class and privilege. He makes forays from the elegant neighborhood of his home to poorer working-class areas as well as to middle-class homes and rural areas. These expeditions expose him to the conditions under which other people live but increase his personal conflict. He experiences what can be called Dostoevskian guilt: at times he believes that he is outside society's norms and is thus permitted anything and everything, but at other times he recognizes his common humanity and moves closer to the notion that each person is responsible to and for all others. His search for his true identity, his overpowering feeling of impotence at not being able to communicate with other people about his inner self, and his vacillating attitude towards Jews are reminiscent (not coincidentally) of Kafka's treatment of similar topics. Wilfred's relations with Jews are in fact a significant aspect of the trilogy, especially his relationship with one of the main female characters, Miriam, who is Jewish and represents wholeness and harmony. Unlike Miriam, Wilfred is acutely aware of his split personality. Elsewhere, Borgen commented on this condition and offered the view (in *Innbilningens verden, The World of Imagination,* essays, 1960) that people have a natural tendency toward schizophrenia.

Lillelord is indeed multi-faceted and many-layered. At its simplest level, it can be seen as the narration of the hero's life from the late winter of 1912, when he is fourteen years old, to the late summer of 1913, when he is fifteen. On a deeper level, however, Johan Borgen is concerned with combining an examination of an individual psychology, sometimes disturbingly real, with more universal social themes set against the turbulent background of his own generation.

In the years following the Lillelord trilogy, Borgen published several more collections of short stories, another *Mumle Gåsegg* volume and brought out (in 1963) what is considered by many to be his best play, *Frigjøringsdag* (*Liberation Day*). He also wrote a number of novels—among them *Jeg* (*I,* 1959), *Den røde tåken* (*The Red Mist,* 1967) and *Min arm, min tarm* (*My Arm, My Intestine,* 1972). All experimental in form, these novels reveal the influence of Dostoevsky and Kafka, and deal with protagonists' quests for identity and their feelings of being split apart. Borgen also continued his journalistic and editorial activities, most notably as the editor of the literary journal *Vinduet* (*The Window*) from 1954 to 1960.

It is safe to say, however, that from all of Johan Borgen's many literary endeavors no single work better introduces him to the English-speaking world than does *Lillelord.* It is a modern Norwegian classic which could well become a universal classic of twentieth-century literature.

Ronald E. Peterson
Los Angeles, 1981

LILLELORD

1

His uncles and aunts came in, puffing from the cold. Their breath hung around their necks like smoke as they passed through the narrow entryway where the maid was standing and showing them the way in. Then they came tramping into the big, square hall with tapestries on all the walls and the head of an elk over the fireplace in the middle. It was warm there; they were inside.

Lillelord was standing on the carpet in the middle of the living room; he heard them coming through the closed door. He knew precisely what happened when they gradually came and inhaled the fragrance of woodwork and carpets and the discreet humming of the approaching family dinner, asparagus soup, trout, venison. He knew where and how Lilly, the parlor maid, helped them off with their wraps, how Uncle René said with gentle coquetry: "No, thanks a lot young lady, I'm not that old yet . . ." and went off with his sable-lined topcoat and hung it in the wardrobe to the left of the doorway, while round Uncle Martin—although he was much younger—let himself be helped with natural delight: anything that could make it easier for him . . . and his aunts, how they greeted each other quickly before the mirror, greeted a mirror image after it appeared—in order to shake hands so prettily right after that with the real person—how some of them said things about how cold it was and that there was snow in the air. Lillelord could see the scene in his imagination more distinctly than if he had really seen it and hear more fully and richly from the middle of the floor where he was standing, precisely where he should stand when they came in and where he would be the little host, in a way, fortuitously present when the maid opened the door in a moment. A ritual every time—so that his mother could come in from the interior of the house, a little surprised, a moment too late, the busy housewife . . . . He was standing in the middle of the floor and enjoying it. A nervous delight, because of the sociability just beginning, tingled all through him. He heard the train pass by—a train for those going out towards Skarpsno—right below the windows that faced Frognerkilen. Any other time he would have run to the bay window, which was a step higher than the room itself, to see the shower of sparks from the locomotive's high smokestack dance out into the dark winter afternoon, to go out later in the air or along the snowy edges on both sides of the roadbed, often far up in the garden, between the pavilion and the old fountain with the walnut tree towering right beside it.

Not today, no sparks today. Nothing more than standing in the middle of the floor because he should stand there, and because he enjoyed it, and someone would say, "The house's little lord"—it was Aunt Kristine who would say it, "The house's little lord, already in his place," she would say, and there would be a stupefying scent of cocoa and vanilla around her—or perhaps it was just something he believed because she made "homemade candies" in her tiny kitchen and had a sales outlet on Kongensgate, and everyone said she was "admirable"; she had once played the lute and sung in elegant restaurants abroad, and once someone had said that she was admirable, but perhaps a little, well, yes . . . and then one of these quick glances to the side from his mother who would say that there was a child here listening. But Mother knew that the child knew that Aunt Kristine's eyes became as soft as velvet after dinner and her voice hummed, and she calmly kicked off her shoes under the sofa and leaned forward with her décolleté like an abyss.

And he *saw* through the closed door how Uncle René intertwined his thin hands, which were smoothly lost in each other, when he was coming back from the wardrobe, and how he inspected his moustaches which were waxed on the tips as he passed by the mirror and, with a diminutive comb which appeared and disappeared in his magic hands—like everything that could appear and then disappear in his hands—smoothed his gray-blond, thin hair, smoothed it down over his forehead with one of those hurried movements those hands were created for, and how he would stand in the doorway a moment later and be on the verge of going in, while right at the last moment and with marked politeness he would yield to Aunt Charlotte, who in return would rush in with a silken song in her many petticoats—and Uncle René would say, "Mon petit garçon," and raise his dark brown eyebrows that Mother once said that he dyed, and wink down at him with a jocular twinkle that didn't really have any special meaning, but which was pleasant, which was right for the occasion, it too . . .

Then Uncle Martin, with his tight, striped pants that swung out stylishly from the prison of his waistcoat, would speak his piece about "masculinity"; but that was only after Mother had come in.

Only then—and a good while after the others—and he knew that it was to make a point of her modesty—his Aunt Klara would come in, black and insipid, and make herself more and more superfluous the more cordially Mother welcomed her. . . .

Lillelord stood in the middle of the floor and heard the noise of the train grow more distant. Soon the incoming train from Skarpsno would arrive and cast its long strip of light out over Frognerkilen for a moment; the ice there wasn't shiny, yet it was almost free of snow. And he knew that clamor from a world outside merely increased the trembling delight he felt *here, inside,* with all these people, the smell of venison, the recollection of the careful pop as the bottles of red wine were being opened over an hour ago . . . the glow of colored light from oriental lamps in the inner bay window. The light flickered over brass trays and sinister Bengal masks that were now quite pleasant—and porcelain dancers from Meissen, which were gracefully fixed in the uneven gleam of light and danced marvelously, forever and ever, on the bric-a-brac shelves, unnoticed by the adults who walked by them or looked at them absentmindedly, but not by the person who had identified their lovely movement, halting in the act of leaping, with a movement inside himself: something about to leap.

He knew every one of the people who were coming in, what they would say, and their clothes and the smells coming from all of them; he recognized each of his aunts by her perfume. And still it was just before the tall, white door opened—the door with the matte blue and brown decorated panels—this moment was almost unbearable because of the expectation. He had once wet his pants from sheer excitement right at this moment, and he had been obliged to greet them in his warm, wet velvet pants, but that was a long time ago; it was when he was eleven years old, three years ago. Now he was standing in his navy blue, cloth suit with the white linen collar, his ashen curls flowing down over it, in his patent leather, totally smooth pumps, his nails shining—he was standing as straight as a stick, in order to be there and to be the one who received the guests on behalf of the house; equally casually each time, but always just as full of celebration and excitement.

The incoming train was puffing over from Skarpsno. Immediately after that thunder from the train racing by increased under the windows. The sparks were dancing now. He knew it. He stood with his back toward the window and saw it through the three windowpanes; he saw it with his back. Then the clamor faded away in towards the city. The door was opened. Lilly's arm was visible for a moment against the door and disappeared again. Uncle René stood in the doorway and—a little surprised—yielded to Aunt Charlotte, who rushed in with a silken song in her petticoats!

He disappeared in them. He let himself be captured rather willingly so he could disappear in Aunt Charlotte's silken rustling, which was like the ringing of church bells close by when she clasped him to herself, to her waist. She gushed ecstatically then, and when he looked up Aunt Charlotte had tears in her eyes, and Mother had said that she wanted very much to have a child. Uncle René stood behind her during this gush of ecstasy. He came forward, bowed ceremoniously, took his hand and said: "Mon petit garçon. . . ." Then he raised his too brown eyebrows jocularly and let his hands disappear in each other while he walked toward the bay window and looked out towards Oscarshall. Soon—at the table—it would be time to study his phenomenal fingers when they transformed everything they touched, the thin stem of a glass, a fork, or when he raised his hand, almost transparent and therefore doubly commanding, to "say a few words. . . ." Everything Uncle René touched came to life and acquired brilliance. For a moment his hand caressed the icon over the arched portal to the oriental bay window. "Insanely placed," he muttered, as so often before.

Uncle Martin came in. At the same moment his mother appeared in the other doorway. Lillelord had pondered over whether this was an arrangement between them—they had once been siblings, Mother said—yes, they still were, but how could that fat man be her brother? Uncle Martin came towards him. Everything on him was curved and striped, as on that blue lady by Matisse that hung on the wall ("is that supposed to be art?"). Uncle Martin came toward him and greeted his mother over his head, grabbed his curls quickly and said: "Good Lord, Susie, isn't it time to clip young Samson's curls and let his masculine gender show through?"

He knew very well how his mother looked right then, though his own gaze was fixed on a point in Uncle Martin's pants, where the stripes came together in an exciting center and then fell vertically from it. Mother's eyes were cheery then; they were cheerily welcoming and irritated and full of affection when she looked down at him as he stood there and he knew about these eyes, though his gaze was firmly directed toward the exciting point in Uncle Martin's pants.

And Uncle Martin said with diversionary ease: "No. Dear Lord, if you want to continue to let the boy play Little Lord Fauntleroy until he's good and ready. . . ."

But now Aunt Valborg had come in behind her vast husband. She was tiny and was the only one who met Lillelord's eyes at the same height as his; she said: "Martin—!" in her gentle and authoritative way, which got Uncle Martin to stretch absentmindedly and say: "To each his own," and with sudden friendliness go over to Uncle René and confusedly contemplate the pink statuette so alone on its black column under the palm. Beneath Uncle Martin's gaze it became absurdly small, but when Uncle René lifted up the statuette and turned it in his thin hands, it grew and became a tale about a lady who struggled with a swan, yes she fought, but she liked it . . . it was one of the exciting things.

Aunt Valborg offered him her chubby hand and held his for a little while. Aunt Valborg's gaze didn't come from above. Therefore she was like a child. She laughed and said: "You're getting taller than me, boy—well, it doesn't take much." Aunt Valborg laughed at herself good-naturedly.

Lillelord walked over to the platform quickly, turned his back to the window, and said: "Welcome everyone."

"Too soon, dear child!" Aunt Kristine called out, only now rushing in through the door. She embraced him cursorily, filling him with the scent of cocoa. It was as if they took turns drowning him: Aunt Charlotte with her thundering silk petticoats, Aunt Kristine with her cocoa smell, Uncle Martin just with the sight of his splendidly curving paunch. . . .

"And in addition, Aunt Klara—!" Mother said and looked nervously toward the door, where Aunt Klara was now making her entry, in black with a white jabot, insipid, intentionally late, with her lorgnette on a cord, she quickly moistened her lips with a pointed tongue that was almost white and looked like ashes.

Lillelord left his elevated position in the bay window and went to meet her and asked ingratiatingly, because it was expected of him: "Oh, Aunt Klara, can I see your brooch!"

"Later child, don't be so impatient." But she said it with a friendly little pat on his cheek that showed both that she was mollified and that she was still and all a school teacher. She taught German and French and was rigid in body and in opinion. ("Like a grammar book," Uncle Martin said to Uncle René behind the fluttering palm—"just that none of the irregular verbs can be seen by her outward appearance.")

Aunt Klara took out her little lace pocket handkerchief suddenly and let it brush her nose. For Lillelord, that white, slightly arched nose and that little pocket handkerchief belonged together; and the scent of Maria Farina, which at that same moment swept through the stifling room like a refreshing shower. The veins on her hands formed the most delightful landscape—

like a picture in a geography book with rivers and mountains—they also smelled faintly of Maria Farina . . . so different from the beloved, heavy scent of Mother's own Beylie's Es Bouquet. *That* was kept in the next to top drawer of the bureau in Mother's room; when he was younger he could just reach the drawer with the tip of his nose when he pulled out the lowest drawer and stood on it. His mother had been closer to him then than she was now, here in this room where she stood and filled the empty space between his uncles and aunts.

Her scent was generous and omnipresent, not scarce and cooling like Aunt Klara's, which just flitted past each time she opened her little, pearl-embroidered, Bohemian purse and let the Maria Farina waft forth from its lace.

And he sensed a well-being because of these contrasts, a secure balance between all the things in his sheltered world. Now it was time for them to wander around each other a little restlessly and to examine each other absentmindedly, before the tall double doors to the dining room were thrown open by an invisible power, which he knew very well was the maid Lilly, and Mother would say: "Yes, everyone, if you please!"

The time had come now; it was condensed by pleasure and expectation. They were here. All of them. And he was supposed to bring joy to someone by making another childish approach toward Aunt Klara—because it was expected of him—and say: "Can I see your brooch, Aunt Klara!"

He said it, and she said, as she was supposed to: "But dear child, don't you ever get tired of looking at this brooch? . . ." And she drew the thin gold chain over her head carefully and opened the outer locket, which contained another one just like it, but a little smaller, and opened it, and it contained another one just like it. And he said: "Ohhh!" But even the innermost locket had a crack that could mean that it could be opened. Once Mother had said that it contained a photograph and that it was Aunt Klara's tragedy. And Lillelord knew that he wasn't supposed to know or to ask if it could also be opened. He knew it, like he knew a thousand traditional things. A good many things were givens.

His thoughts far, far away, he knew at that happy moment that there was also a world outside—the ice on Frognerkilen, the street, the school . . . and that the boys in his class were dressed differently when *they* had company. He knew it. He knew that they tore things down and they smashed windows and they got holes in their pants. He knew that at Andreas' home there weren't any bric-a-brac shelves with dancers on them, and that they ate herring on Saturdays, and that they didn't drink wine from generous glasses. He knew that some boys called him "sissy" because of his curls and different clothes. He knew that Uncle Martin's "masculinity" was a reference to that.

Once a long time ago, when he was ten years old—it was while they were drinking coffee and Uncle René's fingers were playing best with the thin coffee cup—Lillelord had said suddenly: "And then he fell on his ass and skidded on down. . . ." And Mother had looked like she was about to faint, and Aunt Klara's tongue slipped out and back into her mouth like the cuckoo in the cuckoo clock on the wall in the dining room, but Uncle Martin burst into peals of laughter and shouted: "Bravo, young man!" and squeezed a ruddy hand into his waistcoat pocket under his round paunch and fished out a ten øre piece; and the scene was interrupted by a panic-struck operation because the coin had to be disinfected with ammonium chloride before he could get it and put it in his piggy bank.

Lillelord had felt ashamed then. Not because of the word he'd used, but because he gave them a glimpse of a secret.

For he also knew something the boys didn't know, neither did his aunts and uncles, and not even Mother: he knew a lot of those kinds of words. He had a lot of those kinds of thoughts. He had a whole existence that was *like that*—and not at all like what they thought. . . .

The double doors to the dining room opened up, as if by magic. No hands could be seen. Mother said: "Yes, if you please then . . ." as if she herself were a little surprised. And they began to move, all together in front of him, all toward the door and the delightful scents that billowed forth toward them. And he brought up the rear and seemed to guide them into the Land of Goshen with little directing movements of his hands that they couldn't see. Almost without knowing it, he imitated Uncle Martin's rolling gait, and then Uncle René's gliding, elegant walk, and Aunt Klara's rigid, grammatical steps, and he made himself rustle behind Aunt Charlotte's gentle, silken thunder. He danced behind them with lovable disdain and felt brimful of happiness because of this dual mood of pleasing and scoffing. And right in the doorway, where he passed by the maid Lilly, he stuck his tongue out a little and at the same time made an embracing motion toward her while he drove his flock before him to the table, where the light from the candelabras fell gently over the bluish porcelain.

"Baa-aa-aa!" Lillelord bleated noiselessly behind the dear family that was going in to dinner.

2

Lillelord was standing by the east window in the dining room and willingly let the sharp morning sun cut into his eyes. He hadn't eaten and he felt a sickening disgust for the room itself, its scents, the thought of going to school. He heard the cuckoo ticking behind him and let every ticking second go through him like an ache. His sealskin school bag with the dangling straps lay on the high-backed gilt leather chair in front of mother's secretary. The rigid smell of learning was also noticeable this morning; it bothered him. He heard his mother coming down the stairs and knew that at the next moment she would be standing in the doorway. Irritation flared up inside him.

"But Lillelord, aren't you going to school?"

"Call me Wilfred," he said coldly, without turning around. It was completely unexpected, even for him.

"But my dear boy. . . ." Now he heard her steps coming toward him. His mood changed abruptly. He walked towards her with tears in his eyes.

"Forgive me, Mother."

"But it's already 8:30, and a little bit more."

"Mother. . . ." He let his tears come all at once—not letting go entirely, but just enough so that they gushed out and he felt a nice lump in his throat. "Mother, I can't go to school today."

She laid her arm protectively around his shoulders; they walked to the window together. "See, Mother," he said and nodded toward the wet, dark branches that filtered the sunlight. "Mother, I need a lot of flowers for my herbarium, blue anemone . . . several plants with rhizomes—no, it's not too early in the year—I can dig them out from under the melting snow on Bygdø."

"Then I'd have to write tomorrow that you were sick," she said. "That would be lying."

He knew that she had been won over. He knew it from her eyes. He knew it from everything on her, from her black dress; she was having one of her gentle days, one of the days she would go to the cemetery and remember his father. He shrugged his shoulders.

"It wouldn't be lying if you said I have a sore throat."

She also shrugged slightly, with exactly the same movement of her adult, rounded shoulders as his thin, childlike ones, a gesture of willfulness and irresponsibility.

"And Mother—" he walked behind her from the window into the room. "Call me whatever you want, call me Lillelord."

Mother turned around; she looked worried. "Maybe my brother Martin is right, it's time we began to call you by your real name."

A deep feeling of displeasure seized him, a displeasure because disturbing realities had come and were asserting themselves. He reached his arms out toward her, beseeching, and said: "Call me Lillelord!"

She sighed happily: "All right, if you want it that way, dear boy." Then she walked back to her secretary: "You'll need some money for the boatman."

She reached up into the blue china cup, the one farthest to the right of the cups that crowned the whole cornice, she took the key out of it and unlocked the secretary. The rolltop slid up marvelously; he enjoyed seeing things function in a well-oiled and attractive way. She took out her brown purse from the little drawer on the top, to the left, and took out two five øre pieces from the middle compartment with the little brass snap. The purse smelled sweetly because of the tiny book with the wafer-thin leaves of powder that lay in the open back compartment together with two tiny, pink pencil stubs, the remains of "dance card" pencils, treasured in acquisitive sentimentality from her youthful triumphs at grand balls. Then she shut and locked the secretary again and put the key in its place in the cup on the cornice.

"And you haven't eaten either?"

She pushed the button of the bell beside the buffet, which had carved cabinets and a luxurious silver centerpiece in the middle of an arrangement of silver chalices and Bohemian crystal bowls.

"I waited to eat with you, Mother. I don't have any appetite when you're not here."

And now it became true at once. He felt ravenously hungry, as one does when the worst is over. He felt uneasy about everything that would take place—but now it was like something sweet running through his back and up along his legs. Mother had hot coffee brought in, and mother and son rushed to the breakfast table with conspiratorial happiness, tacitly agreeing to postpone all unpleasantness.

"I don't think you ought to wear black today, Mother," he said.

She looked at him in bewilderment. He had expressed her own thought. He often expressed her thoughts as they occurred to her. "The weather's so nice; you can change, I think."

This "I think" was a bit like a secret code, a remnant of baby talk that had had a meaning at one time.

He got up politely as soon as she did. He heard her go up the stairs and into a room on the second floor. He went over to the secretary quickly, stood on a chair, fished out the key and unlocked it. A moment later he had four twenty-five øre and five ten øre pieces in his hand. Now, when he should put everything back, he was seized by a new thought. He took one of the "dance card" pencils from the back compartment of the purse, found a little piece of paper with purchases made written on it, and wrote—in his mother's meticulous handwriting—three expenditures for one and a half kroner altogether. Then he put it all back where it was, got off the chair, and went back to the window, whistling, just as Lilly, the maid, came in to clear off the table.

She stood still, amazed. "Haven't you gone to school yet?" she said.

"As you can see, dear Lilly," he said and turned towards her, beaming.

"Does the missus know that you're skipping school again?"

"Lilly, what a thing to say—" He walked towards her, smiling. "I'm going to Bygdø today to botanize; the weather's just right for it." She sniffed contemptuously. He came towards her: "You know, Lilly, after Mother, and she's so much older, you're the prettiest lady I know."

"Lady," Lilly sniffed, conquered.

"Yes, lady," he said stubbornly and stood peering at her, quite close. "You know, I think you're the daughter of some—someone highly placed, a minister or a wholesale grocer. Your hands . . . the way you move . . ."

"Are you starting that again," Lilly said and gathered the plates with her chubby, red hands. "You know what I think you are, you're crazy, up here." She pointed up at the golden lock in front of her maid's cap. "Totally crazy," she confirmed quite happily and sensed the minister's daughter swelling up in her.

"So give me a hug then," he said aggressively. She was standing very close to him now. She turned around quickly and bent towards him with sudden warmth. And with a passion she hadn't counted on, he buried his face in her firm breasts and drank her in quickly. Ashamed, she freed herself and straightened up. "I think you're mad," she said in a low voice.

"Yes, or crazy—let's say that." He walked away from her but then turned towards her, his eyes shining with excitement and desire.

At that moment his mother came in; she was wearing a light beige dress and gray shoes.

"Haven't you left yet?" she asked. He said: "I wanted to wait for you, Mother, so you could wave to me from the window. Yes, that's how you should be dressed today," he said quickly. "Isn't that so, Lilly?"

The two women exchanged a quick, confused look. He said: "I'll be going now—sweet Lilly, be a dear and make me three sandwiches; it doesn't matter what's in them, although one with smoked salmon and two with Swiss cheese would be fine." He went out into the hall to get his coat and hat. From there he rushed up to his room, where he stuffed the French flashlight Uncle René had given him for Christmas in his pocket. Mother and Lilly were embarrassed and avoided looking at each other while he was away.

Wearing his new gray overcoat, he walked slowly down toward Skarpsno. The boatman was sitting at the wharf, smoking. He wanted to see the money before he rowed him across. He was used to young boys. When they were partway there and just in the position to be seen from the dining room window back home, Lillelord half got up and waved. He couldn't see Mother, but he knew she could see him. He waved for a long time and said to the boatman: "It may be that I'll come back with you." He put the other five øre piece in the box on the seat in front of him.

"All the same to me," the man replied. The fingers that held the oars had the most remarkable claws and foreshortenings. The whole man resembled a domesticated animal that wasn't like anything else in natural history. The whole year, except when the ice was thickest in the winter, he rowed back and forth and took care of the traffic from Skarpsno to the little cove on the other side.

Lillelord went ashore quickly and stood conspicuously on the stone jetty for a moment. There were four adults there, waiting to go back to the city. He slid down into the boat behind them and hid himself from the sight of the house, in case anyone was still by the window. When he reached land on the city side again, he went over Drammensveien quickly to the first stop on the Bygdø streetcar line. He handed the conductor one of the ten øre pieces and got his five øre change. At the Atheneum he got off and walked over to the Grand Hotel, where he got on a green trolley that had "Grünerløkken" on it; he went up by the driver and followed the track with excitement, as it sucked them towards it. All his restlessness had flared up again, violently. He felt a delightful tingling fill his back and limbs. He stood and sang aloud to the accompaniment of the din from the streetcar. The day was new and in every way remarkable. And this was one of his secret expeditions to the places and districts that his mother and aunts didn't know about, and to the boys and adults that they perhaps didn't believe existed—dangerous, unknown districts full of dangerous, strange smells, and people who spoke differently, walked differently, were different, yes, some of them were quite *different. . . .*

Lillelord got off at Olaf Ryes Plass. He had been here before—four times—and on the same mission. He went into a gateway in Markveien and gathered his curls painstakingly up on his head and pressed his hat over them. Then he went over to Thorvald Meyersgate. There, and in the dirty streets up towards Dæhlenengen, he knew that he would find some boys, either in the vacant lots or along the street, carrying soup buckets or packages. Here he would get together with his unfamiliar friends who spoke differently and were somewhat *different.* Here he would partake of one of the adventures that cost him so dearly a couple of times, but which he couldn't do without.

He didn't search in vain. He had come into a dark and dirty street that ended with some gloomy piles of boards; behind them there was a construction site with buckets of mortar and scaffolding. He had noticed that they were there, in the dark doorways, already there when he was passing by. Now he heard their threatening and teasing shouts behind him; they had gathered in a flock. "Oily snob!" "Sissy!" And the perpetual, mocking shouts about something with "yer mother" that he didn't really understand. He swallowed drily, frightened, erect, walking with his back to them—and he heard the band behind him growing.

These boys spoke a language different from his; they went to school in the afternoon, something called Grammar School. They were somewhat different in every way, and he had detested them joyfully each time he met them. Today he chose to walk straight as a stick in his new gray overcoat and let them tease him till they were at the breaking point.

Soon the voices behind him grew more threatening; the boldest ones moved towards him, a couple of them were already so close they could tug at his coat, one tried to trip as he seemed to be just running by—it was a little guy they called the Rat and who smelled sharply of pepper; perhaps because he wet his pants so much.

"Don't dare turn around! Don't dare turn around!" they shouted behind him, louder and louder. He didn't quicken his step; he stopped himself from doing it; he wanted to run a little, but he resisted. He walked straight towards the enormous piles of boards that opened up a gloomy cavern before him that faded away in darkness. Dignified, he walked in front of them into the cavern. There was no way back from here. There were no adults here he could call on. Here he had to take whatever came, or win right away.

The flock was right beside him now. Some came forward and trod on his heels with every step. It got darker and darker inside the cavern, and the shouts behind him took on an undertone of oppressive hostility.

Just then he glimpsed the end of the cavern; he turned around abruptly, tore the flashlight out of his pocket, and turned its blinding beam of light straight toward the flock.

The effect was unexpectedly strong. The ones in front tumbled backwards. Those in back stood there and gaped. There were nine boys, an incongruous mass of wretched clothes and uncombed hair, dirty fists, and skinny, white faces, full of violence and hunger.

A gasp passed through all the boys. He turned the light off. The darkness flooded over them in red flames that blinded them. He turned the light on again—turned it off and stuck it in his pocket.

They stood opposite each other in the profound darkness. One boy from *his* world and nine boys from *theirs*. He had a momentary advantage. None of the boys had seen a flashlight before. None of them had electricity at home. He knew that. He had counted on it. It was his card. Now he had played it. The gasps of expectation and action were rife around him.

"How much d'ya want for the light?" one of them asked. Another said, almost respectfully: "Can I hold it a little while?"

Lillelord held the light out for the outstretched hand in the darkness. The boy couldn't get the light to shine. "Like this," Lillelord said and pushed the button. The cavern of boards blazed up like a fairy-tale grotto around them, and all their faces became strange and flickery. It was as if the boys didn't know each other any more; their solidarity was broken. Lillelord turned off the light. The boy stood with the magic wand in his hand, a magic wand without magic powers in his hand. Their faces quivered with agitation in the darkness.

"Let's see it," said a voice in the darkness. The flashlight changed hands. Lillelord knew that now—now he'll get the light to work. My power will be gone. Maybe I won't get the light back again at some point. "Well, guys," he said into the darkness, "whatta we do now?"

He heard a strange sound in his own voice; he heard that it was the voice of an unfamiliar boy, a Wilfred perhaps, one whose acquaintance he might make from time to time, and he felt this boy's power in him, his desire to rule.

"Here with that light," he said and stretched out his hand into the darkness at random.

A hand groped for his and found it. Once more he held the light in his hand, he let it shine for an instant. He quickly unscrewed the magnifying lens and took out the light bulb, then he screwed the glass back on.

"Here," he said. "Whoever wants can borrow it."

Eager hands reached out, struggled with the button and the little sliding switch; it passed from hand to hand. They couldn't get it to work, they were disunited, they accused each other of destroying the light. All the solidarity of what had been a flock of comrades, a band, was gone. He stood and felt faces turned eagerly toward him, waiting for a proposal, an order.

"All right, let me have it," he said curtly, he screwed things in properly and let the light shine for a second. He looked into boys' faces that had become warlike faces, ugly with lust for experience. Once he had suffered a defeat among these boys. Some had suggested they play a game with their caps, but he knew that if he took his hat off his hair would come cascading down. It had ended with a fight that was lost in advance—and flight through the long, dirty streets, where his pursuers had all the advantages.

He had to suggest something else.

"Suppose we try the dairy down on the corner," he said coldly.

"Jonsa's?" someone asked.

"Or the Cigar-Jew?" he proposed blindly. He knew there was a tobacconist's with a name that ended in "vich" some place down on Toftesgate. He took a chance on everything: an aversion to "Jews," an appetite for tobacco that he barely suspected, a desire for adventure or a need for goodies, the gnawing hunger of a child or an adult to break out and turn everyday life into something different.

"We'll try the Jew," a hoarse voice in the darkness said. There was an exciting smell of moldy woodwork in the vault where they were standing. The boys' dirty clothes and their excited exhaling increased the atmosphere's heaviness. He sensed in a brief, intoxicated moment that right here and now he could get nine boys to do whatever he wanted, even what they didn't want to do.

"You follow me," he said curtly and cleared his way through them. They backed away timidly and they closed ranks behind him, mumbling. And when they came out into the light, he knew, full of inner jubilation, that the transformation would last even when they came out into their familiar surroundings—especially then, everything would be changed for them, even the streets and houses they looked up at on both sides, only he—before all others—walked ahead, closely followed by two or four of them. He had an idea. "You can be adjutants," he said to those closest on both sides.

Whom had he meant? They began to shout among themselves. Strong guys, who had been somewhat in the background, pushed their way forward in front of the entrance to the pile of boards and asked: "What about me? What about me?"

"You're part of the guard," he said nonchalantly to the big hulk with the hoarse voice; he was the one who had trod on his heels, who had tried to work the flashlight. He heard the hoarse voice repeat: "The guard."

Someone in the back asked what they should do to the Jew. Lillelord had an answer ready: "For the time being we'll just relieve him of a few trifles." Some in the flock solemnly said: "For the time being." They knew it must mean that things would get worse.

At the corner above the tobacconist's shop it occurred to him that they couldn't all come in. He turned around quickly and faced the boys; they formed a circle. "Four of us will do it. The others'll scatter in the park for a while."

Their dull faces glowed in his direction; he didn't see them, not as faces. He saw them as oval discs in the sharp light, red mouths open, ready for his orders. All of them wanted to be one of the four. Or none of them wanted to. He quivered nervously because he knew this, and because he knew the ones who were chosen would tremble with delight and wish they were far away at the same time.

"You," he said and let his hand fall heavily on the hoarse boy's shoulder.

The one they called the Rat was already moving away, but it was too late.

"And *you,*" he said and caught the Rat with a hand that was now heavy with power.

There was one left to be chosen. All their eyes were cast down, with the exception of the gaze of a little, pale boy, beseeching, hypnotized. . . .

"Yeah, okay, you too," Lillelord said, as if he had talked himself into doing a good deed; the pale little boy sank under the grip of the hand on his shoulder. It was the beginning of everything. And the end.

He jerked his head at the rest of the gang. "We'll gather in the park—gradually," he said. "Anyway, take these!" He tossed several ten øre pieces at them.

They threw themselves at the money, and fought. Then they went, they left reluctantly, relieved and unhappy, doubting and believing at the same time.

The four had a brief conference, then they wandered by the shop on the lower corner and spread out, nonchalantly they peeked in. Lillelord took his position and waited till a customer inside came out. Then he nodded his head and strolled in indifferently.

The tobacconist turned politely from his shelves and looked inquiringly at the young customer.

"I'd like to look at some cards," he said and walked up to the counter. "And I'd like four Batschari cigarettes for my father. Four Cypriennes."

"Unfortunately, young man," the merchant said politely, "you are apparently too young to buy cigarettes."

"I have a note from my father," Lillelord said and reached into the inner pocket of his gray overcoat. He heard them coming, they were in the doorway now.

"Those cards on that shelf over there, I'd like to see those," he said.

The tobacconist turned his back to him and, limping and burdened, walked back into the shop towards the shelves.

Lillelord turned commandingly to the hoarse one.

"Take him," he whispered. "Hold him."

The hoarse boy didn't understand and just stood there. The tobacconist got up on a little stool now, to reach up to the cards.

"Do as I say," Lillelord said. "When I say *now*. And you—" he said to the Rat, "take the till just behind the counter, *there,* and grab what you can. I'll say 'now': *Now.*"

The hoarse boy jumped over the counter like a cat and grabbed the old tobacconist from behind. The Rat ran behind the counter and took some money out of the till. The third man—the pale little boy—retreated toward the door, white as a sheet. "Take this, and get lost!" Lillelord whispered and fished out a ten øre piece. The boy shot out the door. His big shoes clattered down the street. Lillelord turned towards the shop. No one was coming in now. The sun had left the area. It had begun to drizzle.

"Come out. Share it with the boys," he said harshly to the two frightened ones who were coming out toward him. Alone, he walked back from the closed door to the tobacconist who came tumbling out from behind the counter. For a moment, they stood facing each other, the fourteen-year-old in defiant panic and the sixty-year-old, embittered and afraid. Then Lillelord raised his hand to hit him. Two times. The tobacconist was stunned and retreated back to the counter. Lillelord walked quickly toward the exit and passed by an elderly worker coming in. He held the door for him politely and then quickly went up towards Dæhlenengen, away from the park where they were supposed to meet.

He paused for a moment at the corner, he knew that now—*now* the alarm would be raised, the shouts would begin, the people would peek out of the doors and stairways. They would go north and east, out toward the vacant lots, where the boys frequently were.

He walked across the street quickly; he had one chance, but it was the last one. He was in the next side street when he heard the shout. He ducked into a doorway, came into a courtyard that ended in a plank fence, where there were two trash barrels. He hopped up on one of them, threw himself over the fence heavily, and was standing in a new courtyard. He went out through the doorway and stood in a new street and tried to get his bearings. He heard the shouts now, several voices, but no words. He walked to the left, straight across the street, cut across the vacant lot there, and came to a place behind some tall tenement buildings. He found an opening and came in among some old wooden houses with an open space between them, with a pump in the middle. He pumped some water on his hands; they were bloody. He jammed his hat tighter onto his head and let some thoughts come forth. A crooked old woman came out from one of the wooden houses with a green metal pot, she was walking toward the pump. "Excuse me," he said and bowed politely, "could I have permission to drink a little water?" He bowed so deeply that the old woman couldn't see his face. She was overwhelmed by the unusual tone and wanted to go in for a cup. She hobbled in after the cup. All at once he didn't have the heart to leave her in the lurch. And when she came with the cup and he had drunk, he fished out one of the twenty-five øre pieces and handed it to her.

"Many thanks. You shall have this for your kindness."

The old woman stood there gaping when he went between the wooden houses and through a long alley between damp, wooden walls. He came out into a street where he had never been before. He didn't hear the shouts now. That was all far behind him, a place in another world. But that world could reach him if he wasn't clever. He walked steadily to the south, and a little to the east. He felt which direction he was going with his body. He came out by the fence of the Sofienberg Cemetery and went in through the gate there, because the street was deserted along the fence on both sides. The drizzle had turned into a dark mist. A little way into the cemetery he crouched down by a grave. Then he heard shouting again. It could be those shouts. It could be him they saw. He lay down by the grave and stuck his fingers into the cold earth and said: "Don't let them come. Not this time."

The shouts receded. It was as though he were a different person now. He read the tombstone: *Rakel Jensen*. . . . He knelt before the grave and said: "Thank you, dear Lord God."

He got up and hurried through the graves doubled over, to come out at the other side of the cemetery. Through the crosspieces in the picket fence by Sofienbergsgate he saw the black helmet of a police constable. The shiny point on the helmet shone unusually among all the grayish brown and leafless branches around him.

The helmet approached quite calmly and gave him an unexpected feeling of security. A policeman—he was there to defend respectable citizens, even in the unsafe and poor sections of the city. . . .

Lillelord stood up fully and walked erectly out of the cemetery, straight towards the police constable, as if he were seeking protection.

There were several seconds of excitement when he neither fled nor fought, but left everything to chance. If it went well now, then everything would go well. And if things went badly—that was something he had never thought about; it was a dark unknown power that he had given himself over to.

The police constable didn't pay any attention to him. He walked in his measured way along the gray-walled row of houses. The boy straightened up at once and felt the scornful expression come over his face. He was still balanced between the fear he pleasantly felt in all his limbs and the longing for his own things, for the secret security that he couldn't enjoy without having something to balance it. Already he was walking and imagining his cozy, bright home on Drammensveien with all the stuffy comfort that he loved; he imagined himself having a secret, another secret—evil deeds that only he knew about.

He went quickly down toward Schous Square to take the trolley home. Ideas popped into his head as he walked. He acknowledged them, took them up, and cast them away. He had done something now, hit a poor old man with his own hands. He didn't sense the least twinge of compassion or conscience. Because the danger wasn't over. He had to look out for himself. He had to protect himself against *something*. He himself had to create this *something* that he had to protect himself against, and he felt very happy with this whatever it was that freed him from the fact that everyone knew everything.

Soon—he knew this—his complete reality would consist of his mother and his home, and this . . . was something else, something left behind.

But only for a while, until a new, exciting idea would slip out, so that all his nice security would be risked in his other world, which had to be rich in excitement and contain things only *he* knew.

And as he walked slowly southward through the city's center

below, a good, benevolent sense of calm came over him. He walked somewhat brightly to meet things and wanted to do bright things. At a stationery shop on Øvre Slottsgate he went in and bought a sheet of paper, an envelope, and a ten øre stamp. He stood by the tall writing desk provided for the customers and wrote with Miss Wollkwarts' elegant, slanting handwriting, which made every letter a friendly being with a smile:

Mrs. Susanna Sagen
Drammensveien
Kristiania

Just a few lines to inform you that your son Wilfred is making excellent progress in all his subjects and distinguishes himself with his pleasant manners.

Gratefully yours,
Signe Wollkwarts

He posted the letter at the corner of Carl Johansgate, before he walked over to the streetcar by the Atheneum. Mother had truly earned this pleasure, he thought, and he let his curls fall into place below the edge of his hat.

3

The doorbell rang.

His mother lowered the *Morgenbladet* over her coffee cup and listened. Mother and son both heard the door from the corridor into the entrance hall open, and then Lilly's steps as she walked across to the little lobby.

The front door as it opened, the hum of the mailman's morning greeting, and Lilly's bright, laughing voice—Lillelord felt a warm sense of well-being at these ritual sounds. This was home—these sounds—they made everything feel like home, even the world felt at home. There was something about this certainty that simultaneously shut everything else out, made it remote, and forestalled the encroachment of reality that gave it weight in his nervously balanced world. This was the place where nothing could happen.

Lilly knocked softly and placed the mail on the corner of the table. His mother looked absentmindedly at the letters over the edge of the newspaper. Letters with firms' names on them, from a world that sought her but didn't break into her life, pleasant offers she could let herself be tempted by or leave alone, Silkehuset and Steen & Strøm recommending their latest creations for the upcoming court ball.

Then she fished out the only letter without a postmark. The slanting, meticulous handwriting on the envelope aroused so much curiosity that she opened it and read it quickly.

Lillelord scrutinized his soft-boiled egg. He was careful to see that every mouthful he took consisted of just the right amount of yolk and the right amount of white for the right-sized piece of toast, with just the right amount of salt on his egg spoon.

The grown-ups always laughed a little because he was so concerned about his mealtime joys harmonizing well. Then he felt his mother's eyes on him and reached out for his teacup that contained half milk and half tea, with a spoonful of sugar.

"Oh, my dear boy!" his mother said. He looked up with just the right amount of surprise: "What is it, Mother?" he asked. He seemed a tiny bit alarmed, and he knew it.

"It's—it's . . . no, I can't tell you." His mother put on a solemn expression.

"Is there something wrong?" he asked, his eyes slightly watery now. He was in fine form.

"No, my boy, there's nothing wrong, you can be sure of that," his mother said. Her eyes were shining now. She was so pretty. He felt sweet joy stream through him because he had made her happy.

"Well, surely you can tell me, Mother—I mean, if there isn't anything wrong," he said.

She stood up and walked toward the window, humming. She was filled with a happiness so great that she had to hide herself from him. No, a letter like this was between the school and her;

it certainly wasn't Miss Wollkwarts' intention that she should tell her son about their secret correspondence. No, she'd write her a letter, that's what she'd do. She would write a letter to his teacher and tell her how happy she was and that she must always take good care of her very talented little boy. And she would do more, she'd send Miss Wollkwarts a gift, something discreet, a pin perhaps—but something genuine, something really excellent.

All of a sudden she felt irresponsible and incompetent compared with such a school teacher—a person with an education and experience and reliable knowledge, all of the things that she had missed in her sheltered life. She was seized by a great pedagogic earnestness, by the need to impart something educational.

"Just look at this in the paper," she said, abruptly changing the subject, "think of the difference between the homes, the milieu—yes, it would do you good to know a little about these things now, Lillelord. . . ."

She settled herself resolutely with the *Morgenbladet* in front of them both. "Just look at what it says here—about some boys in a place called Grünerløkken. . . . No, I don't know exactly where it is, somewhere far away—and what do you think?—they broke into a poor tobacconist's—right in the middle of the day, just think of that, Lillelord—they *struck* him—and *stole* his money . . . and . . . yes, as I said, it's good for you to know that such things happen—just imagine, boys your own age, and younger than you: ten or twelve years old, it says. . . . Oh, my dear son!"

She had gotten to her feet again, overwhelmed by the atmosphere she had created. She bent over him and hugged him. "Poor, poor boys," he heard her say.

It was like listening to her through layers of felt. Nausea was rising in him. It had come too unexpectedly. That it should be in the papers. That she would take it this way, perhaps that most of all.

The nausea mounted, everything in him writhed, and before he could stop it, he had vomited onto the plate in front of him: eggs, milk, tea.

"Oh, Lillelord!" She stepped back, appalled. "I didn't mean. . . ."

"I'm sorry, Mother," he said, through tears that had been squeezed out by sheer physical weakness.

"No, my dear boy, it was my fault—I had no idea it would effect you so violently. . . ." She was standing beside him with a clean napkin and had rung the bell. . . . "Lillelord's suddenly gotten sick, Lilly, would you please. . . ." She gestured toward the plate. "It was my fault," she exclaimed unhappily, "I was reading aloud, about something raw and brutal in the newspaper here, about some boys. . . ."

But Lillelord didn't want to skip school that day. "It's over now, Mother," he said and got up.

"My brave boy," she said proudly, "but don't you think it'll be too much for you?"

All at once he could see the print of Lord Nelson in his bedroom: one-eyed and bleeding, struggling to his feet at the base of the mast while black cannon balls whizzed (though statically) through the air. "It's nothing to speak of, Mother," he said.

He stopped on his way out of the room, a little way from the table. There, on the edge, was the newspaper, a dirty piece of paper against the snow-white tablecloth: it was like a crime against the ivory-yellow purity of the porcelain; an unexpected echo of a world that was not allowed to exist when he was at home where everything was good. "No, Mother," he said again, "it's nothing. I feel just fine. I don't want to miss school for something so trivial."

That diverted her attention back to where he wanted: to the letter. She picked it up again and fingered it for a moment; she felt like it was something good and encouraging in a world that sent them such cruel messages.

"Have a good time, my boy," she said, as he left. "And give my regards to Miss Wollkwarts—for the present!"

There were sixteen boys seated around the table in the fifth form of Misses Wollkwarts' Private School. Misses Signe and Anette Wollkwarts divided the different subjects between themselves. Signe Wollkwarts, who taught Norwegian and religion, sat at the end of the table looking with concern at the row of fair and dark heads, heads with bristly, short hair or wavy forelocks, boys with jagged, dirty fingernails and boys with hands like kid gloves laid nicely on the tabletop in front of them. It was a day when collective absentmindedness reigned, and that bothered her most—more than ignorance and momentary defiance, more than a willful mood. A willful mood was, after all, Signe Wollkwarts' specialty.

Her concern was mostly for that well-bred Wilfred Sagen. He was never up to any mischief; he was well dressed, well brought-up, gifted, but he had a tendency to exaggerate that made his amiability almost a caricature. Could all that be because he had begun with a couple of years of private tutoring and had come under her discipline too late?

She sat and looked along the row of heads down to those fair curls that fell right down over the boy's white collar. She had thought about writing to the boy's mother about the advisability of letting him act so differently; she had consulted with her sister about this. But together the two Wollkwartses had come to the conclusion that their pupils' hair styles were a matter outside the jurisdiction of the Misses Wollkwarts' reputable "Institution for Boys, Providing an Introduction to the Subjects of the First Five Years' Curriculum," which was the way it was still put in the circular that was sent out in good time "before the beginning of the school year to a circle of families that might be expected to be interested."

The air in the classroom was heavy. The window on the opposite side was open a little way behind the tall, straw venetian blinds; but it was as though there was no life in the early spring weather outside. It was mild and calm and slightly misty. The words came and went in Miss Wollkwarts' mind: mild and calm and slightly misty—precisely the mental atmosphere in her own classroom that day.

It was time to go on to the "written part," which even for the higher grades in the Misses Wollkwarts' institution inevitably included penmanship.

Pens scratched in all the notebooks; the pens scratched according to models from Olsen & Wang, short sentences with a certain moral content: "A land is built on laws. The North Pole 90° W," was on one line. And on the next two: " 'Carry,' they said to the camel-bird. 'I cannot, because I am a bird,' it replied. 'Fly,' they said to it. 'I cannot, because I am a camel.' (Arabian Proverb)." The pens scratched. Miss Wollkwarts looked at her watch, a plump silver watch that hung on a thin chain around her neck and was tucked away in a pocket in her white blouse.

"Has everyone written it down?"

The boys looked up, expectant, timid, relieved. . . . On such days it was as if a mysterious obstruction lay over the assembled class.

"All those who have finished, raise your hands!"

Small, ink-stained hands were thrust into the air. A few ducked their heads down and reached for their pens in mild panic.

"Haven't you finished, Wilfred?"

"No, Miss Wollkwarts," he replied politely. And she suddenly realized that what got on her nerves was this self-assured politeness. None of the others called her by name and put her in her place, so to speak, keeping her at a distance with his correctness.

"And why haven't you finished?" she asked with unusual irritation. The boys sent frightened looks at her. They were wary of unexpected changes in her intonation.

"Because I haven't begun, Miss Wollkwarts," Wilfred replied in a loud, clear voice. Some of the boys grinned, others were terrified and just stared straight ahead.

During her Pedagogy Course at the school for governesses, Signe Wollkwarts had learned to count to five before getting angry. When this ritual was over, she asked, aspiring to be kind: "Why haven't you begun?" And when he didn't answer: "Let me see!"

Wilfred stood up obediently and walked quietly along the table. He held out his notebook with its empty page. The perfect examples shone back at her, all alone.

"But what in the world were you doing all this time?" she asked.

"Thinking." The answer came without hesitation or any feelings of guilt.

"Thinking—about what?"

"I really can't say, Miss Wollkwarts. I regret it. Regret it deeply."

But his head wasn't bowed as the other boys' were when they confessed something, and his eyes weren't lowered. Nor was she accustomed to her pupils "regretting."

"I don't understand, Wilfred. You sat there writing."

"I was *pretending* to write."

Was there a tiny, little ironic smile deep inside those clear, blue eyes? Was all this delicately chiselled innocence a cover for concealing depravity and defiance? She couldn't believe it. On the whole Wilfred was a conscientious boy, quick-witted, with an exceptional facility for expressing himself. Her sister spoke particularly highly of his ability in zoology and botany. But he had an aversion to pressing flowers.

Miss Wollkwarts controlled herself. "We'll have a recess now. After that, we shall have Bible history."

The sound of the boys rushing out, bursting with laughter, the buzz that turned into shouting and laughter as soon as they were down the stone steps and out in the open, gravelled yard that was framed by ancient lindens and a green board fence. . . . She loved this sound. It conveyed a message of natural joy and due respect. The Misses Wollkwarts were known for their liberal pedagogical principles, which allowed their pupils to play freely in the schoolyard—provided there was no violence. She peeked out through the venetian blinds, secretly keeping an eye on Wilfred. It struck her that he looked like one of Raphael's angels: his soft, regular profile, his curled eyelashes that were a little too long and strikingly dark against the fair curtain of his curls, his proud yet graceful carriage as he stood there under one of the linden trees. There was something ethereal about his figure, and yet . . . she didn't know; she wasn't familiar with his type: no submission, yet amiable and obedient, and still he didn't really conform. Something almost brutal in a model of refinement.

She couldn't handle that, and even worse, she didn't want to admit that there was something outside her experience and imagination.

Should she write a letter to that Mrs. Sagen? She had seen her once, at a concert. She had been there with Wilfred, and her sister and her husband. They had been pointed out to her by a friend, because of the husband, an old dandy as far as she could tell, the French type that was considered fashionable here in Kristiania, a man surrounded by talk and gossip. And she had thought: how strange, there's a certain resemblance—not really a resemblance but a sort of spiritual kinship between the elderly man and little Wilfred. And she remembered now—almost shamefully—that she had pointed out to her friend that she also knew those people: the young angel was her pupil, one of the very best!

Standing there, looking through the venetian blind, Miss Signe suddenly felt abandoned, abandoned by the Wollkwartses and by a world to which *she* had never belonged, which in fact she despised, but in which she essentially lived. Professor Wollkwarts had been one of those radical Darwinists who could afford to set his daughters outside the best society. Afford it intellectually, but not financially. He left them with the finest inheritance, a good education, but nothing else. They had taken up their pedagogical mission with a resignation that with time turned to happiness.

Miss Wollkwarts went out onto the steps and rang the brass bell. The boys stopped playing instantly. She noticed that Wilfred hadn't joined in. He was still standing under the big linden tree, observing the tumult with a look of absentminded irony. His pursuits weren't broken off abruptly like the others'. He was composed, as if he knew he was being observed; he then walked quietly up and inside. She saw him pass by. He bowed formally as he passed. One of the rules from the school for governesses popped up with vivid clarity: never persecute a pupil! Neither with suspicion nor excessive interest.

The class went smoothly, though there were some gaps in knowledge and little, comical misunderstandings that ought to have been an easy burden to bear for a teacher on a normal day.

Signe Wollkwarts knew that. And she suffered gladly a mistake or two about Jairus' daughter and Abraham's sacrifice. She didn't support the popularization of the different subjects, as in the version by Jenssen and Svensen. But on the other hand—if they were to be given the necessary knowledge of the Christian religion. . . . Her Institution could still be glad that it sent the best contingents to the High School.

The examinations weren't far off, and now it was time for a test that day. She began questioning them about the Annunciation. She reached the delicate point of the angel Gabriel. Involuntarily her eyes sought Wilfred who would tactfully provide the correct answer.

"So he said to Mary: I am the angel Gabriel . . ."

"Who stands for God," he answered.

"Correct, and then . . ."

"Then they cast him into the lions' den."

She stared at him to see if he was trying to sabotage the test: "That was someone else, Wilfred."

Wilfred met her gaze frankly.

"I thought it was the angel Gabriel," he said.

"It was Daniel. The prophet Daniel. They cast him into the lions' den."

"Miss," a little boy said eagerly, sticking up a gray hand: "in the picture in our Bible it says that they threw him into the lions' *pit*."

"Well, den or pit . . ." Miss Wollkwarts fiddled nervously with the silver chain of her watch. "It's the same thing."

"But Miss Wollkwarts, could they really throw him into a pit?"

Eyes full of bewildering eagerness shone on her. She wanted to explain to them that a *kugle* was a bowl, and a *kule* was a pit. . . .

"But it says that *under* the picture!"

"Under Doré's engraving," Wilfred said.

Miss Wollkwarts suddenly felt inexplicably furious. "Wilfred," she said, "that doesn't concern us. It's quite true that the picture you mean depicts Daniel in the lions' den or pit; it was made by the Frenchman Gustave Doré, 1833 to 1883. But it has nothing to do with the angel Gabriel."

She saw his face turned straight towards her now. It was as though it grew into another face, into a portrait she had seen somewhere, the Pinakothek in Munich, or a gallery at the Vatican. . . .

Unashamed, he said loudly: "I was mistaken. Please forgive me, Miss Wollkwarts."

As she went on asking her questions, she thought: I must write that letter. It won't be pleasant, but I have to do it. These people are full of pride. Suddenly her whole gentle being was filled with a spirit of defiance she hadn't felt for a long time. Appalled, she thought: Is it because they're rich?

The door to the classroom next door opened. Miss Anette Wollkwarts was standing in the doorway. She took a few steps toward her sister. "Excuse me, Signe," she said, "but I need a pupil from your class—from your fifth form—to tell mine about the phylum of vertebrates and the class of mammals." She looked toward the open door with a shameless smile—she had spoken loudly on purpose. "Could I borrow your Wilfred for fifteen minutes?"

Wilfred obediently got up, looked modestly at Miss Signe: "If Miss—" he made a slight movement—"Wollkwarts allows me, it will be a great pleasure."

The peaceful school was like a loaded shell. Even the rhythm of the reading in the lower grades taught by the assistant teacher in the other room paused for a moment or two, as if everything were communicated through the walls by telepathy. A transformation seemed to have taken place on the ground floor of the peaceful house. Miss Signe noticed it and thought that there were days when God was gone. Absentmindedly, she let her pupils repeat the same answers because she was thinking—and now quite maliciously: I'm going to write that letter, and I'm going to show it to my sister. She was already composing it in her mind. She knew that it was her duty to inform his mother that there was something brewing.

But it was one of those days when thoughts pass through walls, and feelings guess the thoughts and put them into words. As he stood by the blackboard instructing the fifth grade in an authoritative voice, pointing to the chart hanging there, Wilfred thought: She'll write home, I know it. She'll write this evening and mail it at the corner of Løvenskioldsgate and Frognerveien.

He realized it with that inner calm which is full of resolution. He was used to thoughts coming through walls; they did it at home too. It was just a matter of knowing when they did it. He knew it because of an infectious restlessness within him. He was used to paying attention to that—an anxiety that gave rise to composure. He stood there on the other side of the wall and knew—without having to wonder—that she was going to write home. And a blissful feeling of triumph spread through him because he knew more than they thought he knew. And that made him unique. He knew that she would write the letter that evening. He smiled contentedly at the chart of vertegrates and glanced serenely at the spiteful eyes of the boys who felt humiliated at being put in their places by his obvious knowledge.

He experienced the same pleasant composure that evening as he sat with his mother. She was leafing through *Die Woche,* he was reading an article on the physiology of angels in the *Shilling Magazine.* He had looked quickly, and with terror, into the big, matte blue kitchen where Lilly was taking care of his new, gray spring overcoat. She had two hot irons ready on the stove. He shut the door quickly and left the servants to their thoughts. He had just managed to greet Mrs. Frisaksen politely; she had come from the country to visit the maids and was perched on a corner of the dresser having a cup of coffee with Oleanna, the cook.

"I can't understand," Lilly was saying to her, "how the boy could get so dirty on Bygdø; he must have been lying on his stomach botanizing. There are some torn places too."

Oleanna was sitting on a short bench beside Mrs. Frisaksen, commenting on the worrisome news in the *Christiania News and Advertiser,* to which she subscribed; it was like her personal periodical.

"Those boys at Grünerløkken are just awful," she said to Mrs. Frisaksen. "Now they're putting the blame on a stranger, a boy who they say came there. The only trace of him was a packed lunch, some sandwiches that fell down inside a stack of boards when he pulled a flashlight out of his pocket. One sandwich had smoked salmon in it, it says here, and the other two had Swiss cheese."

Lilly looked up from her ironing board. She said nothing, but thoughts fluttered in her head and a feeling of uneasiness came over her.

And she said nothing the next morning when the postman rang and she found the little darling had gotten there before her; he must have been in the hallway and seen him coming.

"There were only some letters for Mother," he said, quickly going through the letters. Then he turned abruptly and looked at her beseechingly.

"You're not mad at your Lillelord, are you Lilly?"

Lilly tossed her head and walked away.

She didn't like to miss the postman, not for anything in the world.

She didn't see Wilfred stuff a letter in his pocket and walk in, humming, to give the rest of the letters to his mother.

4

Lillelord's hands were quite steady as he opened the letter. He sat on the edge of his unmade bed, his conscience not bothering him at all. He wanted to feel like a mother when he read the letter. Not *his* mother, but any mother. The experiment gave him a pleasant feeling of swaying on a thin cloud in a room full of transparent light that made things dangerous.

Mrs. Susanna Sagen,

I feel obliged to write you concerning your son Wilfred. Lately his behavior has been causing both my sister and myself much concern.

As both you and I know, your son's abilities leave nothing to be desired. In most respects he is far more mature than his classmates. He is also one or two years older than most of them.

But there are occasions when your son is so different from the other pupils that his behavior is unlike anything we have experienced. It is as though he is unable to realize what the position of a pupil at school is like. Today one of those awkward situations arose when he excluded himself from the circle of his fellow pupils. It would certainly be best for Wilfred to tell you what happened himself. This is, nevertheless, no isolated incident. Rather it seems like covert opposition to necessary discipline or perhaps to the school itself. I would like to ask you to forgive my having written, and I beg you most earnestly to take a stand on the difficulties that have arisen. Nothing would please me and my sister more than a talk between you and your son that could cause some improvement in Wilfred's relationship to the school.

Most respectfully yours,
Signe Wollkwarts

Cautiously, he put the single sheet of lined paper to his face and smelled the faint fragrance of school. The joy of something forbidden quivered in him; it filled the room and made it all different. The portrait of his father looked down from the wall indifferently, a little tired, his short beard above the high collar of his uniform made him look gentle and severe at the same time. Thoroughly enjoying himself, Wilfred slipped calmly to the door and locked it; then he straightened up the books on the table, and took a pen out of his pen case, listening carefully to the noises of the house the whole time.

Miss Signe Wollkwarts,

I have read your letter about my son Wilfred with some concern.

I can assure you that I will spare no effort in my attempts to bring about the change in attitude toward his school that you have so kindly suggested.

Meanwhile, may I suggest that you not mention our correspondence to my son or to anyone else.

Regards,
Susanna Sagen

After he had put the letter in the mailbox, Lillelord walked along the street with a sense of relief. The afternoons were starting to stay light longer, and that always made him feel happy and nimble, as if his legs were singing. He had taken a tiny, little leap and set himself beyond the fixed order—a tiny leap, but just far enough so there could be no jumping back, so that no explanation could save him. He was where he wanted to be: something had been done that couldn't be undone.

The streets smelled of fresh dust after the dull, rainy days that were now over. Everything around him was calculated to please, it seemed, just to please him, because he had ventured into something that was ready to burst. He decided to visit his friend Andreas, who lived on Frognerveien, in one of the top blocks of apartments right up by the park.

There was a piano in the living room at Andreas', a dreary, black instrument. They had asked him to play it once, because he was so good. He had screwed down the piano stool, which was up far too high and which must have been used for some other purpose. He played a mazurka by Chopin on the untuned instrument, which sounded so heartrendingly awful that he was doubly delighted by the impossible episode. Andreas' father and mother and his two brothers had listened solemnly, until Andreas' mother half stood up and said: "It's a bit out of tune. But nobody here ever plays. . . ." He had replied that it had an excellent sound; one or two strings could be tightened, perhaps, when they got a chance. . . . Her eyes darkened with gratitude for the breath from a world where people lied out of kindness.

He amused himself as he walked along by peeking into all the ground floor windows where he saw men in their shirtsleeves reading at dining room tables lit by paraffin lamps that cast sad shadows. In one or two of them he saw children tiptoeing through rooms, and the points of palm leaves from a plant hidden in a corner. He knew that the person bent over the table reading was the *father*.

It was because of him that they tiptoed. And the stern men whose pictures hung on the walls right at the edge of the light from the hanging lamps, these were probably their fathers' fathers; they hung there on the walls, admonishing their sons to continue the strictness.

He was filled with cool happiness as he walked along because he had no father. He felt a kind of gratitude toward his mother for letting him be alone with her. When he looked at the old photograph of his father over the pipe rack in the smoking room, it said less to him than the oil portrait in his own room. The short beard over the high collar seemed even more like a sign of that strength he was so glad to slip around him. Wasn't there something else in the portrait too—something almost the opposite? It occurred to him when he thought about it, but he always forgot to look, and he avoided doing so. He continued along, stealing looks through the windows as he passed, peeking at other people's fathers, and at other portraits on stern walls. Having such men in the house every day must lead to fateful things.

Lillelord remembered his father only as a thin cloud of cigar smoke in the hallway in the morning. It was a nice, agreeable smell that disappeared during the day. It faded away, like the memory of his father. He would always remember him as an aromatic haze, noncommittal and fleeting. And he remembered it with gratitude, because it disappeared and didn't linger with the threat of returning and causing a catastrophe.

Feeling lazy and happy, he walked along the melancholy, long street in the spring afternoon. He liked these dreary streets; they made him feel good. There was something about their long, drawn-out sadness that tempted the joy that was in him, far more than things that were meant to entertain him did, even more than a circus, for instance.

Now he knew why it had occurred to him to visit Andreas. He wanted to ask him something about their geography lesson for the following day, but he also wanted to sneak a look at his father. In the evening Andreas' father liked to sit in a dark brown rocking chair in the dining room; it was also the living room. When the boys came in, he put on a cheerful face, winked, and tugged at his thin brown moustache, which had a tendency to droop. Then he asked how things were at home and in general, and that suddenly made everything immensely dismal and dreary at Andreas' home. He liked to go there and revel in the dreariness for a while; it made the walk back home seem good and rich. He would still have the stale smell of the stuffy dining room in his nostrils to remind him of all the sadness he didn't have to share. That would put him in quite a good mood, a mood that made him forget that there was anything to be worried about.

The very smells on the staircase in Frognerveien made him almost moan with delight. It didn't smell poor, like the doorways in Grünerløkken, where he had been a thief. It was a *boring* smell. The word itself thrilled him. Each front door with its frosted glass and gray curtains on brass rods inside, the oblong brass nameplates, worn by polishing around the names engraved in an italic script that was meant to be fancy—it radiated a boredom that thrilled him because it contained the possibility of escaping. This time, as so often before, he didn't believe that he would actually ring the bell at Andreas' door. Panic and fear of the unknown would overwhelm him before he got that far. But then, all of a sudden, he was standing there, and he'd rung the bell; he was standing at the front door, afraid but pleased, staring at the gray pattern of the curtains inside. He heard muffled footsteps from the long corridor inside, where the forlorn brass hooks were; dead-looking overcoats hung straight up and down in eternal gloom.

He could still run away. He had done it once, panicked and happy, he had run farther up the stairs, while a dishevelled old woman's face appeared and looked around helplessly; then the old woman had shuffled out onto the landing in her slippers and peered down the stairwell—just as he had calculated. He was safe behind the next turn of the banister, keeping an eye on events until the old woman had shuffled back in again, muttering to herself.

But when he was back down in the street again, he felt a little sorry for the old woman in the felt slippers.

This time he stood there, letting the footsteps come nearer. The same old head—it was called Marie now—peered warily through the gap. The chain was still connected. He took off his cap and bowed deeply. "Good day, Marie. I'm sorry to disturb you. I only wanted to see if Andreas is at home."

He was looking at a face that suddenly was no longer old. It dissolved into an open, childish smile, though all the wrinkles contradicted the expression, as in a painting by Frans Hals that they had in the smoking room at home. "Well, good day, good day, it's the little gentleman himself, come to call!" the old woman said happily, closing the door momentarily to unfasten the chain. ("None of Andreas' friends is as well mannered as that Wilfred!") "Yes, Andreas is doing his lessons. Please go in."

It was exciting in Andreas' room. The three brothers shared it; everything was divided precisely: books, tools, pictures they had cut out. One of Andreas' brothers stuffed birds. Wilfred smelled the stimulating odor of formaldehyde the moment he came into the room.

"Does it smell awful in here?" Andreas asked. "I don't notice it."

"No, it's delightful," Wilfred said, sniffing deeply.

"Oscar's crazy about them. He's selling them to the museum now." Andreas looked up at Wilfred through his round, steel-rimmed glasses, glowing with bashful pride and ardor. Andreas was Wilfred's closest friend in their form, his devoted and somewhat timid follower. He radiated a goodness that you could almost feel.

The two boys had finished their geography lesson and were sitting across from each other at the worn table. It was that silent pause when each one guesses the other's intentions.

Wilfred felt a wave of shame coming over him, but he had no intention of going away unsatisfied.

"Your mother—is she still in the hospital?"

"Came home yesterday—but she's still in bed!"

"I should have said hello to your father. . . ."

The boys stood facing each other, uncertain. Wilfred knew what Andreas was thinking: Why does he always have to say hello to my father?

"I meant, to say good-bye—or perhaps good day?"

"He's having his afternoon nap in the dining room!"

"We could peek in; we can slip in quietly."

And then the same ceremony: two boys tiptoeing through the

serving area, the bench covered with an oilcloth and the tall blue cupboard with glass doors, the remains of a set of dishes from the old days staring asymmetrically through the small panes . . . the door of the dining room being eased open quietly.

"He's asleep. . . ."

Oh! That picture again: the man sitting in the desolate rocking chair, shoved into the corner under the palm, his left hand hanging limply over the *Intelligenssedlene* newspaper that had fallen onto the floor. His head drooping, his chin thrust into the grayish, starched shirtfront, and his moustache, which was supposed to stick up jauntily, hanging a little below the point of his chin, which was lost in his collar. Above him—half hidden by the palm leaves, yellowed at the tips—the framed photograph of someone who could have been *his* father. . . .

"We have to go!"

A voice whispering behind him. They have to go, can't wake him up. But Wilfred shook it off; he had to stay a few seconds more, to drink in the whole picture: on a little, three-legged coffee table with a white cloth, there was a moustache cup, the gilding worn off, in the saucer the stump of a cigarillo, carefully stubbed out before nap time; the white tablecloth was still on the dining room table ("We might as well leave it there till we've eaten supper!") with the brass lamp hanging above it, not lit now, but its furnished melancholy hummed in every curve of the candelabra and in the mysterious arch of the brass paraffin container.

A nudge from the back. A faint whisper: "We have to go."

The buffet! A miniature storehouse, reflecting a true buffet's excessive tastelessness with a poor sheen that made its severe shape ugly and meaningless.

Wilfred felt a tingle of nervous delight, the onset of anxiety: that it *was* like that, that it could be like that. He submitted to his friend's tugging from behind, closed the door and said: "I just wanted to greet your father, but I see he's asleep."

He looked at his friend's helpless face and the mute prayer behind the round glasses, a prayer that this wasn't the only reason for Lillelord's visit.

"I like it here at your place," Wilfred said. "It's so cozy."

A single, searching glance found confirmation in Lillelord's open, childish gaze. Suddenly Andreas' glance and his glasses became one in a glow of happiness. He said: "Yes, it's rather nice here."

They went down to the street together. It was almost dark.

"So, you'll come to my place someday, okay?" Wilfred said. He was Wilfred now. Only his eyes were boyishly hard.

"You bet!" Andreas said happily. "Wilfred," he added: "there's one thing I have to say: it's really stupid that some of the boys are afraid of you. . . ."

Wilfred raised his hand slightly.

The long street was like a gorge with solitary islands of light from the gas lamps. The brown, packed dirt of the pavement seemed cold and black.

"My Uncle René says when you feel you really have to say something—then *wait,* that's what he says."

"I don't care about your uncle. I like you. That's what I wanted to say."

Andreas saw a thin, white hand in the light of the street lamp. Was it Wilfred's? It rose above him, to one side, like a secret sign. Then it struck him—a tap on the cheek. Half chastisement, half caress.

Then he saw his friend's back a little way down the street, and dull anger boiled in him—against his will; he called softly: "Lillelord!" It could have been an insult; it could have been a term of endearment.

Lillelord didn't turn around. Soon he appeared in a pool of light from the next gas lamp. But he didn't turn around. Andreas thought: will he turn around now . . . but he didn't. Had he heard him?

"Lillelord!" he called, louder this time. But his friend was far away now.

Andreas wet his fingers with his tongue and stroked his cheek. Then he spat. His glasses fogged up and he tore them off. Then he clenched his fists and turned toward the door where they had been standing. A moment before that, they'd been standing there.

He struck his flabby cheek with his fist twice. Then he put his glasses on again and ran his hand over his face lightly. He stamped noisily up the three steep steps.

Wilfred walked quickly down Frognerveien. He measured his steps so that he never stepped on the shadowy edges of the rectangular patches of light cast on the sidewalk by the street lamps.

He did this automatically, but also consciously. He knew precisely the moment when Andreas' eyes left his back. He knew that this time he hadn't done anything wrong, hadn't exaggerated, just put things in their proper places. There had been some excesses, but they were exactly what he'd wanted. His whole being was filled with a peace that suddenly became so enormous that it fostered fresh excitement, and the expectation of unattainable sensations.

He didn't want to hurt Andreas, not at all. He wanted to make him his friend—but keep him uninitiated—to give him something, a gift, some alms, but he didn't really want to bother with him. He had seen his father now. He had inhaled the smell of formaldehyde in the boys' room. He would send Andreas' mother some flowers. He would fill himself with the joy of capitalizing on compassion. He knew that the maid, Marie—the old painting who answered the door and set the table—would help him with his good deed.

He knew too that he was satisfied by this joy when he had done it. "Let the devil dance, Uncle Martin!" he said out loud. "Let the devil dance, Uncle Martin. You're crazy about Napoleon. You despise Talleyrand."

He didn't really mean anything by it. But he skipped along as he was saying it. He skipped down Elisenbergveien and felt extremely happy under the birch trees there. He went on skipping, silently now, all down the street—till he passed the mail box. He made a face at it.

He signaled with his regular ring: one short and long long. He heard Lilly's steps, and his mother's—racing for the door. His mother was last. She beat Lilly by letting her win.

And he noticed the abrupt change in his mother's mood: so

glad because he was home—but then she had to be severe because he was late.

"Thanks, Lilly! Sorry, Mother, but I went to see Andreas, and his mother had just come back from the hospital and she wanted to see me so badly."

"Oh, my dear, good boy!"

And Lilly's quick look as she walked to the door into the corridor.

"Oh, yes, thanks a lot, Lilly, for fixing up my overcoat. I had to climb over a fence, you know, on Bygdø."

Lilly gazed at him, half relieved, half scared.

And as they went into the living room—through the other door, *their* door—"You know, Mother, there's something about coming home when you've been at a friend's house—even the . . . atmosphere . . . isn't that what it's called?"

But when he was standing in just his shirt beneath the painting of his father, he felt shivers running down his back. The whole room seemed to be spinning. He got up on the chair beside the bed, took the portrait off its hook, and put it on a chair facing the wall.

He couldn't fall asleep; he wasn't afraid about anything now, it was just that so much had happened that he couldn't get to sleep.

He turned on the light on his night stand and got up in his bare feet. He was cold. He went over to the desk and opened the righthand drawer where the big family album was. He turned the thick pages till he came to the photograph of a man with a moustache who was holding a child in his lap. *Father and Lillelord* was written under it.

He took a soft, yellow pencil from the pen tray on the desk and drew a short beard on the man in the photograph. Then he looked toward the portrait on the chair and saw the gray-brown burlap on the back. But he saw the portrait of the man even more distinctly than before he had turned it around.

He wrote *Father and son* in his mother's handwriting under the photograph in the album.

5

Could it be such a long time between three Thursdays?

Lillelord could be sick with excitement the whole day before one of Uncle René's musical evenings. Borghild Langaard had been there once. After Lillelord had played his little piece by Gluck, she had said: "That boy is exceptionally involved in everything."

He wasn't meant to hear that. Or was he?

Often the people whose pictures appeared in *Morgenbladet* came every third Thursday—but could there be such a long time between three Thursdays? Time was a hazy concept for Lillelord. He measured it in Thursdays. That also applied to keeping threatening things at a distance. Thursdays were good for that.

Yes, he had to keep everything that threatened him at a distance. Don't let them come, dear God, dear Mother, dear Anyone and Anything, don't let them come.

Or let them come. With a bang. Let the police appear in Uncle René's music room with the gilded legs on all the chairs. Let them appear in the middle of the room—two stern looking men with forked beards wearing uniforms and helmets: *"Is there someone named Wilfred here? We've come to take him away."*

He could see them; he could see it all. He saw the gaping mouths, saw them half getting out of their chairs, felt all of their eyes on him—like steel blades piercing his body—and he would get up from the narrow bench in front of the grand piano and say: "I'm Wilfred. May I be allowed to play my Mozart first?"

The music room had a high ceiling and white walls. Everything in Uncle René's music room was white or gold. Once Lillelord had thought it was heaven—the real Heaven, and even now he was still certain that God must have something like it in His heaven.

There weren't any palm trees in Uncle René's music room, no pictures on the walls, just a bust of Beethoven on the white chest with the protruding, decorated drawers. The chest also had curved gilt legs, as did everything here: legs that seemed to boast of lavish comfort and which had been allowed to harden that way one time when things were at their best: ro-co-co—it sounded like doves cooing, a contented sound, a sound of good humor, a festive mood that gradually spread to all of the people who poured in.

They didn't get a meal at Uncle René's, just tea and toast during the break. Before the break there was usually Bach and Brahms and the other B's. But afterward came the exciting part with Debussy and César Franck, or an unknown sonata, pure in style and somewhat tame, which everyone knew had been written by his uncle. But that was a secret, and God help the person who mentioned it. . . . There were the three regular musicians from the National Theatre's orchestra: viola, cello, and violin. Various guests played the piano, but never Uncle René; he kept to the violin or the flute. And Lillelord knew very well that sometimes they made fun of Uncle René a little, even though he played well. He thought that his uncle probably knew it too, but the strange thing about Uncle René was that nothing seemed to affect him. He was what he was.

Once a poet was supposed to come there and Lillelord dreaded it all day. He knew grown-ups who wrote music, but no one who wrote words. He thought it must be so unnatural. But when the poet read his poems during the break, it was like a piece of music. The man had broad cheekbones and very blue eyes that always looked at you for a long time. And when he read "Gobelin" and then a piece about a girl named Elvire who was going to a ball, Lillelord thought that words could be more than music because they were both music and words.

At other times the music seemed to tell a story: once they played Chopin's Sonata in B Minor, and when they came to the "Funeral March"—the world itself came to an end.

His mother had been reading out loud a lot from the newspaper then, something about a ship called the *Folgefonnen* that had been lost at sea somewhere. And Lillelord sat by himself in the twilight, and he heard the music tell about how the water rushed over the tilting deck and engulfed the people in its sad thunder. And he knew then, sitting there by himself, that nothing that really happened, nothing real, could be as great as the expression it found in notes that became words.

Words became music and music words, but it was more than that: they became everything. Everything was contained in the vault that words and music built up around him, and he knew that he was alone in the midst of everything in that vault, and that nothing could reach him. They could come now, the Misses Wollkwarts and the police and all the old women in Grünerløkken—they wouldn't reach him in his vault, they would continue to circle, fascinated, around him in accordance with a law that governed everything and made all things good in the end.

"And now here is a young man who wants to present his Mozart!"

He was going to play with the "orchestra." For the first time he was to experience the solemn twinge when the others began and then he was to join in and even take over from then on, and lead three grown-up musicians who played for money. He had imagined it many times, always full of exultation, yet frightened of the actual moment, and the continuation, when he was on top, sort of, and alone, the one the others made way for or followed.

But it was all so different. He could dream all sorts of things when the others were playing, put words and images to the music and make it mean something all the time. But not now.

He wasn't standing on a bridge. He was part of a math problem they all had to solve together. And when he joined in at the tangents, he wasn't leading them, he hardly played at all. It wasn't the others and him and certainly not he and the others. It was *them*.

They acted and counted together in accordance with laws none of them could control. And he embroidered his Mozart, following a pattern which he was neither able to choose nor to evaluate, just do right or wrong. And he wasn't nervous about making mistakes, as he had expected. He was ruled by a law.

His fingers obeyed, but there was something else inside him that also obeyed, a sort of certainty that accompanied everything that was going on then and there. For the first time, he wasn't hovering in his vault, among the essences. He was part of an instrument that was a part of a closed unity of instruments where one's expectation released the other's music, following a pattern that could continue into eternity.

And when they had finished and the fat little violist from the theatre stood up and applauded him right in front of his face, and the thin first violinist took hold of his hands and held them up to the light from the candelabra for everyone to behold, he wasn't tired or glad or proud, just filled with a gentle warmth that wanted to come out through his hands and head or his throat. He gave his mother a quick kiss on the cheek. Then he walked out of the music room and ran, almost terrified, to the bathroom and locked the door. Trembling, he sank to his knees in front of the toilet bowl and cried. But when he stood up and had blown his nose properly, he had enough presence of mind to flush the toilet with the porcelain handle, so that if the others heard the swishing, they would think that he'd been there and done something. Because he didn't dare let anyone know how moved he had been.

And the strange thing was that as the water rushed into the bowl, it seemed to sweep away all the Mozart with it, leaving him hard, cold, and a little ashamed. It had never happened to him!

It had never happened to him. He never wanted to play again for others to hear. Those people in there were a closed society, a congregation, and no one disclosed anyone else's misdeeds. Suddenly he realized that there was a line somewhere between the ordinary and the really good, and that he hadn't even approached that line and never would. He didn't know where the line was, or who belonged on one side or the other. He only knew that *he* would never reach the side of the really good. And he didn't suffer because of it. It was almost a relief.

He tiptoed out into the hall, got his overcoat and cap, and quickly flung the overcoat over his arm so that no one could come close and reach him again. He quietly pulled the outer door shut and walked down the veranda steps of Uncle René's wonderful old villa, keeping close to the rail. Now he could hear them playing again behind the yellow blinds. It was Debussy now. The muffled lament of his uncle's flute reached him on the road that led into town.

It was dark and pleasant under the trees by the road. He soon saw the glow of the gaslights in the city. Everything was quiet. Everything was good. He had sinned against someone or something, perhaps against Mozart. He didn't want to commit that sin again. He wasn't sorry, but he wasn't going to do it again.

All the other sins . . . a sudden lust for *everything* flared up in him and set him running in small, wailing leaps of joy and longing. A whole world full of forbidden things, and things that might be forbidden, and things that were almost permissible—a whole world of possibilities awaited him, and it was full of sins and sinners. He looked forward to all of it. He wanted to do everything in front of everyone and behind their backs. He saw a tall, elegant woman ahead of him—alone. He felt a desire to lay her down on the road and have her there, and he walked more quickly to catch up with her. But when he was right behind her, he didn't dare do it. He stopped, bent down and tied his shoelace to let her go on ahead.

But he knew that he could have done it, that he *could* do it, and a sweet pain in him was aimed at everything.

His cheeks burning and his throat dry, he reached the streets of the city and most of the agitation left him. The fear of everything he had done and all his discoveries gradually began to come over him again. But he chased it away, driving it off with dreams of desires that he revelled in and let himself merge with and disappear into. He carefully took stock of the possibilities. The next moment he felt small and weak, but also full of defiance and good, strong willpower. He was going to do everything, just everything.

But not play Mozart again so that people could hear.

6

Mrs. Susanna Sagen lowered her *Morgenbladet* and glanced shyly at the clock under its glass cloche on the mantelpiece. A tea tray laden with china and old silver was already arranged on the round table. Contrary to her normal practice, she had lit an Egyptian cigarette while waiting for her brother. "Martin," she had said on the telephone, "do you have to be so secretive? We can talk when we dine together on Sunday."

But Uncle Martin had insisted. He wanted to talk with her when Wilfred wasn't at home. So it was Lillelord he wanted to talk about, "as the boy's godfather and guardian in the absence of his father." It was a bad omen when he called him Wilfred. It was as though her brother wanted to take away her little boy when he spoke like that.

She didn't get up when the bell rang. During those last seconds of solitude she enjoyed the satisfied atmosphere of those rooms where she had spent most of her adult life. This *was* her life—with all that that implied—she felt like a sleepy lioness inside when she sensed a threat to any tiny part of her surroundings, and that included Lillelord; it even included the regular ticking of the clock on the mantel, every smell, even the unchanging temperature of the rooms.

Martin came toward her, smiling: gray tweed, turndown collar, and a large pearl pin in his tie. So, today he's the prosperous, English-style businessman, she thought involuntarily. She knew her brother's various phases. Each of his roles had an indisputable reality which—no matter what the disguise—was the same: a successful view of life that was suited to slogans like "common sense, practical point of view, stick to reality. . . ." She knew them all, she knew from her childhood that hadn't been very rosy, through a long adult life that actually seemed to have been almost too rosy.

"A cup of tea—?"

"Thanks." He picked up the newspaper that was spread over the chair he was supposed to sit in. He glanced at the section of *Morgenbladet* that his sister had obviously been reading, and read, still standing, in an official voice that was meant to express all the irony possible for his impractical sister:

> His Majesty the King danced the first quadrille with the wife of Cabinet Minister Lindvig vis-à-vis Admiral Dawes and Mrs. Inga Schjelderup, the first waltz with the wife of Squire P. Anker, Rød, the second waltz with the wife of Captain L'Orange, the second quadrille with Mme. Terres Rivas, wife of the Mexican minister, vis-à-vis Prefect Blehr, the third waltz with Miss Hagerup, the third quadrille with Mrs. Scheel, wife of the Supreme Court justice, vis-à-vis Attorney Heyerdahl, Christiania's mayor. The seance with Mrs. Kai Møller, esquire. . . .

"Sit down, don't stand there and be so unbearable," his sister said. "Is it really so ridiculous for a person to glance at a report about a court ball? There was a time when people actually had the pleasure. . . ."

"Who said it was ridiculous?" he said good-naturedly and folded the paper up again. "But I'd be willing to swear that you haven't looked to see the latest total of those who perished in the sinking of the *Titanic*."

"What you call realities, Martin dear," she said, pouring his tea, "are always sad things, never anything else. Really, what benefit is there for me in knowing whether exactly one thousand or even fifteen hundred people died on that dreadful ship?"

"You're right, you're so right. But what's interesting is that those people were sent to their deaths by a mania for breaking records and the desire for profits. And this business of the notoriously false reports that the ship was afloat and safe and sound that were put out so that certain people could have time to work the stock exchanges in London and New York?"

"You must have been reading *The Social Democrat* again," she said lightly. "Really, with your views, it's a little peculiar that you're so open to all kinds of propaganda put out by those people whenever anything happens in the world. But anyway, I'm sure it wasn't the court ball or the sinking of the *Titanic* that made you pause during your busy day in the office, in the middle of the morning, to come see your lonely sister in her widowhood."

A little embarrassed, he looked at her smooth, and in a way, too young-looking face, and while he helped himself to the stipulated two lumps of sugar, he struggled to maintain his train of thought in these surroundings that always overcame him at the same time as they satisfied all his demands for something pleasant.

"What I wanted to talk about is in a way connected," he said, "precisely with the unpleasant world of reality, if you'll allow me to say it, *versus* pleasant illusions. To put it bluntly, my dear, I'm concerned about Wilfred."

"About Lillelord?" It was almost like a correction.

"About our Wilfred, yes, your Lillelord. We're all so fond of the boy—you, his mother, I, his uncle, Valborg, his aunt, René, his uncle by marriage. . . . I don't have to tell you how highly we think of him—each in his own way, yes, each in his or her own way . . . well, let me try to say it now, let me, the one who takes a more practical view of things. . . ."

"Martin," she said, "you have an irritating way of making it seem as though you've been interrupted whenever you can't express yourself properly."

He looked seriously at the teasing expression on his sister's face. It was as if their childhood had remained unchanged in their relationship: they were always devoted, always detached, always on opposite sides of an invisible line.

"It really isn't so easy to express," he said faintly, and fortified himself by drinking the whole cup of tea. "The thing is that I'm not entirely certain myself what I want to say, but if you'll listen to me—well, then. . . . Take, for example, René, with all his magnificent interests: one day he finds it amusing to give the boy a whole course on his French Impressionists—with the result that today Wilfred has at the tips of his pretty little fingers everything about its development from Claude Monet to Gauguin via Van Gogh, from Cézanne to this Henri Matisse who . . ." he glanced bashfully at the painting over the sofa; it always bothered him that this sort of thing should be so remarkable. And now that monstrous Edvard Munch was going to fill the University with his daubings. "Please don't interrupt me."

She sat holding her teacup, self-confident, the same teasing smile on her lips.

"You're right. You didn't interrupt me. It's a bad habit I have. . . ." He pulled a silk handkerchief from his breast pocket and wiped his forehead. "But what I wanted to say is this: you all stuff him with painting, with music, and even with lectures on the vintage years of fine Bordeaux wines. You let him grow curls like a girl, you call him—well, well, I can see that much of this is both touching and—yes, educational, as they say. His Aunt Kristine stuffs him with candy, and more than that, with all her sugary essence which—you must excuse me—is rather foreign to us. What I want to say is that in the middle of a working day that requires a practical approach to life from the next generation and—believe me—this is becoming more and more necessary as the society in which you and I live so pleasantly is being reformed and *not* in our favor, believe me, as I said—in the middle of this working day, you surround the boy with an atmosphere of unreality, of longing for pleasure, yes, you'll have to forgive me now that I've gotten going; but the fact is that everyone loves him, we all think he's charming and gifted—and each and every one of us likes him because of our own special predispositions, but never just because he's Wilfred. One is almost tempted to ask: where is the boy himself, where is *Wilfred* beneath all this contentment, all this pleasure, these perfect social manners and the ability to adapt? Where is he? *What* is he? And what is perhaps more important: what will he be fit for?"

Susanna Sagen sat a little, looking straight ahead. The teasing smile was gone. For a moment she was overwhelmed by the same feeling of inadequacy that she had felt before when she thought of Miss Wollkwarts, the schoolteacher. But at the same time that this feeling arose, something else occurred to her, and her eyes filled with silent exultation that became more and more definite as her brother went on, and in the end the sparkle in her eyes brought him to a stop because he wasn't used to speaking for such a long time on these abstract subjects.

"You know what?" she said finally, getting up. "You've earned one of those light, morning whiskies that you Anglo-Saxons like to impute to their business friends."

She calmly walked into the dining room and returned with a bottle, siphon, and a tumbler. Uncle Martin looked with relief at the things in her hand and happily poured himself a drink, half of which he drained at once. He also saw a piece of paper, a very ordinary sheet of writing paper that his sister had in her hand when she returned. She held it out to him when he finished drinking. "Read this," she said quietly. Her hand trembled slightly.

Mrs. Susanna Sagen. . . . Just a few lines to inform you that your son Wilfred is making excellent progress. . . .

He read it through twice in order to gain time. Then he drank the rest of his whisky and read the short letter one more time.

"I'm glad," he said weakly. "Do I need to say that I'm extremely glad that the boy's making progress at school and that his teachers are satisfied with his conduct?"

"So, maybe it's not so bad that his own mother and a few others take a little interest in his, well, aesthetic education?"

Her voice was gentle and not triumphant. There was no need for exultation.

Martin stood up, took out his fancy gold watch, and looked relieved. He had carried out this errand and been—in a way—defeated. He ought to be satisfied.

"Susie, my sweet," he said, bending down to kiss his sister lightly, "I can't tell you how pleased and relieved I am. Thank you for listening to my views, which—I admit—seem less weighty at the moment. On the other hand, you know that I am the boy's godfather and guardian. . . ."

"And, as a man who deals in realities . . ." she added with her teasing smile.

He paused, concerned once more. There was always something

about her whole atmosphere that worried and irritated him, at the same time that he adored it.

"Susanna," he said, suddenly serious again. "There's one thing I've never been able to ask you—there are often a lot of other people when we meet, and besides. . . ."

"I didn't interrupt you," she said. She stood there in front of him, so self-confident and cheerful. She stuck the teacher's short letter back into its envelope with the neat, prim handwriting on it. For a moment his gaze rested on the address.

"You don't have to answer this if you don't want to," he went on, "but what exactly does the boy know about his father?"

She took a short step backward, then turned and walked toward the window. She stood for a moment looking out over Frognerkilen, where the ice had just recently broken up and the water in the fjord lay like oil in the warm, April sunshine.

"He knows what everybody knows," she said easily and came toward him, serious now, but without any anxiety. "He knows that his father was one of the noblest men that ever lived, a prosperous man besides, who gave his family and society all they could crave and who left a feeling of bereavement that those who were closest to him have found difficult to get over."

There were tears in her eyes as she said it, but her tone was so firm that it seemed almost defiant.

"Does he remember him?" Martin asked quietly.

"I don't know how much he does. After all, he was no more than five when. . . ."

Brother and sister were standing close to each other now. He laid his hand lightly on her cheek. "Strictly speaking, of course, it's not really my business. Well, we've talked about something that was occupying my mind. You let me talk about it and I'm grateful. And you have reassured me at the same time—in a way. . . ."

He broke off and walked toward the door, then looked at his gold watch again, turned by the doorway and said: "Is Lillelord at all interested in Oscar Mathisen?"

She laughed quickly. "What in heaven's name made you think of that?"

"No, well, it just seemed reasonable. Are you aware that he's won all his races again down there in Davos and beat his own world records for 500 and 1,500 meters?"

"You're the most amazing person," she said. "No, I wasn't really aware of it. And why should Lillelord and I think about this Mathisen?"

"Everybody does," he said. He turned toward the door again, feeling a little bad now. "All ordinary people do. They talk about it, they call him Oscar. Well, good-bye and thanks—no, you don't have to ring for the maid, I'll find my own way out."

On Drammensveien, Martin sat behind the wheel of his new car, a Peugeot, having first started the engine with the crank in front. He sped carefully in toward the center of the city, constantly squeezing the bulb of the car's horn. People still strolled casually in the streets and there was some risk attached to driving one of these modern speed machines in Kristiania.

He drove down towards Carl Johansgate. It occurred to him how unaffected the people here at home were, living in their own world; they went around thinking their pleasant thoughts and arranged their own little affairs without a trace of the passion and anxiety that had characterized the people of Leipzig, Berlin, and Paris during his last business trip to those cities that winter. How many of them were concerned about the level-headed article he had recently read in *Morgenbladet,* where B. W. Nørregaard pointed out that despite the British superiority at sea, the Germans would soon catch up with them in regard to those awful war machines, the dreadnoughts and the so-called super-dreadnoughts. According to Nørregaard, the two countries would be more or less equal in two years, at the same time that the deepening of the Kiel Canal would be completed. It would be to the benefit of the English, he wrote, to have a war now and not wait until 1914, if the politicians considered a war inevitable, and a lot of things pointed in that direction.

None of that seemed to worry the citizens of this well-fed city, which was so full of people who were far from being well-fed, especially in the eastern sections. What, for example, did his sister Susanna know about such things? Did she know that these eastern sections even existed? Or Lillelord? He probably didn't suspect that there were boys from a quite different world so close to his own, boys who didn't eat at tables with damask tablecloths or find clean underclothes neatly laid out for them on a chair twice a week. . . .

He tried to think about that letter his sister had shown him, but this thought couldn't get any farther than a vague feeling that something was wrong.

He had to slow down on Stortingsgate because of the number of people on foot, and it was even worse in Prinsensgate below the Atheneum. He steered toward his office on the corner of Tollbodgate and Skippergate, where his substantial import-export firm was located. Solid and substantial—but for how long? It was as though his uneasiness about *everything* was caused by the worries about his incomprehensible nephew.

The traffic was just impossible at the corner of Nedre Slottsgate. In fact, the crowds forced him to stop the car. He used the opportunity to light a cigar and look around anxiously from his high seat. The vehicle was shaking quite strongly beneath him, making it difficult to light the cigar.

A red monster, drawn by four horses and surrounded by a shouting crowd, was slowly moving toward him. He realized what it was almost at once: the fire department's new engine, the first one; he'd read about it in the papers. From his vantage point in his car, he followed the slow advance of this strange vehicle with interest; it was drawn by four strong horses and it paralyzed traffic as it advanced and the crowds rejoiced.

There was something about this sight that fit in with what Martin had been thinking a short time before—power that was still not being utilized here in Norway, people cheering the arrival of a new age without any clear idea of what it all implied.

The rejoicing subsided behind him. Uncle Martin tapped the ash off his cigar and drove on again.

Once more, he could clearly see the address on the envelope of the letter his sister had shown him, and it forced its way into his thoughts. There was something about the ink, the greenish-black office ink that was used in the city—and it looked quite different from the gentle blue ink used in schools. He didn't want to think about it, but it bothered him. Wilfred bothered him.

Other thoughts met him at the corner where his office was, thoughts about goods and exchange rates, thoughts from a world that also existed, and—as it seemed to him—with a clearer sense of reality than the fuzzy world here in his hometown. The smell from the coffee roasters on Skippergate tickled his nostrils pleasantly. *That* was reality.

Susanna Sagen stood in the bay window looking out over Frognerkilen. She was also affected by thoughts that bothered her. Not about Lillelord. She even allowed herself a little smile of triumph as she put the letter back into her desk—but this air of something foreign and alarming that followed her brother around—with all that travelling and those connections, his *world*.

Two quite different trains of thought kept coming and going through her head. Anxiety caused by being reminded too strongly of this *world,* of life in general—didn't she let it all slip away from her, day after day, year after year; on the one hand a simply useless being and therefore superfluous, on the other hand lacking the courage—or a sufficient appetite—to take part in that life, scarcely even its diversions. Though once she had at least travelled. . . .

And then the other thing that always alarmed her about this world, which she could stand less and less and which her brother—and others as well, for that matter—let bother their carefree minds: the fact that this oft-mentioned world of theirs didn't behave according to its own rules. Her gaze fell on the newspaper.

Not that people here in the blessed North were going to get agitated about a tiny war between Turkey and Italy; or about the hunt for those ruthless car thieves through the fertile land of France; or the fact that Amundsen and Scott were upsetting people's notions about geography by dragging the poles into the picture. But there was something in the atmosphere itself that had reached all the way to her home and more or less put an end to the isolation that she had always taken for granted. Previously this isolation was broken only when one wished, that is, when one wanted to go out and travel. And now to have to evaluate these phenomena here at home where life had been so good; that the Germans, English, and French were more or less aimed at each other, and you had to choose: if you preferred one, then you had to condemn the others. These countries with their wonderful big cities and memorable little places, these nations with the characteristics that you either preferred or disliked—all at once they had stepped out of a pleasant coherence that one had until now called "abroad." And now, suddenly, they started to concern her personally. Just as this talk of approaching war had been promoted from a social topic of conversation to one of those subjects that made men raise their voices over their whisky, even to the extent of forgetting that they were gentlemen. . . . That had happened. And over something as remote and irrelevant as that Kiel Canal. . . .

Her worries turned, without any transition, to domestic problems. . . . It was at the same party that the women had touched on the *servant problem*—should they be educated, and then all this time off that was suddenly being talked about. It occurred to her to take a liberal view. But then she also had her two good, steady servants, Oleanna, the cook, and Lilly, the parlormaid, not counting Åse, a transparent little creature who came in to help when they had guests. She had been lucky—here, as in everything. Who was it who had said that?

Kristine—of course. Another alarming phenomenon, this dear Kristine, the widow of her weak, refined younger brother who had died before he was thirty. She was another one of those capable people—whatever else you wanted to say about her. . . . Generally all these things that were irrelevant could get aggressive and try to break into one's sheltered world. She had been lucky. With her maids. With everything. And yet—all these alarming things. And that also included the maids.

One day that Lilly had shown that she could really be impertinent: it was about something or other that had to be done with Lillelord's clothes, some stockings—and this impertinent girl had taken the liberty of hinting that this "golden boy" caused a lot of trouble, or something like that, and that it wasn't so certain he was all that much better than the others.

Just some nonsense, of course; no one paid any attention to it. And the little creature had taken it all back again right away.

But all the same, just standing there, Mrs. Sagen had an unpleasant feeling that all these anxieties were collected in one way or another around her Lillelord, her beloved boy: the Kiel Canal, the distant countries that seemed to be coming closer, the servant problem, all this talk about the working class that had suddenly *appeared*. . . . Well, naturally, it was just because he was a child, he was the future, he was the one who was going to experience the things that the grown-ups almost seemed to be dreading now.

But still: how could her Lillelord have anything to do with class struggle and the Kiel Canal?

She shook off these questions. Was that the bell?

"Mother!" he called from the doorway, "didn't you hear me ring?"

She didn't recognize him at first, though he was standing in the light.

"Yes, Mother," he said and came toward her quickly. "I did it on my own, I mean Mr. Reinskou, the barber at Tostrupgård did it. . . ."

Only then did she realize—Lillelord had short hair; not exactly short, but his long locks were gone, along with most of his curls.

He puckered his lips at her, pouting like a child: "Don't you think it looks nice?"

His head was quite close to her now; she ran her hands over his bristly head. A thought passed through her mind: he looked like his father when he was standing there in the doorway. She'd been so deep in her own thoughts that she'd thought it was him standing there.

He turned his childish face up to her, waiting for her to kiss him.

"Yes, it does," she said and bent down and kissed him. "Lovely!"

"Lilly said I looked like a hobo," he said, and was delighted.

She pushed him away from her a little and looked at that dear head in the failing light.

"Lovely!" she said with conviction. "Now that you've done it. . . ."

He turned abruptly toward the tea table with the empty cups.

"Uncle Martin's been here," he said. "I could tell by the smell of his cigar. . . . Mother, are you unhappy about something?"

"No, dear boy," she said. "I'm not unhappy."

She suddenly thought about the Kiel Canal.

"You know, we'd been talking about it, Mother, that one day I'd have to get rid of my curls."

Of course—they had talked about it, like a lot of other things. It struck her that people talked like that about many things without actually imagining them.

"The barber asked me if I wanted to take the hair home. . . ."

"Did you get it?" A silly hope raced through her.

"No! Mother! What'd we do with it? It's good that we got rid of it."

Of course it was. Her brother Martin would like that, it corresponded to his ideas about being masculine. A big boy with long curls—that wasn't reality, that was a dream.

"I think it suits you very well, my boy," she said. But it didn't sound very convincing.

"I'm not a child anymore," he said, disappointed.

She was still deep in her thoughts. She heard what he said, but the words just floated around her—like so many other things. The Kiel Canal. It was just a phrase. An alarming phrase.

"It will be your first formal dance without curls," she said suddenly.

"Formal dance? Oh. . . ."

"Yes, you didn't think you could get out of it—even if you do think you're so grown-up!"

Her bitterness was noticeable now. Taken by surprise, he felt sad, he didn't dare disappoint her in this too.

"No, of course not," he said. "If you think we should have it . . . we can always say it's the last time."

"As you wish," she said curtly and walked toward the door

into the dining room. Those silly words were still trying to force their way into her life and be accepted. She felt tears of self-pity working their way up, warm and tempting. They would wash away those silly words like Kiel Canal, curls, grown-up, the last time.

Her son watched her, his eyebrows raised. Then he shrugged, walked to the window and looked out. In the transparent spring light, one suddenly realized that there was a world on the other side of Bygdø.

7

The event of the spring in those circles was the final dance at Wilfred Sagen's. Originally it had marked the end of the semester at the dancing school, now it had become an end of the season dance, a true copy of the grown-ups' world.

For Lillelord there were so many duties attached to these dances that he experienced none of the carefree gaiety he normally did at grown-up parties. Besides, all his cousins had to be invited as a matter of course, and that included Uncle Martin and Aunt Valborg's twins, Mikal and Fredrik, who had come home for spring break from the school in England where they were learning to be men of the world according to Uncle Martin's formula. Wilfred always felt that the two bigger boys were merely doing their duty for the provincials every time they attended a ball for the children. There was a bewildering mixture of outgrown sailor suits and imitation Eton suits among those present. The nucleus of the guests, pupils from the dancing class, was a helpless little group—if for no other reason than they knew each other too well and were already unmasked, so to say, despite their clean fingernails and glossy, patent leather shoes.

Lillelord had filled his dance card with an exemplary combination of Cousin Frida and Cousin Edle and the three overgrown daughters of a diplomat from across the street. It was always difficult to market them, partly because they seemed to be all knees and elbows when they danced and partly because they made no attempt to learn Norwegian. Lillelord acted for all he was worth, there was nothing else he could do with people his own age, who left him with no solitude other than feeling foreign. But his mother's eyes were on him from the doorway into the living room and Aunt Kristine's warm velvet gaze rested on him from her place near the buffet; in accordance with an old arrangement, she always came to help. And when he danced by in the dining room, between their watchful gazes, past the table that had been pushed up against the wall, he felt like it was a reward for all his acting and his efforts. Their eyes said: "my clever boy," "my little gentleman!"

It was a little embarrassing that his mother could never resist serving a hot supper before the cotillion, though there was a tacit agreement among the various households to restrict themselves to one sitting with sandwiches and one with cake, serving *bisp* and raspberry soda between the dances. ("If the children are to have half a ptarmigan each now that they cost eighty øre apiece, then it doesn't make any sense to give parties for the children!") And still there was whispering in the halls when the gong summoned them to the splendidly laid table, each "lady" with her "cavalier," as at grown-up parties, a glass of red wine already poured beside each place. All of Lillelord's infatuations at the concluding balls were interwoven with memories of ptarmigan sauce and a sort of jelly that tasted like wine, and a thick vanilla cream that he had stopped liking when he was older. There was something artificial about all this: the little infatuations he built up from year to year; the affected tone of playing like the grown-ups that had little to do with his real desire to act; the merry paper hats and the magnificent cardboard decorations that delighted the others and which his "English" cousins acknowledged with a joy he thought must have been insincere. All this was really far from amusing for *him,* but he was proud on his mother's behalf, as he never failed to emphasize in the little speech he made at the table. It was almost exactly the same from year to year.

The cotillion was over. The dances on the card were all finished. Young men, intoxicated by the food, had forgotten their bashfulness during this last, lawless half hour when the dancing was wild—the unruly finale when anything could happen. ("At Mrs. Sagen's they carry on right up to midnight. What's going to come of it?")

Lillelord—covered with orders—sneaked off to the depths of the smoking room and listened wearily to the uproar in the dining room. It sounded alien and childish to his ears now. It was his first spring dance without curls, and he knew it would be his last. There was an element of finality in everything around him, not just an end to his curls and the "season" but everything that . . . he didn't know. He stood there in the farthest corner of the room and didn't really know. His gaze fell on the terra-cotta representation of Leda and the swan, but he didn't know. It was treason on his part, not to be there with them, not to be having fun; he hadn't enjoyed himself all evening, he had just pretended. Suddenly he felt that he understood something; his mother had been so apprehensive that day. Uncle Martin had been there. There was something disturbing about Uncle Martin's visits. He knew about the world and made his mother feel insecure. For many years now he had been after his curls—Uncle Martin was in league with all the grown-up powers but he was no friend. Uncle Martin's little men had to go through a sort of machine in England; it made them fit for use in the city and in society, but left them without that inner solitude he longed for. . . .

Lillelord heard the din of the now unrestrained guests as he slipped out onto the balcony facing the garden and stood there looking out over Frognerkilen; it looked black and shiny beneath the stars now. Far out on the fjord a motorboat was chugging on its way from darkness to darkness. All he could see of Bygdø was three lights and the soft outline of the ridge by the Royal Forest. Aunt Kristine called it "Ladegårdsøen"; it sounded so alluring. The name became more mysterious because she said it, and it lay over the whole landscape at night, something exciting and illegal that she had perhaps hinted at, some sort of a Saturday sanctuary for the lower classes. Perhaps it was one of those quick looks from his mother—looks that could make people stop in mid-sentence and which she thought he didn't see—perhaps it was only these looks that made some sentences seem exciting and made his throat feel dry. . . .

He leaned over the railing of the balcony to fasten one of the dry climbing rose bushes that had broken loose in the wind. He saw that someone was sitting on the bottom step of the stone staircase by the garden. In the rooms behind him, they had switched to an uproarious two-step now; Mrs. Zimmermann at the piano was doing her best to bring the celebration to a noisy climax. The ringing of the front door bell had already announced the arrival of various servants who were now sitting sleepily along the wall in the hall or peeking stealthily at the dancers through the door—all sent out at night to bring home red-faced little girls with pink bows and overgrown boys in sailor suits who were ashamed of having to be escorted. They were calling for him somewhere in the depths of the house.

He sensed the usual ceremonial with his back as he leaned out over the railing to see better. The suspense down by the garden was heightened by the night's unprecedented event: a stranger on the bottom step. Finally something that he had to himself again—like the promise of a vice. Then he discovered two things simultaneously: that it was Aunt Kristine sitting there and that she was crying.

His first impulse was to sneak back inside. He hated these situations that he always seemed to get involved in, being let in on more than he had intended. But at that moment a feeling of affection welled up in him, making him forget everything else, even the distant voices calling out his name behind closed doors.

He scraped his foot on the floor of the balcony. She got up at once and came toward him, up to the low stairway.

"Kristine?" he exclaimed in amazement, and for once there was something like a lump in his throat. "I just came out for a breath of fresh air," he added quickly. They met on the top step. A gleam of light caught one of her eyes; there were no tears, but it was dark from crying.

"You too, dear boy?" she said and gave his shoulders a quick hug. He felt a warmth all over him, so different from the extraneous sensation he was so used to from thousands of aunts' hugs. His throat tightened.

"Aren't you cold?" he asked into the darkness, towards where her chin ought to be. He reached out in front of him, only intending to make contact with something in this unusual situation. His hand encountered a soft breast. It rested there for a moment before being withdrawn as though it were cut off at the wrist. His body seemed to lift from the balcony where he was standing, head over heels, floating in red, spinning space. And then, before he realized what he was doing, he had put his arms around her neck and drawn her head down to his. He put his lips to hers and again he went tumbling in a great somersault into space.

"But, dear boy!" she exclaimed and freed herself. She smelled of vanilla and cocoa, the scent surrounded him like a defense against the rest of the world. The last desperate bars of the two-step swerved out to them in the night, along with the rumbling noise of feet in their last, insane, leaping race across the floor.

"You aren't angry with me, Kristine?" he whispered to her. "Are you cold?" He could feel her trembling. He realized that he was trembling too. Now they could hear the voices more distinctly, several of them were calling "Wilfred" and "Lillelord!"

"Hurry in!" she whispered. She ran her hand quickly over his head and squeezed his hands in her warm, soft hands.

"I'm not angry. No, not angry. On the contrary. . . ."

He felt a quick nudge in his back and crept indoors. Sneaking behind the gilded portieres, he came in unseen and was standing in the middle of the living room before they had time to call him again.

Where had he been? What had he been doing? Questions showered over him, not severe, but curious. He summoned up all his presence of mind and replied that he'd gone out to get some air, that it had been so warm. I've been flying, he thought.

Most of the guests were already in the hallway being helped into their coats by sleepy, irritable servants in a hurry. Their wraps looked gray and ordinary compared to the festive sailor suits, bright red dresses, and bows. They were like little bonfires of liveliness being put out by ordinary clothes, a conflagration of celebration and amusement that only now glowed on the red cheeks and in the sad eyes as the thank yous and good-byes gradually died away down the steps and the two or three waiting carriages rolled away and the rest of the company went straggling off down the silent, nighttime streets—those with maids escorting them sulky, those who were more grown-up, who hadn't been fetched, in lonely groups of four or five.

Mother and son came back from the hallway. The maids were putting the dining room table and chairs back in place. Aunt Kristine was there too now; he saw her as he glanced through the open door. The refreshing draft from the open windows swept in, under the arching curtains, and scattered the smells of the children's ball.

"Well, my dear boy, was it a success?"

"Splendid, Mother—and thanks a lot for having it."

She looked at him questioningly: "You were gone a long time—?"

"It got so hot in here; all those—kids!"

The word just slipped out. He amazed himself when he heard it. His mother was looking at him the whole time. She went to the door and said: "I think we'll stop now. The rest can wait. And thank you for everything." Then she thought of something and walked quickly over to the desk and took out some money. The extra help curtseyed low and the maids thanked her for their tips.

"And Kristine, thank you so very much for helping me again, me and Lillelord."

He was standing in the middle of the big living room and heard the name Kristine as if for the first time—it was so melodious, so full of song and mystery. Aunt Kristine came in just then. For a moment they stood facing each other. An unusual feeling of shyness passed through him. But the next moment was transformed into a dizzy sensation that came over him again; it filled him with a sweetness that wanted to lift him up. He took a step toward her, but she raised her hand almost imperceptibly. At that moment his mother returned.

"And now, son, it's time for you to go to bed!" the tone was most unusually brisk, like Uncle Martin's when he was being cheerful, and manly, with him. There was something unnatural about it. Instantly he became the well brought-up young boy again. He held out his hand and without looking up at Aunt Kristine said: "Thank you so much!" He turned in the doorway: "Thanks, Mother!" He glanced at both of them. When his eyes met Kristine's it was like something striking him inside. "Good night," he whispered at the door as he went.

The two women stood there, strangers to each other. Susanna said:

"I have a strange feeling that this was his last children's ball." And when the other woman didn't respond: "Well, I think we should have a well-deserved glass of port wine before we go to bed."

"Thank you, Susanna, but I don't think I will this evening," she said unexpectedly. "Besides, I'm rather tired and I think I'll go back to my place tonight."

"But, my dear. We got the guest room ready. You always . . . and then to walk alone—the streets. . . ."

Kristine shrugged: "You seem to think we live in a city filled with robbers. . . . But seriously, Susanna, I would prefer to go home."

Mrs. Sagen remained for a moment at the top of the stairway leading down to the street. Her eyes followed the always young looking figure as it crossed the street; she saw it turn and wave. She stood a moment or two longer. Everything was deserted, not a person in sight; it was night. It was as if the house behind her was refusing her something at that moment, as if something was over. She wasn't used to thinking; she didn't know what it was and didn't understand clearly that there was something wrong.

She wasn't used to thinking. But instinct found its own way and told her something was over and done with, that all that lay ahead was uncertain and different. And as she walked through the rooms again, it was as though there hadn't been a dance here and as though all the young people had been ghosts—as if everything that was *hers* seemed to vanish into something intangible and frightening.

She went to the fireplace and nervously tapped the last glowing log with a poker to be sure that it wasn't going to shoot out sparks. As she straightened up and put the poker back in its stand, her gaze fell on two photographs there: one of her husband, Christian Fredrik Sagen, as a young navy captain, the other of Lillelord with soft curls falling over his collar. She looked from one to the other. Whenever she wanted to keep her eyes on one of them, they moved back to the other, so that in a way they became one; in another way they receded into the distance—both of them.

Then she gathered up the train of her gown quickly and walked alone through the hallway and up the stairs.

8

Things were closing in around him now; he began to recognize them now. It was as though the spring shed its light on them and separated them, so that he saw everything clearly. He would defy them, or he would give in, give in to everything. His own body had become his dearest friend and his bitterest enemy, a source of desire and shame in an order that was unbreakable. And in this tangle of abrupt swings from happiness to unhappiness, his consciousness of the tension around him grew. He noticed the candid scrutiny of him in Uncle Martin's eyes and a certain reticence, even at Uncle René's the last few times he had been invited there to plunge into his uncle's wonderful art books and study with him *The Woman in Blue* or one of Braque's still lifes that made him shiver with delight when he arranged all the restless elements on the surface of the picture in his mind, according to an inherent musical principle.

Scrutiny and reticence . . .

Even his mother wasn't the friend he could naturally go to for everything, and he was deeply ashamed that it was his own fault, because he didn't confide in her, because all his thoughts turned to Aunt Kristine, with her mysterious depths, the depth between her round breasts, the depth in the abyss of her eyes, the depth of mysteries in a grief that only he knew about, and yet he knew nothing when it really came down to it.

He lived in the midst of an intrigue of suspicions that were directed against everything that was secret in his own mind and actions. The world around him was filled with suspicions about his setbacks and his lust for vices, a lurking jungle where *discovery* crouched, watching with yellow eyes, ready to surround him and move in cautiously, a little closer every day, until one day, or night, it would be able to seize him from all directions at the same time and catch him in a net of guilt.

He was making progress at school at this time. He always did better when the summer vacation approached. He was proud of being the best at the exams every year. He used to do it to please his mother; but this year it was to defy her, because he suspected that she no longer thought quite so well of him. Besides, it was his last year at the Misses Wollkwarts' school. In the fall he was going to attend a "proper" school, to Uncle Martin's relief.

It was important to have something in order amid this chaos of contradictions and guilt. He wanted to attend to his *sortie,* as Uncle René had said. One should always provide for a good *sortie.* Especially when everything else was wrong.

But doing well at school didn't make things any easier for him. The constant praise from the Misses Wollkwarts made him think that they might write another letter to reassure his mother. All the nervous speculation made him tired and hollow-eyed. Every morning he waited tensely by the door to see if the postman had a letter that would expose the earlier letter. But Lilly also waited behind her door, and every morning there was a silent, hostile race from their respective doors across the hall to get to the mail first. Lilly hated him now; he knew it. And he felt that she suspected or knew something. Neither was he lucky with all his clandestine projects; it was as though luck and the feeling of being carefree had deserted him at the same time. All his cheerful dissimulation seemed to wear a mask now; it nullified the effect of the dissimulation. No, things weren't going well for him any more. One day when he came home from school, she came toward him, holding the letter. It was crumpled. She must have read it many times; it must have tormented her.

"I don't understand," she said, "here's a letter from your teacher saying that she's satisfied with you now, that you are doing well in every subject and perhaps will still come out on top at the exams."

He tried his old, carefree expression.

"Fine, Mother!" he exclaimed, though it sounded forced. "Aren't you proud of me then?"

"But I don't understand," she repeated, "haven't you been working hard and doing well all the time? After all, it hasn't been so many months since she wrote. . . ."

He could have flung himself at her, could have used the old trick of confessing everything, or almost everything, his eyes full of tears—its effect was always overwhelming. But his urge to surrender was countered by a contrary urge to let the mystery remain open, to frighten her with more leisurely means. He said casually: "Oh, there was a time when things went really bad. Maybe she thinks she wrote you about that."

His mother remained standing with the letter in her hand. He saw very well how her fingers crumpled it nervously. He knew those hands; he had loved them as he had loved everything about her, and her hands told him that she was in a state of great confusion, torn between wanting to believe and not being able to. And he knew that all she needed was a word from him and she'd believe the best with all possible certainty, that she would thrust her doubts aside and forget the unpleasantness, as so often before, in fact, as she always did.

But he didn't give her that word. Something inside him refused to let her have it any more. Something inside him thought defiantly: You'll have to grow up some time too, like your brother, Uncle Martin, like—Aunt Kristine. *She's* experienced a lot of grief.

Grief and sorrow—he wanted that too. Just one proper sorrow and not all these worries that just made him anxious and afraid every time he went through a doorway. He wanted to be like Aunt Kristine and have a sorrow. Or to share her sorrow, comfort her, no, bear it for her—alone! So that she wouldn't have any grief and could just smell nicely for him and have that abyss between her breasts.

"I'll be the best at my exams, Mother, don't worry about it," he said curtly and walked away. He paused for an instant outside the door, and with his back to the closed door he *saw* her standing there in the middle of the room, quite still, holding the enigmatic letter in her hands. He knew that if there had been anything bad in the letter, she would have been his friend in everything; nothing could have broken her resistance then. But it contained something pleasant that she didn't understand. Soon she'd realize everything; that he'd become a different person, that he was an individual, a being full of desires and secret actions. Better to let it come. Better to let his childhood, good as it had been, come crashing down.

He went through the hall and walked upstairs to his room. There he stood helplessly between the bed and the desk. All at once he saw everything differently, this little paradise of his; it had always been different from the untidy, overpopulated dens which he had seen his friends had for bedrooms; so clean and so absolutely his, *here* to such a great degree; now it was a child's room, a room to grow out of.

And still he felt that he could head downstairs; he could still sneak up to his mother and put his head against her and say . . . no, there'd be no need to say anything. It was enough for him to *be* there.

But he wouldn't. His legs wanted to, but his mind wouldn't. His mind was like a pointed ball, like the one on top of the old watchman's staff in Uncle René's hall. A ball with spikes sticking out in all directions, trying to get loose and go and do violent things in the night.

There was a knock on the door. Mrs. Susanna Sagen was standing there. It was the first time he had thought of her by her full name, as a lady. He didn't see that she was different now, that she didn't have a letter in her hand.

"I forgot to tell you that the Sagens in Copenhagen have written to ask if we—or you—would like to go down there for the summer and take a vacation at Gilleleje."

He walked straight into the trap—if it was a trap.

"But aren't we going to Skovly—you and I?"

He saw her eyes fill with tears right away, and only then did he realize that she had been different when she came in.

"Do you want to—like we usually do?" she asked quietly.

Now he was in her arms. Now he was where he had always been, yet not quite in the same way, because he was now conscious of being there.

"Of course I want to!" he said loudly, yet in a strangely flat way, so expressionless that he wondered if she would notice it. But she didn't. She hugged him to her and said, rather girlishly, "I didn't know if you'd want to—this year. And it's so nice of them to ask us."

He freed himself shyly and felt cheated. But he couldn't show it now. He was obliged to keep up the old act of being a good child, so he said: "It's not really summer unless we're at Skovly."

It worked. He celebrated because he realized that he had convinced her, that everything was all right, like before. He was possessed by the joy of making her happy: "Do you remember that one summer we spent at Gilleleje and how we both longed for Skovly—you did too, didn't you, Mother?"

He had carried it off. He saw her getting serious, growing up a little, on behalf of both of them, because he was a child.

"Well, then, I'll write at once and thank them for asking us, but that—well, I'll think of something."

"Of course you will, Mother!" he shouted enthusiastically. "You know best what to say. . . ."

They stood facing each other; she was barely half a head taller than he was now, so young again, so untroubled; they were almost the same person for a moment, a moment of intoxicated abandonment to everything that had taken place.

"Well, it's settled then," she said quickly and turned away.

She was gone. He knew that she had to hide her emotion. He sat down on the edge of the bed and felt a great emptiness steal over him.

That one summer in Denmark with his father's relatives—they had been so kind to him, and so foreign. . . . The painful longing he had felt every day and night for their dear, brown timber house in Hurumland. That was summer itself, with its deep orchard, with its overgrown fruit trees so tall and shady that it was like being on the bottom of the sea when you walked on the lawns beneath them. . . . That had been summer itself, the only one; and perhaps it would go on being that for him, all his life. All the carving on the veranda railing where he used to stick his head through, pretending to be a watchdog, and bark, till suddenly he couldn't get his head through any more! All the gilded paths with the glittering sunshine between the tiny knolls that had been Mount Sinai and the Cape of Good Hope, and the two small brooks that had been the Tigris and the Euphrates, and the old, rotten well where Joseph had been thrown by his brethren and where a terrifying beast called Kakaksaks lived . . . the summer house in the old linden with the sighing in its crowns, day and night the same whisper of voices that he gave names and shapes to. The chestnut tree on the lawn outside the kitchen door—and the green, wooden table beneath it, where they cleaned fish and prepared berries in the autumn. The smell of green leaves assaulted his nostrils as he climbed up the cherry trees and put the fruit he picked into a basket he had hung on a branch nearby . . . the smell of apples, freshly picked apples spread out on an unpainted wooden floor scrubbed and shiny clean in order to receive the autumn harvest. . . . The beach with the scary waves after a big boat had just passed by—waves that used to chase him far up the slope because he was afraid of the sea when it was moving, and it was the sea that stole all his thoughts and challenged him to perform heroic deeds. . . . The old bathing cabin, painted brown, with the rotten railing that was patched up every year but never got any better—the first time he had *dived* from the pier and had come up to the surface after that exciting action, his long hair sticking to the back of his neck—and had looked up and met his mother's eyes, glowing with pride. . . .

And the quiet walks beneath the dark foliage towards evening: the heavy scent of jasmine around midsummer, mysterious shadows under trees that grew absurdly in the twilight and came alive, murmuring beings with messages for everything around. Breakfast on the porch with the little birds that came and dared to eat the crumbs off the tablecloth. The tame hedgehog they called Jonas. . . .

It was all his summers. It was all summers in one, a memory and a state all at once, a state of bliss that was real and fabricated at the same time because nothing was just like it was, not even the flag they raised on Sunday mornings—that was ritual. Nothing was just itself in the summer, because everything *meant* something, *was* something like "make-believe" that was truer and greater than the trees, the sea, and the falling shadows: an abundance without form or limit, all joys in one joy that had no cause and didn't ask why.

He sat on the edge of the bed and experienced a great emptiness. It was as if all the summers had collected inside him and turned to nothing, as if the sum of all joy that had flooded through him when he remembered them had suddenly exploded with a faint pop and dissolved into nothing.

He got frightened, then angry. He knew it now: she had set a trap for him and he had walked right into it. Why not go to Denmark for once and visit his amusing Danish relatives—they could be as foreign as they wanted, it was just fine. It would be a lovely way of escaping everything that surrounded him and threatened him. He was on the verge of running down to his mother and begging her to change her mind. He knew that she would, if he asked her.

But he didn't get up. He suddenly didn't feel strong enough to see that little smile which would hide her disappointment. There was also the point that he didn't really know if she liked his father's relatives, or if they liked her. Then there was all that stuff about his father . . . all the things he didn't know.

And there was another nice thing about Skovly—Aunt Kristine was sure to come and visit them there in the summer, as she always did. This thought raced through him like a flash of lightning, frightening yet sweet. He *hadn't* thought of that. He hadn't taken *that* into account. For once there hadn't been any calculation. He was quite sure of that. He knew it and felt rather proud.

But as he sat there, he became less and less sure that he knew it, that there hadn't been something that had been taken into account. And this suspicion also came to him with a kind of cruel pride.

And suddenly the memory of all the times he had been afraid of the dark at Skovly came over him. And it was more than a memory; it really *existed* then. All that lay in between had vanished and he could smell the aroma of the room with its silk-covered panelling, a conglomerate atmosphere created by a big log hall transformed into a rococo room with a fleur-de-lys pattern on the wallpaper, and sofas and chairs with curved legs; the white paint was scraped and the gilding faded, but it was radiant, shining—a complete contradiction of the fake Norwegian style farmhouse that looked like a cuckoo clock. Logs and silk! Outside a troll's castle, inside a box of candy. Of course this glaring contradiction had always existed, it too was a *state,* the house had to be like that, it wasn't till Uncle René had casually remarked about the style and everyone had laughed that he actually *saw* the house. But he loved it more than ever after that, as a sort of enchanted freak, a castle for the most preposterous of princes. . . .

These late summer nights, when the dusk was tight around the house and shut it up with a fabric of darkness. His cousins had been there visiting. They shared the big east room with him; it had beds along three of the walls. And *he* had to go to bed first because he was the youngest; they stuck to their rights. He had hidden in all the nooks and crannies to avoid being noticed. Until a voice had said: "*Now,* Lillelord!" and it was inevitable.

Crossing the deserted hallway to the staircase with its single lamp burning dimly, only increasing the darkness; the stairs themselves where he kept to the very edge by the banister, so that they wouldn't creak; the long, cool corridor at the top—and then the room. . . . He stood in the middle of it, tingling with fright. The windows were empty holes into the darkness, and outside the linden trees sighed their eternal song. In one bound he had reached the windows and pulled the blinds down, first one, then the other; he shut out the night. But the matte blue surfaces of the blinds had darkness in them. Again he stood there, white with panic, not daring to move, or undress, or light the lamp, or do anything.

Matches on the chest of drawers! The comforting little flame that the next moment became smaller and *wouldn't* shine for him. . . . The lamp shade, big and white, that he lifted off carefully so he wouldn't brush the chimney, and put down gingerly in the dark; he struck another match and was quick to get the chimney on again to help the flame draw air. The warm, blessed moments when the flame grew and he put the white shade on again and the light spread. And the terrible discovery that it didn't spread far enough, didn't reach everywhere, that there were still areas of darkness beyond its light, an eerie feeling lurked in them that was worse than all the other darkness.

He stood close to the lamp, staring at its weak light, feeling the pounding in his temples. His cousins would come soon. He would hear them on the stairs, on the third step from the bottom that creaked because they walked in the middle and not close to the banister. Oh, endless times, endless hours of waiting, and so full of boundless fear. The distant roar of the sea was like thunder inside his head. Hands reached out from the corners and even the locked veranda door was no protection against the dreadful *outside* that was trying to get in. Not a smell reached him, not a sound that could help him. His own enormous solitude grew into a being on its own, a being that took up residence in him, conquered him from within, so that not even his last source of courage had a home in him. Fear dissolved him from within; he felt his own contours being erased and the terrible thing was that he couldn't move and prove that he still existed in this process of total disintegration.

Then he heard the creak on the stairs. They were coming! A kind of jubilation swept through him. Saved! Saved again, but this time at the very last moment. In less than a second he had reacquired his boundaries, his contours, existence; the corners withdrew into their own darkness and became what they were, the limits of a room; the door to the *outside* became a defense and the space inside a place of security against everything that was frightening.

Then a new fear raced through him, the fear of getting caught being afraid. There were fourteen stairs and they had crossed the third one when he heard the creak. They must be halfway by now, or farther. They were coming. They would humiliate him. He acted quickly to save himself: he kicked off his shoes and shoved them under the bed, he dived into bed with his clothes on, pulled the down comforter up to his chin and lay stock still, breathing deeply and regularly as if he were really sound asleep.

But his cousins weren't fooled. "Lillelord," they whispered, testing him. He answered with heavy breathing. "You're not asleep, we know it."

And the horrible footsteps near the bed. The comforter being pulled off with a jerk: "Ah-ha! In bed with his clothes on! Mama's boy's afraid of the dark!"

Humiliation. Humiliated again, God knows how many times. Humiliated in the eyes of his older cousins. "Who's afraid of the waves? Who gets into the tank with his mother? Who's afraid to go to the outhouse in the dark and shits under the willow?"

And it was true, all true. He lay outstretched beneath their terrorizing scorn and let them flay him alive. It was all true, that he was a coward, afraid of water, afraid of the dark, a scaredy-cat. And that infamous, well-bred brood of Uncle Martin's missed no opportunity to rub it in. They knew he didn't dare retaliate, that any attack would mean giving himself away. He had squatted once under the big willow because he didn't dare go any farther on the path through the bushes that led to the outhouse that had the long bench with the little child's seat and the extra step up to it beside the two holes for grown-ups. Hedgehogs and rats had been crossing the path that evening and the bats were darting so low across the lilac hedge that it seemed they were coming to get him and fly away with him. Finally he had squatted down under the willow, but still almost in the middle of the path. And the next day someone had stepped in the result and his cousins had called him Lilleturd whenever the grown-ups were out of earshot, and they had told Erna and Alfhild in the white house just behind the hedge, little girls in light blue dresses that always smelled freshly ironed—and blue . . . and after that they had held their noses whenever Lillelord was around, and their little lips stuck out as they said "turd" to themselves.

And it was true that he had bathed with his mother in the tank in the leaky bathhouse that smelled of damp wood inside. Afraid, he had climbed down the steep wooden steps to his mother in the tank, who was standing up to her chest in water in her red and white striped bathing dress, its pattern turned into checks by the reflection of the sunlight falling in through the vertical bars of the tank's cage—and she had coaxed him down to dance a humiliating "Ring Around the Rosy" on the slimy bottom. And when she said "all fall dow-w-wn" his head had gone under water and the world was shattered by a mortal fear that just made him wish for annihilation. And then his mother's laughing face when he came up again and was still alive. . . . What treachery in her laughter, what a betrayal to trick him into going under and then laugh. And suddenly a great roar of laughter from his cousins who had sneaked in to watch, their two laughing faces high above the tank's hoist with its threatening chain coming over an iron railing painted with red lead paint that was peeling off. And his mother's overly gentle reproach for laughing at him: "Just wait, one day Lillelord is going to swim like a fish, much better than you can."

But no. He would never swim. They could hold him in the harness over the side of the pier like they used to, and he would do the same as last time: let himself sink when they slackened the line to see if he wouldn't float a little, let himself sink to the bottom and cling tight to the rotten tree trunk that had once been used to tie the boat to, but had gotten rotten and was sunk. He had clung to it, intending to die then and there, no matter how much they hauled on the rope up above, he wouldn't budge. He was stronger. He could die. It would serve them right.

He didn't remember how it had ended that time, but someone had jumped in and loosened his grip and gotten him ashore. He had cried with shame and anger when he came to.

No, he wasn't going to swim. He would let them think that he wanted to, he would get into the big, rubber ring and kick way out from the shore, then he would swim a few strokes in the ring, and then he'd slip out of it and let himself sink. Then they would find him in the autumn, blue and bloated, when he drifted by the lighthouse. Then his mother would play "Ring Around the Rosy" with his corpse until it fell to pieces, like the blue body of the dog they had found once on the beach and which he had never been able to forget. . . . And it was true that he ran like a savage, far up the slope, from the waves when they came, those ghastly shadows on the sea that became foaming monsters as soon as they landed on the long bank and came sweeping to get him with their jaws open to gobble him up.

There was a lot more that was true that they didn't know about and which he was afraid they'd find out. He was so afraid of thunder that his body twitched and he ached inside when it was still just building and no one else noticed it, except perhaps his mother; she also got restless in thundery weather. Yes, he was so afraid of thunder that he was afraid of the sun in July because someone had told him once that the sun and the heat charged the air and in that way good weather itself became the root of a fear of what was to come, and so now he was afraid of the sun.

And every time the sun was sinking and the air got cooler, he heaved a sigh of relief: he had gotten a reprieve; it wasn't charged yet, but it would come. Then there were only the long shadows to be afraid of, before dusk fell in earnest. The long shadows were like forerunners of the dusk, gloomy messengers that stole, meter by meter, across the grass and the hills and made terrifying patterns among the trees and whispered everywhere:

We're coming now, we're the stealthy knights, but behind us the great princes are coming. He didn't know where the words came from: they just came into his mind from somewhere and had a terror of their own that he covered up with his other fear, the fear of being discovered.

And when the thunder broke loose and advanced, threatening, he became quieter and quieter inside and everything inside him was scooped out by something that sucked at him, and the first flash of lightning was like convulsions inside him. He had a special way of hiding this fear, because his mother was scared too and always looked for a corner where she could sit and face the wall. He would go there too and sit beside her on a stool to comfort her. No one suspected the connection, except perhaps his mother, because they were both so terribly frightened. Once, when the air was "electric," they had seen long sparks jump between them in the darkness of their corner. They were like the two victims selected by the lightning's threat.

After the thunder—that was the only time when there was any peace. When the wet grass was sparkling again, when the sun was cool and hadn't had time yet to store up more danger, when the birds were starting to sing again, and the air was all fresh and new, then his jubilation was boundless and he would go off by himself among the trees and up the hills and down to the sea and give thanks to God in high-pitched hymns that he made up and chanted aloud: Oh Dear Lord God Your Favor Is Boundless Oh Dear Lord God Your Mercy Is Great Oh Dear Lord God Who Wants To Cleanse The Air Oh Dear Lord God We Are Jubilant On Your Earth. And he would fling himself down on the ground and bore into it with his hands and thank it because it hadn't swallowed him up, and he would kneel down on the beach at the edge of the water and lay his palms lightly over the bright, mirrorlike surface and thank it because it hadn't swallowed him up. And he stood on tiptoe, facing the light and prayed for it to go on being light and not let the darkness come and swallow him up. And he walked around the flowers on the glistening meadows and asked them to forgive him if he had ever stepped on them and then ran back to the path so that he wouldn't step on any more. They were all friends *after the thunder,* for they all rejoiced in unending friendship at having escaped destruction again.

Yes, all the things they said when they made fun of him were true, and a lot more besides. There were no limits on his discomfiture. And the time when he was five and had boasted about how well he could read and his mother had proudly let him read aloud from the newspaper, then in secret he had read eighteen exciting stories about Nick Carter, King of the Detectives. Then he had come to number nineteen, about Morris Carruter, King of the Criminals. And he was supposed to read aloud to his mother and both cousins and his uncles and aunts on the porch. There were two columns on every page and no dividing line between them, just a little white space. And when he had read a good long while, Uncle Martin got up, glass in hand, and said it was a curious conglomeration the boy was reading and came over—glass in hand—and looked over his shoulder. And then he discovered that he had been reading straight across the page, both columns at a time, and that he had read all eighteen stories like that, this gifted boy. . . . Then they started to laugh, snickering in cascades, waterfalls of laughter that seemed to drown out everything; and howls and yelling from his two cousins hiding behind the grown-ups.

Then he had gotten up, hot with shame, and walked out onto the hillside and picked up a stone with his right hand and laid his left one flat on a rock and brought the stone down with all his might on the ring finger of his left hand; the joint was smashed and the nail had to be taken off.

What he had felt was pleasure—pleasure in abasement. And that summer all his shame had a good side, and this gave it a reverse interpretation that made fear and shame bearable.

Just as the sunshine that delighted him made him more and more afraid inside, so too he discovered a sweetness in defeat that made *two* of everything that had originally been *one,* that made delight sad and the next moment fear became sweet. And with all the shame there could be a taste of something like honey spreading through his body. And this taste of honey could accompany him on his flight from the waves and make him prolong it beyond the safety limit, *i.e.,* the barberry bush, which the sea water never touched. And even the lightning had a hint of this sweet power in it that illuminated him from within by the pleasure of fright.

Only the creeping fear that inhabited darkness didn't have even a glimmer of pleasure; and only his hymns *after the thunder* had no fear or pleasure: The Good God . . .

Pleasure in abasement—when he thought about it, he had always felt it. Once in midsummer he had gone alone to the top of a hill facing the sea and had thrown big stones straight up into the air there, one after the other, to see if they would fall on his head. He went on and on, throwing stone after stone up in the air and waiting with his eyes shut in suspense that was intolerable . . . till finally one stone did fall on his head and made his world explode. Bleeding and half swooning, he lay on the mountainside feeling both good and bad pain, streams of blue and red coursing through his body, and the deadening pain growing in his head with its gaping wound and his hair glossy from the blood.

And when he stole—it always filled him with sweetness and terror. He was always stealing something during those terror-stricken years. One warm day in July, when there was a thin haze over the sea, he and his mother had gone to town to do some shopping. At two o'clock they were standing on the Stortorvet outside the Christiania Glasmagasin and saw the gilt ball drop down its pole, then everyone knew it was two o'clock. They went into the glass store, and as he held his mother's hand with his right hand, and she talked with the salesgirl, he stole from the counter on *his* side with his left hand—some little, colored glass saltshakers with a star on the bottom: yellow, green, and red saltshakers; first one, then another, then a third, until the fever seized him and he stole handfuls of saltshakers; he stuck them into the pocket of his loose blue jacket, holding his mother's hand all this time. And it was good, very good. And it was good too, the time he took the little pin out of the spout of the oil can attached to Mikal's bicycle when he found the bicycle leaning against the fence, and he had stuck the pin in the front tire so that the air hissed out. But when his cousin came out and found his bicycle like that, just when he wanted to go for a ride, then he just felt ashamed and didn't feel good any longer, and he couldn't admit he'd done it because they wouldn't believe him, just asked why, why. . . . And once he stole an ivory Indian elephant from Uncle René's bric-a-brac shelf and trudged through the city, all the way to Vaterland, to sell it to a junk dealer, but the man threatened to call the police and then there was nothing but fear and it wasn't good. All that autumn he had had the elephant in his pocket and hid it in a new place every day, then one day he wrote a note "from his father" and went to another dealer nearby and got eight kroner for it, and that was dizzying and terrifying in every way, and then it was all over. But it had been good. Everything dangerous was good. But not the consequences of danger. Going under was good, and never to come up again, to be lost, was good. But it wasn't good to have to come up again and be a part of everything around, with the really good people who had plenty of what was good. That wasn't good.

They knew it. They knew about him: his cousins, maybe everybody did; it seemed like the entire world had a system for knowing all about him.

But not his secrets. Nobody could know those. He had to keep his secrets. They hadn't known about the thunder, nor about him throwing stones in the air—not until that time they found him bleeding and he told them about a stone falling from the air, a meteor, a huge bird; and because they didn't believe him, about a strange boy, a giant with a stone in his hand, a monster. . . .

They didn't know his secrets. They didn't know about the girl with the orange.

The long, deserted corridor with the dim gaslight at the end of it. It was in the place where they lived then—with the outhouse at the end of a long corridor and a few steps out into the raw cold. Along the wall on one side was a shelf of glass jars, one beside the other, that contained adders preserved in alcohol, coiling gracefully in the twilight, and he had a name for them: father.

It was almost bearable on the way out to the cold, because he had the gaslight ahead of him, that was on the way out, and besides, he was going to "the place" as they called it. . . . But on the way back, when the light was behind him and there was only one long shadow that got longer, falling jerkily over the adders in their jars, and it was dark ahead of him, dark for a *long* way, and he couldn't be certain that there was a door at the end or that there would be a flood of joy and happiness as soon as he reached it and opened it to the brightness of the hanging lamp in the hall and the light from the open doorways . . . that was unbearable. The corridor lasted such a long time, and the gaslight was behind him and everything got darker and darker, then he was afraid of what was ahead and not behind; all the things that could swallow him up were ahead of him; it was all hopeless—suppose the door wasn't there? And how could he know there was a door in the darkness, perhaps he had just imagined it?

Then there was a sliver of light on the left side, a glimmer in the gap between the shelves with the glass jars and adders still visible in the fading light from the gas burner, and he could hear voices snickering. The *maids* lived there. Emma and Marie—it was their room. He had never realized that they actually *lived* there, because in the daytime they were just "the maids" who cleaned shoes and cooked the meals and cleaned the rooms and had time off. Now, all at once, they were living there, they existed, they emerged from the night and were real. All he knew was that they were his salvation because there was light in the crack.

It was Emma. He remembered it now. No, he didn't remember it, because it *was*. One doesn't remember. One is, one knows; he suddenly knew it. One experiences something forever or one just passes by. It was Emma.

He stormed in—there were two beds. He had never been in the maids' room before. There were two beds, one on each side of the room, to the right and left of the door. Facing him was a window that had a blind with a vase and some flowers painted on it. There was a chest of drawers by it, and on the chest—two plaster horses with their necks crossed.

The bed on the left was already occupied. That was Marie, the cook. She muttered something unpleasant and turned away; she was asleep. But Emma hadn't gone to bed. She was getting ready for bed. She was standing there in her corset and lace panties, a revelation of grace and something unfamiliar, of security, and—he realized it instantly—of danger.

It was Emma, and she smiled and understood. "Were you afraid?" she had said. And she undid her corset as she spoke, just as his mother did. "Were you afraid?" she said.

And Emma said: "You mustn't be afraid!" She said that as he pressed his head to her belly, almost forcing her down onto the bed. She said: "I'll come in with you and put you to bed: the nursemaid's gone to her room." And now he knew what he'd realized then: that she'd said "nursemaid" with contempt and hostility.

And he had burrowed into her, into Emma, forced her down, terrified that she would leave him or take him back. Because it was good, safe, and alarming, all in one. Then Emma said: "No, dear . . ." in a voice he didn't recognize, and "No, but!" in a voice that he recognized less and less—and again: "No, dear. Dear . . ." in a voice he had never heard while he burrowed and bored into her, afraid that it would stop, afraid of the corridor outside, of the gaslight and the adders in their glass jars that were perhaps called "father," afraid that something that had existed would come into being again, but not the contented terror of sinking under water and clinging to something down at the bottom, inside, the eternity no one returned from.

And the voice that had said: "No, dear!"

And he was lying in the seaweed and clinging to it, and holding on tight to the inner darkness that he couldn't let get away: it was life and death and anxiety and pleasure and drowning.

It was Emma, it was the voice, it was the depths, it was Emma, it was the gas lamp at the end of the corridor and the long corridor and the smell of the outhouse and the good and the bad and everything, everything.

Marie was snoring in the other bed. He knew it now, he always knew it. Marie had been snoring in the other bed. And that too was part of the pleasure: that it was distracting, it created mystery and a space of its own, that everything increased to infinity.

He died there, he smelled mildewed wallpaper and died. He heard the hiss of the distant gaslight and knew everything and died. And it was good to die. He wanted to die. And if he lived again, he would die again. Always.

It was Emma. She was faithless. She said to Marie, who had woken up: "I think the boy's crazy, and he's only five!" One evening she was standing with the gardener under the little roof of the carriage shed, and she said: "No, dear . . ." exactly the same way. He knew it now and always had. Then and now had merged.

But she was nice to him that evening. When the painful moment arrived and he came up to the surface again and he knew that life would go on, that his destruction was over, that it wasn't the end of everything, like it should have been, then she went with him and put him to bed.

Perhaps the world knew everything—that there was a secret system just for pointing out his shame? But she had been nice. She had put him to bed and tucked him in and said: "Because Mommy's not here. . . ." And he had smelled oranges then. He had smelled it, not dreamed it, because Emma didn't smell of oranges. She smelled of honey. It was something else. It was the sight of Emma as he came in.

Suddenly he looked up from where he was sitting on the edge of the bed, looked at the wall and the picture hanging there, a wretched oleograph: "The Girl with an Orange. . . ." Layer after layer, back in time and space. That was *it*—the picture that had hung over Emma's bed. It had followed them around on all their moves since then.

This was the picture, the idiotic picture that had filled him with sweet terror every time he glanced at it; he didn't have the energy to throw it away. The whole picture was an insult, a brown-eyed girl holding an orange in her hand, a cracked oleograph in his room, and he was familiar with Degas' dancers, he had bathed his eyes in the blue of Bonnard. "The Girl with an Orange"—this disgusting creature in a simple gilt frame was Emma and all his shame and his pleasure in the horror of the long walk to the outhouse.

He stood up, furious, and walked toward the picture; he wanted to seize it with both hands, tear it down from the wall, break the frame over his knee, tear the picture to pieces and throw them out the window.

But as he stood there—quivering—in front of the girl with the orange, her expression changed as he looked at her, or rather she *acquired* an expression: it was Kristine, Aunt Kristine—could it be? It was like. . . .

Nonsense. It was a wretched production of some banal "masterpiece," one of those rectangular horrors that go from one maid's room to another to hide the marks on the wallpaper.

And yet: it did resemble Kristine. It had the mysterious humming of her gaze. Did Kristine have brown eyes? Of course she did. Had he always known it? Her hands, rather indolent, clasped loosely around the orange, like Kristine's affectionate hands, they always gripped things so softly: hands without action, but also without merit. Confectioner's hands. . . .

He stood there in unconscious revolt before the picture he hated; he lowered his thin hands, they were so full of shame too. Recently—a moment before—he'd wanted to use them to smash that silly picture; he raised them again now and gave the cracked surface a shy caress. But as soon as his fingers touched the hands holding the orange, a cold fire of fear and pleasure raced all the way through him. The girl in the picture looked at him in serene amazement, the girl in the maids' room picture. It had accompanied him all those years since then: it had persecuted him. So there *was* a secret alliance of powers that wanted to hurt him, to expose him from head to toe and destroy him with shame.

Yes, he'd suspected it. Luck had deserted him, the luck of his dissimulation and illegal expeditions, of his guilty masturbation. They could come and get him now: his cousins, Miss Wollkwarts. He was the only one who knew that pleasure and terror are the same thing and that each desire contains remorse and remorse desire. He wanted to do what was good for the sake of the wicked, and the wicked for the sake of the good. He wanted to drown: to make a mess of himself to get clean, to get dirty to be clean. . . . He wanted to fall, to be able to rise, in order to fall in order to rise.

He wanted to fall. He sank to his knees by the bed and bored his head into the crocheted bedspread. And when the rapture of crying took hold of him, it was like being borne on waves over the land and sea, through realms of sunlight which was blackened by the light and slowly became red: a dark sun. But the waves carried him on farther through the water, through purifying blue sky and patches of light filtered by the branches of fruit trees, to a moon-green land where light was shadow and shadow light and where it was good to diminish gradually to nothing: the cessation of everything.

"Kristine," he sobbed.

9

He woke up on the floor; he had fallen asleep. He knew at once what had happened. It had happened before, once or twice; because of the strong emotion he had fallen asleep without any preparation.

Moonlight was shining in a broad strip across the table and floor, making the plush, bedside rug green. He took out his watch and held its face to the light. It had stopped at one o'clock. Had anyone been in and seen him sleeping like this? The thought made him feel cold and uncomfortable: as did any thought of being exposed.

He went to the door; it was locked, thank goodness. He must have locked it after his mother left, when he was so agitated. He must have slept through dinner and supper and everything. They must have come and knocked cautiously, but they never woke him when he slept like that in the daytime. They knew about these fits of sleeping.

With his shoes in his hands, he sneaked downstairs, through the hall and into the living room. It was filled with moonlight. The clock on the mantelpiece said five past one. He looked at his own watch. It was still at one. It must have stopped when he woke up. The thought was immediately discomforting. He stood there shivering in the cold light and thought: I was asleep, so I was alive, but how?

All at once he felt that there was something sinister about his own room; he didn't want to go back up there. He looked out at Frognerkilen's dark cover, pierced by a spear of moonlight. He would get his bicycle, ride out into the night, ride until he was free. He acted quickly to keep from changing his mind. He took a box of matches from the mantelpiece and, still carrying his shoes, ran through the hall; he took his gray overcoat off the hook, quietly slipped the latch into place, and crept down to where his bicycle was. The outer door was locked.

The inner door had locked by itself. He was in a trap, a trap with eight steps that he couldn't see, but which he felt around him more vividly than any time he'd stormed up them, two at a time, or sneaked down them, deep in thought.

His mind was alert now; he was like an animal in a cage. The pleasure of this unusual situation was like a pleasant throbbing in his veins. He picked out the thinnest key from the toolbag of his bike and pushed it into the old lock on the outer door. He thought intently, trying to imagine what a lock looked like on the inside: he wanted to find out about that when he had the chance. One day, perhaps, it would be amusing to break *into* a house or something—and not out.

A blissful feeling of triumph raced through him when the lock opened. He hadn't expected it. It struck him that he was always amazed when anything succeeded. He wheeled his bicycle out and quietly shut the outer door.

He couldn't get the carbide lamp to work, but it didn't matter. There was moonlight and the night was light. He put the matches in his pocket and hopped on the bicycle. He felt very jolly. He rode across the sharp shadows of the trees on the road, like a flight of stairs without any risers. It went easily; everything was easy. He was almost dancing with merriment, and when he rode out onto Drammensveien he began to sing aloud. Where was he going? He'd let the moon decide!

"I'll let the moon decide," he sang and was delighted with the idea. He felt so strong that he had to go up a hill. He got all the way to Løvenskioldsgate before he was a little out of breath and had used his muscles so much that he had to slow down and just enjoy his freedom.

The Lille Frogner farm was bathed in moonlight. He decided to take the little path that went uphill through the farm, between the main building and the outbuildings: it was muddy there and smelled of warm cows. It was so slippery that he had to get off and pull his bicycle between the buildings. The moon didn't reach there, and it was quite dark. The going got slower and slower on the slippery path. He was out of breath, but he was possessed by a vague desire—for everything.

He stopped to catch his breath among the buildings and to sniff the smell of animals. There was a patch of farmland amid the villas and yellow apartment blocks, and not far away there were fields where sheep grazed in the spring and autumn. He wanted to *see* the buildings, to see the crevasse itself he was walking in, deep in the darkness; he wanted to know it all. He struck a match and looked quickly around as it flared up. He struck another and looked greedily at all the unfamiliar things: the dark red wall of one of the outbuildings rose up toward the moonlight and was lost there—and on the other side, the corner of the main building, gray-white and weatherbeaten. He struck match after match in his desire to see, a desire that suddenly became a strong obsession. He wanted to see everything; he wanted the good feeling of seeing it shine. He began striking matches two at a time.

But he couldn't see enough; he wanted to see more. He used a match to light up the ground and see if there was anything there that would burn and give him more light, so that he could see between the houses, where anything could happen and be worth seeing.

There were some twigs a little way up the hill. He gathered them quickly, his hands trembling. He had only three matches left now. He had to be careful if he was going to get his little bonfire to light. He put his bicycle aside and knelt down. The first match blew out when he struck it.

He was suddenly frightened that he wasn't going to be able to *see.* He shielded the second match carefully with his hand and brought it in under the dry twigs; they glowed, but they didn't burn.

He got right down by the little bonfire. Some long sticks were just barely glowing. He wanted some light in there between the buildings, amid the good smell of animals and manure: he wanted it to flare up into some great happiness only he could imagine. He wanted to hear the fire crackling and see, yes, *see* how the flames brought everything to life, the houses that lived.

The third match really kindled the twigs. He lay flat on his stomach and blew carefully: a flame was born, it got bigger, not large, but bigger. He was filled with a great excitement; this was what he wanted.

Taking his watchful eyes off the fire, he saw that the flames were already lighting up the red wall of the outbuilding that had been just a shadow in the night. It was coming to life in little spots, as if he were creating it out of darkness and making it visible. Everything had to be visible; it had to come to life and shine around him. This liveliness rippled through all his limbs now. He was involved in something highly illegal, but it was also something great and joyous that set it above all his other petty transgressions. This feeling grew into a great flame inside him, shot up and drew other flames after it, drew even the little bonfire with it. All at once it was growing fast.

Then he heard footsteps, a door that creaked. He was startled and was wrenched back to a reality he'd left behind. He stamped on the fire and took hold of the handlebars of his bicycle in the same motion. Then he heard a door open behind him and was aware of a gleam of light from there that fell over his shoulder. But he was already in the saddle! He was escaping into exciting, dark space. His bicycle skidded down the muddy path, then he had firm ground beneath his wheels and swung up Bondejordsbakken. The hill would slow him down, and in a moment or two he would reach the jumble of wooden buildings at Briskeby and could hide among the low houses there, where the trees made shadows in the moonlight.

It was all quiet and nothing was happening when he reached the low wooden houses. He leaned forward and listened, but just for a moment, then he changed directions again, to the left. Suddenly he was no longer thinking clearly—and he'd been so clearheaded! I'm doing something stupid now, he thought. But he couldn't think of anything better. There was open land along Briskebyveien now. The Uranienborg church was bathed in moonlight. I ought to have stayed among the houses there, he thought. The moonlight was falling brightly on the old smithy at the end of Industrigate. He could read the sign: SMITHY, it said. Then there was a whole labyrinth of old wooden houses on the right, but he didn't bother to turn in there either; he didn't have any peace of mind now. He thought he could hear people everywhere.

Uphill it was like a muddy chute, but he kept to the edge where it was firmer. Nobody could have followed him on foot, but on horseback? He had read about the car thieves in France who robbed banks and were being hunted all over the country by policemen with firearms. . . . Now he was a car thief himself, being chased by people in cars. He bent over the handlebars and streaked through the night like the moon's wicked friend, a creature that people feared. Fear and jubilation hummed in him; it created a storm of excitement, of coursing blood in his veins. . . .

He stopped at an unfamiliar street. No pursuers anywhere. He hadn't met anyone, he realized that only now. No one had come after him. The man at the Frogner farm had probably put out the fire and gone in again.

But what had he thought? Who did he think it had been? That

thought took all the joy out of it, leaving him with the empty anxiety about the consequences. Those consequences that he always forgot in moments of excitement; there were many of those moments now and they were still being discovered, but if they were linked together, the *consequences,* all the consequences. . . .

He got off the bike and went right up to a house to read the name of the street on the sign: Sorgenfrigate.

The word sank in deep as he stood there with his bicycle. What a name for a street, what a word: Sorgenfri—free of care, free of sorrow, a dream, a hope. . . .

Or were there perhaps many people free of care? Free of sorrow? He had wanted to get hold of *one* sorrow, but he had frittered it away on cares that perhaps were just fabrications. And with an icy anxiety he asked himself what he wanted to do with that bonfire. He saw animals on fire rushing out, heard cows bellowing in the stalls where they were tied up. Was that what he had wanted? His hands clenched the cold handlebars. The moon had sunk low, and it was almost dark in the streets, but there was a hint of the dawn to come.

As he got on the bike again, the saddle suddenly shifted under him; it must have gotten loose when he threw the bike to the ground by the bonfire. He got off again and took out his heavy pipe wrench to tighten the nut. Right then a policeman stepped out of the darkness and said: "Are you riding without a light, kid?" He was a broad shouldered, little man with a short, dark beard under his black helmet with its bright spike. "And anyway, what are you doing out at this hour?" he said.

Lillelord was cool and calm instantly. I'm Wilfred now, he thought, this is dangerous now. He flung himself on the bicycle and pressed the pedal, but the policeman was even quicker and took hold of the basket. The bicycle tipped over. Wilfred put one foot on the ground, turned quickly with the heavy wrench in his hand, and hit the hand holding his basket with all his might.

It let go at once, and gripped again, but this time at thin air. The boy and his bicycle had a head start of about five paces. The man ran, but the distance between them increased. The boy felt a strength in him that could overcome any force and any distance. He turned at the next corner and sped down a different street with tramlines, turned again and had a long stretch ahead of him. Behind him he heard the lonely sound of a whistle in the night.

Again he was filled with great jubilation. He was riding an unruly horse at a gallop and his pursuers thundered behind him, many hooves! But they couldn't catch up. He didn't look back; the street where he was riding was rough and treacherous. Because he was afraid of being thrown by something unexpected, he kept his eyes fixed a meter in front of him. But they didn't catch him. Everything was lost, or else he had won. Everything was in motion. A wonderful peace came over him as he flew along, yes, he was flying now, like Blériot crossing the Channel. The man with his cap on backwards!

A thought struck him: suppose another policeman stopped him for not having a light. He was the "wanted" cyclist of the night; he was Kristiania's "bicycle bandit." Time and space were fluid, but his brain was working fast and his head was clear.

He stopped and looked around. The street was deserted. He put his bicycle between some bushes in a park, locked it and put the key in his pocket. He walked up a steep slope where there wasn't a path; it was like a forest with short trees. Was he out in the country again? No whistles behind him, no people. Just the low moon that rose and became more visible with each step *he* took.

On the top of Blåsen, he sat down and looked out across the fjord in the faint moonlight, a new world. A world so strange, with the spire of the Fagerborg church and the green cupola of the Trinity church popping up in the middle of the city—it caught the moonlight; so strange and remote that everything floated back to where he had fallen asleep that afternoon with his feeling of loss. Kristine—he had forgotten her since then. The girl with the orange. . . .

Dead tired and wet with sweat, he lay right down on the ground. But he got over his tiredness immediately. All that had happened was almost obliterated or hidden behind a veil. The connection with what he had experienced in his room at home came back. The past—it had overpowered him then, almost like fainting. Now it emerged again, all the things that had tried to force themselves on him, which he had escaped by falling asleep.

There was a certain similarity between then and now. He knew *now* that he was faced with a decision. He sat up and let the light stream into him. . . .

The autumn after that summer with all its defeats—he had become a clever boy then—that's right, the boy who did what was expected of him. But inside he was on the way to understanding that deep within defeat there was a sort of victory, and that fear and pain could turn to courage and something that was very good.

That was how it had been. His first day at school, when his mother had taken him and Miss Wollkwarts had asked him a few questions. Yes, he was a little late starting, but he could read and write everything, and he knew some French. They had had a governess. He was the gifted, modest boy who bowed politely, but without embarrassment. He knew it all now, because from the very start it had begun to take on the shape of a plan.

And the first party he'd been to: the little gallant his aunts adored and his uncles raised their eyebrows at. He remembered his program, how little was left to chance. And everyday life at home—now he dared to meet his cousins from Skovly. When he was seven, they'd been able to terrify him with anything. Now he was eight. From now on he could be conceited, but in moderation. "Thanks" was a good word. "Many thanks" and "Thank you very much"—those were good words, they had a good effect. He learned to say: "Have you got a new dress? It's delightful."

It was worse with ski jumping, worse than learning to swim.

The terrifying abyss of the ski jump and the little platform that swallowed you up as you flew down.

The ski jump at home was in the garden leading down to the railway line, a tiny jump that Dick from the house next door had built on *his* orders and down which they went whizzing—or so they thought. Dick was from Holland and didn't know what a hill was, and he himself . . . yes, Mother, his mother sat in the bay window there, sewing and giving him encouraging looks through the window. But she couldn't see him on the slope itself, and he jumped and fell and brushed the snow off him at the foot of the slope where she couldn't see him, then walked quickly up under the jump and skied down with a swish all the way to the fence, so that she wouldn't think—did she really believe it?—that he hadn't fallen.

Over and over again. He fell and brushed the snow off, ordered Dick to measure the distance, climbed up a little ways, pretending, and *sped* down again, skiing well when his mother saw him. He waved from where his mother could see him, and she waved back. Up again. Up again. Jumped and fell. Fell. Fell. And laughed at Dick from Holland; he fell before the jump and didn't know what a hill was. . . .

His cousins took him to the big ski jump on the Stasjonsbakke at Huseby and all those nasty slopes where his mother couldn't see him. Mittens and a cap with ear flaps and sandwiches in his pocket. And the awful jump, an abyss of fear. The last abyss—being engulfed.

The cousins at the foot of the slope after having jumped themselves. The cousins jeering, exultant. "Aren't you coming?" "Don't you dare?"

The sliding, the inexorable slide towards the abyss, the jump, the brink . . . and then—the great nothing. The flight, death. "Four meters, a-w-w!"

The happiness of discovering that he was still alive after slithering on his back with his skis spread apart down to the end. The bitter, quick scissoring up to the top, past the jump, past the jump, up. Once more. The terror. The shout from below: "All clear!"

Jump. Fall. Jump. "Keep your weight forward, Lillelord!" Keeping his weight forward. Falling on his back. Up again. Jumping and falling. Up again. Dreading it. Jumping, soaring, dying. Falling. Keeping his weight forward. Falling on his back. Being afraid. Being afraid. Terrified. He had made up his mind to do it. Stand up.

Why? He had made up his mind—to jump, to swim, to be best.

Best of whom? Of all of them. At school. On the ski slopes. In the water. Best.

A year of fear. A winter. . . . A year of applying himself, of wanting to kill anyone who threatened to be better. . . . And a break with all earthly things when he learned to swim the following summer. A flight, a baptism, a victory. . . .

To feel water flowing freely between his legs, to know there were dark depths beneath him, to be in the sea, to be independent of the land—and not to be afraid. . . . That was his greatest victory, his greatest experience. It had gotten rid of almost every other anxiety that summer—until being able to swim ceased to be a novelty, and the old fears came back, reaching out for him.

And Uncle Martin had said over his glass on the porch: "The boy's a real man!" He seemed to doubt it a little, but he said it anyway. And his mother had said: "Yes, why not? I've always known it."

His little Aunt Valborg, however, was the only one who was worried about his progress: "I think Lillelord's forcing himself to do all this; he's wearing himself out for us."

And it was true that he was wearing himself out, but not for them, for himself; he wanted to grow up and not be made fun of, to be able to develop and do all the mysterious things that awaited him, all the base things that attracted him. He avoided Aunt Valborg's scrutinizing smile that winter; she was the only one who had discovered a part of the truth, no doubt because she was so short that she didn't look down on him from above so much.

He avoided scrutiny, kept out of sight, and was very eager to serve. At school he displayed the will to be best, it couldn't fail to carry him forward; and he knew it all the time, and he knew well that the Misses Wollkwarts didn't like it, no matter how much they praised him. He knew it because it was a part of his program, which was to dazzle them, so they couldn't see inside him, so that he could keep his secrets to himself.

And he stored up secrets as a revenge for this scrutiny. He made secrets out of everything, even the most innocent things. He politely ate food he found tasteless and didn't like so that they'd think he liked it. ("Lillelord's so fond of tomato soup. . . .") He found secret delight in pulling the wool over their eyes and was delighted again when he noticed how easy it was, provided he paid attention all the time. ("The boy's rather nervous, Mrs. Sagen, I'm afraid he's being pushed too much. . . ." "On the contrary, doctor, he really loves his school, and contests, and ski jumping!")

He hated it. He was scared to death. As the jump got nearer, it was as if his stomach was being sucked out of him, and the first time he took part in the class competition he made a mess in his trousers as he stood waiting for his turn among the trees above their homemade jump at Tryvann. But afterwards he eagerly polished the tiny silver cup and cast loving glances at it in its place on the shelf, the evidence: fifth prize. He would never do any better, he knew that. He knew that when they were ten and had to use the real jump at Lille Hegghull, he'd be discovered; it was impossible to lean forward far enough when a person was as afraid as he was.

But the cup was proof, proof of a step forward on the way to being safe from exposure and mockery, so that one day he could live his own life in a world of secrets without anyone suspecting what or who he was.

He collected evidence, good reports, recognition. He was weeks ahead of the others in his lessons; he read the encyclopedia at home, column after column, and he learned to say foreign words from Meyer's dictionary: "exceptionnel" and "variable" and "retrospective" and "interieur," all without batting an eye and without that shy look up at the grown-ups that usually accompanies children's more daring efforts.

He had crushed one of his fingers once because his bluff had been called, but it was the last time. He discussed representatives of Neo-impressionism with Uncle René and knew what he was talking about. He had discovered that everything could be learned by heart, even a manner, a nature.

He got up shivering from the stone on Blåsen. The moon had set and it was beginning to get light in the northeast. He must have been daydreaming, as he had beside his bed at home, or had he?

All at once the events of the night were perfectly clear to him. He was in danger now. He may have set fire to a farm; he had struck a bearded policeman wearing a helmet. He was being pursued. There was, in fact, a word for him: *wanted.* . . .

No, he hadn't been unconscious, but gathering strength from thinking about all his defeats and how he had risen above them. Now, just like when he was six and seven—and all the years of false progress since then—he was faced with a choice, he had to embark on a fresh struggle for his secret world. He had all the advantages, and the others had none because he alone knew everything, and because he was clever and well brought-up and obedient and well dressed. He wasn't a poor boy with patched clothes who looked down at the ground when he was questioned and proved his guilt that way. He was the only one who had no accomplices and was never suspected, provided he kept to himself and was false and showed no signs of weakness—none of the passionate self-contradiction that seethed in him and at times threatened to make him explode. . . .

He soon found the right way home. The morning was bright and chilly. He walked along and felt the key to his bicycle in his pocket. The bicycle would have to stay where he'd put it, in the bushes; he could get it later. A boy with a bicycle would possibly be in jeopardy this time of the morning on the empty streets. . . . Or better yet, he could get someone to fetch it for him—Andreas. It would be a dangerous bicycle to ride for some time. It was the only Raleigh in town that he knew of. Andreas could borrow it for a while, until after the final exams. He wouldn't need it much during the time left until they went to the country. And Andreas would be happy and grateful. He walked home, shivering, but he also trembled with warmth at the thought of making Andreas happy.

But it wasn't safe for him to be out on the streets. He had to get home now. If only he had some excuse for being out. Someone might appear—a bearded constable.

He heard someone coming down the street and dived into a

gateway. The footsteps were coming closer, the footsteps of a policeman. He darted into a courtyard, there were three steps leading up to a door. The door was locked. But he squeezed into the niche and listened to the footsteps approach and then go by. He ran back to the gateway and peeked out—the back of a woman delivering newspapers, keeping close to the walls of the houses, the bumping of a heavy bag slung from a strap over her shoulder. He breathed easier. The woman stopped and took off the bag; then she took out a bundle of newspapers and let herself into the house, leaving the bag there in the street.

A new thought occurred to him. The woman had let herself in with a key. The building was a block of apartments, so it would take her some time to deliver the papers if she had to stuff one under every door there.

Quick as a cat he was over by the bag and had snatched a bundle of newspapers. He saw the key in the door—she would lock it behind her. For a moment he toyed with the idea of locking her in to gain time. But that wouldn't be necessary; he had at least a ten minute head start. Besides, she wouldn't notice that any papers were missing until she got to the end of her route. He ran around the nearest corner and came out at Teresegate. It was deserted and dreary in the growing light. He took a chance and ran at first, then he turned onto Josefinegate, by the Bislett. If he met anyone there, he could slow to a walk instantly and pretend to be looking at the houses he was passing to see if he was supposed to deliver a paper there. . . . He was the clever boy from a modest home delivering newspapers before he went to school. He sneered with distasteful exultation and looked around guardedly. He should play his part fairly well, but not to the extremes. He had to act according to the part. Had he read that somewhere? That's what he had to do—and he knew it now—to play his role properly.

He didn't meet anyone. He didn't need to play any part. No one in this section of the city had to get up before sunrise. He sneered distastefully at that thought too. There was so much to make fun of: of people who were different, of your own people, of yourself. There was a lot to make fun of. He could laugh at anything when he wasn't afraid.

And he wasn't afraid. Because he had made up his mind. Like that time before; and all his thoughts of the day just past, and the night too, they had been leading up to the realization that that summer and now—these were two almost identical times for him, all he had to do was hold his ground, boldly and with his talent, so that no one could get near him with guesses and suspicion; so he would keep to himself and be able to do remarkable things behind everyone's back and laugh at them secretly.

All at once he thought of the stupid criminals in the Nick Carter books. They brandished revolvers and made a lot of noise in the dark; they made themselves so conspicuous that any bearded constable could discover them, and basically it didn't matter if you read books like that across or up and down. That thought made him feel better. It lessened the pressure on him, the remains of pressure from long ago. He shifted the bundle of newspapers to his right arm and held up the disfigured ring finger of his left hand to the morning light. The tip was still rather flat, and the nail had faint, lengthwise streaks in it. But it wasn't deformed. No one who didn't already know could see it.

He smiled stiffly. That was exactly it: no one could know about anything if he or she didn't know or suspect something. He had a secret finger, but he also had a secret soul. All of him was secret.

Then he reached the tree-lined avenue that led down to his house. He looked around quickly, then he stuck the bundle of newspapers in the ditch under the footbridge to the next property. No one would find it there, and anyway he could always remove it some other time. He looked at his watch: a quarter past six. The maids would be getting up in fifteen minutes. Then he would ring the bell and Lilly would come and he would say that he'd gotten up early and gone out for a walk; he had slept so much the day before that he couldn't sleep any longer. He would say all that, or just part of it, depending on Lilly's mood. He would be friendly, maybe even ingratiating—or just conceited and authoritative—according to how Lilly acted. He was fully confident of his luck now, and of his ability to dissemble; he wasn't indecisive now; that had been a weakness, but it was over.

He opened the door, the one with the lock he'd picked. The *Morgenbladet* was stuck behind the door handle. There weren't any newspaperwomen with keys here, he was sure. He smiled at that thought too. He sat down on the steps to wait till it was half past six. He would ring the bell then and get Lilly to believe him. Then he would throw himself on his bed for a while and then wash and go down early and meet his mother, rested and resolute. He would make her happy by talking about the summer. He would coax her into telling him whether Aunt Kristine was coming to Skovly this summer.

That thought made him feel hot suddenly. He would see that his mother invited Kristine, like she did before, and why shouldn't she? But first of all he had to make his mother happy; she deserved that. He had made her anxious before. That was no longer necessary. That had been because he had vacillated and been divided in his own mind. Now he could make her happy just by being what she wanted him to be and still have his secrets without her or anyone else being aware of anything.

He sat down on the steps. In five minutes it would be half past six. He yawned and glanced at the newspaper he was holding. His gaze fell right away on a small headline:

BICYCLING PYROMANIAC ON THE LOOSE

The stairway swayed for a few seconds; then he collected himself, it was like ski jumping. "Lean forward!"

Slowly the letters came to rest again in front of his eyes. The tenant at the Lille Frogner farm who had woken up to find a huge bonfire. The pyromaniac who had been frightened away and hopped on a bicycle. A young man, might have been seventeen . . . vagrants seen in the area. . . .

That's what you get! The stiff sneer appeared on the boy's

face again. They couldn't imagine the arson being committed by someone who was fourteen, for example; couldn't imagine that it was a schoolboy, a resident of Drammensveien. He almost laughed out loud, until he noticed the short article underneath:

CONSTABLE ATTACKED

The steps began to rock again, and the letters danced until they turned into stripes. He pulled himself together again and stopped the swaying: ". . . knocked him down with a heavy object . . . escaped into the night. Was it the pyromaniac from Frogner?"

He tried to smile; he thought that they had made the most of that too.

But the smile wouldn't come now. He had to learn that, had to learn to smile at all times, even when no one saw him. Just to be prepared. . . . He read: "Well dressed, about sixteen, but of course it was very dark on Sorgenfrigate. . . ."

Now he managed to smile, now he could do it. It had been dark on Sorgenfrigate—that was good—it had been pitch dark and dreary on Sorgenfrigate. Perhaps there were vagrants there too. Vagrants in the darkness of the carefree street—Sorgenfrigate, Nick Carter in Kristiania. Dark men of seventeen who escaped into the night after violent crimes and arson. Wild delight shrieked inside him.

But even delight had to be tamed, everything had to be tamed, fenced in, to protect his secrets. He looked at his watch. Twenty minutes to seven. Yes, he would choose the free and easy approach with Lilly, no matter what mood she was in. He was triumphant now, an audacious lad who had been out for an early morning walk.

He got up lightly and ran up the steps with the newspaper in his hand. He rang short and hard. The approach of footsteps:

"Good morning, Lilly, here's your paper boy!"

10

Examinations were being held at the Misses Wollkwarts' private school.

Both of the tables had been removed from the big corner room that had windows facing both the street and the schoolyard. In their place, chairs had been set up along the walls for the parents and judges to attend the oral examinations. The teachers sat side by side along one short wall behind a little table covered with books and gradebooks. Miss Anette put her lorgnette on and took it off as she glanced down at the books or out into the room. This movement helped to give the ceremony its rhythm of efforts and evaluations. The pupils were called in by twos from a side room and stood in the middle of the floor while they were being examined.

Lillelord enjoyed this ceremony. He enjoyed the presence of strange grown-ups; it made it seem like appearing on stage, and he knew his part by heart. He enjoyed having his mother enthroned in the middle of the row of mothers and the one or two stranded fathers with umbrellas between their feet. He enjoyed noticing his mother's discreet elegance in that gathering of strangers all shooting stealthy glances at each other. With his back to the audience and looking at the expectant faces of the Misses Wollkwarts, he was faintly aware of his mother's scent enveloping him and giving him its own soft assurance.

But even more enjoyable to him was the ceremony afterwards, when the results were read to the parents and judges, accompanied by various degrees of silence. Then all the pupils were assembled in the big corner room and stood, groaning weakly, in a cluster around the window facing the schoolyard. One by one they stepped forward then and recited a poem of their choice—it could be something they had done at school that year or something they had read at home. Many of them chose a psalm, partly because much of it was incomprehensible and it stuck in their minds better, and partly because they had a vague notion that they would gain some sympathy by siding with the angels.

Lillelord experienced a peculiar, buoyant calm as he stepped forward—this time facing the circle of guests—and announced the title of the poem he had chosen:

" 'In the Power of the Farmer's Daughter'—an old Danish folk song," he said firmly.

A buzz of anticipation passed through the classroom. Miss Anette Wollkwarts nodded confidently and glanced quickly at her sister, who also nodded, though she was a little uncertain. Why did the boy always have to choose something unusual? But the words *folk song* inspired respect and confidence in his very refined manners; he was one of those pupils who worked at his subjects on his own.

Lillelord began:

Once I journeyed from the town
To a farm I had to go
The farmer's daughter took me in
Better had she done not so
For sleep I did not know.

One or two people cleared their throats as Lillelord continued:

I asked her where her father was,
"He is gone to the court," quoth she.
I asked her where her mother was,
"She is in her bed," said she.

There was a certain restlessness here and there. He was aware of it in front and behind him; he saw the Wollkwarts sisters exchange a wary look, but he continued indefatigably:

When I had drunk a little while
But not so long, you see,
The maid she went to her father's barn
And there prepared a couch for me.

People were whispering loudly now. One of the Misses Wollkwarts almost got up, but Lillelord stared straight at the wall in front of him. His persistence gave him a delicious fiery feeling in his veins. Never yet had a pupil been interrupted at the examination celebrations because of his choice of a poem:

"Listen here, my handsome young fellow,
This hour thou shalt pleasure me
Or with this hand of mine
Thy life shall forfeit be."

"Lillelord!" It was Miss Signe who had finally gotten to her feet. "How many verses are there in this ballad?"

"Seventeen, Miss Wollkwarts."

Miss Wollkwarts' mouth trembled. She was momentarily unable to make a decision. The judges were either looking at the floor or glancing dejectedly at eath other. Lillelord went on:

One hand grasped my hair
The other held a knife,
"Now thou shalt pleasure me
Or pay forfeit with thy life."

"Lillelord! I think—I think we've heard enough of this!"

It was Miss Signe's voice. It had acquired a metallic ring, but even so, half of what she said was lost in the buzz from the audience. He might not have heard it because the pupils were often excited during this part of the celebration.

So I drew off my tunic
And off my doublet red . . .

"Wilfred!"

This time no one could have missed hearing it. He seemed to come out of a deep trance and looked straight at Miss Signe.

"Yes, Miss Wollkwarts?"

"That's enough of your Danish folk songs. I don't think you really understand. . . . I mean, they're scarcely suitable. . . ."

Her bewildered gaze strayed over the gathering. There were one or two barely concealed smiles on the lowered faces. Birds were twittering in the old trees in the schoolyard. Wilfred walked back to the semi-circle of boys at the end of the room.

"Next!"

Andreas stepped forward. He was pale.

" 'Flower-Ole,' by Jørgen Moe," he said, in a low, mumbling voice.

"Louder, Andreas."

" 'Flower-Ole,' by Jørgen Moe."

It wasn't much louder. Outside the birds were chirping in a frenzy.

"All right. Begin."

They all knew about his strange fascination for that poem, though no one had heard him recite it. It was just something that he mumbled to himself during quiet moments.

"I remember so well," someone whispered, to get him started.

"No whispering, thank you!"

The Misses Wollkwarts were again in control. There had been one unprecedented incident; now they had to see that everything else went smoothly, so that the end of the year celebration would have its traditional effect. All eyes turned hopefully toward Andreas standing there in the middle of the floor. You could see the lips of many of those present forming the fateful first few words. Then suddenly it came, as from a machine:

> I remember so well from my childhood days,
> A badger that came . . .

There was a burst of laughter from the group by the window. Parents and judges snickered, though with some restraint. Signe Wollkwarts drew herself up and fired off a "Quiet!" that had more effect on the parents than the pupils.

"You happened to say 'badger,' Andreas. It's easy to do and nothing to laugh at." She reprimanded those present with a look. "It ought to be, of course . . . well, go on—or rather, start over."

> I remember so well from my childhood days,
> A badger that came . . .

This time the laughter was uncontrollable. Even Miss Anette smiled. But her sister's voice cut through the merriment: "You mean *beggar,* of course, don't you Andreas? The poet is recalling the tragic story of the thoughtless children who nailed Flower-Ole's wooden shoes to the steps, so that he fell down and was killed, isn't that it?"

Andreas blushed in waves. His fists opened and closed. Opened and closed.

"Isn't that it, Andreas?" The voice was so gentle that it was threatening.

"I always thought it was a badger," Andreas said quietly. "That's why I liked it so much."

There was another explosion of laughter that seemed to come from the walls and corners. Andreas, the arithmetician, the geography expert, perhaps a poet in his own way—stood there utterly helpless, it looked like a world of mysticism and beauty had crashed around him. "Badger," the word spread from mouth to mouth, a sarcastic, wicked sound, a teasing, jeering sound. The Misses Wollkwarts realized that the boy must have really labored under that extraordinary misconception about Jørgen Moe's childhood reminiscences.

"But that's quite impossible," Miss Signe said coldly.

Lillelord, standing in the group, felt that she had betrayed them, betrayed her pupils to the mockery of the others and the laughter of grown-ups and strangers.

"Miss Wollkwarts," he said in a loud voice, "I always thought it was a badger, too."

Suddenly it was deathly silent.

"Nonsense, Wilfred," Miss Signe said calmly.

"Excuse me, but I have. I can't help it."

This was another unprecedented situation. The end of the year celebrations at Misses Wollkwarts' preparatory school had always been characterized by harmony and competent presentations. What was this spirit that had suddenly come into the gathering? Parents exploding with laughter and pupils who acted like idiots or rebels.

"Next!" Miss Anette said. Her tone was neither loud nor sharp, but it carried something definite: there would be no more scandals.

Thoughts tumbled through Lillelord's head throughout the rest of the ceremony. He listened lethargically to poem after poem, some recited monotonously, others with an artificial meaningfulness that bothered him even more. He knew them all and had his own way of saying each one of them. But behind his listlessness, his thoughts intersected in an expectation of catastrophe.

What had he wanted with that peculiar folk song? It was true that he loved these semi-incomprehensible examples of the oral tradition in that old volume with the fantastic drawings. It was up on top of the bookcase, on the right. Those books were his, but they were put where he couldn't reach them easily.

He liked the racy "In the Power of the Farmer's Daughter," but he wasn't interested in defying the Misses Wollkwarts on his last day at their school, where in general he had been content and learned so much. He had trembled for days and nights, afraid that his teachers and his mother would somehow come in contact and discover the game he'd been playing all year with his letters and messages and the foolishness that was over now. He vaguely sensed that if he tipped over the first stone, there would be a landslide; he would be exposed as a depraved young boy in the eyes of all the people he was fond of.

He stood there among the other students, suffering, coolly pondering whether it was this catastrophe he was longing for: a revelation that could put an end to all his misery. . . .

But this wasn't it. He had made himself a life of necessary secrets and had lived it on a modest scale that winter and spring. That was just a prelude to all the debasing and liberating events that were to come in the immediate future. He didn't want to defy these people now, no matter what the cost, now that it depended on them that nothing went wrong.

And yet that was what he'd done. For the first time during that spring of crime he felt apprehensive about himself, because he didn't have control over the things he'd started. He knew that the silly joke about the folk song had been carefully planned, but the other thing, about the badger, that had come on its own. Both were equally risky and almost equally incomprehensible to him. What had he expected from the folk song? And the other one: wasn't that his system, that no one should ever catch him doing anything spontaneous—that everything must be calculated beforehand. . . .

He noticed Andreas looking at him. For a moment he half turned towards him. His eyes were shining with gratitude and despair. He saw a wan smile flit across his face—he was condemned to being dumb.

Lillelord thought: He is grateful to me. I can use him for something when I need to.

He stuck close to his mother during the good-byes. He was ready to use any means to prevent a conversation between her and his teachers. While his mother was still shaking their hands, he interrupted her with a clumsiness that was quite unlike him. He begged their pardon, but he couldn't be avoided. He succeeded in reducing the ceremony to the minimum. "But, Lillelord, I think you're crazy," his mother said. "The grown-ups have to say good-bye first, you know that very well."

But he persisted and got her away. The Misses Wollkwarts were left with their sour-sweet smiles, fighting for authority. "Examination excitement," Miss Anette murmured with panicked geniality.

Mother and son walked down the street in silence. There was an air of desolation about everything in the sunshine. That good time—the day that had always been so good—had suddenly become a threatening day.

She stopped. "Now, Lillelord," she said, "I want an explanation."

"But Mother, Miss Wollkwarts was being so nasty to Andreas."

"It's not that. That can pass, just barely. You did it to help a friend. You know perfectly well what I mean: the folk song."

They were standing on the gravelled sidewalk; they had walked along here many times; four of those times from the end of the year celebrations, always in high spirits and full of expectation.

"Aren't we going to Rolfsen's for pastry?" he asked.

"I don't know," she said and started to walk slowly. Two big, horse drawn wagons clattered heavily over the uneven pavement. The din they made gave him time to think.

"Mother," he said, "if I had recited that folk song at one of Uncle René's musical evenings. . . ."

"Well, what?" she said coldly.

"You would have all laughed."

"We certainly would not!"

Mrs. Sagen felt powerless again, and she was aware of her own inadequacy, as she had been for a moment in that stuffy classroom among those serious parents. She had always had reason to be proud of her clever boy at the exams. But now this feeling came over her again.

"Are you sure of that?" he said quietly.

She looked down at him, worried. It was no longer so very far down. When had he grown up so much?

And again the unpleasant feeling that everything was heading for a change.

And then suddenly, the opposite: a feeling of joy that everything was still like it had been.

"Of course we're going to Rolfsen's."

His hand slipped in under her arm—the warm, trusting grip of an escort's arm, a feeling of loss and satisfaction at the same time.

"Four pastries?" he said temptingly.

"Four pastries."

"The biggest ones, that cost 80 øre?"

"The very biggest."

"And hot chocolate with cream?"

"In this heat?"

"Mother, it *has* to be chocolate and cream."

"All right, that's what we'll have."

They fell into step and walked on, arm in arm like an engaged couple, leaning slightly inwards toward each other. At Rolfsen's on the Egertorv they went to the back room with the marble ceiling and gilt-framed mirrors. With bits of pastry tumbling out of his mouth, he said: "You know, Mother, no matter where I go in my life and whatever I get to eat or drink, I think nothing will ever be as nice and good as this."

She looked at him, touched and yet troubled. There was something fanatical about his need to enjoy and relish things that frightened her at times, and a thought occurred to her: What will happen when it's no longer a question of chocolate. The day it's no longer me. . . .

But then her thoughts came back to the kind that just came and went, and when they were gone, they'd never really been there, they'd only knocked on the door, like the times you're expecting the arrival of some tiring relatives and you're always thinking someone's knocking on the door. Her mind wasn't trained to deal with what was unpleasant, so when she opened the door a little, she saw that no one was there. . . .

"And after this, Mother, we'll walk home along the waterfront; it's been a long time since we've done that."

They walked along the waterfront, the whole length of it from east to west. Full-riggers with bristling yards rocked romantically by the huge red buoys in Bjørvika, and the old *Kongshavn I* with its dirty, gray hull was being painted and having an awning stretched over her afterdeck—she was being outfitted to ferry people over to the Kongshavn Baths, where there was a theatre and park. Lillelord saw signs of summer everywhere, but they were most evident in the smells from the sea, hot and sweet now from all different kinds of tar and rope. And all the big iron hulls with black funnels sticking up threateningly, and grimy men in wool undershirts and trousers on the decks; the foreign languages. He had often sneaked down there at dusk and seen strange ladies being helped on board and heard words that could have meant just about anything, judging by the tone in which they were spoken; he had toyed with the idea of creeping aboard a ship and going out into the world. He had met other boys who roamed around on the quays with the same fateful yearning in their eyes; they recognized each other by that look and they tried to make themselves seem manly by using the words they'd picked up and telling tales about the sea. Probably no one believed what they said, and it didn't matter anyway. They were all at the frontier of the same strange land and didn't mind each other being there.

Once in a while they whispered about someone who had really managed to do it. Once in a while he read articles in the newspaper. . . .

Now he was walking along here, arm in arm with his mother. The sky was high and bright, the day was gently declining. It struck him as he walked along guessing the names of the ships before they could see the lettering, that a waterfront was two things, according to how you experienced it; a boat was two things; he was two quite different persons. And his mother? He studied her face, elegantly raised above the narrow velvet edging of her clothes; her face was covered, and yet perfectly visible behind a gray veil as thin as a suspicion. Was she also two different people? Was everybody? Was absolutely everything? Two or three or infinitely many? Was the *Bonn*'s yellow foremast only yellow in his eyes and, for example, blue in another's? Or if it was yellow in everyone's eyes, was that just because they had agreed on it—and what was it like being yellow? Was the definition of Mrs. Sagen a stylish lady in blue-gray with a youthful curve in her cheeks and gentle gray-blue eyes that matched her clothes? Was she "good fun," "kind hearted," "easy to persuade," "lovable. . . ." Was that her? And why, in that case, when he was here walking along at this wonderful hour and had almost nothing in common with the one who roamed the streets and waterfront in the dusky afternoons with his throat dry with delight and his eyes shiny with the desire for everything, the familiar and the still unknown things that were gathering in a glowing focus. . . .

"Lillelord, you're forgetting to guess!"

"The *Bonn*."

"I can see that too." She was as absorbed in the game as he was. "But what about the one way out by Vippetangen?"

"That's the new *Kristianiafjord,* everybody knows that." Tall and straight and elegant, the nation's pride towered over the others with her two yellow funnels. Until just recently the Danish-American boats had predominated there, the *King Frederik of Denmark* and the other big, black boats with the red ring around their funnels.

"But that one behind there?" he asked. "The one where all you can see is its steam whistle?"

"That's not fair, all you can see is the steam whistle, as you said."

"King Ring," he said triumphantly.

This time she thought he was bluffing. She was going to catch him red-handed now. They walked more quickly now; she was filled with a malicious excitement that she couldn't explain: it must have been the residue of her bad conscience because she hadn't been stricter before.

But it was the *King Ring*. When they came close enough, the name shone clearly—gold letters on a black background.

"Lillelord!" she said, disappointed and relieved at the same time. "How have you learned the names of all these ships?"

"The boy has a talent for it," he said, mimicking Miss Signe's slightly squeaky voice. Mother and son gave each other a quick look. She shook her head slightly and let her gaze rest on the summery fjord with its reminder of the carefree state that had *been*. . . . Without daring to admit it to herself, she was afraid of everything that wasn't that, everything that was different, a fear of the inevitable.

"Mother," he said, "let's go home on Ruseløkkveien and see the place where little Gudrun disappeared."

"But dear boy, that's all so unpleasant."

"Let's do it, Mother. Shall we go through Vika?"

His mother looked at him indignantly: "You know perfectly well that *I* can't go through Vika."

The low wooden houses lay ahead of them, the narrow alleys teeming with strange people, the *other* people, who weren't like them. They walked away from Søgate, past the West Railway Station, and up to Ruseløkkveien. There they peeked into the excavation between the marketplaces; he spoke in a low voice about the sinister door that led down into the sewers, the door that wasn't locked on that fateful afternoon when little Gudrun had run there to hide, and when they found her body, it had been half eaten by rats. . . .

"You know so much about it!" she said, worried, as they shuddered and walked on. "We've talked about it as little as possible."

He was seething with a sensation he couldn't explain. It was as though his two personalities were beginning to unite, as though his mother was out with him on his illegal errands.

"Mother, can we go to the Tivoli Theatre?" he said breathlessly.

She looked at him in horror: "The Tivoli Theatre? When you come with me to the National Theatre and you've been taken to hear *Lohengrin*? How many of your friends do you think have done that?"

"I know that, Mother, but can't we go just the same? Go and see the 'Divertissement Exotique' and 'Life in a Moorish Harem' and a teahouse in Nagasaki with genuine geishas, five of them?"

"Tell me son, are you crazy?"

"Let's go, Mother. Then you can tell Uncle Martin about it afterwards. About the Indian fakirs' mystical secrets. . . ."

"Is this something you're making up?"

"Cross my heart, Mother, that's what's there."

Again she felt like she wanted to catch him red-handed. This was invention and fantasy, the worst kind of attempted bluff. She turned abruptly and said: "Okay, we'll go and see what's playing there."

A heavy silence hung between them. There was no sunlight between the houses there. When they came out on Stortingsgate and went into the illuminated brick entryway to the Tivoli, the gas lamps on the balustrade of the open air restaurant were already casting a dull light. A working class crowd reeking of beer flocked around the posters.

"Now you can see, Mother," Lillelord said, a little offended. It was the first thing either of them had said for a long time. Her astonished eyes read the posters in their ornately carved frames:

DIVERTISSEMENT EXOTIQUE
INDIAN FAKIRS' MYSTICAL SECRETS
LIFE IN A MOORISH HAREM
FIRST TIME IN EUROPE
A TEAHOUSE IN NAGASAKI
GENUINE GEISHAS

She felt almost as if she should beg his pardon, then she was confused: "Yes, but Lillelord, how did you know?"

"It's in the newspaper, Mother, every day on page four of the *Morgenbladet*. Do you know what's playing at the Bio-Cinema? 'Broken Hearts.' "

Then the laughter finally came. His mother's childish, trilling laughter that recognized only fun in the world. It was like a lid being taken off her, leaving only ineffable relief; all these mysterious things were printed every day in her own, safe *Morgenbladet,* and her gifted son, her avid little reader, had read them. And at once she seemed to have found an explanation for the indecent folk song that had agitated the prudish Misses Wollkwarts. Yes, leave them in peace, they did their best. It was as though she had to forgive a whole world now that she could forgive her beloved boy, who had only been using his sharp eyes to read the names of ships, advertisements, poems, and posters. What in the world had she been worried about?

She squeezed his thin arm, and all at once she felt she wanted to do something unusual, like in the old days, as they used to do often abroad; in the good and terribly bad, old days when her life had been a gush of days and nights, a cascade . . . compared to the quiet flow of a stream here in Kristiania, the calm passage of time to an old age that she seldom thought about.

"Yes, why in the world shouldn't we go to the Tivoli Theatre?" she said tentatively, but stopped herself: "But it's a long time to wait until eight o'clock."

"But Mother, don't you see? It's Saturday and there are two performances. It says so on the poster."

That too had escaped her attention. All the things she didn't see! All her boy's eyes saw and his ears heard!

"Yes, of course, it's Saturday," she said, so she wouldn't seem dumb to her quick-witted escort. They pushed to the window of the ticket office along with all the strangers, and the strange smells. They were like two lost children as they went inside and up the stairs to the theatre. A doorman in an admiral's uniform tore their tickets. Then they came to the auditorium of the theatre with its silver painted tables and chairs with curved legs. A waiter in a gleaming white apron came over, conjured a note pad out of his apron and a pencil from behind his ear.

"Have a glass of sherry, Mother," Lillelord whispered.

"A glass of sherry please," she said automatically.

"And for the young gentleman?" the waiter leaned over the table and smiled cordially.

"A glass of sherry for me too!" Lillelord whispered.

She had said it already. The waiter, naturally, had raised his eyebrows: Was she mistaken? "I think you're crazy," she said happily.

"You can easily drink two glasses of sherry," he said. She looked around furtively at the strange place. The air in the hall was thick with smoke and smells. A huge man with a roguish, beery look stepped over her feet, with his back to her, and she shivered with happiness. For some reason or other she thought of Aunt Klara and her grammatical finickiness. Lillelord was singing softly to himself amid all the noise as the theatre filled up, and tobacco smoke began to create a haze among the tables, uniting them in genial companionship.

"Lillelord, you're singing!"

He sang louder. He sang *Die Angst, die Axt . . .* to a tune he'd made up with its own rhythm.

"I was thinking of Aunt Klara!" he shouted up toward her face.

It was like lightning striking her.

"*Why* were you thinking about Aunt Klara?"

"Die Zusammenkunft, die Feuersbrunst!

"Don't know. Don't know. . . ." He sang that too. He was possessed by the fever of expectation that grew with the noise around him: loud voices ordering beer and herring, drinks and meat patties and herring and beer, toddy and coffee and herring and beer.

There was a buzzing in the theatre. He saw the conductor's baton between two thick necks wearing bowler hats. It was as though that thin stick was slashing away at the curtain of haze to obtain some silence. And the next moment the brass instruments blared forth. The din and the shouting increased simultaneously and began a mortal struggle with the music. Arms motioned at the waiters gliding among the tables, balancing shiny trays on the palms of their upraised hands. Everyone knew that he had to get his order in before the curtain rose. Shouts and music joined in an ethereal unity. The din made all conversation impossible. Large sherry glasses were placed, with a flourish, on the tabletop in front of mother and son. They looked at each other; there was a delight in everything.

And suddenly it was as quiet as a church. The red curtain parted and revealed the stage, bathed in blue light and peopled by four demonical fakirs in shiny yellow silk. Shouts and applause thundered out, then everything was quiet again, except for the men smacking their lips and sucking the beer out of their beards —this sound ran through the auditorium like an agreed signal. Then one of the fakirs raised his hand. The act was beginning.

Their performance was gratefully received, though the audience was shocked. Lillelord was bewitched and stared at the eerie things, and when the fakirs finally went backstage, his hands were wet and numb. He couldn't clap; he couldn't say a word. The pierced cheeks, dancing snakes, swaying, weightless limbs, as in his—and everyone's—secret dreams, that filled him with terror and a joy greater than even Peter Cornelius singing in *Lohengrin* at the National Theatre. He had caught occasional glimpses of his mother's face through the smoky haze: when the fakirs' tricks were too much, her face was bent down toward the table. She whispered into his ear: "How's it going, son?"

"Fine, Mother, fine!" He was afraid that she'd want to go.

But when it came to "Life in a Moorish Harem" and five skinny girls, obviously of Germanic origin, appeared onstage decked out in orange silk pantaloons, she suddenly burst into hysterical laughter. People turned toward her indignantly. They were all thrilled by the flame-red lighting on the stage and the cardboard Moorish walls behind the girls. Mother and son stared at the tabletop in anguish and didn't dare to look at each other. They didn't want to challenge the plebian surrounding they'd ventured into, not for a moment. Lillelord carefully laid his hand on his mother's and gave it a squeeze. Even that was enough. The next moment they were doubled over again, giggling. But fortunately the ladies of the harem had started singing a monotonous oriental song, supported robustly by the orchestra's woodwinds. The spectacle and the music kept the rest of the audience spellbound.

The jubilation culminated with the genuine geishas. They utterly captivated the audience. They moved around the stage so gracefully, taking tiny, Japanese steps, that the two necks in front of Lillelord began to glisten. He stared at them, entranced, every time they came so close together that they blocked his view of the geishas. It was like looking at a landscape with rivers and mountains and damp valleys with deep craters full of undergrowth all around. It gave him the same terrifying thrill as that time at Kunio's menagerie when he got to hold a month-old lion cub: it was frightening and delightful. . . .

"Lillelord, what are you looking at?"

He pointed discreetly. He saw his mother's eyes narrow in disgust. She picked up her sherry glass, it was empty. He quickly pushed the other glass in front of her. But then he noticed that she was pale.

"Do you want to go, Mother?"

She nodded. As carefully as possible, they picked their way over the feet that didn't move an inch and the feet that only reluctantly moved as much as necessary.

As they were walking together along Drammensveien in the

late spring evening, filled with light and with the red sunset blazing, the same uncontrollable giggling came over them. They walked along, laughing at the light, and people turned to look at them, but they weren't bothered by anything.

They walked along arm in arm, laughing at the sunset, they were on their way home, back *from* an exciting expedition to a foreign land, *to* a world that was safe and was theirs. They turned down their own driveway with its old trees and old wheeltracks, dry at the edges now, toward their house.

"I'll never forget this evening, Mother!" Lillelord said.

THE GLASS EGG

11

He recognized her the moment the boat swung around the headland. She was standing on the foredeck among the crates and barrels, the only woman, surrounded by men in work pants. She was wearing a narrow-brimmed straw hat with a veil tied somewhere at her neck and a cape with a yellow lining over a green dress. He saw it all like a picture he had anticipated in his mind, and he thought there was always something "indoorish" about Aunt Kristine, no matter how she dressed for an outing.

But as the little fjord boat got closer, he suddenly no longer recognized her; he began to think that it had just been his imagination because he had pictured her standing like that. The woman on the foredeck suddenly looked shorter than Kristine and perhaps a little older. . . .

Then she waved. And he was disappointed. He was amazed that he had seen everything correctly at that distance.

But as he held his hands out to help her, as the little gangplank was put ashore, it was Aunt Kristine after all, no, it was Kristine, not "aunt." During those last weeks of longing and dreaming, when everything was transformed, he had stopped thinking of her as his aunt.

The boatman handed up two big suitcases—so, perhaps she intended to stay a long time. His tanned face sought hers, to give her a kiss that was returned.

He looked up and noticed that the people sitting on the deck were looking at them.

"Yes, actually I've travelled second class all the way. The fresh air. . . ."

That stung him. Was it true that Aunt Kristine was poor? The word itself was so strange when it was applied to a member of his own circle. It wasn't possible that anyone who was poor wasn't also—well, different. They walked up the steep path toward the house together—she graceful and light-footed from just being in unusual surroundings, he the gentleman carrying the heavy suitcases.

And she seemed to be continually changing as they ate a late breakfast of small lobsters (trapped illegally) and then tea and marmalade on the veranda, where they sat facing each other across the slatted table with a gray linen tablecloth.

Aunt Kristine got up to fetch her purse, which she had left in the hall. When they were alone, his mother looked at him, irritated: "Why are you staring at Kristine like that? You look like you're going to eat her!"

He looked away when she returned. He looked everywhere but at her, out over the sea, then the other way, toward the garden, where the birds were getting quieter as the sun rose higher. It was going to be a hot day.

He felt hurt and ashamed; he'd been caught red-handed. With just his mother and a few friends from the neighboring houses, he had relaxed his feverish defense precautions during the vacation. Nothing had confronted him with that dangerous reality from which he had fled—all the unexplained things. It was all different here at Skovly; it was a sanctuary. And what had his mother meant when she said Kristine and not "aunt"?

When the maid came to clear the table, his mother went with Kristine to her room. Alone, and feeling more lonely than he thought was possible that day, he wandered out to the garden and took the path that went down past the old well with its worn brown pyramid of a roof behind the tall clump of grayish-white aspens.

And now he sensed what it had been at breakfast: Kristine had been changing the whole time! From the moment she met his mother's outstretched arms at the white gate: she was "Aunt" Kristine then, a lady, someone who had come with the boat. But later, when he handed her the marmalade and toast and their eyes met for a second, then she was no longer a lady but the "woman," the person from his risqué dreams since that cold early morning when he sat on top of Blåsen steeling himself for now; waiting, he'd been spending the happy hours at Skovly alone, on the pretext of botanizing, roaming around by himself so he wouldn't have to join the ecstatic games the young people and children played on the first boisterous days of the vacation. Those were the days when life began again for many of them. They never saw each other all year in the city, but out here they knew each other from all the previous summers, and it was as if there had been no winter, no school, and no lies. *That,* at least, was the same for all of them.

But now and then—when they told each other some of the things that had happened since last autumn, he couldn't help feeling utterly alien to young people his own age and to the older people as well. Their innocence was foreign to him, as were their childish tales about school and tiny excesses. He hadn't realized this properly before, and he suspected that it was because this was a summer of decision for him, a summer that would change him once and for all and complete the *other* person in him—and how horrified they'd be if you mentioned *that* to them!

He could see them from the garden now: they were standing by the big window upstairs, his mother and Kristine. He could see that she was being an "aunt" from more than a hundred meters away. He heard the voices of his companions on the other side of the tall hedge, the loudest voice belonged to boisterous, serious Erna. It stung him, Erna always did that. There had "been something" between them from summer to summer ever since they were small, something that existed but never became anything, a childish infatuation that he liked to have there, but which had suddenly become more compelling these last few weeks. He crept up carefully to the elm hedge and parted the leaves. He saw Erna in the middle of a circle, flushed and eager, in her faded blue dress that only reached to her knees. A child, he thought. But suddenly (and for the first time)—even though he had seen her every day for the last two weeks—he saw that she wasn't really a child, like he'd thought. Then he also remembered the look she had given *him* the first time they met this year, a look that measured him from the top down, like the one his mother had given him last spring. . . .

They were going out to the little islands, two boatloads of them; they'd take some food along, collect feathers and swim; they were going to *capture* the islands—a game they played every summer, a game with drama and affectation—there was no one who would refuse to let them conquer those two bare rocks in the fjord with their innocent white boats and picnic baskets and bottles of fruit juice!

Another twinge. He wanted to call out to them, as they stood there on the gravel path with its trim edging of white shells along the grass on either side, to let them know he was there and to tell them he wanted to go with them.

Then one of the boys said: "We should have taken Wilfred."

But Erna pouted and said curtly: "He's having that aunt visiting. . . ."

And she said "aunt" in exactly the same way as. . . . But was it possible that he had given himself away like that? Could it be possible that these "women," his mother and this little girl, that they were so clever, so suspicious or sure of their instinct—whatever they called it. . . . Could they possibly have guessed the connection that was his secret dream to such a degree that he himself was scarcely conscious of it—at least not on the level of consciousness that dealt with everyday realities? He had never even linked these two things, not even by himself: his resolve and painful desire on the one side, and on the other, he saw himself as he *was;* it wasn't clear to him that he was the one who was involved, the one who would experience those joyous and scandalous things. For when his thoughts were on them day and night, it was as if they were about someone else.

Tenderness and irritation rose in him. He let the leaves fall back into place. He looked back toward the house. There was no one by the window now. At that moment the young voices on the *other* side began to recede, down toward the water and the boats.

And what about it? He got up from where he'd been kneeling on the grass: wasn't this just what he wanted—to be alone, to be someone they didn't know? He noticed that it hurt to be less like a child, but he knew that he didn't belong among the grown-ups, so what? Why should he belong at all? He should *be*. . . .

Suddenly self-assured, he walked back to the house to make himself useful and be unmoved. It was when he acted cold and thought quickly that things went right for him; it was in his weak moments that he bungled everything. . . . And as he walked along—with a new, somewhat elastic gait, holding his head abnormally high—he suddenly thought about everything that had happened that spring and about the reports in the newspapers about his "arson," the worried articles in the *Morgenbladet* about depraved young people, and those children from better-off homes who indulged in shady activities, about a new spirit these days. And that the police had a lead.

He laughed; his head tilted back: if they did, it wasn't leading them to him. They were on the track of all the childish braggarts who told secretive stories on street corners at dusk. Not on *his* tracks, because they were covered by the circumstances themselves. No short, bearded constable with a black helmet could find him, not with all his tracks. It was the poor boys who were caught, the grammar school boys and the stupid adventurers from his own class who did little things for the fun of it and couldn't keep their mouths shut.

He quickly scrambled over the uncut lawn that was always left as a sort of wilderness for them to play in. He snatched up the flowers he could see: pansies, red clover, daisies and buttercups. Poppies and flaxweed added to the confusion of a bouquet that was like a child's shout. "Hallo!" he called out happily as they came out onto the terrace. He ran up the steps—and knew that his "shining" face was obvious when he reached them, breathless, and held out the bouquet deferentially: "A little bouquet for you, Aunt!" He noticed his mother looking at him; all her irritation was gone now; now her eyes were saying: "My own good boy." And he saw Kristine's eyes; they said something quite different. Now she was Kristine again, not aunt—though she was standing right beside his mother—almost on fire—and took his offering. He saw that she had a dark red bathing suit over her arm.

The *bathhouse* became the place where anything could happen during that summer of sharp desire. There was something mysterious about everything in the bathhouse: its stuffy smell—a combination of sun, hot timber and salt water in the channel into the tank; even the walls with their pattern of scraped paint and knots in the wood that could be turned into something sweetly indecent; the comically shimmering oval mirror in a green papier-mâché frame with *Pellerin's Margarine* on it; even the cheap, wobbly surface of the mirror that distorted your image—there was something sinister and tempting about everything that he hadn't noticed before. And the tank with its heavy mechanism of steel beams and chains and the restlessly sparkling green light down there where he had suffered defeat. . . . There was something enticing about the very recollection of those disgraceful scenes, precisely because they were ignominious. And the seaweed poking in through the ribs of the bathhouse, swaying and waving, always moving—everything spoke its own exciting language: the narrow couch covered with an icy waxed tablecloth for people to rest on after a bath, with a bath towel under them. There were possibilities everywhere: memories and possibilities merged into something sweetly depraved that possessed him all the time. And the colored panes in the windows, green, red, blue, and exciting yellow squares. How wonderful and frightening to look at the beach and the knolls and the willow trees through them, and to move from pane to pane, from fiery red to estranging blue, to cool green . . . and then a quick shift to dark yellow that produced an atmosphere of thunder and terror that affected every fiber in his body, and then, finally, his eyes were disappointed by the ordinary glass, which suddenly made all of nature seem innocuous and silly, just ordinary. . . .

He circled around the bathhouse while Kristine was bathing. He didn't peek in. There was nothing to peek at, for Kristine began to swim from the opening in the tank and even her shoulders were covered by the dark red material of her bathing suit; even her hair. . . . There was less of her to see then than there ordinarily was. But to stand behind the knoll when she was inside and know that she was there. To stand up confidently and walk over there, fling the door open and see her standing there, white, soft, and naked, and then. . . . There were as many variants to his fantasies as the situation permitted: a smile, the open arms, two breasts and a crotch; or a horrified shriek, two arms coming together and trying to conceal; or another form of consternation that he could pretend was feigned: anger, anger and indignation that were possible to overcome. . . . And his part: a pretense of being aghast, or even amazed, as if he hadn't known she was there; ecstatic surprise that she was *so* beautiful—an attitude that could cover a lot of things; blind determination, violence, force!

Anything was possible, anything *should* be possible. But in the end, at last!—just one thing, the unprecedented thing that would consummate everything and make it different.

She was always alone in the bathhouse. His mother complained about her rheumatism, but only because she didn't know how to swim. He felt sorry for her about that, otherwise she always bathed. But his sympathy was overshadowed by the dark delight of his fantasies. . . .

. . . Or *he* could be there. He could be standing there when she came, in the middle of the floor and obviously excited, a condition that was almost permanent for him now. He could stand there like an unexpected, grotesque indecency that would scare her out the door, or better yet, make her swoon a little. Then he would storm her and tear off her clothes, the loose summer dress with its cloth buttons on the back, at the top—he had touched them and knew how to deal with them. . . . Or, even better, she'd stop, paralyzed, and look him over for a moment; she'd understand and be conquered by his appalling, childish desire that would drive out any notion of childishness.

He had thought out every way and every possibility in his feverish fantasies, seeing misery and delight, his throat dry, sometimes being drained in moments followed by shame and disappointment—like that final look through the pane of plain glass. Every possibility was accompanied by aching loins and a sore throat. It was her and sometimes it was him. But just as often it wasn't him or anyone definite, just someone filled with his bitter sweetness; or it wasn't exactly *him,* but certainly not anyone else! Someone in him. *The one* in him. The one *on* him, who was bigger and stronger than he was; the stubborn animal on him; and the stomach, thighs and breasts . . . things boys joked about secretly on street corners in the twilight and shyly exchanged experiences about, but he wanted to know about them, use them as they were meant to be used—that was the only thing that could consummate the springtime aching in him and make him really alone.

But there was another Kristine too; not only the white, imaginary figure in the suggestive shadows of the bathhouse. There was the Kristine who had cried, the little girl who sat at the foot of the stairs by the garden and cried; and he could love her with tender innocence, with an affection that was full of comfort and manly advice about life's adversities. He had the words to say to her, masses of borrowed and experienced words, words that he had read and words that came on their own, full of comfort and wisdom and chivalrous tenderness towards the weaker being who had suffered.

A Kristine like that lived in him now and then and with full intensity, but not even she was his "aunt"; she was a woman, a defenseless woman, whom life had dealt with harshly and whom he should take under his kind, strong wing. And there were intermediate Kristines, just like there were parts of him that were mixtures of his different personalities: the ravisher, the lover, the protective brother, even uncle or husband. There was an infinity of transitions corresponding to the ones in both of them and to the wealth of possible situations, so inexhaustible that all the days and nights in the world wouldn't be enough time to dream about all of them. He concocted all these variants, according to the secret recipes that were his life and served them up for himself in consciously graduated helpings.

And everything was full of words, but not words he could say to her.

He could pass her the salad bowl across the table and not be able to say "help yourself." After lunch he went out under the trees and let the incomprehensible folk songs overpower him again. He only half understood them, they were vague and exciting:

Skammel he lives in Ty,
Rich and lecher too;
Five stalwart sons has he
And evil are their deeds.

There was something good about that: the incomprehensible "lecher" and the grim drama of "evil are their deeds," but in his perverted circling, when he knew she was in the bathhouse, there was another song about Ebbe Skammelsøn that totally obsessed him:

And there in the open yard
He shoulders his sheepskin coat
And up to the hayloft
To Maid Lucy he goes!

There was an entrancing ring to the name and Lucy became Kristine, both the one he would defend and the one he was going to rape in the hayloft or the bathhouse.

"Get up, Maid Lucy,
Give me your troth . . ."

That was when Kristine stood up, appalled, naked, with outstretched arms:

They drank the betrothal beer . . .

The words came against his will, raged in him *against* his will, and he liked to intoxicate himself with words, words that were indifferent or that brought evil, disappointing warnings:

Ebbe Skammelsøn was troubled,
Tears ran down his cheeks:
"I have intended you for wife
And not for mother mine."

He couldn't prevent them from coming, not even this verse, even when it affected him unpleasantly. He was young, but also a lover—and Kristine was in many ways a child, with her soft hands and smell of cocoa in dim rooms.

She was his Lucy! He sang the name. It tasted like honey and vanilla cream; it tasted like looking through the red pane of glass. He could rock in it, fall asleep in it like a sweet melody of woven lianas, and he woke up to it: then it was a fanfare. He dramatized it and hunted her down with this name till it was bloody and ominous. Tragic.

Yes, it had to be tragic! It had to end horribly. There had to be cold steel at the end, and tears, tears. . . .

Then Ebbe Skammelsøn
His sword he drew
And fair Maid Lucy
He to the ground did strike.

He met Erna in the pine forest. She was wearing her faded blue dress, as cool as oats; she smelled of washing and young skin. He was immediately entranced by the contrast, the plunge from hectic red into a blue bath. She said: "You never come over to our place any more." They stood quite close to each other in the sunlit woods with its steep paths leading down to the water. She made him long to break out of his prison of lust and wild dreams. She said: "This aunt of yours. . . ."

They stood there, kicking at roots and twigs. She made him feel ashamed. Why had she said "aunt"? What was it about women, what was it that made his mother and Erna, a middle-aged woman and a young girl, guess things that he didn't even want to admit to himself, even though he was experiencing them. Instinct—the word struck him again.

She said: "We could have rowed out to the islands together."

"We?" he said vaguely. "All of us?"

"Us," she said. They just stood there getting nowhere. Suddenly she began to cry.

"What is it Erna? What's wrong?"

She turned and walked away from him. He followed her up the steep path. The accumulation of many summers of lukewarm infatuation suddenly hit him and became a wave of compassion, shame, wonder, and guilt. This wasn't part of his plan; it had taken him completely by surprise. But the bright woods around him were like before, and so was the sparkle of the water between the tree trunks and the smell of pine needles and ants and resin. Nothing was bewitched any more.

They came to the old stone table in the no-man's-land between the two properties.

She sat down on the wooden seat on one side. He didn't dare sit beside her, so he went around to the big stump that made a stool on the other side. Some small, sharp stones were lying on the dark tabletop. They had used them to play tic-tac-toe; the tabletop made an excellent slate.

She didn't look up at him, just sat scraping on the table with one of the sharp stones. He picked up one and did the same thing. It was like an agreement between them. Without realizing it, he had written: *I love*. He didn't know what he meant by that. He sat staring at the tabletop with the words there.

Finally she looked up, eyes shining. "I've written three words," she said, covering what she'd written with her left hand.

"So have I," he said, and hurriedly added *Erna,* pretending he was making something plainer.

"Can I see what you've written?"

"If I can see yours. . . ."

They got up slowly and changed places. They went around

opposite ends of the table, their eyes fixed on each other all the time. They arrived at exactly the same time and bent over to look at the words at exactly the same moment.

"Wilfred!" she wailed and ran around the table to him, where they met. They fell into an embrace that neither one had expected and clung to each other. His mouth groped in her flaxen-clean hair that filled him with the smell of blue. Neither one dared move his or her head even a tiny bit away from the other, so their mouths moved slowly over their cheeks until they were in the right place, against each other. Her mouth was a little hard and a little rough, and salty from the sea. It was a kiss that didn't grow or develop, a condition that something in them had longed for through all the summers since their childhoods. They had no body, no hands, just two mouths that were one.

Just as suddenly they released each other and stood there, embarrassed. Then their eyes fell on the tabletop again. The words were equally visible on either side. They stumbled towards each other again, but this time they didn't embrace, they just stood close, very close, with the top of her head under his chin.

"Is it true?" she gasped. "Is it true that it's me you love?"

And he gasped in reply: "Is it true that—that you love me?"

They stood there saying "it's true, it's true" again and again, until the words became meaningless and they had to laugh, embarrassed but happy. Standing by the table, she said: "Are we engaged now?"

The word danced in him, so unexpected and hurried. "Yes, we're engaged now," he said decisively. He wanted to hold her close again, but she went away and solemnly put her tanned, salt encrusted hands together, and said quietly: "Thank you, God."

"Thank God, why did you say that?"

She faced him squarely and said: "Because I've prayed to God for this since the first summer we were here."

Terrible innocence! They held hands as they walked quietly around in the little clearing that surrounded the stone table.

They scarcely looked at each other; they looked at the sea glittering through the tops of the low pine trees on the slope below them; they looked at the short, coarse grass they walked on, at each other's feet in the grass. Their happiness was so great that they didn't dare to use any of it for words about that happiness, but only for little words about other things; the feeling was so total that only tiny caresses, forehead touching forehead, and a hand cautiously stroking hair could be allowed to intrude and seal it. Their expectation embraced everything: they could afford everything! afford to wait all their lives and beyond, and it would never end.

Binding innocence! The song of all those summers was in them. It was a song about childhood; it colored their love light blue and kept their minds in a captivity full of sweetness. They had played hopscotch here. They had drawn colossal lines with the edges of their shoes in the coarse turf. Paradise now arose again. And if there was a serpent in their paradise, it kept at a distance warily, outside the bright circle where they walked, child's hand holding child's hand. Their minds like one mind. Yes, the heaven of their innocence was a heaven of childhood and vanished summers that came to life again and made that blissful moment a game like all their games, and yet a game that contained a threat because they weren't exactly children. They were playing a part to some extent, and they weren't grown-ups; they were playing a portion of the grown-up game and had played it with grown-up words, scratched on a stone slab, words that until then had been unheard of. The biggest word—was it already too big?

Hastening innocence . . . they circled closely around the stone table as if they were drawn by a magnet, and they stopped—at exactly the same moment—and *saw* what they had written. Together they felt a shameful pride that they had dared to do it. And when their eyes met again, across the table, they blushed hotly; only then was it really true, the recognition was complete, it became dangerous. . . .

Treacherous innocence!

They walked toward each other stealthily now, not into an open, incorporeal embrace like the first time, but a closed, flaming hot one. And they had arms and legs now, their mouths met without the clumsy fumbling; they were suddenly all body now, and they were possessed by their bodies; everything went around as they tumbled over onto the hard grass. "No, no!" he whispered in their embrace that wasn't loosening. "Yes, yes!" she wailed and pressed him to her thin, girlish body. All the scared serpents looked eagerly into paradise, their tongues flickering.

A moment—then they let go again, simultaneously and as if they had a common will. And as they stood facing each other, panting, this time they looked each other in the eye and there wasn't any shame, but there was fear, and they were filled with a new realization that made everything different. Now DANGER DON'T TOUCH was painted on them in huge letters, on every inch of their trembling bodies. And when a hand or an elbow happened to touch as they walked, breathless, along the narrow path, they struck sparks that could have set fire to the whole forest.

They parted at her gate. The summer day had been dulled by a light mist that came in from the sea. A pale twilight had begun to creep in among the fruit trees and berry bushes. They parted with a shy look that was heavy with assurance.

On the way home he remembered the words on the tabletop, words that announced their wonderful new secret to the whole world. He turned back into the woods to erase them. Dusk was falling quickly among the trees, and the water no longer glittered so gaily through the tree tops. When he was almost at the top, he heard someone coming down towards him. He looked at the ground, hoping to slip past, but something about the approaching footsteps made him look up:

"Aunt Kristine!"

The words were supposed to sound free and easy, but they came out like a husky blast. "Good evening, Lillelord," Aunt Kristine said calmly. And as they stood there, she slightly above him, so that he suddenly felt like a child again compared to her: "Aren't you coming back with me?"

He looked up at her in panic, unable to relax: "I have to go back to the woods and get something," he said. He walked on quickly without waiting for the effect of his meaningless words. He heard her walk on slowly, humming to herself; as if she had a secret, he thought.

When he reached the stone table, the three words had been rubbed out on both sides of the table. All that was left were two damp spots.

12

White flowers of panic blossomed in him. He had been discovered. More than that: there was something he couldn't keep to himself. And what had been discovered, moreover, wasn't necessarily true, not exactly. It had been true a few minutes ago, joyfully, painfully true, brimming with truth. But being exposed in *her* eyes made his love for Erna seem like a misunderstanding—in *his* eyes.

It couldn't have been anyone else. She came straight from there, and she'd been led to the table by . . . oh, he'd heard that word but never actually understood what it implied. Instinct, a desire for truth, for a debasement of everything that was secretly golden.

Because the words had been there, hadn't they?

He bent blindly over the table and didn't really know. He bent right down to one of the damp spots and barely made out his own hair-thin handwriting, the three impossible words—they meant nothing to him at that moment—she no longer really existed. The dusk was silvery gray over the transparent woods, and the sea no longer winked gaily at him; it was like a dull slate.

He wailed loudly—little gasps of pain. Then he turned and ran back, taking long strides and desperately hoping he could catch up to her before she reached the fence where the big path began. It was only a short way home from there, too short for any explanations. But almost at once he saw the back of her light dress on the path ahead of him. What did that mean? Had he been up there such a short time? Or had she been walking *that* slowly? And anyway, what was there to explain—to the person who could never know the secret he had from her!

Then he saw that the back ahead of him knew he was there. He had run quietly in his tennis shoes. She couldn't have heard him. She had been *aware* of him all this time; she had sensed him with her back.

And suddenly he felt his own face smiling; he was filled with a wonderful feeling of certainty.

"Listen, Aunt," he said, confidently sticking his arm under hers. She wasn't frightened. She didn't even bother to pretend. "What do you say we go back the lovely, long way, along the beach, before it gets dark?"

Had he really felt her arm quivering against his? He wasn't going to think it through; he didn't want to put his great invincibility on the line, when he'd just gotten it. She obeyed the slight pressure of his arm and let him lead them down the path through the thicket of aspens that were so close together they formed a tunnel down to the water. Was the path so narrow that they *had* to walk this close together? Questions appeared like ghosts to him; he didn't give them a chance to shake his new calm. There were explosives at every step. They walked in step, slowly and easily, toward the water; it enticed them with its soft, evening murmuring.

There were worlds within worlds, but only he and she were in one of them now. And these worlds revolved in some kind of joined relationship. But this was the only one that existed.

Did she stop—or was it him, did he stop her? They had almost reached the sea, and then it was too late. Suddenly they stood still, facing each other, the same height, eye to eye. He took her head with both hands and felt weak, like his body was melting away under him.

"You're a naughty boy," she said in a low voice.

"Yes," he whispered.

"A really naughty boy."

"Yes!"

No parts of their faces were touching except for their mouths, which were cautiously sinking into each other, holding each other softly. Then they both seemed to fade, collapse suddenly, and dissolve.

"A really naughty boy," she kept on saying, when they had freed themselves and were standing there, breathless.

"Yes!" he whispered again. And as he said it she kissed him on his open mouth, and then slowly opened hers too.

"Really, really naughty."

"Yes, yes—"

"Naughty!"

"Yes."

"Naughty, naughty boy!"

He met her mouth on that "boy" with her lips pushed forward. He laid his open "yes" over her inviting "boy."

"Naughty . . ."

And he finished it with his "yes" while her mouth was forming the "au!" It was like thrusting a dagger of excitement into a smile. Every cell in his body was alive with that kiss; it spread through them till it had taken all their strength. But his numb hands were clumsy instruments for getting through the armor of clothing he was feeling. Soon it would be too late for his inexperienced organ; it was reaching its limit in frightened jerks. And she wasn't helping him; she just kept whispering meaningless words in a final, bursting embrace that released everything and splintered his world into weakness.

And just then she pushed him away from her and stood facing him, quivering. Suddenly her eyes were strangely cold, her mouth loose and moist. She looked so lonely and helpless at that moment; he came out of his trembling confusion and took a step toward her, with a different intention—a caress, reconciliation—he didn't quite know what: a feeling of compassion, for her or for himself, and already there was a hint of fresh, awakening lust. . . . But she raised her hand and slapped his cheek, fairly strongly, almost like a box on the ear. Then she set off quickly up the path, walking more and more quickly beneath the thick ceiling of leaves, until she was almost running. She didn't turn around.

He suddenly didn't feel like he was anesthetized; all he felt was childish wonder. He walked slowly down the path toward the sea, across the sloping rocks and over the line of seaweed, out into the water that rose around him and cooled him off, until it was deep enough to swim with his clothes on. He scrambled onto a skerry and lay down on the sun-warmed side away from the land. No one could see him there. He couldn't bear the thought of anyone being able to see him. He was open, transparent. But even there he felt there were eyes looking at him. He pulled his shoes off, tied them around his neck, and slipped back into the water, away from all the staring eyes in that un-secret place.

Afterwards he lay in the last bit of the evening sun, below the lighthouse on the headland. He had his clothes beside him and was waiting for them to dry and for something to change inside him, and outside him too. But nothing changed, and his clothes didn't really get dry. The sun had lost its strength, as he had lost his. He sat on the rock in a world that seemed to be ebbing and turning into something jelly-like and shapeless. There was no shame and no comfort slowly oozing in on the tiny excuses designed to triumph in the long run. Nothing to dread, but nothing to be happy about either—just a defenseless openness that made him empty and deprived him of the secrets that had to be defended and hidden away, an inner delight.

"Isn't that Wilfred sitting there?"

He jumped up, frightened. The voice came from the water. It

was Madame Frisaksen rowing her boat. Several times a week she inspected the three lighthouse lamps. She always rowed with shirt cuffs on her oars; people called them Mrs. Frisaksen's wrist-warmers; they said that since her husband was lost at sea she couldn't stand the noise of the oars in the oarlocks. Her brown face with its spider web of wrinkles glowed in the red evening sunlight as she turned towards him. "Did I scare you?" she asked gently.

In a moment he felt strong enough to master the situation, naked as he was. "Excuse me, Mrs. Frisaksen," he said politely, with a slight bow, "I got wet and so I took my clothes off." He made no sign of bending down to get them.

"You don't have to be bashful because of me," Mrs. Frisaksen said cordially. She glanced at the lamp making its pale rounds behind six lenses. She didn't land; she just let her boat drift. He saw that she had fishing gear lying on the seat. That suddenly became the epitome of well-being: Mrs. Frisaksen in the white boat surrounded by reflected sunlight; comfort and security and everything that had no fear or desire.

"Well, I have to be off, if I'm going to tempt any whiting before the sun goes down," she said in her invariably dry voice. "Give my regards to the people at your place."

"Good evening, Mrs. Frisaksen," he said politely and this time he bent down for his clothes, so that he wouldn't be left standing so utterly naked, lit by the setting sun. That, he felt, would have been ostentatious, theatrical.

She silently rowed out to the whiting grounds right across from the headland with the lighthouse on *this* side and the little skerry on *that* one. It was at the point of intersection that the whiting came up. She had an unshakable faith in that. Toward evening, in rainy weather, the fish were everywhere and would bite at anything. But in the golden, summer evenings they were only at that one place. He stood and watched her take aim and settle down to row, and then let the grapnel go, bait the line, and pay it out. There was something happy and confident in every movement, a certainty about a world order. He had never thought about it before, just that she was part of the picture, a woman in a boat.

Did that mean then that something in him had changed?

Had Aunt Kristine—had she felt the same as he did after all? Or something like it—something *they* felt—something like what it should be, or should have been? Had something changed after all? So that she was neither angry, nor sorry, nor ashamed—that they should have a deep secret, so close together that it was almost like having it to yourself—or that it was more than having it alone? Because when the great secret came, then he would have to share it with someone. That was what was great about it, that it was two that did it. Two! Two! The word became a song for him, an incantation, an indecent juxtaposition of letters that were mystically related to each other. He hadn't thought of that before either, that there were two letters in the Norwegian word for two—*to*. A hard, firm "t" that met the open "o" and melted into it. But there were three letters in the Norwegian word for three—*tre*, a combination with at least one intruder, an "r" that sort of peeked in between the two other letters—E*r*na! The tight sound of the word "two" which became the mysterious union of two people of opposite sex, an atrocious indecency of a word that he had to repeat over and over until he reached the limit of excitement: *Two. Two.* And he had to say it twice every time. *Two. Two!* The letters' magic, which had only occurred to him in an incomprehensible verse, now became an opening into a whole world. He wanted to transform the word into action and the action into a word and give both the word and the action their full value, each in its own way. Equal: to say it was to do it: *Two! Two!*

He saw Mrs. Frisaksen and her boat in the streak of dying sunlight, a little woman in a saucer of gold. He saw her pull a flashing whiting over the edge of the boat. She was one and only one, a secure but solitary outcast in a boat. He pulled on his damp clothes. He had dreaded doing it, but now took a certain pleasure even in that. Having dressed and pulled on his wet tennis shoes, he straightened up and waved arrogantly to the solitary woman in the boat. She waved back and held up a fish; she was overbearing too. He clapped his hands noiselessly, making broad gestures so that she could *see* he was applauding. She nodded gratefully from her boat. He turned and walked inland thinking about the curious word that excited him so much; it filled him with a fresh surge of sweetness.

Two. Two.

"Well, have you been flirting with Mrs. Frisaksen?"

He didn't jump this time. It was his mother's voice. It came from the "Bastion," a knoll facing the sea where she often went alone. He smiled up at her with feigned assurance.

"Where have you been, Lillelord?"

The summer evening and the voice were one. Sunset—Mother. . . . He ran around the gloomy hollow where he had played as a child (as a child, "a child!")—wide awake and happy that he was able to comfort someone who was alone, a woman he loved.

"But all your clothes are wet! Did you fall in the water? . . . And all evening—where have you been?"

"And you!" he said, his voice aiming for a pact with the evening's soft calmness to ask a question without obligations, an attentive question, a caress that she would fall for: "What have *you* been doing all day?"

He knew that she would fall for it: "Not all day," she said. "It's only been since dinner. . . ."

He knew it, he knew that he could lure her onto the defensive. But it wasn't meant to be deceitful: he didn't want to be investigated. And all at once he saw that she didn't want to find out either. She had asked him out of habit and because she missed him. He put his arms around her and realized that he was practicing being spontaneous: "I'm so fond of you, Mother!"

"It's been a long time," she said quietly.

"Since what?"

"Since everything, since you said that."

They walked together up the gravel path to the house, away

from the water, the sunset, and Mrs. Frisaksen. "Aunt Kristine's gone to bed," she said lightly.

Too lightly? Why was he always suspicious? He jubilantly answered his own question: because he had a bad conscience. He was a victor, a deceiver. He loved her, loved her as a mother, lady, father. "I'm still a bit taller than you," she said with a laugh. "Shall we measure—properly?"

They stood back to back in the dull light of dusk, feeling the crowns of their heads with flat hands. But they couldn't agree who was taller, they quarrelled about it and boasted. He said: "We could get Kristine to decide."

She seemed to shrink momentarily. "Your aunt's gone to bed," she said in a low voice. "One can't wake people."

They walked toward the house with their arms around each other's necks, and they felt a happiness that was new again. It was physical, but without the disturbing sweetness that otherwise always possessed him. Her hair brushed him with every step they took. They had the gentle peace of an old loving couple in a life that *wanted* to be without passion. As they walked to the house, he could see her walking restlessly out to the Bastion, as she had hundreds of times when he was small and in danger because he couldn't swim yet and she overestimated the dangers of the beach because she had no sense of the sea. Something sang in him: "It's *her* I love!" And Erna popped up—her hard kiss. And, for an instant, so did the city: a fire behind a dreary outbuilding in the night, solitary expeditions in the twilight—it all appeared and reminded him of the uncomfortable simultaneity of everything. He saw the light in Aunt Kristine's room, softened by the dark blue blind. All his worlds became one and he knew that he had to keep them separate. After all, every world had to be secret for it to count. It had to be his alone. "Mother!" he said. "Mother!"

She said: "Come now, Wilfred."

He switched abruptly: "Shall we have some of that cold fish for supper?"

She looked at him happily—a mother's look at a son who is in the process of leaving her; this was her last anchor: "Are you hungry?"

"Yes. Very! And you could have a glass of Liebfraumilch!" He was inspired and was testing her.

"And you?"

"Milk. I'll get them both."

"Yes, but to open a bottle just for me. . . ."

He had her now. He knew it, though there was no triumph, only affection.

"I can decant it. And you can give me a tiny, little glass as an excuse."

Yes, he had her now. And as he dived into the icebox with its mixed smell of new ice and old zinc and cold meat on boards like bridges over the ice—he saw the amber bottle lying there like an extra temptation for just that evening—an extra temptation for every single evening he could remember—he thought about Kristine, quickly and hard. Come down, he thought, come down and destroy it all in a second, my love, that's what you're here for.

"Come now, let me open the bottle since you really want me to have it."

"You go in and sit down, Mother!" he patted her gently on her rear end. "What sort of son do you think you have? Are you afraid I'll screw the corkscrew clear through the cork?"

He said it rather loudly because he was happy. She had to hush him. They were conspirators gathered around the old ice-box. He whispered: "Yes, if you'll go in and sit down."

"Walk quietly," she whispered, "your Aunt Kristine can hear us."

He quietly got things ready. He was freezing in his damp clothes. He arranged the things on the tray, remembered the jar of vinegar, and forgot his glass of milk.

"No, not there!" he whispered dramatically when he came in with the tray.

He motioned with his head that she should sit on the white rococo sofa. Then he arranged the things on the table; he poured the wine, only a little in his glass, his mother didn't want him to drink. He filled up her glass and held the dish with the cold trout for her. While she was helping herself, he reached across the table and stroked her golden-brown hair with a happiness that remained in his hand—it wasn't brutishly transmitted to his body.

His mother ate. All at once she was eating so greedily that he was shocked. She didn't give herself time to chew, but ate like a starving man, dropping little pieces of fish. "I think you were hungry!" he said. The summer night sighed outside. Dusk had fallen at last. Only now did he see the two candles she had lit on the table where they were eating their little feast.

"I feel like I haven't eaten all day!" she said happily. "As if I'd been afraid of something."

"Afraid?"

She raised her glass. "Damned instinct!" she said lightly.

He was afraid. "Instinct?"

"You don't know about it," she said. "You're a child, you can't know, but it's like a fear of something that's over, a fear that everything's over . . . but now you should taste the wine, just a sip."

He sipped. They looked into each other's eyes across the table.

"Skoal, son!" she said, and her eyes were warm in the candles' gentle light.

"I'll tell you one thing, Mother," he said seriously. "You're the prettiest."

"Of whom?" she said, surprised.

"Of all of them."

She said: "Lillelord!"

She had wanted to say it lightly; he'd heard that and acted as though she *had* said it lightly. He raised his glass and put it to his lips; he felt the cooling peace of the yellow liquid, a thirst for more. Erna! he thought suddenly.

She said: "What were you thinking about?"

"I don't know, Mother. That it's so nice out here."

"Erna's a sweet girl," she said.

He started slightly, but he saw that she hadn't noticed. That damned instinct, or—was it a coincidence? He wanted to know if everything really was revealed the moment it happened, or before, if people who were on the same wavelength were so attuned that nothing was hidden from the person guessing.

"Why did you say that?" he asked. He *could* hear that his tone was forced.

"Why?" She looked at the clock and was horrified. "Do you realize it's high time you went to bed?"

He knew what she meant, and that she knew he knew. It was like an agreement that all the words and sentences were a code they used, the two of them. *Two. Two.* That exciting word. It brought it all back.

"She was here asking for you."

"Who?" He came tumbling back through the worlds.

"Who? Erna. That's who we were talking about. . . ."

"When, Mother, when?"

"Oh—a while ago, an hour. She didn't really ask for you."

"Well, what did she do?"

That damned instinct. Damned, damned instinct. What had that bashful girl gone and guessed at. . . . She could never be persuaded to come in. . . .

"What did she do? She came to see—me, I suppose. She brought some sweet anemones."

He followed her gaze to the bouquet of flowers in a green vase on the white baby grand piano. He hadn't noticed them before. So Erna had brought a reminder. In a way, she was there with them now.

His mother emptied her glass and began collecting the dinner things. There wasn't any enchantment between them any more, just open suspicion—or? He couldn't believe that she thought or knew or merely suspected anything.

"Oh yes, they were going to take a trip out to the little island, I remember now she said that. I think it was tomorrow."

"Are you coming too, Mother?" he asked suddenly.

"Me—?"

"Don't say that now!" he said quickly.

"What?"

"You know."

"All right. I know. But I still think I'm too old for pirate expeditions. So we'll stay at home—Aunt Kristine and I."

"Me too," he said.

"Why?"

She had expected it. "Maybe we'll come," she added. "Kristine in any case. She wasn't here when Erna came. . . ."

It was as if she had said: You and she weren't here. . . .

"All the better, Mother, then we'll stay here, just the two of us!"

But he wasn't certain of any victory, and this time he didn't win. You have to believe in the deceit if it's going to last.

She said that it was late. Her voice was small and certain now; there was no longer a code. They sat silently at the empty table, unable to collect themselves and go upstairs.

"No . . ." was all she said and stood up. They went upstairs together. He saw a light under the door of Kristine's room. Their hands met in a weak caress in the cool darkness. "Good night," they whispered simultaneously.

Like a prisoner! he thought as he stood in his room. Like a prisoner who has been investigated and everyone knows a little about—or suspects, or guesses. They all knew something, but all he knew was that the desire in him sent him tumbling helplessly between the women he was fond of and made him the only one who was exposed and who had no secrets.

His whole body ached from his knowledge about everything and that he was the property of others in a little world where mighty things happened, and he didn't have any control over them. He walked out onto the curved balcony facing the linden arbor: it sighed constantly—the slender music of murmuring voices that must have lived in the trees themselves—they sighed even on windless days.

The sea was opaque in the faint light of night. Gulls were complaining in the distance around a net. A narrow, brighter strip in the opaque water showed where Mrs. Frisaksen had rowed silently away from the whiting grounds.

13

Wilfred woke up. He didn't want to go with the children to the little island. This was the first thing he realized. He called them children now. The previous day had provided experiences for the night and new possibilities for the coming day. Exhausted, he was trying to balance on a borderline where he had to be alone with his skirmishes. On the other side was good old solitude.

He looked over the books in the bookcase, sat down with a history of art in French that Uncle René had given him. Neither the pictures nor the subtle descriptions that he only half understood had much to say to him at this moment, but he plunged into them absentmindedly, just waiting for something to happen. It was a fresh, cloudless morning outside, but he wasn't going to let that concern him. The time for playing was supposed to be over.

But when he began rummaging in his closets and shelves and came across all his old toys that had piled up over many summers and stood holding them in his hands, he was filled with a blissful sadness. There was the battleship *Akasa* that he had built himself, with long nails through the funnels and a complicated system of ladders and bridges, and on the top there was a Japanese admiral, carved out of a root, that had a head with slanting eyes. There were also wooden boats and celluloid boats, merchant ships with sails and propellers and thwarts and rigging—the other boys had envied him because of all these things, and he had generously let them destroy the boats gradually. They had never amused him.

Then he heard the noise of the young people and children

outside. They were laughing and rejoicing on their way up the path from the sea. He heard the sound of the oars down there. They were after him; they'd come to take him with them. He was scared to death, scared of meeting Erna and not only her, but everything she stood for; he was tired of it, he'd simply had enough of it. He began fashioning excuses, one after the other: a headache, he had to do some reading, just wanted to stay home. . . . He looked out and saw them coming, girls and boys, some big ones too, older than him, with red and blue and green clothes and towels and fishing rods and lines and scarves, and one had a trumpet he kept blowing. His mother was calling him. He heard her talking with them. Now she was saying that he was up in his room, that she would get him. She was calling him again.

He felt like a trapped animal. There wasn't anyplace to hide from this avalanche of goodwill. Aunt Kristine—where was she now? Was she in bed with a headache? That thought made him feel uncomfortable; he couldn't meet her in the house; he had to meet her somewhere else, in some imaginary place beyond the limits of all possibilities, in a gambling casino. . . . The fantasies trickled through him as he stood, helpless, between the table and the window, not daring to look outside or to hear his mother calling.

And she was calling. Talking with them out there and calling:

"Lillelord! Wilfred!"

All at once he felt he couldn't leave her in the lurch either. He couldn't bear to shout or be shouted for. Holding the history of art, he went down and met the whole flock on the veranda steps. His mother was standing among them. Terrified, he looked for excuses, but here in the sunlight, among all his companions, none of them seemed to hold any water.

"Well, here's Wilfred now. Just a minute and I'll fix his lunch."

He glanced quickly at his mother, but she looked away and let the young people rush around her. Then she went in to get something for his lunch. He felt a cold anger because she had done that. She had promised him away, sold him, to make it easy on herself and to put him back with the children again, just to get rid of the great anxiety she had revealed the previous evening.

"Erna is down by the boats," someone said.

Why? Did someone know something? Was there something to know?

Again he felt a dull rage because of the suspiciousness that was beginning to possess him. He was tarnished by it; he was losing his good, indefinite solitude.

"Well, what about it," he said coldly. "I'm staying home to read art history."

Those closest to him gaped. It sounded simply affected and incredible in the sunshine. Then his mother came back again with a picnic basket and a thermos full of cold fruit juice, with all the things that meant she wanted to force him back into childhood.

"Now, hurry up, Lillelord . . . no, no we're staying home; Aunt Kristine's not up yet; she had breakfast in bed; she has a headache."

"But Mother, I did ask you—"

She stuck the basket in his hand and turned immediately to the others, a young, healthy mother among these young people. "Come with us, Mrs. Sagen!" someone shouted. Others joined in. But she defended herself with both hands. Words and excuses came to her easily: she was expecting visitors the next day; she had some weeding to do; she had a visitor sick in bed, yes, Wilfred's aunt. . . . And they had to be careful, and what about that old motor in Jørgensen's boat, could anyone work it properly? Her voice was drowned out by exultant shouts—just what she'd wanted. Everything should be drowned out by noise and the young people departing; there shouldn't be a moment's peace, and in a way she was the one who'd arranged it all, although it had been planned in detail, and they had only come to fetch Wilfred, because Erna had come and told her.

Yes, she'd done that—they got to talk so rarely. But now here was Wilfred. He thought he would spend the morning at his schoolbooks. Had they ever heard of such a thing? Ha, ha! Ha, ha! Suddenly they found it incredibly comical. The always young Mrs. Sagen put her worried son on display and liberated them with this.

She went with them down the path, in the center of the group and as far as possible from Wilfred. She drove them, urging them on with her bright laugh, her delight in everything that *gave* pleasure. A young fellow in cream-colored sailor's pants, who had the beginnings of a beard (he was staying with the Jørgensens), had fallen for her in those few minutes and was openly flirting with her on the way down to the wharf where the boats were. The Jørgensens' old tub was supposed to tow two fishing boats, while three of the boys absolutely insisted on trying to sail out in a little boat with a spirit sail; they tried to predict the weather according to an almost invisible shadow somewhere out in the fjord that was supposed to mean wind.

They put out like a high-spirited wedding procession. It was almost their duty to rejoice as long as the invincible Mrs. Sagen stood on the wooden pier where the sunlight was reflected around its pilings. They remarked merrily about the motor that started with angry explosions and sent out clouds of blue smoke into the summer day. Then they saw her going slowly up that path from the pier. One more shout from the water—but it didn't reach her.

The voices on board abruptly fell silent. The heavy thumping of the motor sounded angry in the summer air. The last Wilfred saw of his mother was her slender back on the path and there was no exultation about it.

"Your mom's a spry old lady," someone shouted over the noise of the motor and gazed cheerfully at Wilfred. That stung him. His bitterness about his mother's treachery was replaced by an urge to seek restitution for that remark. But when he looked at the freckled face of Tom, the gardener's boy, he could see nothing but admiration and childish respect, though it was accompanied by an audacious expression. He could feel Erna's hand on his over the edge of the boat. Her hand was cool. He had scarcely looked at her. Now he looked at a shy, little girl's face that had the grayish tan of people who lived here, so different from the sudden mulatto brown that visitors acquired over a weekend. There was something so fundamentally healthy about this girl that it set him on fire in a different way. Flaxen hair, linen dress. The whole girl was flaxen. Cool and innocent and yet combustible, with cool, blue eyes that revealed everything.

"Didn't you want to come?" she asked.

"You weren't there, you know," he said enthusiastically. Once more he felt the delight of duplicity overpowering him, challenging him to act and go on acting. Or *was* it duplicity? Couldn't he be extremely fond of her just now, in a setting of blue and silver? She was just made for it—she was freshness itself, summer from head to toe. He bent towards her confidentially and spoke over the din of the motor.

She put her mouth close to his ear. It wasn't so conspicuous because they were sitting near the thunderous motor.

"I've been thinking about you the whole time," she said seriously.

Why did that irritate him? Because he hadn't been the first to say it—or simply because it was a challenge he couldn't refuse—?

"And I've been thinking about you!" he whispered back flatly. "All night!" he added. That didn't sound very likely, but it made her eyes grow dark and moist. She stroked his hand on the outside of the boat. Her hand was hard with dried salt. . . .

"All night long!" he assured her hoarsely.

"Haven't you slept at all then?" she asked anxiously. To him it sounded like the most banal irony. But he knew that it was simply concern and innocence and nothing else. He tore off the short silk cord from the front of his sport shirt and tied it around her wrist. As a reward, or to comfort her? He didn't know, but he tied it carefully with a type of fisherman's knot he had learned.

"There!" he said, "now you can never take it off."

She gazed at the yellow-white cord, moved and speechless. She stroked it with her other hand, put her cheek against it and looked at him, dreamily and sincerely. He was looking at her all the time again. Now he had convinced himself that he loved her.

They took the little island with loud battle cries. The boy from the city marched in front with his trumpet, then came Tom, the gardener's boy, with the flag, a painted skull and cross-bones, that he planted on the cairn in the middle of the island. They held hands and sang a subdued, mystical song to show that they were the masters of the island. Totally childish. The bigger boys bashfully let themselves be caught up in the game and soon were the most enthusiastic participants. Wilfred also let himself be caught up. He suggested that they play a tracking game. One group was supposed to leave behind pieces of paper and the others were supposed to find them. But they had to put the pieces of paper under rocks to keep them from blowing away in the light breeze, and anyway it was almost impossible to hide on that flat island. Only in two places was there a sort of gully with water in it, full of driftwood and glass floats from nets. The ones marking the trail were so easy to find that they had to switch to other games the whole group could play; the games weren't exciting and had no purpose other than working off surplus energy that had accumulated during the long winter of lessons and stuffy classrooms.

Erna called to him quietly. She was bending over the rocks right by the water and signaled to him to be quiet. In a few silent bounds he was beside her, gazing down at a gull's nest with an egg that was moving all by itself. It was obviously in its final stage: the chick was about to hatch.

Soon a group had gathered and was watching the mystery in that windblown little nest. They solemnly watched the miracle take place, the chick, far too big, struggled out of the egg, wet and sticky; all at once it was twice the size of the egg it had been in; it stumbled and crawled and tried to stand up. Erna had taken hold of Wilfred's hand; she was weak with emotion. In some obscure way it had become a ceremony that was minted just for them; it was as though they were standing over their first child, helpless and touching, watching it crawl out into an existence that was full of grown-ups and dangers.

At that moment there was a violent uproar in the air above them. Before they realized what was happening, they had an umbrella of screaming, angry white birds over them; a few of the birds dove frantically and threatened to peck them. Some of the boys picked up rocks and sticks to protect themselves from the angry birds, but Erna was indignant and stopped them.

"Let's go away," she said, still moved and very serious. "They're only defending the chick. I think it's the last one this year. We have to leave it alone."

The flock of birds followed them, screeching angrily until they were a reasonable distance away from the nest. She sat down on a rock and looked out to sea, filled with a peace he had never seen in her before.

"Have you ever seen anything so touching?" she said. "The poor birds were courageous to the point of being crazy, just to defend one helpless, little chick. Do you think it's only instinct?"

That word again. It stung him. "Instinct?" he said. "Where do you get that from?"

"Well, isn't that what it's called? Things they do, things *we* do too—without knowing why? Things we guess. . . ."

"What do you mean—guess? The gulls just defend their chicks, isn't that simple enough?"

"Yes, it's simple. But somehow they knew that the chick was in danger."

"But they didn't know. Because it wasn't in danger. None of us would have harmed it."

"Yes, but if we had. . . ."

"We wouldn't have. I think all this guessing isn't very impressive," he said. "Anyway, you always guess wrong, all of you."

"All of who?" she said. "You're not angry with me are you, Wilfred?"

He took her head and drew it toward him. They looked

around quickly, then their lips met in a quick kiss. They heard shouting nearby. The others had begun to look for chicks in the crevices and had obviously found some.

"Why did you say *all of you,* Wilfred?"

He stroked her hand.

"I just think that everyone guesses too much. People shouldn't do that."

And as he said it, he was thinking: It's strange, we're just like old people, sitting and arguing about something really important, but we don't dare say it.

Now the others had found a lot of chicks and were obsessed by the idea of guarding and protecting them. The chicks, terrified by all the protecting, dashed on their long legs from one crevice to another.

"Let's eat!" some of them shouted.

"No, no. Swim first!" others shouted. There was a tumult of swimming suits and trunks. Before, when they were children, they hadn't worried about that sort of thing when they were alone. Now they suddenly realized that they were more developed. And all at once there seemed to be so many strangers.

"It's the same with people, I think," Wilfred said tentatively. "I don't like being protected so much."

"You don't want people to guess about you or protect you then?" she asked. And he was moved by her naive, trusting face. What she had said was precisely the most important thing for him. She stood and fiddled with her yellow swimming suit. A mother, though she was too young, who had become superfluous. But the first ones were already in the water and they had to hurry. It was just awful to be the last one in. Someone had to be, but let it be someone else.

The bigger boys from town did what they called Indian swimming, which meant splashing a lot more than the others without getting any farther. Soon everyone wanted to swim like the Indians, and there was a lot of noise and splashing; the flying water made a rainbow over the bubbling mass of bodies and panting faces. They tried to see who could swim the farthest under water, and then they played tag. Panting and exhausted, they gradually dragged themselves ashore and made their way up to the sheltered hollow, radiant and spitting, where some of the girls were already mixing all the lunches together, so that no one would know who brought what or would eat just his own.

"Tom," someone said. "Where's Tom?"

That question was first asked down on the beach. Those up by the food were talking and shouting. "What's happened to Tom?" someone up on the rock asked; there were four of them sunning themselves there. Suddenly it was quiet. Someone said: "His clothes are lying up here." Then there was an outburst of hurried cries: "Tom! Tom!" And some drawn-out calls: "To-o-o-om!" And finally a roaring chorus from throats choked with panic: "Too-om! T-o-m!"

Then it was quiet all over the little island. Someone went quietly, barefooted, to the top to look, others went down to the beach or out onto the rocks. No one was shouting now. They *looked*. But no one saw Tom anywhere.

Wilfred felt an icy hand on his wrist. He looked into Erna's eyes; they were filled with desperation, but there was also something else. An appeal?

He was afraid too, but he didn't lose his composure. Now he heard random shouts again, some whimpering, some commanding, as though they wanted to conjure the missing boy out of the rock on which they were searching.

He collected his thoughts, straining his will so that it almost hurt. Tom's clothes? They had found them far away from the boys' and girls' clothes scattered behind rocks and stones on the south side.

Then he realized something with absolute certainty, something only he could picture: Tom hadn't had any swimming trunks. He imagined the little living room in the gardener's cottage. They didn't have things like swimming suits there, and Tom, of course, had been too embarrassed to swim with the rest of them. . . .

Wilfred realized that he had been squeezing Erna's arm. Now

he let go of it abruptly and ran off without saying a word. He ran towards the northern end, where the little island ended in a narrow promontory of rocks that sloped down into the sea. He ran softly and quickly over the little hills, but he was careful where he put his feet. He ran, jubilantly certain that he was right. The others were just groping blindly, but he knew. He could picture the little gardener's cottage all the time. He ran as fast as he could, but he saved a little strength so that he wasn't all out of breath when he reached the promontory. There he stopped abruptly and looked down into the water. Here, on the leeward side, it was smooth and crystal clear. He could see the bottom plainly for some way out; brown seaweed was swaying gently in the water moving beneath him. He stepped from stone to stone out into the water. Looking down in front of him, systematically searching sector after sector of the rocky bottom under the clear water and the seaweed.

And there he saw Tom. He was lying face down, white and naked. The refracted light distorted his thin legs, making them longer and making them look like they were quivering.

Wilfred turned around to look for help, but the shouts and cries on the other side of the island barely reached him. He waded out, being careful about every step so he wouldn't fall. It was deeper than he'd thought. He had to tread water before he reached Tom. Then he dove under water quickly; he took hold of Tom by his neck and raised him up until he was kneeling on the bottom. He thought in quick, sharp spurts about everything he had ever heard about lifesaving, about getting the victim on his back and swimming under him.

Tom was heavier than he'd thought. He just sank. But just as he was going to change his grip, Wilfred touched ground with one foot. The next moment he had Tom half out of the water on a rock right by the promontory. All he had to do was wade ashore with the cold body, heavy and limp in his tired arms.

Just then he saw Erna appear over the ridge. Her yellow swimming suit flared up against the blue sky. His tired body felt joyful at once: he was going to overcome everything.

Now Erna had turned and was waving. Breathless and exhausted, Wilfred hauled the lifeless body in, but he concentrated all the time on what he had read about resuscitation in his first aid book.

When the first of the young people came rushing down the slope, he had Tom, lying on his stomach with his head lower than his feet, on the outermost strip of dry rock behind the promontory. He was on his knees, straddling the naked body. The boys came out to the promontory. The shouting stopped. The girls came storming up, hard on their heels. He sensed that a group had formed behind and around him in a semicircle, row after row of tense, expectant, helpless children, just waiting for him to perform a miracle. He worked with the boy, rhythmically and deliberately. Was he doing it right? Was this what it had said in the book?

He was so tired now that he was close to collapsing over the wet body. But he didn't dare let anyone relieve him, or stop and ask if anyone knew more about it than he did. A dark voice from somewhere gave him good advice—but it was hesitant. It was as though it wasn't a matter of Tom's life being at stake any longer, but his own. Was he going to manage to do it, was *he* going to manage it. . . .

Then water began running out of the mouth of the lifeless body under him. He couldn't remember any longer who it was. It was just a body with its head on a rock. Now a lot of water was being regurgitated. The boy was vomiting it up.

Wilfred turned him over. He got some help now. They laid him on his back with his head turned limply to one side. Wilfred lay over him and tried to listen to his heart. He couldn't hear it beating, but he felt that it was beating. A red mist filled his eyes. He wanted to look up for help, but he slipped away into oblivion. He probably vomited himself.

"But Mother, I didn't jump in at all. I didn't do anything like what you're saying. I just walked out into the water and took him out!"

It was becoming quite a burden for him. His mother, Aunt Kristine, and he were having coffee after dinner. The children were still roaming around, noisily telling their parents and anyone who would listen that Wilfred had saved Tom from drowning. Tom's parents had come as quickly as possible—they couldn't be away for more than a half-hour—and both of them wept with gratitude. The doctor said that it had been touch and go. If a brave young fellow hadn't come in the nick of time, they wouldn't have Tom now—and he was all they had in the world.

The actual trip home—the contrast with the anxious minutes that had ended with muted exultation—had been a triumphal procession with everyone suddenly wanting to pay homage to him. He had told them as soon as he came to, there on the rock, that he hadn't done anything special; he hadn't even swum, just pulled Tom up. The more he protested, the more certain they all were that he had performed acts of heroism. This glorious commonplace had to be even more splendid. They *wanted* to elevate him to the rank of a hero. He could still see Erna the way she was in the boat coming home: her blue eyes clinging to him, not saying a word, blind and deaf with admiration and happiness because he had done it.

He would have liked to take the sunny path across the fields to the gardener's cottage and pay Tom a visit, to *see* that he was alive; but he didn't dare because of their gratitude. He knew that Tom's parents would treat him like a gift forced on them, like someone on whom they had to lavish all their love for Tom. Tom himself was in bed and wasn't allowed to get up, though he insisted that he was fit as a fiddle and wanted to go out and enjoy himself.

But Tom's parents were very concerned: he had to stay in bed for a few days. It was as if they wanted to tie him to them and couldn't bear to let him out of their sight, though they hadn't been aware of missing him until after they knew he wasn't gone.

And Wilfred's mother was nearly bursting. It wasn't that she boasted or said much, but she kept telling Kristine that she was proud of him. Kristine had listened to the account with a bashful smile. She somehow had no right to share in the admiration. She was just a spectator, and not even like the other children had been; they had witnessed the misfortune. She wasn't able to talk about cramps or resuscitation either. But still she also seemed to radiate happiness towards him, as he sat there knowing what it was like for her.

"So in other words you did nothing at all?" Kristine said ironically. "You just happened to stroll out into the water, pick him up, and bring him back to life again?"

"Not happened. I *thought* it out. That's the difference. I thought he would be embarrassed about swimming naked. And I also thought that he didn't have any trunks."

"And so all you had to do was go out there and pick him up!" his mother said.

"Exactly."

"And how could you guess that he didn't have any trunks?"

"I didn't guess. I saw it."

His mother and Kristine exchanged looks over their liqueur glasses. What did they suspect; the area of conjecture was vast and they were on different sides of it.

"You're always saying that," his mother exclaimed, rather bothered, "that you *saw,* that you *see.* . . ."

That scared Wilfred. He realized that they were guessing about him. He knew perfectly well inside himself that this delight in being able to *see* was one of the paths that led to the land of secrets. That's how it was for him. It was different for other people no doubt. *See* and *know*—these were good words to be certain of. To see with something other than your eyes. To know more than just what you were sure about.

"I'd like it if no one talked about this again," he said. "I'm glad Tom's alive. I'm sure he's a great fellow, but I hardly know him."

He got up and walked out into the garden. He knew that they were silently looking at each other now, that they thought they knew. And what they thought they knew was that he was a modest boy who didn't want praise for something any boy would have done—and could have done—if he just acted thoughtfully. But at the same time as he *saw* them sitting there giving themselves up to their need to admire something, he also knew that they were painfully wrong; it was painful for him. Precisely that kind of falseness wasn't a part of the plan he had made for himself. He found a word for it: *trite*. He made a face. . . .

But there was also something in him that was just the opposite, when he thought about it by himself. Something that had streamed through him during those precious seconds when he was concentrating hardest out there on the promontory and hadn't yet discovered what it was. Something about *not* destroying. But there was something else too, something that bothered him. He was walking in the failing light now—down to the beach again, toward the piers where this brief adventure had begun. Yes, this was it: had he wished that someone would come and help him when he consciously waded out into the water to search for Tom? And how could he have *known* that the boy was there precisely?

He hadn't wanted any help.

But if he hadn't managed to get him out on his own—would he have preferred that Tom die, rather than have the others help him?

He didn't know. But he knew that he was glad when he saw there was no one there.

And afterwards? When he was kneeling over the "corpse" and working on it according to instructions he only vaguely remembered and which he certainly had never put into practice before, had he wished for more experienced help, for guidance . . . ?

He hadn't wanted it. When that big, strange boy with the deep voice had given him some advice, he'd been irritated and he listened reluctantly.

Besides, the boy hadn't known anything for certain—he'd just said what he did for the sake of saying something.

But if there really *had* been someone better, more experienced, better trained, and strong. . . .

There hadn't been anyone.

But if—?

Would he rather Tom had died than accept help?

Did he just want to assert himself?

Again he had to take little steps on the path wailing all the time; it relieved an inner unrest that couldn't be stopped. Because wasn't it true that he had actually almost been prepared to kill Tom—although he had saved him so courageously? Wasn't that the real truth, which bothered him so much that he couldn't bear to be praised for his resourcefulness and decisive action!

In a strange way Tom had become dear to him—now, afterwards, although he had never paid much attention to the freckled boy with the white body when they were swimming. When he had knelt over his half-dead body and, in a way, rode him back to life—wasn't it precisely that he had sat on dead Tom as on his own property, his heroic steed, and just ridden him, for all he knew, straight into death?

He wailed softly as he walked along. Although he still didn't know for certain that that was how it had been—he was almost sure. And he got more and more certain as he was forced to throw off layer after layer of excuses and self-praise. These things came from what the others had said and all the cheerful slaps on the back he got on the way home, and Erna's admiring gaze and his mother's understanding way of interpreting his modesty. He had to reject it all as nauseating and preposterous: it was foreign to him.

Because of a need for absolute honesty?

He kicked a stone contemptuously and the stone went sailing out into the water.

That was just it: when he tortured himself this way, it wasn't to be honest "through and through," but to destroy something that had gotten misshapen and big enough to be an accepted truth. It was to make this thing small enough and mean enough, so that he could be alone in a place where no one could reach him and share with him—the innermost shallows of his solitude, where nothing could shine unless he gave it a radiance. And then *it* could be as "false" as it liked.

He had come clear out onto the promontory with the lighthouse. He felt a cool satisfaction at having reached what seemed to be the final layer. All the exultation was gone from him now. Instead there was a good, hard stone in him, angular and sore, a place to stand, where he could always be. A stone as hard as the rock he was standing on, but it wasn't long and didn't come to a point like the headland, caressed by the sea at sunset. A small, hard stone with sharp edges to have *inside* him, a place to be and at the same time a weapon. . . .

He heard the soft swish of a boat on the other side of the promontory. Just then Madame Frisaksen's white boat shot out from behind the lighthouse. Madame Frisaksen sat there, brown and parched, her back half turned toward him, making her way noiselessly to the whiting grounds. Across from the promontory, she caught sight of him in the reddish evening light and she rested her oars.

"Well, isn't this the fellow who goes out and saves people from drowning?" she said gently—or was it ironically?

He felt himself blushing terribly. What was it about this unpopular person that made him so happy?

"Good evening, Mrs. Frisaksen!" he called and bowed to her from the rock where he was standing. "Are you going to try the whiting again?"

"Is it true what I hear, that you pulled little Tom out of the water?" she asked over her oars.

"Yes, Mrs. Frisaksen. I hauled him ashore. He'd slipped, I suppose."

"Ah, yes," she said quietly. Sound carried so well across the water. "Ah, yes," she repeated and took up her silent oars again. She paddled gently against the current to keep herself clear of the headland. "He was lucky, perhaps, Tom was," she said.

"I hope the fish don't bite, Mrs. Frisaksen!" he shouted happily. "Not a bite all evening!"

She nodded slyly. She understood him. It wasn't right to wish people good luck fishing. Nothing good could come of it.

"Phooey!" he shouted and spat into the water towards her.

Mrs. Frisaksen's whole face opened in a smile, so unusual that it seemed like it was going to split. Then she nodded once more and rowed silently out to the whiting grounds, playing there in the red reflections.

And again he was left staring at this solitary being in a boat who belonged to another world—not the noisy world of the vacationing visitors, hardly any world at all. It was as though she floated into a shimmering land of something missing, something that existed by itself and bore no relation to any other person or thing. She rowed quietly into a cold sun.

"*Perhaps,*" she had said. "*Perhaps* he had been lucky."

Besides, she hadn't praised him in any way; she'd just seen it from Tom's side, from that of his parents perhaps. They were the only ones who knew her there.

But what did she really think about the day's great event, which would be the topic of summer conversation for a week and maybe more?

She probably didn't think anything.

Suddenly, as he stood hypnotized by the sight of the little craft, like a drop of gold in the evening blue, he realized jubilantly that Mrs. Frisaksen was someone *who didn't give a damn about anything*. Not a damn, not a damn! She had had enough in her tiny little existence.

That's how it was. She radiated the mysterious pleasure of absolute indifference, of relaxation. It was the same with his Uncle Martin, only somewhat differently. *His* circle was big; it comprised stock exchanges and foreign firms, and a whole basketful of cares and joys on his own and on other people's account. But those were really just things with which he surrounded himself so that he could be left in peace and because those were the things people talked about. Actually, he didn't give a fat damn about it. Exactly—it was his own expression. Music, the delicate little works of art that made other people react so violently and changed Uncle René so much that you could see him go white while the impressions were still in him . . . and even all the poverty and the danger of something breaking out—all the things Uncle Martin talked about so earnestly and at length . . . he didn't give a damn about it, not at all. He, Wilfred, realized that as he stood there on the shore, empty and yet filled with an inexplicable inner delight that people were like that. Weren't they the world's real egoists?

The grown-ups had often spoken about egoism. When they said the word it was like picking up a rotten apple.

And they didn't even know what it was! They thought it was thinking about what's best for you before anything else. They had no idea of the passion he would experience when he walled himself in behind layers of solitude, where only he could fit inside and be a hard stone, glossy with all the polish and politeness and consideration they required of him. When he had become independent, when he had become a stone that didn't have to think about other stones, no one would be able to see anything but kindness and friendliness and heroism. He would be rich, like Uncle Martin—he really was rich—and live simply, so that people could correctly say: See how modest he is; he does a lot of good things behind the scenes. Rich and certain and never ever asking if something was right or wrong. Why else had they let him learn so many things—things the others didn't have, his music, that spring in France with his mother—before school . . . if he wasn't supposed to use all his precocious gifts they spoke so much about to become as hard as a stone?

Everyone was so stupid! So easy to see through with their guessing. They always looked for what they *wanted* to guess. And when they were wrong, they adjusted the result so that they had guessed nearly right after all! And so they went around knowing nothing about each other, less than nothing, because what they knew was wrong to begin with; they were led astray by rough guesses and wishes that were acceptable, for everything petty, that is.

But they thought they knew! Mother thought she knew about

him. Aunt Kristine thought she knew about him. Uncle René thought he'd gotten a young aesthete he could manage. . . .

Mrs. Frisaksen was the one who knew it. And no doubt she had only arrived at it because of bitterness and the contempt of others. They said it hadn't made much difference when her husband drowned, and he didn't *quite* know what they meant by that either. But he probably knew as much as all the people who said those kinds of things. He knew—because he had discovered Mrs. Frisaksen's secret at this exciting evening hour—that people just said things, and said them, and said them. And the more they said them, the fuzzier they sounded. It was only when something got really bad or threatened them that they were different. Then they made heroes of people—everything that they longed for. . . .

He came up onto the road again. Erna's parents called to him over the fence to come in. They were having supper at an unpainted table under the big chestnut tree where things always dropped into your food. They were eating something called "health food," a sort of cereal with milk poured over it. Wilfred was forced to swallow a tiny helping of the health food; it stuck in his throat like a cork. Erna's father was in charge of an institution and knew almost everything about education and bringing up children, and the little he didn't know he learned in England, where he went every year from the fifteenth to the thirtieth of June, on a scholarship, to find out a little more about education at an institute there.

He talked about character and training and something he called purity of mind. He was the only one there who walked around naked from the waist up and scrubbed himself with sand and never ate anything cooked. He praised Wilfred's achievement in educational terms; apparently it was the result of Baden-Powell's positive sportsmanship that never left a person in doubt about what to do.

Erna's nine year old brother listened slyly from the radish patch, where he'd been sent to pull weeds.

Wilfred looked cautiously at Erna. For the first time he could remember, he saw an expression of something other than frankness. Surely she wasn't ever ashamed of this soothsayer who sounded like a phonograph. They laughed so much at him—his uncles and all the other self-assured gentlemen who knew everything *their* way—when they were sitting with their whiskies on the veranda at home. Even Erna's mother, who humored her husband by wearing a kind of folk costume when they had guests, sat stirring her health food absentmindedly. Was it really true that what he said was so silly, just because everybody thought it was? If it hadn't been for his grating voice, Wilfred wouldn't have minded admitting that he was as right as all the soothsayers at home.

"I quite agree that one shouldn't beat his own drum about naturally assisting a companion," Wilfred said, thoroughly enjoying using Uncle Martin's phrase "beat his own drum." When he used a grown-up's phrase with other grown-ups, he always noticed an uncertain look in their eyes. Erna looked at him quickly. Was it gratitude, or anxiety that he might be making fun. . . .

Erna's father chuckled with appreciation and put a spoonful of cereal and milk in his mouth. It reminded Wilfred of a cow chewing. He took the opportunity:

"But I'm not so crazy about this English scout movement," he said thoughtfully.

Erna's father displayed that indulgent smile that pedagogues have when a layman doubts their ideas.

"So—our young friend doesn't like the scout movement?" He looked around at his family and motioned for the nine-year-old to come out from the vegetable garden so that he could benefit by the instruction. He was a wiry-haired little ruffian who was only interested in the bowl of black currant jam. "May I ask if our young hero has acquainted himself with Baden-Powell's principles?" He now had a firm though friendly grip on his youngest son's bristly head.

"I have read them carefully," Lillelord said easily. "It seems to me that everything there about honesty and purity is pretty much the same as what everyone else says. But I think it's too simple for ordinary boys. It just sounds like an echo of old maxims."

Erna's father actually jumped slightly. It was amusing to tease him a little, but not too much.

"I think that people—especially very young people—are a little more complex than you think and have many motives for what they do. They're really pretty indifferent about all of Baden-Powell's very obvious goodness."

Erna stared down at her plate, her little brother shrugged—because he was enjoying it, or was he impatient? Their father was going to say something sharp. But all of a sudden he seemed to be thinking about something else. All he said was: "You probably hear opposing views at home. A young person's point of view is influenced too much by his milieu."

"Exactly," Lillelord said, mollified.

It was time to thank his hosts now. He knew that children and young people were invited here by Erna's parents just to hear a lecture.

A little devil jabbed him when he was getting up. "We children are certainly most influenced by what we hear at home—probably quite often in the opposite direction than intended."

He shook hands politely with Erna's mother and thanked her for the fine food. Her father looked at him graciously. Wilfred felt like a butterfly pinned to a board. If he stayed ten more minutes, he would undoubtedly become one of the pedagogue's "cases" that were so frequently discussed in a monthly magazine about spiritual and physical health. They received it at home on Drammensveien all year. He'd never thought it was probably Erna's father who published it.

He was strolling home between the two elm hedges, almost bursting with joy because of Erna's healthy father, who got his patent wisdom from a course in Kent every year in June. All of a sudden there was a rustling in the leaves and Erna came right through the hedge and stood on the path in front of him.

"It was awful for you to make fun of father," she said. Her cheeks were ablaze with anger. She was lovely.

"I didn't make fun of him. I just contradicted him a little." He was annoyed too.

"That's the same thing when it comes to my father. You have to remember that no one ever contradicts him."

"Then it was high time somebody did," Wilfred said indifferently. "You all seem pretty bored with that health stuff too."

They were standing close together now. She looked sad and soft. Her sudden anger had subsided. "Do you think he's terribly stupid?"

He looked at her and was pleased. This devotion served no purpose. She was apparently ready to say that everyone was right.

"No more stupid than other people who act like that," he said. "Do you know Mrs. Frisaksen?"

"That dreadful person—?" She looked up at him, frightened.

"She doesn't act like that," he said. "Nor do you, for that matter, but you're not a grown-up."

Now she was both happy and confused. "But you, Wilfred?" she said. "Are you just acting?"

"Yes!" he said and quickly took hold of her hard little neck. They stood for a moment, their heads facing each other. Someone called her from the house on the other side, and Erna was already halfway through the hedge. It certainly wasn't *only* theory that accounted for the obedience in that house.

"Give my regards to that little rascal you have for a brother," Wilfred whispered, "he'll never be a scout."

She turned in the hedge. She was like a part of her surroundings. "Wilfred," she said in a low voice, "can you lend me one of those histories of art—?"

He was struck dumb for a moment, then he was moved. "Ugh, don't read that stuff. I'm just showing off when I do it," he whispered. The person calling her was closer now.

She shook her head helplessly. Then she dove quickly into the hedge.

"I was just looking for the kitty," he heard her shout back.

Honesty! he thought merrily. And because he was in a good mood, he dared to continue his thought now:

I was only acting a part when I pulled Tom out of the water. I knew she would follow me.

14

Aunt Kristine had a migraine.

She could get a migraine on the shortest notice. His mother smiled slightly when Kristine sailed through the room sideways, looking for the nearest place where she could collapse and lie down. Kristine maintained, with some resignation, that it was bitter to suffer from the two ailments that people always suspected you of putting on: insomnia and migraine. There was always someone who heard you snoring at five in the morning.

It was a relief for Wilfred. When she was sick it temporarily put an end to his incessant lust. On the other hand, her condition wasn't so pitiful that it evoked the chivalrous side of his feelings for her. And besides, she described her symptoms in such a drastic way. He could never see why people should go into details about their illnesses.

His summer world at Skovly was divided. He had looked forward to it as a way of forgetting his old sins and as a prelude to a great transformation. Kristine was a disappointment when she drew away from him now because of his unsuccessful attempt to conquer her. Erna was a disappointment because her touching affection disarmed all his violent initiatives—he had visions of vice and had been given a butterfly to play with. His mother was a disappointment because she guessed things he wasn't even really guilty of. But he had outgrown the summer playing that they had both looked forward to.

It was all because he was a disappointment. His visions never came to anything. His childhood treasure chest didn't shine like it did before. Even his old game of playing with everything that washed ashore had taken another tack: the fantastic things from the sea, from boats and distant lands—they always had an aura of adventure when they reached the shore, even if it was just an old mattress. There was always expectation in things that came from the sea. It was as if he had been expecting everything from the sea, as if a childhood would come back in the form of everything with which he used to rush home: glass floats, kitchen utensils. He knew it was self-contradictory to expect splendor from those things that had vanished when he was trying to obtain a new world. It didn't help. The things he found were just what they were, a lackluster protest against the dream he still wanted to enjoy.

Once he had brought home a float from a net. Had anyone asked if it was something to collect? A world could have collapsed, but he felt certain of his victory; only the grown-ups with their insipid stupidity could take such a poverty-stricken view of phenomena. Now it was as if the things on the beach were on the point of acquiring a meaning, of transforming themselves as he expected, but strange voices, which were *also* his voice, were whispering to him: Can that be anything to collect. . . . There was treachery inside him, two forces betraying each other. He sided with them alternately, with the glory and the thing that killed it.

There was only one thing worth striving for: the dry, dark red taste that ravaged him; it possessed his body and his thoughts; it couldn't be collected, couldn't spring to life in the glow of anticipation. It had to be *done*.

Aunt Kristine had a migraine and Erna was a butterfly.

Nothing helped him to flee from anything. The stupid stories from the spring were popping up in the newspapers again. Now that the three-week visit of the British Fleet was over, readers wrote column after column of letters to the editor about misguided youth, a theme that alternated with Elias Tønnesen's latest escape from prison. They said that this master crook was every boy's hero and that even the sons of good families were suspected of robbery and even worse. Kristiania was more or less marked by young people who imitated French gangs as a sport.

Sport—!

And Uncle Martin had quoted his perpetual *Social Democrat,* saying that the public wouldn't tolerate any coddling of upper-class children. Poor boys, his mother had sighed.

He knew that her worried looks contained nothing more than concern, but that bothered him because her concern made him a child again. Just the summer before, he had loved that concern; as late as last spring, he had needed it for a change. Now that he was only staying in the country and doing things he was praised for, it was annoying that she protected him. The skinny boys from Grünerløkken, he thought, they would have been suspected, not him. He could do what he wanted. He *would* do . . . but he didn't want this concern.

One day there was a letter for Lillelord. He discovered it in the yellow, wooden box by the wharf. When you opened the box, it smelled of shut-in sunshine, almost like the bathhouse.

The letter lay by itself on the bottom, its only company was some shreds of the issue of *The City Missionary* that had been delivered by mistake weeks ago. He read the address again and again before he dared to pick up the letter. A hand gripped his heart. A letter meant something wrong. The large, round, rather irregular letters showed that it was from a child, a boy in his class—all the possibilities whirled in his mind. Deep inside he knew who it was from.

He didn't open the letter right away. He picked it up carefully and looked around. The south wind gently ruffled his hair; nothing had changed on the wharf, where he knew every stone and all the deep marks made by the mooring ropes on the posts. Everything was the same and everything was different, all because of a letter; a new state had come about, suddenly transforming the existing one, which had been full of conflict. In time the new state displaced everything. It put him back with all the unpleasantness from the spring; it was something undiscovered popping up again; it gave him a gnawing feeling around his diaphragm.

He went up a path at random with his letter; he found himself between two gray boundary fences that needed paint. Up on top there was a kind of lookout point, where everyone went, except on Sundays. It was like a little crater with trails, with dust and trampled grass. Suddenly he took out the letter, dropped it on the ground, and walked away. He got the idea that maybe nothing existed if you didn't let it, and that when he turned around a little ways away, there would be no letter, just the brown, dusty crater with its thin covering of grass. But when he did turn, the letter was lying there, and he ran back quickly to pick it up before anyone else got there. He knew right away that no one should get there before him and discover that it was a letter for him. Letters were events during the summer. Everyone had a right to at least hint about what was in them.

Then he opened the letter and saw at once that it was from Andreas, and he knew right then it was about the bicycle that he had let Andreas borrow in return for retrieving it from up by Blåsen after that disastrous night of what the newspapers called arson and "resisting arrest." Andreas wrote that the police had come twice and asked about the bicycle. The first time was a while ago, a couple weeks after the examination ceremony at the Misses Wollkwarts, the second time when the family returned from their short stay in the country with Andreas' aunts at Toten. It seemed that someone from the police had noticed the smart English bicycle and recognized it. Andreas admitted that he had been riding it a lot.

At first Andreas denied everything, but then he had admitted borrowing the bicycle from the park by Blåsen but said that at first he'd always put it back in the evening. They knew, of course, that the bicycle was English and a little different from the ordinary bicycles people had in Kristiania. And Andreas' father was insisting now that he should tell the police the truth, or at least tell him, but Andreas wasn't going to tell anyone the truth, because he thought that maybe there was something Wilfred had done, and he, Andreas—he wasn't the kind who betrays a friend. . . .

Signed: *Your friend Andreas.*

Wilfred stood there, trembling inside. But his hands were steady, they weren't trembling. Friend, he thought, and felt a surge of shame and guilt. But the next moment he was hard again, cold and alert. A friend. What do you use a friend for? He had lent Andreas the bicycle for an indefinite period. That was really something for Andreas; he didn't have a bicycle. Now Andreas happened to get involved in something because of the bicycle. That wasn't his business. Had he intended simply to shove everything onto Andreas in case the constable had noticed the bicycle? Had he intended to harm Andreas?

That wasn't what he had intended. Standing there in the little crater on top of the lookout, he was quite sure of that. And he knew too that he thought it was clear Andreas was the one to go and get the bicycle—for various reasons. He had had so much to do right then. But he wasn't the kind who betrays a friend. . . .

Who wasn't the kind? He, Wilfred. He wasn't the kind. Nor was Andreas. They were friends; they stuck together through thick and thin. Andreas and he stuck together. Now it was his turn. Or maybe it was still Andreas' turn for a little while longer. Andreas wasn't through with this business yet. He would have to manage the best he could. Afterwards it would be *his*—Wilfred's—turn. Then *he* would have to manage. They stuck together through thick and thin.

He tore the letter into little pieces to show that he was done with it. What was Andreas actually expecting of him? Nothing. There wasn't a word in the letter about him expecting anything. Or was there? In any case, it was too late to look now. And really, what could he do? Soon, very soon, the police would stop worrying about it. There hadn't been any fire and the stupid constable must have done a lot of things since then. Nobody was really interested in it. It was just something the newspapers wrote about. Besides, he was finished with it. He was occupied with something quite different and more important. . . .

And suddenly he could see it all. It swept over him like a huge wave that you couldn't hope to see the limits of in any direction:

Erna, Kristine, his mother, the police. . . . Feelings, words, all the things that he'd said and done as though someone else had said and done them for him, had led him deeper into a thicket of absurdities. He stood there holding the pieces of the letter in his fists: "What's the matter with me?"

Fear came over him the next moment. He knelt down in the brown dust and dug under the gravel with his fingers, under the grass, he wanted to bury the remains of that wretched letter, to bury himself with all his worries and bad conscience. "What is it? What's wrong with me?"

All at once he got up, victorious, filled with an impotent anger at them all. He would kill them, yes, kill them, one after another, in a cunning, unprecedented way, and kill all the concern with which they were smothering him, and all the temptations—until he was standing alone and clearheaded, without any family or devoted friends, their knees knocking because of his iniquities. He would get rid of all the attachments around him and be alone in a world that was stupid, stupid, and which he could destroy as he wished.

He had a wonderful sensation of floating as he stood there by himself in the shallow crater. Snatches of motifs from music he had heard came to him and were changed to a new music that originated in him; words that he had read came sailing up and broke out of their context and formed new sentences with dangerous significance. The cool summer wind became a storm that roared around his ears and made the friendly day a violent one. He was filled with a desire to erase everything; it filled him up and spread him out until he became someone he didn't know. He experienced a marvelous growth inside, and it didn't stop. It made him bigger, very big; it was no longer a question of being grown-up, but of being *big*. He was powerful. He could do anything. He could soar, judge between life and death. He could assert himself a thousand times against all the people who wanted to violate his right to develop and be big.

He saw the little, white steamer put out across the fjord. It rounded the buoy in the middle of the fjord, and every pane in its windows flashed; then it turned in towards the other side and was gone. He suddenly felt tired and abandoned. All his overflowing thoughts of vengeance vanished with the peaceful little boat. Andreas, he thought, is there in the city now, on Frognerveien, at his wits' end. And he saw Andreas' timid expression when he was reciting "Flower-Ole." He saw Andreas' father under the palm tree in the dining room with the tarnished silver plate on the buffet; he had sat there once with a piece of newspaper over his face to protect himself from the world.

And now the world from which this man tried to protect himself was falling over him like a landslide, and all because a boy from another street, a quite different world, had dislodged a stone—out of a need to stir things up, to upset the balance of his secure surroundings, which found no sympathy in him. No wonder Andreas' father demanded an explanation. He had enough cares already under the palm tree.

And still it seemed like a profound injustice to Wilfred that he, who trembled with the knowledge of a ruler, should collapse in misfortune for the sake of peace in a dining room in Frognerveien. What was so remarkable about his friend Andreas? He couldn't even really remember what he looked like.

Betray. Betray a friend. . . .

Mere words, perhaps? Wasn't this just one of those words with which they surrounded everything, so that people like Andreas' father could sleep in a rocking chair with a newspaper over his face to keep off the flies? People have to get along somehow, Uncle Martin had said. People have to stand on their own two feet. He glanced down at his own long legs: brown, no stockings. Was he really standing on them? Were they really his?

Yes. All this was just temporary, something he could get out of—until he found his great independence where he would be alone. That confounded letter. It was as if he couldn't get rid of the pieces. He couldn't think of a single place where he could get rid of them. He threw them in the air, but they blew back to him like a cloud, almost grouped together, and settled around him, all the white pieces of paper with the stupid, blue handwriting of a schoolboy on them. A strange wind that blew against itself. . . .

Once again he collected the pieces and crumpled them in his fists. Then he stuck them in his pocket. He would take them home and burn them, obviously. Nothing could be simpler than that. Just put a match to them—somewhere or other and—presto—the whole letter would be gone.

Gone, wiped off the face of the earth. But not gone for Andreas, whose world at that moment probably consisted solely of fright and ominous warnings. That tortured letter was no warning, but a final cry for help from a person who wanted to be rescued. This was no case of lying white and mute, face down in the water. And there was no question of heroic deeds, just decency instead.

Decency—? Now who was it who used that word. What a bother always having words buzzing just under the surface, other people's words trying to get out and be used, and in a way create notions themselves. How could he know what everything was, when they were covered with so many words, the grown-ups' words he had adopted before he had acquired words of his own, because he had always been among grown-ups.

Uncle Martin. Uncle Martin again. He was the one who talked about decency. But he was rich; he was secure; he was fat. . . .

Maybe a person should be fat?

Fat like Uncle Martin, or poor like Mrs. Frisaksen, or both. Invincible. He felt like the sun was shining right through him as he stood there, unable to decide. Lobsters changing their shells—he had read about them. They hid under rocks and stones, defenseless even against weak fish. And he'd thought he was. . . .

Yes, but he was! He wasn't transparent. Miss Wollkwarts had said, though without much conviction, that God saw everything.

If this God, in whom not even his mother believed, saw right through him at that moment—and didn't pay any attention to him or his letter. . . . Then he was the only one who knew anything. The little scaredy-cat in the city and his spineless father—what did he, Wilfred, know about those two that wasn't in a letter that almost didn't exist? It wasn't *his* palm tree and smell of soup, but a conglomeration of disorder and poverty where he had gone exploring for the fun of it. Besides, Andreas had warts on his hands. If it had been Andreas lying there, face down in the water, he would have been careful not to touch his hands. He could have always saved him from drowning, but he wouldn't have touched those warts.

The badger—! He could see Andreas' doomed expression at the examination, and he realized again how the bottom had dropped out of Andreas' world when he found that there was no treasure in his treasure chest, "Flower-Ole"—just as it had happened to him long ago with Nick Carter. Yes—he *would have* saved him from dying. Warts or no warts.

That darned badger. That darned, confounded, damned desire of his to butt in. Was that the way for someone who wanted to be alone to behave? He should have left the fool alone with his badger. Would fat, good-natured Uncle Martin have done that? He could certainly betray the whole world and then sit in a comfortable chair and smoke a cigar and talk anxiously about the poverty of the masses and its threat to existing society, about this war he was so preoccupied with. Maybe a war would be a good thing . . . something that swept away all the stuff people got mixed up in, so that they could go out and save their country. . . .

Suddenly, the letter seemed to mean everything else possible for him. He knew that he had to choose now, between everything: Mother, Erna, Kristine, school—the conservatory that Uncle René had written to his mother about; there was a place for him now. But he didn't want to meet that Mozart again, that boy wonder they had let him read everything about, who was driven on and on by a father who wanted to turn him into something remarkable. The letter—he had torn it to pieces. Like all the rest. It was all torn to shreds. Each time he had to choose between something, he had torn everything up instead, to keep from having things around him, from having to choose. Maybe that was all the others did, and that was why they went from one thing to another, just *pretending* all the time.

But not Mrs. Frisaksen. Not Andreas' father. They were what they were.

But when people were what they were, that meant they must be failures. Everyone else pretended and went on pretending as long as they could. But maybe they just didn't do it enough! They didn't bring it off, not all the time. And that was when their faces suddenly got so sad and they answered at random or were absurd. Like Mother. Like Aunt Kristine. Like Miss Wollkwarts when she was all gentleness and understanding, and so—all at once—there was no gentleness any more, instead she was curt and resolute, and behind the kindness there was a repressed anger that made the boys stiffen, afraid of the unreasonableness that was coming. . . .

As he walked along thinking about all this, he had come to the other side of the narrow isthmus. The rock stuck out here and made things gloomy even in the middle of the day. There were no houses on this side because the ground was marshy and rocky until you reached the other side of the flat space by the long, shallow arm of the fjord, where the water swelled and bubbled over a muddy bottom. Mrs. Frisaksen lived right up there; but in the middle of the level expanse was the gardener's cottage, in the center of a piece of cleared land, drained by years of toil.

He made a wide detour around the gardener's house. He couldn't bear the sight of Tom any more and certainly not his industrious, grateful parents. He heard the gardener's dog barking between the houses. But when he found himself standing outside Mrs. Frisaksen's red cottage, he was seized by a sort of weakness. He had no idea why he had wanted to go out there; none of the summer visitors ever did. Now he noticed that the cottage wasn't red after all, but gray; it had just a few patches of red on the short wall that faced north, where there was the least sunlight. She must be so poor that she can't afford red paint. Or maybe she didn't want to take the trouble? No doubt she thought the cottage would last her long enough. She was one of those who didn't pretend. . . .

That was just what he had wanted. He wanted to see her house. It was gray. The gray color suited it, and actually it was pretty, almost silvery gray. One of the windows was covered with pieces of boards, another had rags and newspaper stuffed in it. He saw Mrs. Frisaksen's white skiff, clear out where there was enough water for it, and it was gray too. Lying there in the shadow of the rocks, it wasn't a golden bowl any longer. It must be a long way to row every day, around to three lighthouses and out to the whiting grounds.

Well, it was a long way. The cottage was ready to fall down; the boat was old, and it was a long way to row. That was what she worried about. He knew that now. It was no more remarkable than that. She had found her solitude out there. When she couldn't control her existence and compete with everyone else, she got by without them. It was just a question of overcoming what there was, of giving way until you could overpower what was small enough and easy enough to overcome. Everybody could be in control that way.

Well, now he knew. He turned and was about to walk back in a wide arc across the flat clearing. The cotton grass nodded at him from all the little tufts, redshanks flew up, shrieking, from the pond in the middle. He felt the pieces of the letter in his pocket. He noticed them at the same moment he felt someone was watching him.

He turned just quickly enough to see Mrs. Frisaksen move her wrinkled face away from the one window that wasn't broken. He made up his mind quickly and walked straight to the door on the south side and knocked firmly. Mrs. Frisaksen came to the door at once. "Is this the fellow?" she said. She didn't seem surprised.

"Yes indeed, this is the fellow," he said gaily, mimicking her tone.

"Does your mother need some help? A big wash or something?"

He thought for a moment. "I came to see you, Mrs. Frisaksen."

Was she suspicious, or perhaps somewhat moved? It wasn't possible to tell. "Come in then," she said.

He went inside with a feeling of uncertainty. He was so accustomed to guessing what people were thinking. They said the friendliest things when they were full of dislike, or they hid their delight with indifference, but Mrs. Frisaksen didn't even ask him to sit down, not that it would have been easy to do. The table was covered by a tangled fishing net, and it overflowed right onto the wallseat and the floor. Otherwise, it was nice and tidy, but there was nothing to sit on. The brass rod on the stove was bright and polished. There was a sweet smell—like at Andreas' home on Frognerveien.

"Well, this is it," she said. "You were curious, I suppose, about what Madame Frisaksen's home was like?"

"Yes," he said.

"Does your mother know you're here?"

"No."

He stood in the middle of the roomy kitchen and enjoyed being honest.

"Well, that's it," Mrs. Frisaksen said. "Now you've seen how I live."

Was there a hint of unfriendliness in her tone after all? The door to her small bedroom was ajar. You could just see in and glimpse a bunk against the wall and a dark gray woolen blanket.

"That's just the bedroom. There's no more," she said.

"I know," he said.

"You know?"

"I could figure it out."

There was a gleam in her eyes now, a gruff friendliness that reminded him of the expression he had put in them when the sun was low and she was on her way out to the whiting grounds.

"So," she said, "you go around figuring things out, do you?"

"Yes."

All his glibness had deserted him. He couldn't think up anything or pretend. He stood there as if in a trance.

"Mrs. Frisaksen," he said finally, "is this it?"

"Just this?" she looked at him searchingly. "You mean, is this all I have? Yes, my boy, this is all—since Frisaksen died."

He thought: She could have permitted herself a sigh here. My people would have.

"How long has that been?" he asked.

"Fifteen years this autumn."

Her unfeigned hardness was going to his head. "And no one comes here to visit you—what if you were sick, Mrs. Frisaksen?"

"You mean, if I lay down and died? It could be four or five weeks before anyone noticed it."

"I would notice it," he said, "if I didn't see you come rowing in your boat."

"Think so?" she said curtly. "There's a big difference between noticing that a person is there and *not* noticing that someone *isn't* there."

He was angry because it was true. "*I* would notice," he said.

"All right, we'll say you would."

It occurred to him that they were discussing a rather painful subject. Why was he bothering this poor woman?

"Please excuse me," he said. He turned towards the door to go. On the wall, right beside the window, was a photograph stuck there with thumbtacks. There was a young man dressed like a sailor, a boy almost, taken in front of a cafe signboard, and there were three women and a man walking by on the sidewalk in the background. He stopped pointedly: perhaps he would get an explanation now.

"From Portugal," he said.

She walked over, took the photograph off the wall, and looked at the back.

"Now how could you know that?" Her eyes twinkled almost good-naturedly.

"I didn't know, I guessed. Those women who carry things on their heads—I've seen some pictures from Oporto."

"O-p-o-r-t-o," she spelled slowly, holding the photograph at arm's length, as far as possible from her eyes. "You're right. That's my son Birger. Yes, it's long ago."

"I see that."

"You do?" Now she was really surprised. "How do you see that?"

"It says 1910 beside Oporto and that's two years ago."

"Imagine, has it been two years . . ." she said and stood there, holding the photograph in her hand, now she held it lower. "Was it so long ago?"

"Where is he now?"

"That's the last I've heard from him. He was a cabin boy then."

The two steps to the door seemed like an enormous distance. He didn't know how he was going to make it.

"Things must be hard for you, Mrs. Frisaksen!" he said. Those damned tears, now they were filling his eyes, an old habit, his way of pretending, when he knew that tears would be effective.

She stood there, looking right at him. Her thin mouth suddenly came to life—a faint quivering that made her lips fall inward—like a seam hemmed on the inside, he thought, to keep his tears back. "Well, good-bye, Mrs. Frisaksen," he said and held out his hand. She took it quickly. Her hand was like a hard root. He went out quickly and shut the door quietly behind him. He slowly walked away from the house, somewhat dazed. The gardener's low cottage seemed hazy, the greenhouses floated like mirages on the plain. He had to get away somewhere by himself, where he could cry. Suddenly he couldn't see any way out and just wandered slowly inland. Seabirds were coming in off the fjord, low to the ground. There'll be rain, he thought.

Then he heard someone behind him; he turned quickly. It

was Mrs. Frisaksen. She had something in her hand, a glass snowstorm in the shape of an egg. "I thought maybe you could take this," she said, out of breath, holding the egg out, "he had a lot of fun with it, Birger did."

Those damned tears—it was too late to hide them now. He held the egg and let the tears roll down his cheeks. She stood in the coarse grass facing him and only now did he realize that she was shorter than he. And all at once he wasn't embarrassed any more by his tears, which no one else in the world could see. It suddenly didn't matter with Mrs. Frisaksen.

It lasted only an instant, then she turned away again, dry-eyed, all of her was dry. She muttered something as she trotted off again—not running, not walking, but trotting with small, even steps. He saw that she didn't have any shoes on, just some oversocks tied with string.

"Thanks!" he shouted. But it was like in a dream. His voice stuck in his throat and wouldn't come out. He took a few steps after her. But then she was inside and her door was shut. As if she had never been there.

He stood holding the glass egg, not daring to look at it yet. Again he felt that certain beings around him could see right through him. A lobster without a shell. Mrs. Frisaksen's cold gaze had been replaced by another that came from all directions, a mighty eye that closed around him, so that it could observe him from all sides. He raised his hands over his head to fend it off. But it was there. He walked along with his hands raised, but the gaze was all around him. He walked faster and faster, broke into a run, all the time keeping his hands raised and holding the smooth, glass egg with his right hand. He ran faster and faster over the clearing, past the low greenhouses, over the marsh towards the cliff where it was dark and cold. All the time he had his arms raised. After a while his tennis shoes were sopping wet. The gulls flew up as he ran along and circled low around him and over him, followed him like a hostile cloud. They weren't aggressive, just something that hung over him and behind him; they were also a part of the inquiring eye, with their angry squawking—until it was like all the space around him was a white eye turned toward him.

When he reached the cliff, he flung himself down to catch his breath. He lay like that for a long time. It was like a cave here, no eye could reach him. Then he took the glass egg out from under him, warily; he had kept it there to hide it from the eye. He held it up to the gray light outside the cave. There was a little, white house inside the egg, a fairy-tale house. When he turned the egg over, it filled up with snow. The tiny house inside was covered by swirling snow, a whole world of its own, protected by the snow and the outer form of the egg. A world in snow. He let the snow fall calmly on the house. Then he gently turned the egg over again, and again it snowed. He stared at the egg, hypnotized, and was slowly filled with joy and terror—they were the same sensation and they contained everything—Birger, the dead cabin boy—or was he still sailing on the high seas and couldn't afford even a postcard? Had he also taken refuge in a world that was only his, like the glass egg with its miracle of snow, which had certainly been his entire world on many black, autumn evenings by the paraffin lamp in the little house by the cove, while the lighthouse keeper sat trying to untangle a net that finally seemed to enmesh and capture him. Yes, didn't people say that they found him in a net at the end, caught in it like a fish? Deep in his soul he heard what must have been his mother's voice—the voice of every mother, calling and calling because of a longing that only pushed you farther and farther away. Couldn't he hear the voices now? Or was it music: humming Mozart, humming, humming, an infinite filigree of notes. . . . No, it was rain. It was the rain falling outside the cave he was lying in. It had finally come, the release of summer rain—tears from the enormous eye that surrounded him.

He put his hand into his pocket and felt the damp pieces of Andreas' letter.

The world of the egg—that was what brought everything together. He saw another cave open up, in the darkness of a pile of boards where he had played, enticing little boys to commit violent acts. Andreas' letter. Mrs. Frisaksen's husband who had gotten caught in a net. Birger who had gone deeper and deeper into his lonely world, where he was probably stuck so tight that he didn't have a guiltless thought to spare for his wrinkled mother in the gray house that used to be red. Andreas' father, alone under the palm tree. He held the egg up again and let the snow drift down over the tiny house. There was a fascinating loneliness about that enclosed space full of falling snow. Maybe Birger was sitting in an empty bar in Pensacola now, remembering the egg and feeling as if he were in a world like that, hypnotized by his misdeeds and incapable of even the least communication. He had gotten caught in *his* net.

Now he could feel the net around him. It seemed like it was being drawn tighter and tighter; it was going to close off the mouth of the cave under the cliff soon. He got up with the egg in his hand and ran out into the open, bent over. Rain was pouring down. It had washed away the whole staring eye that had surrounded him. The gulls were low to the ground and paid no attention to him as he made his way back to the isthmus that led out to the island.

The moment he came into the house, he knew that something had happened. There was no one in the hall, no one in the living room or in the dining room, no one on the enclosed porch. His mother came downstairs quickly. She looked serious.

"Why didn't you come home for dinner?" she asked.

"Is it that late? I didn't know . . ."

"Late—dinner was four hours ago. Where have you been?"

"At Mrs. Frisaksen's." It just popped out.

"At Madame Frisaksen's—why?"

"I don't know. She gave me this."

His mother took the egg without looking at it. "Aunt Kristine is leaving tomorrow," she said.

He knew that he had to ask why, but it was like he didn't really want to bother asking. He still seemed to be in Mrs. Frisaksen's little house; he could smell the sweet scent of thyme.

That was it! It smelled that way at Andreas' place too. They put thyme in pea soup.

"I should go to town tomorrow too," he said.

"To town? What for?"

"I got a letter from Andreas. There's something I have to help him with."

He saw that she was going to demand to see the letter. He turned his pocket inside out and some of the pieces fell out. He scraped out the others. "He asked me to come. It's something about school."

"Nonsense," she said. "Anyway, not tomorrow. Maybe later. Kristine's going to the mountains, to visit Aunt Valborg and Uncle Martin."

He thought quickly: What did she say—that I can go to town another day, when she isn't there. He had to take the plunge now.

"Why is Kristine leaving?" he asked.

His mother almost sighed when she said: "Your aunt thinks it's a bit dull here with us, and she has such a short vacation."

Could she have told her? Just straight out—or maybe not directly? Had she really been insolent to avoid having to reveal that she felt uncomfortable because of what had happened and because of what hadn't become something more—after all, she had kept away from him ever since that afternoon.

"I have to go to town one day anyway," he said coldly. He clutched the shreds of the letter.

"That suits me fine," she said. "I also have to go one day, so we can go together; you can see Andreas while I'm having my hair done."

She was still holding the strange egg in her hand. He couldn't understand why he'd let her keep it. He held out his hand. But now she held it up and looked at it in the fading light. She turned it in her hand and a snowstorm began.

"Just think," she said, "an egg like. . . ."

"I'd like to have it back, Mother," he said. "It's mine. It was Birger's once."

"Birger's?" she said and stared at him. Now he could see that she was examining the egg. Her finger followed a thin line scratched in the glass. He hadn't noticed it before. It formed an S.

"It was Birger's!" he said again. He was angry now. She wanted to take away everything that he had to himself.

"Your father was holding this egg when he died," she said.

15

From the moment he and his mother parted at the Egertorv, Wilfred knew everything would be successful. The actual ceremony at the pastry shop hadn't gone very well. No matter how hard they tried to recover the old mood, it just went farther and farther away. It was easier when they both realized it and gave up.

Now she watched him crossing the street, so straight and free—a young man!

The three days since that evening at Skovly had been less difficult than she had anticipated—it hadn't really been clear to her that one day her little boy would have to know about his father. He displayed a maturity that would have frightened her six months ago. His first question wasn't about his father's death, but about Birger and Mrs. Frisaksen. He seemed to be obsessed by a woman she had gradually forced herself to forget. He had only asked how old she was, and when she had replied that she was about her own age, which was true, he seemed to know all the rest: "Is Birger Father's son?"

She couldn't understand it afterwards, but it was as though this "affair" had never been completely true for her until he asked her about it. Affair was the right word. She had always thought of it as an "affair"—not that there was a living person, six years older than her beloved son, who was his half-brother, if you looked at it that way, and people did. . . . And now, after all these years, it had become a far more commanding reality than it had been at the time, to say nothing about all the years of remembering vaguely since then; it had suddenly stopped hurting. The insult that had been encapsulated inside her now somehow turned into a slight curiosity: these people had continued to live a life much like before. This despised Madame Frisaksen was suddenly not just a concept in a boat, an image one was forced to accept as a rather disfiguring part of the evening landscape that had an extremely vague connection with something or other in the past. She was the same person who used to come and do odd jobs in the big houses there and had attracted improper looks from some of the men because of her tramp-like beauty—the kind other women hate and which comforts them by fading quickly. She was lighthouse keeper Frisaksen's lifetime punishment for a youthful indiscretion and—as people said, in any case—the real cause of the gruff faun's melancholy that had gotten worse and worse until they *found* him one day—this euphemism was always used that autumn. The details were always avoided because they were too unpleasant. But the fact remained that this "person" was still Madame Frisaksen and had to be regarded almost as the widow of a respected public servant. And her son. . . .

But when Lillelord said: "But isn't his last name Sagen then? Why shouldn't he have things like I do . . . ?"—this had really been too much for Mrs. Susanna. Was that fair? What kind of ideas were these he had about the world? Scandalously enough, these ideas had even reached all the way to the Storting, even though all decent people disassociated themselves from them, and anyway, how could a boy like him be aware of them?

Yet, what had he actually learned. . . . Later that evening, when she asked him how he happened to think so much about this business, he had answered: "I haven't thought it, Mother, I guessed it inside, without realizing it, I suppose, because we're always guessing, because we prefer to guess and hint instead of asking or saying, because that's a part of being well brought-up."

She hadn't had much to say to that. Six months ago—she knew—she would have been crushed by these words, not by grief, but by disappointment that the boy lived in a world by himself, along with the one they shared, a world full of guessing and God knows what. Maybe a whole different world, for all she knew.

Now, in any case, she suspected this was true, but not to the same extent that she would have thought if it had come to her as a shock. So she must have been guessing too—also without realizing it—that a lot had changed between them and in general. She had to think of her brother Martin when they were sitting together in the living room and things had settled a little more. Was this what he had wanted to prepare her for with his continual reminders that her son was getting big now and that he had developed unusually early? It was true that she had thought of him as a little Mozart at the spinet. He had grown up early, yes—but in his own way, or rather, her way: a dream.

She had only realized just *how* mature he was when she gratefully found herself faced with the question she had always thought would be worst of all: it hadn't even come as a question. He had said, and obviously meant it as a final remark: "I suppose Father's death was a surprise. Don't tell me any more about it this evening, Mother."

All the tears—she'd rather forget them now. All the questions that weren't asked. She preferred to remember how he had come over to her chair, sat on the arm, taken her hand, and said: "Poor Mother, it must not be very easy for you either."

But that "either" continued to torment her. Who had he been thinking about? That woman in the boat or her bastard at sea? Or had he been thinking about himself? Wasn't her Lillelord happy? Was their whole life an illusion, a tangential existence that only counted sometimes; at times she felt that her whole existence had only the validity she herself gave it in her indolent aversion to everything unpleasant.

She watched him walking across the Egertorv in the dusty,

August sunshine. She saw how straight, lithe, and tall he was, how easy his movements were. She looked around stealthily to see if other people noticed these things. But they had enough to do, of course, watching out for cars and horses, which were in constant conflict at the corner of Akersgate and Carl Johan because of the difference in their speeds.

When he got to the Storting, he turned and waved. She felt a surge of pride, a mother's pride, and at the same time a young girl's, and immediately afterwards she felt abandoned. She watched him walking along quickly to the Atheneum, where he would take the Frogner trolley car up to that friend of his with whom he was suddenly so occupied.

As Wilfred was getting off the trolley car at Frognerveien, he saw Andreas and his father coming out of the house where they lived. He was on the other side of the street and didn't know what to do. He had a feeling that one way or another he was going to succeed in what he had to do. He was in a victorious mood; he was certain about the convincing childishness he would use to cover up his hardly childish thoughts. But he had counted on finding Andreas alone at home. So stupid. The two hours he had before he was supposed to meet his mother at their house on Drammensveien were precisely what he thought he would need to settle this matter one way or another.

But how? He had no idea. No thought of sacrificing himself or being noble. Just that he would go and see his friend and let fate take over. Now it looked like fate was behaving very differently.

Andreas and his father walked over towards Frogner Plass. He cut across the street and followed them at a safe distance. It was the middle of the day and people were on vacation. There wasn't anyone to hide behind if either of them decided to turn around.

But neither one did. They walked slowly, stooping a little, and seemed to be heading somewhere. They certainly weren't just out for a walk. Then they turned down Nobelsgate, and he ran as fast as he could so he wouldn't lose them around the corner.

As he rounded the corner they were right in front of him, so close that he fell back and waited a bit. Then he fell into step behind them, only ten or fifteen meters behind. A little way down the street they turned to the left between the small houses. He followed them quickly. When he got there, they were gone. There was a little building with a modest sign on it: POLICE STATION.

He felt a chill pass through him. So this was it. He had come in the nick of time, or maybe even too late? The most important thing was that he'd come. It was always different before—now he wasn't playing a game, pretending that he could change his mind, not for a second. He knew it couldn't be any different. He saw Mrs. Frisaksen's face before him all the time.

He came into a vestibule with three pegs and a spittoon. He knocked on a door. A tall policeman in a uniform opened it. He looked inside quickly. Andreas and his father were sitting there on two kitchen chairs. They looked so forlorn. "Those two," he said to the policeman, "I saw them come in. I'm the one who owns the bicycle. He's a classmate of mine, Andreas, he wrote to me. I let him borrow it. . . ."

Then he was in it, just as he had imagined. The short constable with the beard was there too. He was in civilian clothes now and looked like a lost, little troll. Lillelord stood as straight as a ramrod and answered all their questions: what his name was, why he had put his bicycle there, what he was doing in that part of the city. He answered politely and unhesitatingly that he had been riding around, but he'd strained a tendon in his leg and put his bicycle away, locked it and taken the trolley car from Bislett into the city and the Bygdø trolley home from there. It was because of the strained tendon that he had asked his friend to fetch the bicycle and had let him borrow it for a while. The little constable-troll was asked if he thought it was the same boy he had seen that night. He stared at Wilfred from under his bushy eyebrows and tried to look severe. Wilfred had filled out considerably since the spring. The constable looked into his open, honest face, so different from what he thought he remembered that night on Sorgenfrigate. Then he shook his head. "It wasn't him," he said.

Andreas' father invited the boys to have sodas and cakes at the pavilion in Frogner Park. He produced a brown leather purse, the kind that you tilt the money out of, and paid as soon as they'd gotten what they ordered. "You don't have to be so modest," he said to Wilfred, when he didn't want a whole bottle of red soda. That was the first independent remark Wilfred had heard him make. The actual invitation had been aided by his son jabbing him in the ribs. Andreas beamed behind his glasses, bursting with a desire for confiding. He drank so much soda that he had to go almost immediately to the little shed clear over by the main part of the park. Wilfred remained behind with Andreas' father, who was tired and rubbed his white forehead.

"So you're the one they call Lillelord?" he asked. And suddenly his face opened in an angular smile that seemed unnatural, as if his whole smile-mechanism hadn't been used for years.

"My mother used to call me that. In fact, she often still does."

"Andreas talks so much about you. It's good he has you for a friend."

Wilfred felt terribly uncomfortable. Just the word "friend" made him squirm. The confident lie he had told the police had succeeded beyond all his expectations, or rather precisely in accordance with the vague expectation that always built up inside him on his lucky days. But he hadn't counted on this, that he would get stuck on fairly intimate terms with this wretched man he disliked so much.

"Andreas is a fine fellow," he said in a husky voice. He dreaded the return of this fine fellow, relieved and full of energy, ready to go out fraternizing again.

"Is—is Andreas' mother better now?" he asked cautiously.

A shadow passed over the older man's face. "She'll never be healthy," he said. "But don't tell Andreas."

So those two also pretended, playing the same game that they did in Lillelord's circle. But when he thought of the brown dining room on Frognerveien, it made their pretending seem so mean and poor. Couldn't they have been like Mrs. Frisaksen—forthright and unpleasant?

"Oh, well—" the father sighed and squinted at the August sunlight falling through the trees. "It's not so bad for us with this lovely park so close," he said. Wilfred swiftly reconstructed the train of thought that lay behind his statement: everybody was in the country; they had been at Toten for a while—it didn't sound very inviting. Now they were back in their good, old apartment—but that didn't worry them because they were next door to this lovely park, with the tram at the door and a dairy in the same building. . . .

"No, if you live where you do, you really can spend the summer in town," Wilfred said.

The man's face lit up. "Yes, that's just what I say—this lovely park and . . ." he gestured uncertainly. "Besides, we were at Toten," he added. "Andreas likes Toten so much."

Did he believe that? Wilfred stole a glance at him. Andreas could think of nothing worse than Toten. His aunt was a "fat old woman" who spent most of her time in the barn and wanted them to fetch water all day long. And the house was full of flies. . . .

"And in town you don't have the flies," Wilfred said.

"Exactly. Flies!" Andreas' father was more and more pleased. Andreas came back just then, ready for cakes and more soda. "Your friend and I have just been saying how nice it is in town," his father said, "just think of the flies!"

Andreas glanced at his friend quickly. Had he revealed that Andreas thought Toten was a fly-hole and an unbearable place to spend a vacation? Wilfred saw anxiety almost like a layer over his face. So he wanted to spare his father the truth too.

". . . so, I mean, even if you're fond of Toten. . . ."

Again that flash of gratitude in his eyes. Would he ever be able to stop meddling and having to save other people from their own deceit? Why couldn't these two losers play an honest game with each other?—Why shouldn't Andreas find out that his mother was hopelessly ill?—Why, why should they play and pretend day in and day out, when they didn't even get enough out of it to let them stop being careful not to hurt each other every hour of the day?

Andreas' father looked at his watch. Wilfred thought: You know perfectly well what time it is, you office rat. You have a watch ticking away inside your head, buzzing like a fly. You always know what time it is. Now you're going to say: Well, I never! Is it so late . . .

"Well, I never! It's getting so late . . ."

Wilfred looked at his own watch.

"Half past twelve!" he said and pretended to be horrified. Was that another little look of gratitude from Andreas' father, who was so easy to see through?

"Your father has to get back to his office . . . and I have to meet my mother," Wilfred said. He thought it was best to save them all the words and at the same time make it easier for himself to get away. But it was easy to see the disappointment in Andreas' face. They were so easy to read, these two, that it made it feel like you were cheating.

"It must be awful to be guilty of something," Wilfred said, boldly looking the man straight in the eye. "I mean, when you see how easy it is to have appearances against you."

"You're a clever lad, all right," Andreas' father said calmly and held out his hand. Wilfred took it. It was a limp hand, limp and slightly clammy.

The two boys sat there for a while. There was a faint sighing in the old trees. A wasp was swimming in some soda on the table. The clinging, August sun was dazzling. Andreas' eyes smiled invitingly behind his steel-rimmed glasses.

"Jeez, it was great the way you answered that policeman!" he said.

Wilfred looked at him coldly. "There's nothing to it, when you're telling the truth," he said. Andreas looked like a bucket of water had been tipped over his head. He started to say something, but he stopped. Now he looked the same as he did that time at school when he recited his poem about the badger.

"I'm going to earn enough to get a bicycle of my own," he said instead. "I'm going to start at the warehouse where father works."

At last, something proper. Wilfred glowed with delight. "That's really swell," he said. "Well done. Nice of your father too."

"Nice?" Andreas obviously hadn't seen it from that angle.

"Yes, nice of him to do it, instead of letting you loaf around and live off your family, like . . ." Wilfred grimaced. He realized that he was making too much of it, but he had to go on now: "My Uncle Martin says that we live in a time of change, that the working classes . . . well, I mean that everything's going to be different and that people like us, who still own things from before, are going to find it terribly difficult, that the people will demand their rights. He says there's going to be a war between England and Germany. England has sixty-six battleships and Germany only thirty-seven. He says that England ought to strike now, before Germany gets any stronger and before this Kiel Canal is opened."

"War? Is there going to be a war?" The boys looked at each other tensely, excited by their visions of war and violence.

"Well, not here in Norway, but between England and Germany, and then the others could join in too, he says. Russia has fifteen battleships and Austro-Hungary thirteen. . . ."

"How do you know all this?"

"Don't you talk about this stuff at home? Uncle Martin. . . ."

"They don't talk about war. Father says that politics. . . ."

"And art. . . ."

"They don't talk about art."

"What do you talk about then?"

Andreas thought about this for a while. "We don't talk very much," he said. "You know, Father . . . there's so much. And then Mother."

"Is she a little better?"

"That's what Father thinks. My brother heard the doctor . . . it's hopeless . . . but you mustn't tell Father!"

Wilfred looked into Andreas' open face, which struggled to keep its secrets. The dislike of Andreas' father that he had felt before evaporated now. Andreas played his part as well as he could behind his glasses. It wasn't much of a performance, but obviously it was good enough in that family, where they accepted dissimulation, no matter how simple.

Then the two boys walked down Thomas Heftyesgate talking about the war that was coming. All of Wilfred's eagerness was gone now. He no longer believed so firmly in Uncle Martin, nor, to tell the truth, was he so absorbed by it; it had been a sensation. But Andreas couldn't stop fantasizing; he seemed to gorge himself on the word war, as if it would make everything better in the world and at Frogner. When they came to Elisenbergtorv, Wilfred slapped Andreas on the shoulder; he didn't want anyone with him now; he had to be alone for a while and make up his mind about whether what had happened was a good thing or just made everything worse.

"But you shouldn't run to your father and tell him there's going to be a war tomorrow," he said gaily.

"Oh, no," Andreas said, "Father's afraid of everything. We never tell him. . . ." He stood there, clinging to Wilfred's company, sentimental and inquisitive.

"Didn't you dare get the bike?" he said suddenly.

Wilfred had been prepared for this a while ago, but not now. "Dare?" he said, "what do you mean?"

"Well, since I had to. . . ."

Irritation flared up in him. Best to attack at once and be rid of him: "Good thing you're getting your own bike now," he said, "so you won't need to borrow other people's."

He hadn't taken the outstretched hand. He didn't want to touch those warts. When he turned, Andreas was standing on the same spot, still holding out his hand. Wilfred waved quickly.

Andreas looked at his hand and waved back absentmindedly, like a grown-up. Wilfred didn't turn around again. He slowly walked down the hill towards Drammensveien. As before, when he had walked away from Andreas, he could feel the enmity in his back—enmity and admiration, curiosity and a willingness to make sacrifices.

"To hell with him," he said to himself in Uncle Martin's voice.

16

That autumn confirmed many things for Lillelord. He found it extraordinary the way things turned out to be connected that couldn't have had anything to do with each other. He was in a hurry, therefore, to get ready, so these unexpected connections couldn't come up from behind and tear everything apart, like people were always complaining about. "If only *that* hadn't happened," they always said. . . .

The people in the city seemed to be afraid of something after the summer, and at his new school on Skovveien, there were boys from many parts of the city; they sniffed each other over expectantly.

The French airman, Pégoud, was going to perform at Etterstad; he would turn his airplane over on its back and fly with his head down. It was set for a Sunday in September. The new boys at school didn't get acquainted in the usual way, indirectly at first, then with a sudden attack; they only asked who was going to Etterstad to see Pégoud. Everyone asked and no one had any answers because grown-ups take such a long time to decide on important things. The newspapers wrote that it would be dangerous for the public, but the promoters replied that fliers like Pégoud knew perfectly well where they were in the air and that the French flier would keep well out over the fjord and unoccupied areas, and that in any case the field would be blocked off so there wouldn't be any danger to the spectators.

Lillelord said nothing at school about his family's plans. Late that summer Uncle Martin had been visited by a French lawyer who looked after his business affairs in Marseilles; he looked just like people think a Frenchman ought to look: he had a narrow, dark moustache and pointed shoes and wore a morning coat. Lillelord was sent to show him the Viking ships, which were lying under a corrugated iron roof at the University moorings, and Monsieur Maillard was delighted at being shown around by a courteous young man who spoke French, to a certain extent, and could distinguish between a few red wines. Wilfred upset many of the ideas with which his fellow countrymen had filled him before he embarked on this journey to the ice-covered country where the people wore animal skins all year round and lived on raw sheep bones and hard liquor.

The French lawyer had promised Lillelord that he would get to meet Pégoud and come right up to his airplane on that great day. So, when they asked him at school, he just replied: "An airplane—is that something to go and see?"

"Yes, but just think, he's going to fly *upside down.*"

Wilfred was terrified when he imagined himself being invited to go up in the air. He admitted vaguely that maybe it would be rather exciting to fly upside down. Now on Sundays he went out on Bygdø in Uncle Martin's open car. Only a few of the boys had gotten to ride in a private automobile. . . . But they knew each and every taxi, those with numbers from 200 on up. Someone said there were over thirty of them now; but not many had actually been in one.

The second time M. Maillard and Wilfred were in town together, they met Aunt Kristine at Halvorsen's pastry shop. "Well, it's Lillelord!" she exclaimed and clapped her hands. He realized that it wasn't a chance meeting. She hadn't called him Lillelord for years and ordinarily she was never that surprised at a chance meeting. Besides, she made a big fuss about ordering glasses of sherry for herself and for Monsieur Maillard, and a vanilla ice cream and two cakes for him: "Aren't these the best cakes you've ever tasted?"

The three times the Frenchman had been at their houses—once at each of the two uncles and once on Drammensveien—Aunt Kristine had sat beside him drinking coffee and letting him laugh at her clumsy French, which she made sound more childish than necessary; in fact, Uncle René had said she spoke quite excellent French. Now she sat there at Halvorsen's puckering her lips over her glass of sherry and pretending she couldn't pronounce the open French vowels they were always so careful about at home when they had "French Days." And the lawyer, with his slightly nicotine-stained fingers, sat there, finishing off the vowels in the air. Once or twice he touched her mouth with these fingers, sort of pushing the sounds into place. All the people there turned and looked at them. Wilfred thought it was highly unpleasant. He sat silently and stared out the window at the Masonic Lodge to have something to think about. But all the dark passion surged up in him again. Kristine was no longer an aunt, and everything that made her seem helpless, like a young girl, was swept away as she sat there with her tight veil drawn up over the tip of her nose, sniffing at a glass of sherry which seemed to last forever.

All of Kristiania seemed to pour out to Etterstad about eleven o'clock on that sunny September Sunday. Wilfred, his mother, Aunt Kristine, and the French lawyer rode out in Uncle Martin's car. But when they came to the last hill over Vålerengen, some policemen in shiny helmets made them detour. The muddy road was so crowded that it was difficult enough for people to get there on foot, much less in the cars.

All the flat ground at Etterstad was roped off, and people pressed forward impatiently as far as they could, without thinking that everything would take place in the air, so that it didn't matter whether they were in the front or the back. At the top entrance on the other side, the French lawyer produced a card, and they were all shown through a special opening, and Wilfred found himself standing beside the plane, before he had even looked down the slope with its thousands of chattering, expectant people.

Inside a wooden shed there was a little man dressed from head to foot in leather, giving angry orders to three French mechanics, who were running back and forth between the shed and the plane. But when Wilfred was nudged forward to say hello to the aviator, a brown, muscular hand appeared out of the leather and the manly face in the helmet broke into a sudden smile. The aviator and the lawyer knew each other, and Monsieur Maillard introduced Wilfred as his French-speaking friend from the North Pole who really wanted to take a trip in the air.

Wilfred felt a sudden chill of terror. Fortunately, the aviator just threw up his hands and raised his eyebrows in a sort of mute gasp and said something unintelligible, which all the Frenchmen laughed at. Shortly afterwards they heard the roar of motion and excited voices from the field. The mechanics had pushed the plane out into position and had begun to swing the propeller, while the motor gave off a few muffled hiccoughs. Someone stuck a bag of hot peanuts into Wilfred's hand. He had never seen this kind of nut before, but his mouth was so dry with excitement that they just turned into an inert mush as he chewed. The next thing he knew, the flier was out of the shed, and when they went out and saw all the people behind the ropes a hundred or so meters away on the slope, the leatherclad god was already sitting with his gloves and goggles on, strapped to a seat between the four wings of the fragile machine which was so full of ribs and poles that it looked like he was sitting in a cage. The man and the machine together resembled an enormous grasshopper.

The plane drove off into the sunlight. It leaped from tussock to tussock as its speed increased. Only then did they see that the ground was covered with tufts and tussocks; at that speed, the fragile apparatus could turn over at any moment. But then it made a long leap and was almost up in the air. Only once did it touch ground again; its thin wheels got quite a jolt. Then it soared over the sloping runway towards the north and was free. A roar of enthusiasm rose from the field and Wilfred felt (more than he heard) his own shout of joy and happiness as the grasshopper took off. For an instant it was like he himself was soaring; he noticed that he was standing on his tiptoes and straining to help the plane up. But it no longer needed any help. Triumphant, it circled out over Bjørvika and the fjord. When it flew into the sun, everybody raised his hands, almost in a military salute, and shaded his eyes. Some pointed: *there, there. . . .* But others just laughed: the plane was already *there,* over Nesoddland. Now it was coming back again. A man said: "It goes at one hundred fifty kilometers per hour, think what that means. . . ." A lady right beside him replied: "Don't say anything, just pray that he comes back alive."

Then Wilfred noticed a tight grip on his right hand. It must have been there a long time. He looked down at Aunt Kristine's flowery blue hat—a whole garden of tulle and flowers on top of matte yellow straw. Her hand squeezed his and their arms quickly moved close to each other.

"Are you afraid, Kristine?" he said, momentarily overwhelmed by tenderness.

There was a gleam of something on her face; she turned toward him and he saw something he'd never seen before—it was transfigured. Her lips were parted and moist. He could hear her breathing quickly and irregularly in the solemn silence while the plane came toward them again, so fragile there in the sky. Some people looked at their watches. The man who had spoken before said: "He's been in the air ten minutes now." "Ten minutes!" the anxious lady said. "How do you think he'll get down again?"

A roar of sensual terror rose from the slopes as the plane came in over the field again. Everyone ducked as it passed; then they straightened up again and turned their heads the other way. The machine was over the farms at Østre Aker. The stranger said: "He'll start flying upside down soon."

The plane turned north, then it swung around so that it was

obviously coming toward them from Grefsen. Now it was flying into the sun, and the September sunlight was playing on its matte yellow wings; they seemed as thin as flower petals and so delicate that you thought they had to give under the violent pressure. People howled and meowed with delight and terror as, for the second time, the machine approached the place where they were standing. No heads were bowed now because they knew that it might happen at any moment, this miracle that was even greater than what they were already witnessing. Wilfred glanced quickly at the group around him and at the flat faces out in the crowd. Insatiable in the lust for sensations, they turned toward the incredible, while the shouting changed to a dark roar in the field.

And then suddenly there was silence. He looked up quickly, just in time to see the plane turn over and fall on its side. It was right over the field now, and a moving wave passed through the people standing under it; they fled from the horror they couldn't take their eyes off of. It stopped falling the next instant and the plane was flying on its back out toward Ekeberg. They could clearly see the pilot, with his head down between the bars of the machine. Then it went up into the sun again, and the next thing he knew it was coming toward them once more, but this time right side up. The cheering from the field was like a fabric of sound and reverberated as if there were a roof over them.

The next thing he felt was his hand being broken—it was being crushed. Kristine's arm was like a strong snake coiled around his arm. Now they were slightly behind the others, who had moved forward in their excitement. Now they were standing almost face to face, hers turned up, groping and confused with ecstasy and distress.

He didn't know how it happened, and it probably lasted only a moment, but that meeting of their bodies in those few seconds was so violent that it seemed there had been no time between then and the bad time among the alder trees. It was as though he had been flying in the air and had landed, safe and sound.

Not burned out and confused, but full of blissful excitement, a state that was complete in itself and yet held a promise of the sweet catastrophe.

And in a way he now knew that she felt the same as he did—like a promise of consummation between equals. She was also standing as though she'd made a temporary landing on ground that was safe only because it offered the possibility of continuing.

The plane must have also landed during those seconds. Soon afterwards the aviator was standing beside them at the entrance to the shed with flowers in his hand, while his countrymen, men and women, hung on him, kissing him on his cheeks and everywhere. Wilfred and Kristine also went over, but she didn't kiss him, just took his hand in a friendly way and mumbled a sort of thanks for the demonstration.

Wilfred walked across to the machine, which was now being attended to by the three mechanics. At that moment a triumphant roar came from the crowd. They had broken through the ropes and were surging over the field. Wilfred stood beside the airplane and watched them come; they seemed like a huge, black animal possessed by the desire to get closer. But now the police and guards with cords on their caps came from all directions and blocked the way with long arms and hard fists. Wilfred leaned slightly against the machine, watching the scene. It occurred to him then that he seemed to always be on the side where there were few, those who were permitted, who were smiled at and not kept out.

Was that what it meant to be the lonely one—was that what he longed for?

Some boys were shouting from the crowd. He saw a little flock of boys from his class who were trying with desperate courage to get around the wall of policemen's backs and then reach the paradise where the aircraft had landed. They seemed to be setting their hopes on Wilfred, standing there like a second St. Peter by the gates, with an aura of divinity around him, or so it seemed to the boys' young eyes.

Now the police had seen the boys, and they were forced behind a chain of uniformed arms that were thrusting the crowd back brutally at such a speed that some people stumbled and others fell on top of them—and the enthusiastic horde was suddenly transformed into an angry, howling mob that felt it was being kept away from what really mattered.

Then the leather-clad aviator stepped out from the shed where he had been. He looked out wearily over the crowd and gave the people just a hint of an ironical bow. That placated them, and the next moment fresh cheers rang out; delighted whistles and happy laughter rose like doves into the clear, September sky.

No, no! Wilfred thought, suddenly oblivious to his surroundings because of the fierceness of his impressions: that wasn't the loneliness he wanted, to be favored. He had a sudden impulse to go and find his classmates beyond the ropes and give up his favored position. The triumph he had already experienced was enormous. But he didn't care about it.

And because he didn't care, he didn't act on his impulse. For the first few minutes they would regard him as the next best thing to a god; he had touched the plane and spoken with the miraculous Frenchman who flew in the air upside down. But what did he get out of being set apart here, like so many times before? He wasn't concerned about being over anyone, not over his classmates—he could just as well be under them, or to the side, far away, remote. Only not *among* them. Not among anybody. Not a part of anything. Not a part that was ruled by other parts. He was completely indifferent, for better or worse.

His body was still on fire after that intimate contact with Kristine. It was all so different than that time in the summer because now it wasn't like a boy half-choked with lust striking sparks off a reluctant adult. It was a situation that had ripened in the actual atmosphere around them, a situation that was inevitable and that they were a part of *together*—driven towards each other by forces they had set in motion long before and which neither of them controlled or wanted to control. *This* way of being part of an instrument (he wanted it to be fate) was something quite different than being just one among many, feeling and doing things. It was like being the one chosen by fate to go under or be lifted to the heights, where everything glitters and from which the world must seem cloudy and dull gray.

The people who'd been invited onto the field chatted away, unconcerned. The police and guards had rigged up the ropes again and the tense crowd gradually calmed down after the rush of breaking through. Everything was full of excitement on that glorious September day with its high sun and miracles in the sky. Boys with colored trays of nuts and chocolates on their stomachs shouted and got merry replies from all sides. Three drunk tramps with heavy moustaches wreaked havoc with their swearing, and children in sailor suits stood with their legs crossed, needing to go to the bathroom, to the despair of their parents who were afraid of missing anything. It was like having the 17th of May independence celebration in September.

They were saying that the Frenchman would go up again and this time with a passenger. At that moment the lawyer and the aviator came out toward the flying machine again. The muttering behind the ropes spread feverishly. The French lawyer led a little group that made straight for Wilfred, who was standing close to the remarkable machine. He was about to move away politely when the lawyer saw him.

"Here's our young friend I was talking about," he said and gesticulated eagerly. The flier, Pégoud, came toward him and asked in French: "Are you the young man who wants to go up with me?"

Wilfred felt giddy. He saw his mother and Kristine over by the shed behind the group. They had glasses in their hands: champagne had been served to the diplomats and guests. He saw that Kristine was looking at him between the heads of the men who had come over to him. The lawyer smiled: "Isn't that what you wanted?"

"*Oui, monsieur,*" Wilfred said, half choking. He knew that he had said something like that in a moment of exuberance one day in town when they were discussing what would take place. The men nodded at each other and quickly looked at his mother and the other women. Wilfred noticed Kristine's burning gaze. Did she have any idea what they were talking about? These incredible men who seemed to have accepted them in their circle and talked to him as a grown-up. At that moment he felt a rush of genuine desire to go, not only fear and a hope of getting out of it.

"My mother . . . ," he said in a low voice.

"Of course—we have to ask your mother!" The lawyer was about to walk back, but Wilfred managed to stop him. "I meant that my mother—it might be just as good. . . ."

The men looked at each other quickly and smiled enigmatically. Then they nodded and muttered something. From then on, it all went so quickly that he hadn't realized what was happening before he was being led up the low steps across the ribs that led into the machine, to a seat half behind and half to the side of the pilot's. They had wrapped him in a leather coat like the flier's, which was far too big for him, and put a helmet on his head. Now he looked at the world through a pair of huge goggles that already cut him off from his surroundings and made everything unreal and remote. Then he turned in the seat, as far as the straps they had fastened to him allowed; he could see his mother, still surrounded by men in top hats and ladies with open parasols, and way out beyond the ropes he saw the crowd—something thick and dark that didn't concern him or belong to his world.

The mechanics were doing something to the machine; one of them was already in front by the propeller, which he turned heavily, the wrong way. The motor coughed and started to run smoothly.

Wilfred shut his eyes as the machine jolted across the bumpy ground. Once he glanced up and saw the great trees at the edge of Etterstad coming toward him at a tremendous speed, but he quickly shut his eyes again and the only way he noticed they were off the ground was that the jolting stopped. His hands, enveloped in stiff gloves, were clamped to something in front of him. He was stuck tight in more than one way: between rigid terror and a strange feeling of heedless joy that wasn't quite strong enough to loosen his cramped body. He quickly realized, rather proudly, that he hadn't prayed to God, but just as quickly realized that it was only because he'd forgotten. And now, in a way, it was too late. They were flying in the air now. He knew it only because the pressure of the wind was so tremendous. And in any case, no power in heaven or earth was going to get him to open his eyes. That would be the end of everything.

Then he heard a voice from somewhere. It was a human voice shouting through the roar of the wind. It was only the reflex of a good upbringing, but he opened his eyes like lightning for a second and *saw* the ground below and ahead of him. That must have been the green cupola of the Trinity Church he had clearly seen the instant before he shut his eyes tightly again. But he heard the voice again, this time quite close; he opened his eyes once more and saw a jumble of dark green treetops.

This time his eyes didn't close automatically. They remained open for a few seconds; he saw the fjord swinging toward him like it was on a disc, and he caught sight of some lines down below and some red specks on the blue sea. Those had to be sailboats by the red buoys in Bkørvika. Now he could also see a steamship alongside the quay, like a model, like the one he had admired so often in Bennet's window on Carl Johan. And now he saw the city itself, the streets; it was like a drawing beneath him. He saw the Palace. He saw it swing off the disc and disappear. The main island with the red roof of the powder magazine was almost right under them!

But that also made him look *down,* and this time he shut his eyes for good. He had seen something very different than the distant, unreal panorama. He had seen the thin floor under him and the latticework that kept the wings of the biplane in position. And at that moment he felt that he was up in the air for the first time, and that there were only a few pieces of wood that separated him from space itself.

Then the voice called to him a third time, and when he opened his eyes, once more a wonderful feeling of happiness spread through him and freed him from his cramped position. His hands relaxed their grip on the handle in front of him, he let his body fall back in the seat and *saw*—saw with insatiable eagerness that the city came towards him again, that the blue, blue fjord and the islands were sort of swallowed up by the speed and replaced by brown and green forests that came rushing straight toward them. This time he didn't close his eyes. The ground was coming toward him, and he couldn't take his eyes off it. It grew into something more than a hillside; he could see a lot of houses, scattered and in clumps. It was something delightfully irrelevant, something tiny and insignificant that suddenly gave *this* the status of reality—that he was up in the air, in the sky itself, that everything had changed places and found the proper place, and that *he*—alone—was soaring over all this irrelevance that had arranged itself in a comical little pattern under him; just as he had known it must be, a pattern of tiny things with no power, all they had was an order that he had been placed above. Placed above and separated from, excluded, but in a way that was subordinated to his will and not to everything else. It was no longer the things and the petty stuff that controlled him and put him in his place among them and made him a part of something; it was his power to order that put all those small, remote things in their place under him and made him the soaring, separate ruler of all things.

He leaned forward to catch the pilot's attention, so that he could see that he was a part of it now. He shouted several times with joy and fear simultaneously, with a jubilation that surpassed the limits of everything people had experienced or could experience.

But the flier paid no attention to him. He sat leaning slightly over a handle on a rod, one hand seemingly locked on a little apparatus a little lower down and on the other side. At that moment the flat ground of Etterstad appeared under them and Wilfred realized that Pégoud was tensed and ready to land.

A new wave of fear swept over him. He had read that this

was the most dangerous part. Actually flying in the air suddenly seemed safe to him, something to rejoice about that should never end. Now the ground down there was rushing at them, but as he was about to close his eyes again, he happened to see the crowd in a three-quarter circle around the field, kept behind the ropes; he saw upturned faces, white ovals in a dark mass that sped towards him like something threatening and spiteful: the invincible. Death.

But the torment was shorter than he had expected. After the first three strong jolts that made the machine quiver, he felt the speed slacken abruptly and then they were hopping over the ground. He must have shut his eyes again, for when he looked around everything was exactly the same as when they had led him up into the plane with the huge leather coat. Now he swayed out from the machine, the sleeves dangled well below his hands, everything swayed and dangled; even the ground he was standing on gave way and he sank to his knees with a feeling of muted merriment. But now he also heard the cheering from behind the ropes where all the people were. He forced himself to get up to a sort of twisted position. His mother was running toward him, and Kristine and the lawyer. . . . He stood up and was released from the leather coat. The next thing he knew was that his mother was holding him close, pouring a barrage of Norwegian and French words over those standing close by, Kristine, the lawyer, and the flier. Her eyes were shining with anger, pride, and champagne. "My little boy!" she sobbed hysterically. "My own little boy. . . ."

Wilfred freed himself manfully and held out his hand to the aviator, Pégoud. *"Merci!"* he moaned. *"Merci beaucoup!"*

At that same instant he noticed that his pants were wet. Since it was so cold, it must have happened on the way up.

"Do you think we'll be going home soon, Mother?" he asked unhappily. That humiliation hurt him, just when everyone was looking at him. "How did it feel?" "Were you frightened . . . ?" The questions danced in the September air. A little French lady drowned him for a moment in a buoyant embrace and called him *"Mon petit héro,"* though she was almost a head shorter than Wilfred.

"Yes I was frightened!" he said suddenly in answer to all the questions. His reply was translated and it buzzed in the air. It evoked wails of delight from the ladies. But Pégoud came forward and shook his hand once again. "He's the bravest novice I've ever seen," he said calmly. "He sat there with his eyes open almost all the time!"

Again the mood changed to happy laughter. It was as if they had all performed an heroic deed. The only one who wouldn't accept any praise was the aviator himself. His role was almost over once everyone had assured those around that there was nothing he or she would like better than to be taken up in the air. Meanwhile, the mechanics had wheeled the plane back into its temporary hangar, so people could feel safe that they wouldn't be taken at their word. The crowds were surging back toward the city.

Mrs. Sagen and Wilfred were invited to the legation, where there would be a reception for the aviator. "Do you think I can get out of it?" he whispered to his mother.

"You don't want to go?"

"No. I feel so. . . ." He grimaced. "It's almost next door, so I can just slip away when we get there."

She stared at him, inquisitive and worried. Again and again she had seen that gloomy expression pass over his young face like a cloud, a face that more and more resembled one that was heavy with clouds.

"You'd rather be alone, is that it?" she said.

"Yes, that's it—alone." He saw her disappointment. She was like a child; she had wanted to enjoy her triumph, to let herself be seen with her heroic son who had flown in the air. If she had known about this in advance, she would have swooned if necessary, to prevent this; now she couldn't resist giving way to the temptation to shine.

"I'm really sorry about it, Mother. For your sake."

"For my sake? Is there anything wrong?"

Again that worried scrutiny, the attempt to get at his essence. He realized now that this little accident in his pants wasn't the real reason why he wanted to avoid company. Something had happened to him up there in the sky, something that provided an explanation, or an invitation.

That made it all the easier to tell his mother the shameful little secret because *that* wasn't the real secret.

"I'll whisper it to you," he said and pulled her head toward him.

Mrs. Sagen jerked forward with a happy laugh and looked around stealthily. His charming honesty enchanted her so much she was about to tell someone else, but she pulled herself together and looked him in the eye with the same furtive seriousness as that time when they went on the spree at Tivoli that spring evening.

"Slip away, then, when we get there," she said happily and gave him a little pat. He stood looking at her, filled with surprised distrust. Could this adult woman he was so fond of be *so* easy to fool? Was it possible that everyone was *always* ready to believe what he wanted to know?

Yes, it was possible. That was always his experience. The triumphant deceptions of his childhood were due his early discovery that he should never tell the whole truth, never give himself away. This discovery was one of the building blocks for the solitude he was constructing for himself, where he could get away from people and circumstances. He smiled back secretively and put a finger to his lips, and his mother crossed her heart in reply. The game between them was on once more, again and again—as it always had been. The glorious game that made everything different from what it really was and strengthened his certainty that it was possible to live a lie, if only you were alert enough.

"The only thing is that I let both the maids have time off to go and see the show at Etterstad," Mrs. Susanna said. Given his train of thought, this little remark struck him as incredibly funny.

"You're right, Mother," he said, deathly serious, "it would be a great pity if an heroic young fellow like me would perish from lack of concern while his mother was being feted at the legation."

She lightly tapped his cheek again, happy and relieved that the last objection had been dealt with. It was so seldom that she went out with real strangers; she had been concerned about so much—the way things were changing as she watched indolently. . . . A real need for participation was stirring in her on this day; she had to be involved in things, as she had once been, long before, when all the hundreds of little events in Kristiania were a part of her life.

Wilfred let himself into the empty house and gave way to the relief and enjoyment of expanding on his own restlessness. He took a long bath and then went downstairs to the living room, naked under his robe, which flapped around him in a way he found grown-up and dashing. He felt the temptation of his own body like a cool joy because he knew that he could overcome it now. Feeling sublimely adult, he stood by the big window facing Frognerkilen; he looked at the sky, now being covered by blue-gray clouds. The September day had been hot until then. Suddenly dark ripples ruffled the water down below. He watched it as if from another world, from above. He stood there and relived the joyful panic of the moment when he had seen the slender plane under and around him. He was standing on his tiptoes again, as if to stir up his longing to soar, to separate himself from all that bound him, then to collapse and perish in a solitude that the presence of others always limited. Yes, that was what he'd wanted. He had sat in Frogner Park once, drinking soda with some ridiculous people. They were content with that; they had talked about war; they had shuddered at the word, as one should. But for him—he realized it now—the actual word had been an enormous relief, a possibility, a flight, and a catastrophe. All his daring little adventures with fire and violence had been infantile steps towards this state of terror and independence.

He went over to the cupboard and poured himself a glass of sherry from the decanter. He drank it with joyful disgust. It helped him at once to soar a little more; it let his nerves remain in that unreal state he was so afraid would come to an end. He wanted to force the restlessness of his body up to an oscillation so strong and violent that he would have to follow it like a—like an airplane that was forced out into empty space by its roaring motors.

The bell rang. He swore softly, like an adult. He went to answer the door nonchalantly, dressed in his robe. He was acting a part now and he knew it, but he hadn't yet decided which one. Being who he *was;* he could be the master of any situation.

"Kristine!"

He knew that his tone of voice sounded exaggerated—not because he was surprised but rather because it confirmed something, as though she had come as a result of his will. She walked breathlessly into the hall with its sound-deadening tapestries.

"It sounds as if you were expecting me?"

"In a way. There's no one at home."

"I knew that."

That said everything. Nothing could be changed. All the old doubt and anxiety hung like memories in the warm air, but they weren't strong enough to stop anything. He took her in his arms.

"We're crazy," she said, childishly trying to excuse herself.

"Do you think so?"

He led her inside like an adult. She was still wearing her blue, flowered hat from Etterstad and had a light beige cape over her shoulders. He didn't help her off with any of these things; he gently and expertly led her to the stairs. But when they reached his room, he tore off her hat and flung her cape on a chair.

"Don't be so violent!" she said sharply, trying to be the dominant one.

"No?" he said ironically. He noticed that a stranger's power had possessed his body. Who was this stranger who gave him the authority to exist outside himself?

They kissed without restraint. Suddenly all the difference in their ages had disappeared. It wasn't like that time in the alder trees; there was no impermissible lust that he had to be ashamed of.

"What's come over you?" she said, whimpering tentatively. It occurred to him that maybe she didn't even know then what she wanted—perhaps she still just wanted to play.

"What's come over me?" he said in a hard voice. He was full of will and knowledge. "You know very well what's come over me, Kristine!" he whispered into her skin and clothes. "Everything."

Then she stopped acting. Not helpless, not surprised. She helped his terribly urgent hands with almost maternal slowness. The slanting rays of the sun came in through the curtains and fell like spears of holy light over the white body in which he began to systematically drown himself. She whispered once that someone might come. He knew coldly that all her resistance had been broken by then, if there had been any. "No one can come," he panted back. They were words without any meaning—a ritual: he could just as well have said something else—anything—the words weren't his, nor were the actions. Slowly and with a conscious gradualness that surprised him, he knew what to do, as inherent knowledge about the decisive step was revealed to him, so different from his hot, excited dreams where each stage came headlong and out of sequence. He was possessed by a strange will to be perfect in the act, without any of the beginner's haste and spoiling uncertainty. He was suddenly no longer an adolescent grabbing at unfamiliar female charms. The stranger was in him, whispering wise counsel in his ear, that he had to be slow and keep himself under control, had to give and not just take. He felt the enjoyment in *her* body and in his own—carried through bluish rings of sweetness in their minds and bodies, where he could record their passage and have their common body under blissful control.

Their embrace dissolved into languorous enjoyment. Together they glided back through the spheres without any abrupt transition from sweetness to shame. The experience had been so much greater than he had imagined. The reaction was also a surge of happiness that conquered him completely. She lay and let him discover all the secrets of her body, totally without bashfulness. The transition to gentle intimacy without excitement became an initiation between equals for them. And he knew it. He knew the whole time that he had given her pleasure and there was no shame on her side. The stranger was still in him, for it was like having a real stranger in him, another being who had guided him and was still inside him with an erotic wisdom that had been passed down from generation to generation. It filled him with a fresh, happy certainty of having conquered. . . .

Whom? His thoughts returned jerkily—but slowly too, without revelations or anything depressing. They returned in mild wonder that this, the greatest thing of all, really was so great and yet no more difficult than that. There had been no catastrophe, no falling down from inexperienced heights. The degrees of ecstasy themselves were chiseled in his memory, as if it had been about climbing towards a peak made possible by ledges and firmly anchored ropes.

But when his erotic activity began to appear again, she freed herself gently and sat up in bed beside him and looked at him searchingly. "Wilfred, this was terribly wrong—of me. But you've made me feel it isn't wrong."

He knelt beside her in gratitude; he bathed her body with gentle caresses, not intrusive and hard with demands as they had been, but idolizing and full of gratitude. He needed to show her, to show his gratitude, but he was also calculating: that this was the right thing to do, that this was what he should do. It was the stranger in him telling him what to do and how to act like a lover. There was a strange power giving him gentle orders.

But it wasn't a commanding power that endangered his own independence, but a being who wished him well.

"You have initiated me into life," he said seriously. And when she wanted to smile, so that things wouldn't get too solemn: "No, I mean it, this isn't a childish outburst, and you know it. You have initiated me."

She took his head tenderly between her hands and looked at him for a long time.

"I almost believe it's true," she said quietly, "I almost believe that you're freeing me from the need to regret it and feel sorry."

"But you shouldn't be sorry!" he said, unexpectedly ardently. "You have made something that for most young men is shameful and frightening into the loveliest beauty in me. Don't you believe I know that?"

"Wilfred," she said, "you are the dearest person I know, and you must never say you love me, because you don't. But you are the most adult child I've met, and the most childish adult."

And *she* said it in such a way that he couldn't be hurt, even by what she said about him being a child.

"You remind me of *him,*" she said and smilingly pushed his face away from hers.

"Who?"

She had to smile again, but this time at his comical jealousy, that really did make him seem childish, though in a different way.

"No one—that I've known this way," she was quick to say, "but there was a man. . . . Oh, I shouldn't have said that."

There was a frightened look in her eyes now. She stared out into the room, which had a sort of autumnal twilight from the last sunlight shining in through the windows. He turned involuntarily to follow her gaze: it was as though she saw someone there, someone he didn't see or know.

The slanting rays fell on the portrait of his father on the chair against the wall. The red sunbeams played on the short beard and gave the brushstrokes a life that wasn't in the oil or pigment. It was as though the face—so weak and at the same time masterful—came out of the frame, out of the shape the painter had created for it, as though it could speak to them at any moment, as though it were saying something to them both with its sorrowful eyes so full of bursting life.

And he knew him then. For the first time he knew him. For the first time in his life Wilfred felt a dark current of affinity with this painted being that had once frightened him—as if all the age, time, and distance were erased. And he knew that here was the wise stranger who had inspired him with his skill in the unknown things, a lover among men, a man who had brought shame and happiness to his fellow beings and was like a mystery in them every day he was mentioned.

Slowly he stepped out of bed. She followed and snatched up clothing as she went. With a feline litheness, she was in her burdensome clothes before he had time to cover anything. Naked as he was when God made him, Wilfred stood in front of the portrait of his father and saw his sinful eyes examine him expertly, yet without the irony with which grown-ups always threaten you. Maybe it was a look of acceptance. In any case there was no reproach or veiled talk about guilt.

He turned towards Kristine joyfully and was filled with an affection that blotted out his own bitter impulse to assert himself for the first time. A door opened and closed down below. It was Lilly coming home. He knew it at once by her footsteps and wasn't afraid, and when he wanted to reassure Kristine, she raised her hand to show that she'd also understood.

"But your mother can come at any moment," she said in a toneless voice.

He looked at the clock. An hour had passed. For the first time he had a vague notion about the enigma of time—that it existed in your own blood and only there.

"I don't think so," he said lightly. "Mother was really ready for a good time today. It was so nice to see her like that."

He flung on his clothes without embarrassment as they talked together quietly. He felt all the calm that comes from experience and not having to be ashamed about the mysteries of dressing.

They kissed quickly in front of his father's portrait, then turned—simultaneously—toward it once again. The sun had left it now. It lay in a gloom that seemed completely dark compared to the blinding rays of sunlight up on the wall. It was as though this man had said what he wanted to, had given his son the benefit of his experience as long as there was a need for it. Wilfred picked up the painting and put it on the hook where it had been all those years without him seeing it.

"I'm going now," she whispered. "I want to go alone."

"I'll meet you at the corner, at the Skarpsno cafe."

"No. I want to go for a walk, a long walk by myself."

"A long walk with me."

"By myself, do you hear me? Good-bye, Wilfred—dear."

He stood by the narrow window in the hall and watched her walk up the drive. She didn't seem lonely now. She walked quickly and lightly. Then she had reached the street. He felt a dull sweetness rushing through him. He stood for a long time gazing at the empty road. He painted her into the picture, exactly as he had seen her, the cornflower-blue hat, the cape over her shoulders, the light footsteps that contained his secret in their very rhythm. He stood there by the narrow window and watched the dusk come and the pale glow of the gaslights as they were being lit on the street. He was still standing there when his mother came walking down the street.

"Anything happen?" she asked, as he helped her off with her wraps.

"What should happen? I've been here all the time. Have you had a good time with the Frenchmen?"

"I got so restless. Well, it was quite pleasant. I don't know. I'm too old, I suppose, for such gaiety."

"Nonsense, Mother. You're only saying that to make me say that you're not too old."

"Well, say it, hurry up and say it!"

They stood facing each other, mother and son, as so often before, as they always did, playing the old, old game between the lady of the world and her *ersatz cavalier,* as Uncle Martin put it.

"You were the prettiest of all the ladies up at Etterstad," he said and put his arm around her waist as they walked into the living room. "Were you drinking champagne all the time?"

"Nonsense!" she said. "Kristine was prettier, they were all better-looking. No, they don't drink much. The aviator was a teetotaler. They talked and talked, and I'm out of practice. My French has gotten a bit frayed with the years."

They faced each other, happy and oblivious. All the quick remarks, so easily made and so soon forgotten, all the good, fulfilling security—it had been a torture for him for a long time now, when he had to pretend again—but now he suddenly noticed that it didn't bother him any more. His dissimulation came naturally, like before. Or maybe it wasn't dissimulation? This was no lonely entrenchment he had to defend against a mother, or uncles, or schoolteachers who wanted to force their way inside him and control him and his life.

"Aunt Kristine wasn't at the reception," she said, "they'd forgotten to ask her. They were really unhappy and tried to ring her up a couple of times."

He glanced at her fleetingly but inquisitively. Was this that damned instinct coming out again? The restlessness she had mentioned. . . .

"But Kristine doesn't have a telephone," he said defiantly.

"They rang up the candy shop. She's often there on Sundays to put things in order."

"So she wasn't there today," he said. He heard that his tone was a little more intense than he had intended.

"I guess not," his mother acquiesced.

But he wanted to know now. To know if there were mysterious forces at work, forces that could tell people everything that another person did.

"But you could have sent someone to her home—I mean, if you had to do it over!"

But she shied away again: "We could have," she said wearily, "fancy me not thinking of it."

Was that irony? His suspicion flared up again.

"But it's not certain she was at home either!" he said.

"Lillelord," she said—he noticed that she called him that again—"you're making quite a fuss. . . ."

Row ashore now, row ashore, he thought. Don't let her catch on, don't tempt fate when you hadn't intended to give anything away. Because he hadn't had he? Of course not!

"Sorry," he said, "you can see I haven't really come back down to earth yet."

Did she glance at him to see if there was a double meaning? Oh, if only no one had ever mentioned the word instinct; if only they hadn't said it so often. There was always guessing in the air, something cloudy that made certain situations unclear. If people were forthright and used few words, like Mrs. Frisaksen, like Erna. . . .

"Do you know who was at Etterstad today? Erna! I saw her in the crowd behind the ropes. The whole family was there."

"I'm sure her father told them that it was the airplane's great speed that overcame the law of gravity."

"Ssh, Wilfred," she said, "I'm sure Erna was awfully proud of you."

"Were you, Mother?"

"Terribly proud. But you haven't told me a thing about how it felt. . . ."

There wasn't any danger now. They weren't talking about Kristine any more. The temptation to take risks arose in him once more.

"Felt?" he asked.

"Yes—to fly!"

"Oh, that—!"

It was as if his thoughts were drifting toward the inevitable again, as if the actual situation was gone and he had to summon it up again in the half-dark living room. He could see the last light-reflections on the water outside in the mirror with the matte gold frame.

"It felt—wonderful. . . ."

"Wonderful? But you were frightened!"

He looked into the mirror. The soft gleam of silver off the water was changing the whole time.

"Frightened? Yes, of course I was frightened. The climb. . . ."

"The climb—yes, but weren't you dizzy then?"

The sea reflected in the mirror had turned gray, so the last rays of the sun must have left the water.

"Yes, I was dizzy. I was—soaring. It was blue."

"What was blue? The sea?"

"Blue! Everything was blue. It was like huge—rings . . . they grew in me and outside me at the same time."

"Your stomach!" Mrs. Sagen said, "that must have been your stomach."

"Stom—yes, of course. . . ." But again the picture in the mirror seemed to be calling him, as if it had more to say. It was a different picture that he saw in the dark mirror now, the picture of the man on the wall up there, the one he had once taken down.

"Mother," he said, "you mustn't mind me asking, but Father—was he a good-looking man?"

She got up at once and walked to the window.

"What do you mean—good-looking?"

"I mean, was he the kind of person who—did people really like him?"

"Who?" Her voice was dry and curt. She looked out over Frognerkilen.

"Well, people, women and. . . ."

She turned but remained standing by the tall window. She looked pale and slender against the darkness outside. He couldn't see her face properly.

"Why do you ask?" she asked.

He tried to fix on her face. He hadn't meant to hurt her. But he felt obstinate.

"Is it so strange that I would ask? You've never told me anything."

She certainly must have wanted to come over to him now, but she stopped. It was as though she was looking for an ally out in the darkness. "Did I scare you, Mother?" he said and went toward her instead.

"Why should you have scared me? Of course you didn't. No—it probably isn't so strange that you'd ask. . . . Listen, son. . . ." All at once she put her arm around his neck and they stood there, both turned toward the window: "Has someone been talking to you about your father?"

"That's just it. You, for example—never have."

They stood together, facing the dark water with the pale streaks of a fading day. It was as if they were talking to a mirror together and therefore were less alone.

"Your father was very popular," she said, "with people—women—and so forth."

It hurt him that she tossed it off so easily. She spoke to him like a child, yet with a sort of veiled anger.

"All right, you don't have to tell me anything," he said angrily and walked away from her again. The clock on the mantelpiece ticked sadly, filling the room with silence. He knew that he was tormenting her now, but he also knew that it was unfair that he should know it.

"It was just because of what you said about the egg." The words slipped out of him. He wanted to go now. He didn't want to come down from the heights where his body and his soul were still circling. He wanted to be alone and revel in it.

"But you know about that business with Madame Frisaksen," she said.

"You're right, Mother," he said. "It was silly of me, and really I'm not that curious."

He wanted to be done with it all. His good, old indifference had returned. "And anyway I've forgotten to work on my lessons for tomorrow," he said.

He had given her an excuse, she could say: Heavens, then it's high time you did them; or she could release all her irritation and say that a person shouldn't neglect his duties for the sake of sensations and amusement.

"Oh, your lessons," she snorted. It was as though she was prepared for a battle, while he just wanted to smooth everything over and be alone. She came to him from the window, went to the fireplace, and lit a cigarette; she seldom did that. . . .

"That affair wasn't the only one," she said. "It wasn't just an isolated 'affair'—it was the rule."

He gave up and sat down then, feeling tired suddenly, and slightly curious. She sat down, too, and stared at the glowing end of her cigarette: "People liked him much too much—and he liked them, in a way. That is, perhaps he despised them, I don't know, perhaps he didn't bother about them at all, or even about himself either. They became a part of him in a way. In another way, nothing like that happened. But you wouldn't understand that."

He moved closer to her and politely pushed an ashtray over to her.

"Maybe *you* didn't understand it?" he asked cautiously.

"No. I didn't. I don't understand. I never think about it now—almost never."

"And now I've gone and ruined your peace of mind?"

"Yes!" she smiled. "You've ruined my peace of mind. There's always someone who does that when you want to run away the most."

"But Mother, it's so long ago!"

"Yes, it was long ago. It's something that doesn't exist. Not anymore. But sometimes it does anyway."

"I understand that very well, Mother. Your mistake is that you think I'm a little dumb."

"No, son, I don't think you're stupid at all—just the opposite!" she sighed, resigned. "It's just that you are a child; you're the only person I have . . . no, I know what you're going to say, that you're not a child, maybe that's right, I don't know. I don't know anything; that's what's wrong with me, I don't know anything."

He moved closer beside her on the sofa. He knew that she was almost crying now, that she would cry if he kept asking . . . and he knew that she did *not* want to cry.

"I don't give a fat damn about Father," he said—"as Uncle Martin would say!" he added conciliatorily.

"Oh yes. Uncle Martin!" she said and saved herself. "He's told me so often that I ought to have a talk with you." She sighed again with resignation.

He said: "Mother do me a favor: don't tell me the kinds of things grown-ups feel they're obliged to tell their children when they aren't children anymore."

Did she laugh? Was it possible that she had laughed frivolously in the semi-darkness right beside him? He had spoken in anger. And she thought it was funny! What a mother—she was the most delightful one in the world . . .

"There was something about your father," she said with a sudden energy. "They wouldn't leave him alone."

"Who wouldn't?"

"People."

"Women?"

"Yes, women," she said, enjoying it sort of like a vulgar word. "You know that he was an officer in the navy?" she added, as an explanation.

"In the portrait upstairs he's wearing a uniform."

"Yes. Of course. . . . But he wasn't there long. He—gave it up."

"Didn't he like it?"

"No. That is . . . he didn't want to stay any longer. Then he went into shipping and made a mass of money. It surprised everyone. He was so clever."

"Did you get rich then?"

"We spent an awful lot too. An awful lot. That was my fault just as much as his. We were never alone."

He was on tenterhooks now. There was a lot he had suspected

at one time, and then he'd forgotten it all for something more important.

"We went everywhere, you see. I don't know why, but that's how it was. We just had to be there—and we had to—travel a lot too. Those modern paintings—nobody has things like that here but us. . . . Did you know that your father played in public? That he gave concerts?"

He didn't reply. He had known it, but he'd never paid any attention to it.

"Could he do a lot of things, then?" he asked weakly.

"He could do everything. I mean he *could* have. He had a talent for everything. Everything turned out *successfully* for him."

She paused again—as if to catch her breath each time. Now he was afraid she was going to stop.

"Wasn't that fine though, Mother?" he asked.

"No, it wasn't."

The confidences came in spurts. He thought: She's been waiting for this for a long time. And yet she's just sitting there covering things up.

"Well, now you know everything about your father," she said childishly and, full of childish satisfaction, she added: "It was really a good thing you asked."

"I don't know anything," he said. "The glass egg. . . ."

She got up immediately and went back to the window.

"We've talked about that."

"But not about the connection between it and—well, the other stuff!"

"We've talked about everything. Someone must have taken the egg—stolen it. . . ."

He went and stood beside her. The pleasant feeling of soaring still hadn't left him. He didn't know why he had asked that question just then. It could have been for her sake: so that she could get it out of her system; it could have also been because the good, wise man up on the wall in his room had advised him to do it.

"Did you lose all your money then, Mother?" he asked.

"Lose it? No. Not all of it. What do you think we've lived on?"

They looked out into the night together. A solitary light on the Bygdø side laid a shaft of light across the velvety water. He looked straight out into the darkness and asked:

"Why did Father shoot himself?"

"He didn't shoot himself." The reply was a made-to-order lie. They didn't look at each other, just out into the darkness with the quivering shaft of light on the water. A train thundered past on its way from the city. The sparks were like stars settling behind it and then dying out.

"Well, good night, Mother. It must be getting late. I'm still up in the air."

He had almost reached the door when he heard her say:

"It wasn't my fault."

She was pale against the window when he turned. She slowly came toward him and took both his hands in the darkness. "We were so happy, you and I. You were a child."

"Yes, Mother, but I'm not a child anymore."

She examined his face in the darkness; it felt like fingers searching over his face.

"Aren't you?" she asked.

"No, Mother. And you know it. But we can be just as happy—you and I. . . ."

"No," she said.

"But Mother, why are you saying that?"

"We can't be as happy. The trouble with me, don't you understand, is that I don't pay enough attention. That's what my brother Martin's always saying. I don't pay attention to the consequences, he says."

"Not of Father dying."

"No. For me he went on living. I couldn't believe it. Not until I'd forgotten him. Almost forgotten him. And then in a way, he'd never lived."

"I think I understand you, Mother. You only acknowledge what you have close by. You don't want to know about the rest.

When something changes, you don't want to go along with it."

"How long have you understood that?"

"I don't know. On the other hand, you go and guess about a lot of things that may be true. But you certainly don't know that they are. Not until you have to. And then you either reject them or feel insulted."

He was on thin ice now. He was guessing, as he always had, and as she had—it was the family disease. He guessed that it must be like that. But if it wasn't right, she would pooh-pooh it.

"Well I think you're acting a little too shrewd," she said with some of her old lightness.

"Why did you say that about Erna—that she was at Etterstad?"

"But, my dear boy—I just saw her."

This was where they had to be, though he hadn't wanted to get there now because he was still up in the air and it was his greatest day. Whatever she says, I'll give in and not cross-examine her. . . .

"Actually, there was something completely different that I wanted to talk to you about," she said suddenly. "Confirmation."

"Mother!"

"What is it?" she said, irritated. "We've talked about it before."

"I don't want to hurt you, Mother; I'll do anything not to hurt you. But as you say, we've discussed it before."

"Yes, but why, son—why don't you want to?"

"If you have to know, I don't believe in God."

It sounded too pompous; he hadn't wanted it to. He just hadn't wanted to offend her. Now it sounded like a declaration before the altar. She just dismissed it:

"What kind of nonsense is this? Who believes?"

"I don't know; I have no idea. But I don't."

"It's not a question of believing or not believing. Your Uncle Martin, my brother, what do you think he believes in?"

"Stock prices, I suppose. What's he got to do with this?"

"He's your guardian, son—in place of your father. And he thinks. . . ."

She sat down but got up again restlessly and walked over to

the fireplace. "There's another thing; it's just as well that it comes out now—you've never been baptized."

He had to laugh. And when she didn't join in, he had to laugh a little for her too: "You say it as though it's a disaster."

"It is. It was your father. He was very obstinate about certain things. I. . . ."

"What do you mean 'I'?" He walked after her and comforted her.

"I had so little will power. I forgot about it. But don't you see that you can't be confirmed without being baptized?"

She was wringing her hands, actually standing there with her back to the mirror, wringing her hands. He just wanted to help her when he said: "And so you've been thinking of having me baptized quietly, is that it?" And when she didn't answer: "Mother, have you already spoken to the minister about this?"

"What else should I have done?" she said, annoyed. "It's not at all unusual, he said."

But now irritation was rising in him.

"So you agreed to wheel me into church in a baby carriage and put some diapers on me? Seriously, Mother, I give in to you in most things. . . ."

"You give in! Aren't I the one who lets you have everything? That dummy keyboard to practice on because you can't stand hearing all the music—I've ordered it now." Something brushed him, tenderness, shyness.

"It came a bit suddenly, Mother, and really, there's no great hurry. . . ."

He was soaring. He recognized his superiority; he could afford concessions. Something had happened to him that set him above all the other children. "There's no real hurry," he said. "We could always postpone it. I mean so that it comes a little more gradually."

He'd won her over a little. He saw that. A little.

"And I'll promise you something in return," he said. "I'll be the best in everything I do at school. I'll go to the Conservatory and be best there too. At everything."

She shivered slightly; she seemed to gather a nonexistent shawl around her.

He saw that she was frightened. But at the same time he had made a decision.

17

Wilfred was the best in his class at his new school.

He divided his day up differently now. He did his lessons for half an hour before dinner and one hour after. Then he went for a short walk, and after that he practiced for two hours, partly on the grand piano downstairs and partly on the dummy keyboard upstairs. The one day of the week he didn't practice was his day at the Conservatory, and that was on his teacher's advice. In the evenings he read French and the history of art by turns, except one day a week when he went to the gym. It was hard to be the best *there* because he always retained a certain anxiety about the trampoline and the horse.

At the Conservatory he met a girl named Miriam. She was in his violin class and her father sold knitwear. On their way home he used to carry her light violin case as far as Oscarsgate, and often they went around the block on Metzlersgate and Riddervoldsgate, even around the Uranienborg Church in the dark autumn evenings. It was only October, but it was already below freezing. Some evenings they stood up on the wall in front of the church and watched the northern lights shimmering over Tryvannsåsen. They always talked about music on these walks home, but when the northern lights rose over the ridges to the north and east, mysterious waves seemed to sweep over both of them. Then they could hold hands and feel a deluge of cold light pass from one to the other. And just then neither of them could find much to say.

Kristine had gone to Copenhagen shortly after that day of

initiation in September. She had come once briefly and she hadn't said anything about going. His mother had mentioned it later, one evening when he was busy with his French. It came out casually, along with some other minor things she found to interrupt him. It struck him that she mentioned it a bit too casually. It didn't matter much to him that Kristine had gone away. The one time she had come to see them, she'd seemed tired and a little old. He was grateful to her inside, but he didn't love her.

He thanked her every time he thought about it, and he thought about it often. The boys at his school were always talking about "doing" it and some of them thought you could have children all your life after you'd done it once. They also drew sexual organs on pieces of paper and passed them around the class. He smiled the first time he got one of them, then he folded it and carefully tore it across and dropped it into the front of his desk. They didn't pass him any more after that.

He thanked her, too, because it helped him to keep the wall close around him; he had decided to build it that evening when his confirmation had been mentioned. He had gotten out of going to see the minister for the time being; he had gotten a postponement for the baptism. He knew by experience that in a family that didn't approve of any annoyances, postponement could mean the same thing as having it forgotten.

And he thanked her for his whole physical well-being, for having helped him to become a person they were entirely satisfied with. Sometimes in the evening his mother would glance at him suspiciously—she seemed to be thinking that all his diligence and goodness were really too much of a good thing. Several times, too, he had heard her cut short a telephone conversation, when she noticed that he was nearby. That was when Uncle Martin had recognized his responsibilities and inquired about the great progress he was making, or maybe it was Aunt Valborg; she wasn't quite as enthusiastic and said that young people ought to do some crazy things in between all the good things.

When his mother looked up at him like that, he knew that she was thinking the same thing, too. She might say: "Do you have to work *so* hard on your French?" She might tempt him with a film at the Cosmorama. And he didn't always refuse. He wasn't very bothered by the fact that she had to see through him. He humored her in everything, even her frivolous little ideas. He told her about Miriam and the brief walks they took together in the evening. He made it a point of not keeping anything secret, and yet there wasn't a thing that wasn't false from beginning to end. He had finally reached the stage where she knew nothing at all about him. She didn't. No one did.

One day he met Erna as he was coming home from school. She went to the Berle School on Professor Dahlsgate and lived on Lyder Sagensgate. What was she doing between Vestheim and Drammensveien right after school? He was on guard the moment she turned up on Skovveien.

"I was just going another way," she said. It sounded like an excuse.

She was still tan from the summer. She was always tanned and had a healthy, cool complexion that reminded people of her father. They walked his way together for a while. She happened to be going that way. She was going to see a dressmaker. He really should have been at the dentist, he remembered that now, at the dentist down on Observatoriegate.

Now that she thought about it, she had to go that way too.

They walked down towards Lapsetorv, slower and slower. The dentist—it wasn't really that important. He had to hurry home. They were having guests. They stopped and faced each other. She was wearing a medium blue cape with a very narrow fur edging; it was all very sensible. She rolled up the sleeve from her left wrist and held out her hand.

The silk cord from that summer. White and dull from many washings, it was still around her wrist. Indignation raced through him like a rain of arrows. He jerked her hand up with his own and in one movement he undid the fisherman's knot he had tied that day in the boat and snatched off the thin, braided cord. Tears sprang into her eyes, tears of rage and offense.

"Give it to me," she said. He threw it in the street. It landed on the trolley line and a trolley came right then and ran over it.

"You can't walk around with something like that," he said in a hard voice. He took three steps away from her, then he turned and laughed. "You'll get a diamond ring from me someday!" he said, and turned on his heel. Then he walked away from her again, quickly. But in that brief instant he had seen that she was bewildered. A little spark of light was on the verge of lighting up her eyes just because of that. He laughed loudly as he walked down the street. He stopped and laughed again while he knew she was still standing and watching him.

The musical evenings at Uncle René's had begun again, every third Thursday. They seldom had professional musicians playing now; Uncle René was no longer so anxious to have his own little compositions performed. One of his pieces had been played at a concert once—as an encore. He preferred more and more to see himself as an artist now, and he forgot some of his former deference to people with names. Wilfred was also required to play. He played Chopin and Debussy at the Conservatory in October. He was set to do Bach's preludes and small etudes in November. He never played Mozart anymore, and when they asked him about it, he said that he'd forgotten it all. He did assignments from Buxtehude and at the musical evenings he gave impromptu lectures (without being asked) on polyphonous music. That irritated Uncle René, but his mother looked stealthily from one to the other, her eyes shining.

At family gatherings he was careful to attend to all of his little duties. He told Uncle Martin how much all of Uncle René's teaching had meant to him—just loud enough for Uncle René to gather what they were talking about. He fished out little items of news about the stock market and business which he served up for Aunt Valborg, who clapped her hands and called over to her husband: "Martin, did you hear what Wilfred knows? A thousand things that I don't even know about!" Wilfred hushed her quickly then and said, while it was still quiet: "It must be terribly interesting to be in on the things Uncle Martin knows about. I don't know anything, but I've understood a bit of what he says."

He said to Aunt Charlotte: "I don't think you ought to change your perfume—yes, I like this one too, it's lovely, but somehow it's not you. . . ."

When Lilly came in with the tray, he quickly collected the cups and saucers and helped her with the ashtrays. He had made Lilly an ally, though for a time it had been difficult. It was during that time in the autumn when his mother was so irritable and nothing was ever good enough. There was quite a bit in the newspapers then about young people who had gone astray and he knew that Lilly had a lower-class shrewdness; she didn't let herself be impressed. He knew that it was only *his* look that had saved the situation once or twice, when she was on the verge of answering back and saying something about certain spoiled children.

She was his ally now, all he had were allies. He had no friends at school; he kept his distance, but he acted friendly and honest and often had to be a referee in the schoolyard because he had no interest in favoring anyone. Only Andreas went around looking like he knew something. But Andreas had to struggle like a drowning dog to keep his head above water. Besides, he couldn't get rid of his warts. He used acetic acid made from glaciers on them, and that made them black.

Sometimes when he and Miriam were walking home from the Conservatory on Nordahl Brunsgate on dark evenings, he was just about to open up, a little, to say something real. That little, brown-eyed girl with the soft eyelashes had a marvelous feeling of calm that was transmitted to him. She told him little things about her home, about her father, who was orthodox and went to the synagogue. She was so brimful of music that it seemed to overflow into her voice and fill her whole being. She played at concerts for the poor on the east side of town. She told him about the shining eyes she saw there. And she told him about the solemn Sabbath rituals at her house and how everything got quiet between her parents and brothers. And then things got very solemn between them too as they walked along. He wanted to be included, to share with people, to let them give him something and he would give in return. But then he quickly thought about everything as it was; it was just as he'd decided it should be. Sometimes he had to look around at the dusty streets to get out of this mood. He could say: "Really, what's the point of all this music?" Things like that! But the soft little girl seemed to understand everything about that too; she knew why he'd said it. She never turned to him, with blue eyes full of tears, and looked hurt and wounded. She could laugh, quite softly. She could laugh softly at everything. And when she said something, it wasn't a definitive statement like he was used to. She said it because it occurred to her. If he said the opposite, it was as if she'd never said anything, as if her whole being was filled with the knowledge of many things. Once—it was in the sparse woods on the back side of Uranienborg, he put his arms around her and gave her a long kiss. She let it happen and returned his kiss. They stood embracing each other on that icy evening—violin case and all. Finally he put the violin case down on the ground. She laughed a little then, but she didn't make it difficult when he wanted to hold her again. She met him full of unembarrassed delight: he was aware of a tender desire that contained everything that had been. Then she moved her face away from him and stroked his cheek. She took her glove off and stroked it again. When he bent down for the violin case, the ground was covered with snow, it was deep everywhere. They had snow on their heads and wherever their hands hadn't been. Then she laughed: "Winter's certainly here," she said.

He had told his mother about Miriam. Not that he was in love with her. He talked about her so he wouldn't fall in love with her. He told his mother about school, exactly as it all was, about the fat instructor at the gym who wanted to be the most active of all of them, about all the music that poured out of the Conservatory and reached him from the windows there, and they played music like that everywhere. . . . And all the time he kept noticing how it was possible to tell things exactly as they were without actually saying something as it really was. Sometimes he felt an urge to lie, like he used to do, so that there could be something that was genuine. He knew that if he did, she would be filled with gratitude and happiness: He had given himself away!

But he didn't lie about anything. He was careful not to because he wanted to lie. She wasn't going to tempt him into a cozy little lie that could be their code.

Snowy weather came early that winter. On evenings when they had made plans to go to the theatre, they could suddenly look at each other and agree that it was nicer indoors. They said nothing, but once Wilfred added: "Besides, I have my math to do." She said: "What do you mean 'besides'?"

"Well, we'd decided we weren't going to the theatre, hadn't we? It's snowing and the wind's blowing."

"Did we decide that? We haven't said a word about it."

They looked at each other. Then he laughed. "Didn't we?" It was all the same to him. He had wanted to make her happy by showing how close they were.

"Wilfred," she said, "I think it's uncanny."

That was good. Everything was good. Everything went well. He could make her think that they were close, that there was contact. That made her glad, so glad that she could be happy even with something uncanny.

"You're right," he said, "it is strange!"

Would she bite? She did. She bit at everything. People always bit at things they wanted. A fish swimming in a never-ending search for something to eat—didn't it have the same suspicion when it saw a silly hook dangling in the water? It took it. It wanted to believe the best and a little pang of regret passed through its fishy little brain as it felt the pain in its mouth: I saw there was something peculiar about that. . . .

She said: "Aunt Kristine—I probably should have told you this before. . . ."

Something flashed through his mind. Was he the fish, and not her?

"What about her?" he asked and opened his case to get his compass.

"You know that she went to Copenhagen—?"

He drew his circle. His hand didn't shake.

"She's home again now. . . ."

He picked the thin ruler out. There was something about the hypotenuse. He was thinking about the hypotenuse now.

"Those two ladies of hers looked after the shop," she said. "Want some coffee?"

"Please." He held out his cup. Usually he poured the coffee. He got up to help, but she motioned for him to sit down. "How did they manage with the 'homemade' candies?" he asked.

"Oh, you know perfectly well that most of her 'homemade' stuff comes from a factory," she said. "It's a swindle. Even that's a swindle."

He was using the ruler now. He carefully made a thin line, his tongue in his cheek. He knew that she was looking at him.

"What else is a swindle?" he asked.

"She went there with the French lawyer."

Now the hypotenuse. The radius. Diameter, circumference. . . . "She went—when did she go?"

"But I told you dear—it was just after that aviator was here. Then she and M. Maillard went to Copenhagen—together."

Ruler. Compass. A circle is a round ring. No, it's a line that meets itself. And a line is the extension of a point. And a point is nothing.

"And so?" he said.

"You probably don't understand. You're a—you're young. It's painful."

"Mother." He looked up from his geometry. "What's painful?"

"You don't understand this. I mean, we'll invite her here like before, and talk like before. But—well, don't you see? It's rather painful."

"Then you didn't have to tell me," he said, "then I wouldn't have known."

He was looking down at his geometry problem again. Not all the time, though. He knew that instinctively. He mustn't seem *too* uninterested.

"I never met your brother, the one she married," he said, getting up, "but don't you think you're making too much of this, Mother?"

He'd won now. He must be bleeding somewhere inside. He could feel a warm fluid making its way through his tissue. In a little while perhaps something or other would come out of him. But he had won now. It was the easiest thing in the world to stifle a volcano.

He put his hand on her arm, forced her back into her chair, and held out the sugar bowl. He went over to the fireplace and took the Egyptian cigarettes off the mantelpiece. He'd won now. She thought *she* was the patient. He lit her a cigarette. He went to the window and said: "Look at it snow. You can't even see Oscarshall." He came right back, so that he wouldn't overdo it. He lit the lamp to work on his geometry problem, to be sure he'd see the line that met itself.

"Copenhagen—" he said and looked up, as though distracted by thoughts: "Then they've walked on Hyskenstræde. . . ."

"Why do you say that?"

"Don't you remember Hyskenstræde? Don't you remember Overgaden on the water? Or Violstræde—you bought the Baudelaire—?"

Yes, he'd won now. He had been on the verge of overdoing it. Now he had her back in his childhood again.

"If I only understood you!" she exclaimed and sipped her coffee.

A net again. A net to get caught in. "Sorry," he said, "it was this geometry. . . ."

"This Miriam—?" she said. "They say she spends a lot of time with her violin teacher. . . ."

The hypotenuse. Radius. Circle. His hand reached for the compass, but it missed. She said: "And Erna's mother called. They're having a party, yes, the grown-ups—she asked if maybe you. . . ."

The net. It was everywhere. A circle—people made circles with compasses. But inside the chilly circle there were a thousand little meshes. People thought it was empty, a mathematical possibility. But there were meshes in it, everywhere. So no doubt she thought that she had filled his little circle with a net now, that she *had* him.

"If only I understood why you're telling me all this," he said.

She said: "I don't understand you!"

As if it was his fault. As if it was his fault that she was trying to rummage around and pry into all of his tiny world, and that she could never stop trying to smoke him out, to catch him in some trap or other, and then he'd sit there—as the others did—each in his own private little trap that it was impossible to get out of, that was how people sat, each in a little trap, waving feebly and assuring each other that they were doing exactly what they wanted to.

"You mean to say that everything's a swindle?"

"Are you crazy?" she said quickly. "On the contrary, I mean that people have to see things as they are . . . tell me, are you really so busy with your mathematics?"

He stood up. He could really tell her everything "as it was." He could let his world collapse, the one he'd built up so carefully all that long autumn, a whole world of dissimulation. He could get her to see a few things as they really were and leave her sitting there with her hands empty and her mouth hanging open. It was within his power to make her an old woman with just a few sentences.

He said: "I think my math is quite essential. I'd better take it up to my room for a while."

But as he was walking up the carpeted stairs, he knew that any step could give him away. Not too quickly. She was listening, without realizing it, to hear when he reached the top, to hear his door being shut. It was as if she were there, even in his room; there was someone watching. They wanted to catch him, something in him wanted it perhaps. He was being watched by the *thing* inside him that was responsible for seeing that everything went properly and was false. He sat down at his desk, dead tired, but he kept himself under control the whole time, while he let his thoughts come one by one. Kristine . . . a few days after, maybe only one, and maybe she'd planned it that very day. . . . Miriam—he could take it all if it just came in small doses. A fiddler. A grown-up. . . . Erna, they were bound and determined to link them together, to tie his childhood to something they thought was coming and didn't know already *existed*. They wished him well; they wanted to catch him. That's what it meant to wish a person well: to try to catch him, until they had him floundering in a net and could say: See how well off you are; you're in a net now, just like us. . . .

He went to the medicine cabinet in the bathroom and took two of his mother's sleeping pills; it was the first time he'd done that, and after the first, false excitement, tiredness came like a shadow over all his thoughts. He didn't have time to undress properly. He awoke a moment later and looked at the clock. Ten hours had passed.

He emptied his piggy bank and went to school, but after his first classes he made himself sick and got permission to go home. He went to the West Railway Station and had to wait an hour for a train. There weren't any boats to Hurumland in the winter. The tiles on the waiting room floor were brown with slush, and so was the corridor on the train. At the tiny railway station in the country, the snow lay high around the flagpole, but the road inland had been plowed that morning. He had ridden there on a bicycle once, one summer evening when he'd missed the boat. It wasn't the same road now. You couldn't believe that it went out to Skovly.

Roads to farms and little places away from the coast branched off every once in a while. His own road got narrower and narrower, until at the end it was just a faint path of human tracks in the snow. It had begun to snow again, and for long stretches the path was covered over. When he got to the lane where people turned off to the right to the summer villas, there certainly wasn't any track at all. In winter, the country belonged to the people who lived there year round.

He didn't even notice where the summer path turned off. He realized a little later that it must have been by the gnarled, old pine tree. He hadn't really recognized it with its topping of snow. But it was too late to turn off now. And that wasn't actually where he was going either. It was just that he had thought of Skovly first to get his bearings, and maybe to see how the house looked in winter; he had never been there then—he scarcely thought of it being there in wintertime too. It was snowing harder now, but he knew that he was going toward the isthmus between the houses and the peninsula. He had realized the whole time where he was going: to Mrs. Frisaksen's place, to see how she was. He would walk in and say: Here I am. He would paint the cottage for her; he would fish for her, besides, he had some money, and not just a little bit either. He could go and break into Skovly, there were plenty of cans and things there, so they could live all right. She would certainly be glad he'd come; she wasn't one to surround herself with surprise.

It didn't matter to him if what he'd heard about Miriam was true; it was enough that he'd been told. It didn't matter if Kristine had planned her little escapade the day she'd initiated him. Why should he grudge her an adventure? It was all the same to him that they couldn't stop trying to squeeze him and his little world into a trap—where he would be at home and behave according to the rules of the game that they had made, because they were trapped. They were like that; *it* was like that. If he built all the walls in the world around himself, they would continue to bombard them with their tiny, little artillery and try to force their way into his world and make it the same as theirs, sheltered by all the meshes they had spun around themselves.

He would knock at Mrs. Frisaksen's door. It was really true that she wasn't old, even though they called her "Madame." He had seen her little boat at sunset, a saucer floating in gold. He had seen her red cottage that was really gray, and he knew how it looked inside; he had seen the picture of Birger. His father had walked through that low doorway; he must have bent down quite a ways into his stiff collar. But maybe he wasn't wearing a collar then; perhaps he had put all of his dignity aside?

When he reached the isthmus, the snow was blowing straight at him. He had been on the leeward side of the rocks until then, now he got the full force of the weather. The snow was so deep that he had to lift each foot up a long ways vertically before he could put it down in front of him. That made his steps ridiculously small; he scarcely made any progress at all.

He stopped to catch his breath. It must have been the sleeping pills he'd taken the night before, they made him shortwinded; and they also made him lightheaded, now that the exertion had really started his blood circulating. Even his thoughts couldn't break out of the circle where they had been since the previous evening. The point had become a circle around him; he was walking along the edge of the circle, deliberately heading toward something or other. He didn't find a path over the isthmus, but he had no hesitation about his direction. Soon he could make out the low buildings at the gardener's place in the middle of the level area. There wasn't any smoke coming from the chimney or any tracks leading to the door. The dog wasn't barking. Maybe this kind of gardener went into hibernation during the winter? Maybe they all got into the big bed and spent the winter in a dark clump, hibernating. Perhaps they were a kind of flower that blossomed in early summer and closed up in the autumn along with the other flowers and just stood there under the snow, gently breathing, without any idea of whether it was day or night above the snow.

But to be on the safe side, he made a wide detour around the buildings. Gratitude might give people like that long feelers. They could open their eyes and invite him in for coffee. He wrinkled his nose and noticed that his whole face was covered with a layer of wet snow; he was all covered with it; he only barely stood out from his surroundings. If he stopped, he'd become a part of them.

He didn't stop. He walked on. He wasn't off by too many meters. Shortly afterwards, the cottage appeared just to the left of him. There was no path cleared to its door either. The snow had drifted against it, so that it was half buried. There was plenty for a boy to do there, if he wanted to lend a hand.

He knocked. He knocked again. Then he pounded on the door. He kicked the snow aside, brushed it away from the step itself with his hands, then he tried the handle cautiously. The door wasn't locked. He knocked again and listened. Then he pushed the door open wide and walked in. It was empty. The fishing net was hanging neatly on a forked branch that had been wedged in a crack in the wall. The brass rod on the stove wasn't quite as bright as the last time he'd been there. The door to the tiny bedroom was ajar. He opened it a little more and saw Mrs. Frisaksen. She was lying on the bed with a gray wool blanket over her. He recognized her more by her hand, hanging over the edge of the bed, than by her face sticking out from under the blanket. She must have been dead a long time.

He walked backwards out into the kitchen and closed the door after him. When he turned towards the outer door, he saw the picture of Birger on the street in Oporto. Maybe he did look a little like his father; there was something about the forehead.

It was snowing harder now and he couldn't see the gardener's house. But he went in the direction where it had to be and came right to it. He was filled with astonishment and fury at these people. How could they sit there all by themselves and let their neighbor die just a hundred meters away? Without noticing that there was no smoke coming from the chimney, without asking. . . .

But when he was standing in front of the house with its low mounds (those were the greenhouses covered with snow), he realized that no one lived there in the winter. The gardener was a caretaker at a hospital somewhere inland, Tom went to school there. He had forgotten that until just then. He never thought about the country except as a memory or an anticipation of summer.

He didn't give fear a chance to overpower him. He would make it to Skovly and ring up someone from there, the sheriff. He walked on past the gardener's house and headed for the narrowest part of the isthmus. Once he got there, all he had to do was follow the line of the rocks and the houses would appear, one to each little valley.

He had walked to the gardener's fairly quickly. The snow on that side of the marsh wasn't so deep. On the far side, however, he sank in so deep that he couldn't make any headway. He circled back to find his own tracks, but the circle wasn't so wide that it could bring him back to Mrs. Frisaksen's cottage. Just a little short cut, so that he wouldn't have to see the cottage right now.

But he couldn't find his tracks; they must have been blown over. The snow wasn't as thick now, but it was blowing a bit harder. It had gotten colder and his cheeks were burning, but he could tell from his hands and feet that it had grown colder. Patches of clammy mist were coming in off the sea. As long as he kept on with the wind coming from his left, he would come to the isthmus and then all he had to do was follow the line of the rocks.

The sleeping pills' ill effects came again in little waves of drowsiness. It was like a poison being pumped through his body by all the exercise. He went slower for a while to calm down, but then he scarcely made any progress; so he tried running for short distances, but the snow was too deep and he only stumbled. The best thing was to keep an even pace, as if there were no snow. After all, he knew every inch of this ground in the summer.

Yes, he'd wanted to see Mrs. Frisaksen. It was a vague desire that had come over him the evening before, when the meshes were tightening around him. One thing had come right after another—all of his mother's efforts, one hard on the heels of the other, and it wouldn't have taken much for him to give himself away. Instead he'd made a quick decision. He had known there must be a way out somewhere, if only for a short time, time for reflection, maybe until he'd gotten himself onto a ship. During those light-filled evenings the boys on the waterfront whispered stories about people like him who had done that. They also must have been caught in a kind of net. They must have done some crazy things that would be discovered in time; they were the kind that were suspected.

He wasn't the kind that was suspected. Others might suffer because of his whims; it was all the same to him. But he lived in a world where there wasn't any peace, everything wanted to trap him. He had musician's hands—they were held up to the light. And when he had gained some peace for his world with falseness, *they* would arrange things so that that also became a crime; it was a crime to be well-behaved and clever and considerate; it was the greatest crime of all. He tortured himself systematically with all the duties he performed; it made them unhappy trying to find cracks in his mask.

He had only wanted to see Mrs. Frisaksen. He had longed for her, for that face that was old and young, depending on how he looked at it, for Birger's mother. He loved her, in a certain way. She had rowed past him when he was naked on the promontory. She hadn't been surprised. She had been stern, maybe even unpleasant. But that was the way she was. Then he had opened the door into the little bedroom. He had never seen a dead person before. But she must have been dead a long time.

The isthmus wasn't where he'd thought it was. There was open water with a wafer-thin film of ice that ate up the snow with its wetness. He couldn't get over that either. So he walked along the water to one side, but there it opened out toward the damp mist that was coming off the sea. The isthmus must be on the other side.

He walked along the water to the other side. He was going to find the cave under the rocks. He could rest there and maybe wring his socks out. If the gardener's family had been at home, he would have asked them for a cup of coffee; they certainly would have given it to him—and perhaps some bread as well; no one lived there in the winter. He had to find that cave and maybe wring out his socks there.

The cave wasn't there. There was no way across to the other side either. It was as though his whole summerland didn't exist on that side; it was like something that he had dreamed. All of Skovly. There weren't any rocks to follow, just the same flat land with deep snow and water to one side, with a chilling wind blowing in off the sea all the time.

He must have gone in exactly the wrong direction. He tried to turn the landscape around and see it that way, but it didn't work. But he had to act like it had. The way to do it was to stop and think; he had read that in his pocket guide for boys: you mustn't lose your head. He had brought a boy back to life once by not losing his head, by thinking hard. But then he'd had other people watching him. There had been people around him.

There was no one around him now. He called out quite softly into the falling snow, but he didn't stop to hear if there was an answer. He couldn't remember the outline of this peninsula; it stuck out into the sea on three sides, with one long arm along a shallow bay. That was where Mrs. Frisaksen's boat was when she wasn't at the whiting grounds. But the rocks lay in from there, on the other side of the isthmus that formed the boundary of his summerland and theirs.

He didn't find the rocks. He walked toward where he thought they must be, but he didn't find them. It began to snow a little harder again. He couldn't feel his feet, even though he tried hard to go forward. He chose another direction and was sure he would come to a sheer wall of rock, where the cave must be. But it wasn't there. It was snowing so hard that maybe he couldn't see it. He quickened his pace, dragging his feet heavily out of his wet tracks, but the cave wasn't there.

It was a good thing he'd been training at the gym. He was very tired now, but he thought it was a good thing he was in shape. He went a short distance in every direction, but he didn't come close to the rocks or the sea. He began to feel like he was enclosed in something, and all at once he realized what it was: the glass egg! He was in the glass egg and that was why he was drowsy the whole time: he wasn't getting any air. Now that he knew he was in the glass egg, everything else was explained too: you couldn't get out of something like that. The more he moved, the more it snowed. It snowed and snowed inside the egg. The only difference was that there wasn't a little house inside this egg, the house that the snow was always covering up.

But there *was* a house! So it all fit. He saw it straight ahead of him in a clearing. Then it vanished again in the swirling snow, but it reappeared. That was the house all right, and inside the egg the snow was falling and falling.

It was Mrs. Frisaksen's cottage. He realized that. In any case, he realized it right after he had gotten his bearings in the egg. It was darker now, so he had probably been walking a long time. The train had left at half past one. He turned up his sleeve and looked at the Swiss wristwatch Uncle Martin had brought back with him from Berlin. He had to wipe the snow off its thick leather case. It was six o'clock. He'd been walking quite a long time. It wasn't so strange that it was getting dark.

Suppose he knocked again? The door was shut. It wasn't certain that what he remembered was really true. Those sleeping pills had made him feel funny; he had only dreamed it. Step by step, he trudged towards the gray door. It was almost free of clinging snow now. He was the one who had brushed it away. Suddenly he felt so sick that he had to kneel down in front of the step and let something come up. After that he felt heavy and exhausted. He wanted to crawl away, just a little ways—so he wouldn't have to see the cottage. But then it got darker around him. Instead, he crawled back on all fours. He was so tired. He had to get into the cottage, whether he had dreamed it or not.

It wasn't easy to reach the latch. Suddenly it was so high. He supported one arm with the other so he could hold onto the latch when he reached it. Then he got the door open and crawled inside, onto the floor of Mrs. Frisaksen's cottage. It occurred to him that he should have walked in cheerfully and offered to paint the house for her, or fish for her. He had come crawling over the threshold. Snow was blowing in through the doorway behind him. He turned on all fours and brushed with his hands to get the snow away so he could shut the door, but more snow came in. He lay on his back on the floor and looked up at the roof.

It was dark when he woke. He was shaking so much that he couldn't get his hands together to close the door. Then he remembered the snow that had blown in, and he was able to do it then. There wasn't much more snow. It must have stopped snowing. A little later the door was shut. He was on his feet now, but his clothes were sticking to his body. He let his teeth chatter, almost on purpose, to keep himself warm. Then he felt around the tiny room, inch by inch in the dark, until he found the matches on the shelf above the stove. Then he got down on his knees again and crawled around, feeling for firewood. He found some kindling almost at once, in a box at the side of the stove. He didn't dare use the matches to see by. He could feel that there was only one or two in the box. He had never lit a stove before.

He had never lit a stove. But he had made a bonfire. As he laid down the thinnest sticks across each other in the stove, it occurred to him that he was good at making fires. He built his fire carefully before he lit it. The first match started the fire. It began to crackle and roar. Mrs. Frisaksen had dry firewood inside; she was an orderly person. She had to be, of course.

As the stove began to spread warmth, he realized that he was never going to get the chill out of his wet clothes. He undressed, garment by garment, and hung them up on the string over the stove that he'd discovered in the dark. Mrs. Frisaksen was an orderly person. She lived alone in a place all by herself and had to be able to deal with unforeseen circumstances. He groped around and found everything. He whimpered slightly when he searched, and the little sound kept him from thinking. His teeth were chattering the whole time; he got it to be fairly regular; it made a tune: ta-ta-ta-*tum,* ta-ta-ta-*tum*—the Fifth Symphony. . . . He saved the last match. He took a stick out of the stove and used it as a light to see if there was a candle anywhere. But his hand was shaking too much, and he didn't see a candle. When the fire on his stick flared up, he noticed the gray net on the wall. Then he put the stick back in the stove.

There was more warmth in his body now that he was naked. His wet clothes were dripping onto the stove. The hissing sound gave him a cozy feeling. In Paris they had roasted food on a spit. It had hissed in the fire. It was one of the nicest things he remembered. . . .

But the warmth wouldn't stay in him in the darkness. Now that he was dry, he could feel long, cold chills coming from the walls, along with an uncontrollable drowsiness that paralyzed his thoughts. He strained his eyes to see if he could discover anything to wrap himself in. He sharpened all his senses to stay attentive during those moments, which he knew were critically important. The glow of the fire lit up the net on the wall. It seemed thick and compact hanging there on the wall, almost warm. And there was nothing else, not the smallest little cloth, except the one he knew that was stuffed into the broken window in the little bedroom. But his mind avoided it; he had to stick to what was close by.

He got hold of the net, pulled the branch it was hanging on out of the wall, tried to spread it out and make it something he could wrap himself in. But it just got tangled in his hands. They were trembling again now, so much that he couldn't do anything. He pulled and tugged at the tight net to turn it into something useful. He found an opening and got into the net's meshes. There really was a kind of warmth in it, at any rate it was something to have next to his skin.

Then the drowsiness came over him again so violently that he had to use all his powers of concentration to remember the fire. He got on his knees and fumbled for wood. The net hindered him; he couldn't get his hands out; he had to pick up the sticks one by one, with his hands still in the net, and make them travel the long way between the wood pile and the door of the stove.

He woke up once more, the light outside was gray. He was lying on the floor in front of the stove. It was bitterly cold, but the embers were still glowing. When he rolled over—in the net—toward the wood pile, he saw that he had been lying in his own filth. But he couldn't do anything about it. He built up the fire again, stick by stick. The warmth spread and he slipped back into a pleasant weakness. Another time when he woke up it was dark again. The fire in the stove had gone out. He was shaking so much because of the cold that just the idea of building another fire made him feel powerless. He crept around in his tight net, searching for something to wrap himself in. He held his hands together in front of him. They were stiff; they wouldn't grip things by themselves. Then he remembered the little bedroom, it was deep in his memory. He crawled in there and tugged at the corner of the blanket hanging there. But it wouldn't come off. He tugged again and felt a great weight, as if there were someone holding on to the other end. But he couldn't see who it was—someone who was lying there, in the way.

He crawled around to the short end of the bunk and heaved himself up into it with all the strength he had left in him. It was dark in there. His hands were tied up, but he could feel the hard blanket that refused to budge. But on that side there was a larger corner of the blanket free. He tugged at it and got a few inches; he tugged a little more. Soon he had conquered a whole flap from the person holding on to it. He groaned with the effort while he struggled. During fits of shivering, he could feel his forehead, wet with perspiration, and the whole time the motif from Beethoven's symphony throbbed in him, and it found a sort of outlet in his breathing: ta-ta-ta-*tum,* ta-ta-ta-*tum*. . . .

Once he heard some intense chattering—sparrows or some other birds. It was lighter then and he wasn't quite so cold. Another time, a mouse squeaked nearby; it was dark then. He had lucid intervals while he slept, and in between he was awake but delirious. He knew a little about a lot of things, and he knew more every time he slept, weighed down by the scurrying pictures that rushed through his mind in hot spells. But he never knew everything at the same time. It was like the pieces of a puzzle—when you got some into place, the others were pushed out of alignment, so that they wouldn't fit. Sometimes he felt his legs clinging to something stiff, like sticks, and it seemed to him that he'd put his feet into the stove and that the fire was out and the sticks were cold.

Once he also heard a dog barking. It barked and barked. It occurred to him that it must be Cora, who had barked like that when he was a child and had come and put its wet nose next to his. But it wasn't supposed to do that. He mustn't kiss Cora. Cora was dead—that was long ago. That was what he was meeting now, and no one could forbid him kissing Cora's cold nose.

He heard the dog barking, in the distance and then nearer—far away and then much closer. Very close. It was like that in the egg he was in—in a snowstorm that came from all directions the whole time, and in a house, a tiny, little cottage in the snow, with an old woman inside, so cozy and nice.

THREE

WILFRED

18

It wasn't true that he was crazy.

Not that they actually said so, but why did everyone at the hospital wear noiseless shoes?

They asked about too many things too, things that he knew must have been explained by the grown-ups already, by his mother and Uncle Martin. They just wanted to hear his version.

But they didn't get to hear it because he didn't answer them. Not them. Not anyone. He was mute.

The day his mother had come to visit—he'd had an attack then, wasn't it genuine enough? It was in the afternoon, on Christmas Eve; he knew that very well. It should have been even more touching that way. He had shaken his head. Then, and afterwards. It was real enough.

Real? What had been real about this hospital? And then—he hadn't answered anything. He was mute. Result of an accident.

They thought he was pretending, especially Dr. Danielsen; he had an unpleasant expression and thick, convex glasses that made his eyes seem to grow preposterously. He actually *tempted* him to talk; he set traps for him. He had to smile at it now. This fellow obviously didn't know with whom he was dealing.

Besides, he was mute. He was enclosed inside a glass egg. People couldn't talk there.

Andreas—here was an unexpected fellow. He came to visit him at the hospital. Wilfred didn't shake his head then; now he wanted to know things. Andreas had talked and he had written questions and answers on pieces of paper. Andreas was taking business courses in the evenings. He was going to be someone. He had new glasses and didn't look so stupid in them. He had been to a surgeon for his warts and had clean bandages on his hands. They were better than the warts.

Andreas had also come to see him at home later. He told him

things. He was better at saying things in a connected way now. He was the one who did the talking now. Wilfred was mute. Andreas grew in stature because of that. In fact, he had grown in every respect that winter. It was because of Andreas that they'd found him.

It turned out that Andreas knew little Tom, the gardener's son. He was taking courses, too. He was learning bookkeeping and was also going to be someone. He had been at Andreas' place on Frognerveien when Mrs. Sagen rang up. The last resort. . . . And Tom had used his grateful brain, his faithful brain that never stopped being grateful for something or other. It must have happened long ago. Sometime in the summer. Tom noticed a little bit of everything that summer. He had noticed Wilfred's solitary excursions to the "wrong" side of the summerland. He had seen Wilfred through the window, making long swings around the gardener's place.

The two boys had talked a lot about Wilfred.

And when they heard that the family had tried everything except the police (Police! The police . . .), it had struck him that maybe out there—there was something out there. . . .

They had gotten together with Tom's father. They had taken Fatt with them, their hunting dog that always barked when anyone came near the house on the marsh. Tom's father had wanted to see about their house, but the dog had gotten restless. And it looked so strange and shut-in at Mrs. Frisaksen's.

When Andreas spoke her name, Wilfred's mouth quivered. A word wanted to come out. He opened his mouth to say it. He could have, but he wouldn't do it. For a moment he had wanted to, but then he was inside that glass egg. He couldn't.

Outside it was frosty and there was bright sunshine now. It wasn't snowing.—*That hospital?*

That hospital had been real enough. A good hospital. Andreas could swear to that. A bit small—someplace in Asker. Perhaps because it had been close by—not far at all. A perfectly good hospital. But not as big as the one his mother had been in.

Andreas talked. They were sitting in Wilfred's room. Wilfred wrote notes, asking his questions.

Your mother? Wilfred wrote on a piece of paper.

Thanks. His mother was home now, not all right—but he mustn't say that to—oh, no, that's right. . . .

An embarrassed smile flitted over Andreas' open face. He didn't look so stupid now. Wilfred didn't want to torment him so much anymore.

And your father?

Andreas' face twitched. Why was Wilfred so preoccupied with his father? His father wasn't any worse than most fathers. He'd been a little unlucky. Even very unlucky a couple of times.

What was it like having him there every day?

Phew! What a strange notion. People had their fathers there every day. It was like that with fathers. That was what fathers did. They were there. Worked most of the time. But then they were there, every day.

Wilfred thought about this. He hadn't seen it that simply. He was sitting in the big chair in his room on Drammensveien with Andreas, who had come to see him. He had wondered what it must be like having a father around every day.

They sat and talked. Outside there was sunshine and hard frost. A new year.

Andreas chatted and Wilfred wrote. Andreas thought his friend had never said so much as now, when he was mute. Not that he seemed to be opening up to him either, but it seemed that he liked him to come. He came once a week.

To say nothing of Mrs. Sagen. Wilfred's mother wasn't frightening anymore; he didn't have to swallow twice before he dared to speak to her. Not that she hadn't always been kind or anything with him, but so different.

She was different now too, but in a different way. Andreas struggled to find words, both for himself and for Wilfred. It was good not to have Wilfred finding all his words for him.

Did Wilfred want to hear more about his mother?

Wilfred shook his head. But Andreas had a little will of his own now. He was taking courses; he was going to be someone.

Wilfred was being too hard, refusing to let his mother come up to his room. It wasn't good that he refused to go downstairs.

He couldn't just sit there shaking his head when his mother was mentioned. At home, it was his mother who shook her head. She didn't mean anything by it. It was part of the disease.

Would Wilfred like him to ask her to come up?

Wilfred shook his head violently.

Andreas bought cigarettes for Wilfred. He took the money and bought Sossidi, which cost two øre apiece. The boys smoked boldly while they sat together; otherwise Andreas never smoked.

But he grew during those visits. He was trusted now. Would Wilfred like Tom to come? Wilfred shook his head violently. Anyone else? Anyone from his class? Wilfred shook his head.

Andreas was the only one. He was curious too. They sat for long periods without talking, just exhaling thick clouds of smoke.

Was it really true that Wilfred *couldn't* speak?

Wilfred was on his guard at once. So he'd let the fellow go too far, like that time when he'd asked about the bicycle: whether Wilfred hadn't *dared* to get it. Wilfred shrugged his shoulders and smiled contemptuously. Then he walked over to the dummy keyboard and played Bach with his fast fingers.

Andreas watched him striking silent keys. He was gripped by an eerie feeling.

Andreas was the one who had come with the news about the foreign doctor. He overheard it one day as he came through the hall. Uncle Martin had been there, and Dr. Monsen, the family doctor—he was just about to go. Dr. Monsen apparently didn't have much faith in this miracle doctor Uncle Martin had been talking about. He just called it foolishness and bluffing. He said something about a good thrashing.

Wilfred smiled with appreciation.

But Wilfred's uncle had kept on about this doctor; he was clear down in Vienna, Austria; Andreas didn't exactly remember what his name was, but it was something strange. It wasn't so good for him to know either; they said so many strange things in this house that he didn't understand.

Wilfred nodded absentmindedly. It was all the same to him

what the doctor's name was. Dr. Monsen had been pretty offensive several times. He had spoken to him like a naughty child, so this business about a thrashing sounded probable. He'd said once: "You can't do this to your mother. Have you *seen* her?"

He had seen her. It was the hardest thing he'd been exposed to when the Housecat (that was what they used to call Dr. Monsen) had said that. Dr. Monsen had a little gray beard and looked British. He had large pores around his nostrils, and when he'd said that about Wilfred's mother, the pores seemed to open up. Have you seen her? he'd asked.

He had seen her; his mother was beginning to look like an old woman. She had a wool shawl on and looked like she was cold. Her rounded cheeks were straight and taut now; this woman with curves who had been his mother was gaunt and angular. She wasn't the same person who had drunk champagne at Etterstad, or the same person with whom he used to play let's pretend from morning till evening. He wasn't her little knight. He wasn't anyone's little knight. He was mute.

Erna had been there. That had been on his birthday. He had shaken his head violently. Miriam had come once and he had shaken his head. There had been a period when he started shaking his head in the morning, and it went on all day, even when there was no one in the room to see. He thought: I can stop shaking my head all right. But he couldn't.

He wrote to Andreas on a piece of paper: *Do you think I can speak?*

Andreas raised his hands as though to defend himself. Then he shook his head too. Maybe everybody did it, maybe it was a new age.

Andreas had never meant that at all. He had just asked. He'd thought it was so sad.

Wilfred appeared satisfied with that, but Andreas' eyes were questioning him—he wanted to hear more. . . .

It was just that it was all so remarkable. Wilfred of all boys. He had spoken so easily; he'd known all the words other people had to search for. It was so remarkable to think, to know that he sat there and was unable to form the words that used to come so easily. He wanted to do something to help him.

Did he? Wilfred wrote and asked if Andreas didn't really enjoy being able to speak up whenever he wanted?

Andreas shrank in his chair. This was the old Wilfred again; he had to be on his guard against him. He had felt so important a little while before, like a person who spied for his friend, who brought him secret information. But the mute ruler could put him in his place again with a tiny change in his expression.

Father also thought there would be a war soon, he said.

So he was trying to assert himself! He and that father of his! He went to evening classes and learned business correspondence and foreign words, he could say c.i.f. and f.o.b. and invoice; he'd actually tried out some of these simple terms, which he thought were a secret language only for the initiated.

Wilfred laughed silently. But he didn't want to mock the boy now; he was too easy game. But he couldn't use him for much more. He had gotten him a good supply of cigarettes. Andreas was getting along well. He went to evening classes and was working his way up. Andreas was the future!

The next time he called, he'd shake his head.

When Andreas was gone, he sat for a long time, smiling his wicked smile. It did him good to smile like that. He went over to the mirror and looked at himself smiling. Then he moved his lips slightly, forming words with them. If he forced air through his larynx at the same time, it would make sounds, words. Then he would just have to open the door, stand by the banister, and call down, and a whole world would be changed.

But no breath would come up through his larynx. Not so he could make sounds. It was no longer snowing inside the egg where he was, but he was there. It had come as soon as he saw them around him; it must have been at the hospital—if it had been a hospital. It occurred to him that in a way he could just not answer. Then he had liked the idea better every time. If they had been firmer with him then, maybe—he didn't know.

But some days had passed, some weeks perhaps, and he had noticed the mute question in their looks every time his mother or one of the doctors sat down beside the bed to try and get something—then it had been more and more as if he absolutely couldn't answer them, couldn't make a sound.

Because as long as he didn't answer, it kept the world out. What wasn't said wasn't real. It didn't exist.

It also kept the pictures from coming. There was the stove. The net. It had surrounded him, as it still did in all the linked dreams that made up his sleep. . . .

Dr. Danielsen had asked him if he knew that Mrs. Frisaksen was dead. He knew that. He nodded. Had the doctor expected tears? He would have liked to cry, but not while the doctor was here.

Had he been fond of Mrs. Frisaksen?

He grimaced. These people asked questions from their world and expected answers from his. Could a person answer that, for example? Or why he had gone there that day? He could have answered in Arabic—perhaps. He could have done what boys did when they were small and wanted to be free of the grown-ups: they invented a language with a mass of consonants, and gradually, as they babbled in this language to each other, it took on a significance greater than that of the words into which they could translate it. It became a language for outsiders, a secret language without a real meaning for the words; though taken together they gave the impression that those who spoke it stood together in everything and against—yes, against anything at all. . . .

He could have answered in that kind of language. In its simplest form the name Danielsen would have become Dodanonieloso-senon then. Thieves' cant, they'd called it; it was for the littlest ones. But bigger boys invented greater languages that were so difficult that they didn't understand each other. And the best of all was the language you made up yourself that even you couldn't understand. That was a perfect expression of immurement, a withdrawal from the outer world that was manifested in everything, but which could become real over long periods. He had amused himself once by speaking one of these languages in the yard at the Misses Wollkwarts. He'd made all the boys desperate; their little faces got skinny trying to guess what he meant.

He hadn't meant anything. And yet the language itself had been full of resistance.

He could have answered this Danielsen in this language. Besides, the man had a slight cast in his left eye behind his convex lenses. He quite simply squinted. God only knew when he was looking at someone. He was a traitor.

They were all traitors. His mother paid them. Maybe they didn't know it, but she'd known how to catch them in her net—them too. The idea was that everyone should flounder in that net. Not because she wanted to rule over everyone, but just because people ought to sit in traps. Everybody did. Then you had them in their places.

But when Uncle René came with that new portfolio of colored reproductions made in France by a new process—he'd lost all his desire to resist. He had cried then. And poor Uncle René with his magician's hands, he hadn't known what to do. He'd held out a handkerchief scented with Aunt Charlotte's light *eau de cologne*. He sat there waving the thin handkerchief, hoping that Wilfred would dry his eyes with it. He had swallowed and blown his nose on the edge of the sheet, then he bowed to say "sorry." And they sat all afternoon with the wonderful reproductions.

Uncle René was a good man. As he sat interpreting the mute pictures, he, too, had become mute. He didn't notice it himself. But he had nodded and gesticulated and asked with eloquent mouthing, as deaf-mutes do. He was so full of insight. And when he had to go, he had held up the portfolio with the reproductions, asking in that way if Wilfred wanted to have it.

He had been touched then, so moved that he'd pretended not to understand. He thought the most decent thing to do was to be unable to imagine such a big present. Then Uncle René had asked him with words and so he had formed his mouth into a thank you that was almost spoken. And Uncle René had tears in his eyes, and his transparent fingers played with the air, as if fashioning it into a thousand bright hopes and possibilities—so different from the words of solid comfort brought by everyone else, words halfway between reproach and personal magic: that if they only wished it strongly enough, he would get better. They each had their belief in this. Not Uncle René.

He heard steps in the corridor. It was his mother. He wouldn't shake his head now. He would go downstairs; he'd like to go outside for a little while. Out in the street, he could hear the frozen crunch as people and carriages went past in the cold February air.

She knocked. She stuck her head in, just a little ways, prepared for a refusal. A flood of loathing swept over him. He nodded fiercely.

She'd just been on the point of leaving. Now, instead, she came in a little ways; she opened the door a little farther, surprised.

He nodded and nodded. His throat seemed to be filled with disgust. He smiled and nodded. He was Lucky Lillelord. He signaled for her to come right in; he stood up; he wanted to throw himself around her neck, but the "thieves' cant" held him back.

She shut the door behind her and color came into her cheeks. All at once some of the old Susanna Sagen was there again; her cheeks and body got curves as she stood there. He showed her to his own good chair. He paced nervously between the mirror and the window. The desire to act grew and grew in him, so much so that he interrupted her when she began to speak.

He tore a sheet from a pad and wrote: *I've read about a doctor in Vienna, maybe he can make me better.*

She looked like she would faint. She gasped several times; now she was mute. Then a little, lace-edged handkerchief appeared, Aunt Klara's annual Christmas present. . . .

"But how in the world!" she gasped. "That was what I came to tell you, to ask if you wanted to. Uncle Martin has heard about him; they say he's fabulous—Wilfred, where *did* you learn about him?"

He shrugged. They had said so much to each other without words through the years. Actually, he didn't need to write. Since this had happened, she'd been able to see better just how brilliantly they had gone around each other in that house. . . .

Read it somewhere, he wrote and held the piece of paper out to her.

She read it again. It occurred to her that all things could be arranged in a world where everyone was willing to bear with others and forget.

He was going to suggest that they go downstairs for a while together. He was going to write it. He made a move—that was enough. Couldn't they basically be mute, both of them?

She followed him happily. In the doorway, she said: "Your uncle's downstairs."

He stepped back and made a circular movement with his hands.

"Yes, Martin," she said. "He's the one who found this Austrian doctor for you; he says he's a miracle doctor."

She took him by the arm. He shuddered, but he went with her. Uncle Martin stood up when they entered the living room. That was just it. Nobody could be natural. Uncle Martin got to his feet as seldom as possible. He was polite in his own way, but he didn't usually stand up. He said: "Well, here's our big fellow!" Wilfred grimaced. He did it to warn him. Uncle Martin had mouthed the words at him; did they think he was deaf? He was dumb. But they didn't really believe that. They behaved consistently with something they didn't really accept. Strange.

"Do you know—Wilfred knew about the doctor in Vienna. In fact, *he* was the one who suggested it—!"

She wasn't acting naturally either. Uncle Martin looked hurt. "Okay," he said. "Of course, his name isn't known here at all. But there. . . ." He flung out his arm in one of those gestures that was supposed to be eloquent. Wilfred went close to him and strained his throat. His mother brought some paper. He wrote: *I'm very grateful, Uncle.* Martin looked up, surprised. They smiled at each other. What a lovely smile. Could people smile like that in offices—didn't they spend their time cheating each other, and what was an invoice anyway?

He went to the bookcase to get his Salmonsen and looked up "invoice." Andreas probably hadn't understood it properly. He seldom did. Wilfred wrote on a piece of paper and handed it to his mother: *Do you remember the badger?*

The story was retold. Uncle Martin had heard it. He laughed too much, as if he hadn't heard it. Wilfred laughed with his face. The patient should be all right, in a bright mood. They were easy to gauge; they were a little afraid of him. That wasn't malice. Maybe he was crazy.

Could you go with me, Uncle?

That was exactly what they'd planned. He knew it. Andreas had told him. Now it seemed like spontaneous confidence. Uncle Martin became gentler. He was given his whisky. He and Mother always played a little with the serving of the whisky. Uncle Martin shouted, as at a deaf person: "I have to go there anyway. We'll have a fine time in Vienna, the two of us."

He could always put his hands over his ears. At least Andreas spoke quietly. Uncle René spoke a deaf and dumb language with his mouth. He was always insightful, he understood. Martin shouted.

He didn't put his hands over his ears. He listened gratefully.

When?

Uncle Martin pulled out a small pocket calendar and pointed, as though he was half blind too. His finger pointed to February 17. In three days. Wilfred nodded repeatedly to show that he understood, that the idiot understood. He went on nodding until he was overdoing that too. So he continued to nod. The two grown-ups looked at each other. He nodded for a while and thought: Am I putting this on? He didn't know. But he couldn't stop nodding now.

He made one of his very eloquent movements toward his mother: I think that I'll go upstairs for a bit. . . . A glance at them both, awfully sorry, a little nod of confirmation to Uncle Martin as a sign that the idiot hadn't forgotten Vienna.

All at once he had an indescribable longing for his dummy keyboard upstairs. It had become his compatriot in his secret language. He played the beginning of one of Bach's fugues slowly and with the most careful fingering. But he couldn't get it right. When he made a mistake, his face twisted in a grimace. He couldn't keep his mind off the two sitting down there worrying. Uncle Martin, that rational and profoundly simple man—with the goodness of his heart he no doubt imagined an overstrained brain as a chaos of impulses. For him a nervous mentality was undoubtedly surrounded by mystery and horror. His eternal striped suits helped to keep things in place, and everything was in place for this splendidly stupid man, who knew everything about progress and that the world was facing a change now. He had secretly been busy the last year, reinvesting the family's money. His mother had hinted about this with solemn expressions. The very word "par" made her head swim with incomprehensibility, as if it had been a Chinese character.

Bach died beneath his fingers as he sat at the dummy keyboard, knowing everything about those people. Why did he know it all? They'd never told him anything, really.

Maybe that was why. Maybe you never learned anything about people except by guessing. Maybe it came too easily otherwise—it wasn't credible. But what you guessed, you knew. The mute person held all the possibilities. Nothing was expected of him. He could *see*.

He could see the world that they hid from him with thoughtful kindness. They had always instinctively hid as much of this world as possible. Because there was something that he mustn't find out about. Because of that it had become a habit to let him know the least possible about everything, and so—just because of that—it had been so easy for him to know more about his own people than children did in families where everything was evident and nothing was exciting.

That was how it was. He had always known it, but not for sure. This mute keyboard that was so full of unspoken information sharpened his guessing powers because its song was secret. It spoke the forbidden language, the language that was inaudible to everyone who only heard what was audible. There was an affinity between him and this mute keyboard that made them brothers, joint conspirators in a world that was without expression for the others. Never, never again would he touch an ordinary piano with all its noise that was only suited to destroying the secret sources of music that sprang forth for the initiated. Never again would he let his enclosed world be confused by expressions that spoke to people in general. He realized now that he was starting to reside in a realm populated by beings and things that didn't use violence against the senses.

How the portrait of his father on the wall had changed!

Where was the severity he'd ascribed to it? He had put it there himself—in his naive fear of fathers. So, no doubt it was wrong for a family not to have a father. Some corrective was needed. There ought to be someone you could dislike in a family. A father could serve well for that purpose. Without one, a mother could easily be substituted. He had looked into rooms and seen fathers during his wanderings through the west side of town. It was as if they had judgments hanging over them, a weight that they quietly distributed as guilt to their sons. In return, they were treated with respect—in order to make the burden of guilt easier to bear. Wasn't Andreas' father that kind of man? He went around, stubbornly innocent, demonstrating his misfortune so that everyone could know what he suffered and how much they were to blame. These men chose wives who were ill, or they made them ill with the pressure of their lack of success. Some took to drink in enraptured sorrow, so they could sit and mope in cafés on street corners, where white-coated waiters went around silently pouring oil on the fires of their self-pity.

He had seen them through the curtains of the living rooms; he had peeked into their cafés. They sat there mutely, making a mess of themselves with a devilish glimmer of happiness, so that others could perish slowly beneath the weight of their degradation. He knew them. He knew them. They were the good ones, the ones who never developed, who just suffered.

His father hadn't been one of them. She'd said that they

wouldn't leave him alone. No—and he hadn't been able to leave *them* alone either. He hadn't loved them. But had he? No, he hadn't loved them, but he hadn't despised them either—she was wrong there. She didn't know that. She said herself that she didn't know. He had developed out of sheer defenselessness; he'd been the enchanting one—the one who charmed them. Why? Because there was nothing else to do with them, they were so easy to conquer. And of course he was a polite person. Too polite to assert himself in the long run. And young—he must have kept young the whole time, since he thought he could get out of it by dying with an egg in his hand, a glass egg, where the snowstorm subsided when the hand holding it was still. . . .

Yes, he knew him now. He wondered if they would have told him if he'd just *wished.* He wondered if he hadn't told himself that, as the Housecat had told him, Wilfred, when he fired off a look at him that was supposed to be hypnotic, no doubt, to get him to talk. . . . And no doubt he had answered or told himself: I don't want to want. I don't want to want so much. *You* do it! You do it with all your power! He wondered if he hadn't said something like that.

He wondered if his suitable brother-in-law Martin hadn't irritated him to the breaking point with his efficiency, his all-around admirableness. He wondered if their perfect specialties hadn't gotten on his nerves so much that he'd been forced to glimpse a totality that was fatal to those who saw it. And, afterwards, he'd taken refuge in his egg, with Mrs. Frisaksen, in an uncomplicated love that was more dangerous than his whole cultivated pasture of a marriage with all the faithlessness and brothers-in-law that were attached to it.

He knew him now! A man who had seen the parting of the ways and didn't know what to do because of all the possibilities, a man who had seen no way out, who had closed his eyes, as he had done up in the air with Pégoud, because it makes you dizzy to see more than you're supposed to see at one time: a future for him and his. . . .

Yes, he began to know him, to guess. Once they had lived under the same roof. Then he had been cigar smoke that disappeared in the morning, a pleasant haze that was pleasant because it was the smell of someone who was gone.

What if he'd stayed?

He'd have been a father like all fathers. A man with his eyes shut. A blind man who saw precisely what he was supposed to see and who said the necessary words. A mute man. And a deaf man, who heard and didn't hear what was said and meant to be heard, yet who listened in constant wonder for the sighing of something unspoken beneath the stars. Until the sighing of the unspoken became too heavy to bear and he had closed his ears to it and become a father in shirtsleeves sitting in a living room beneath the picture of a father in a room. Blind. Deaf. Dumb.

Such a father in a family—who had asked him to come and go? Who had allowed an Andreas to take him for granted under his palm tree, a slightly awkward occurrence who felt obliged to have set higher goals for himself once upon a time, without noticing that he had never striven to attain them? Who had given an Andreas permission to let himself be treated to a soda in a park, expecting that the inevitable would pass—dependent as he was on people and things that weighed him down, weighed and weighed according to the law of bearing your own burden right to the threshold, to the grave.

And because he knew him, he went over to the portrait, which was more him than he himself had been, and caressed it slowly, time after time stroking the face's short beard that had been painted in oil by an unknown artist who had scarcely been a master except in one area: he had wrested a look from his oils that must have dwelt somewhere inside the artist, a look that had glistened like—well, a glass egg, where all the crackling flames had fallen silent and calmed down, like snow that *had* fallen.

He realized many things as he stood there beside the portrait. That face had lived in his room and had seen things. It had seen everything that a face can see in a boy's room. It had watched with an enigmatic smile that may have become more and more gentle. Horrified, it had recognized itself and looked anxiously into a future. But also cheerfully. Because there was a secret merriment in that look, which the artist might have put there inadvertently, in a stroke of unconscious genius. There was a certainty about the inevitable in the whole position of the head, halfway between cheerfulness and resignation.

A father like that, a being. What was he in relation to his family? They weren't his. He was theirs. Caught. But then he hadn't let himself be caught, not like the lighthouse keeper, in a net in a green sea in October. On the contrary, he had examined his nets. Without malice. Because it wasn't his intention to catch people. He'd merely watched them get caught. And he smiled, cheerfully and resignedly. That was the kind of man he'd been. And that couldn't continue. No, it couldn't go on like that. Not when the world had become an egg with a snowstorm.

Certainly he knew him. A little better with each depraved excursion to the edge of the permissible. Why had he never confided in him? A portrait on the wall—just a picture. Yes, but more than a person, because that portrait had been made with secret knowledge of hidden things that people put a mask over, a mask that becomes their nature and moves the person farther and farther away from the person it covers. That's why a portrait becomes more truthful if it knows the secret, or suspects it, or gives it away without realizing it. That was why the portrait became more intimate at times than one of a father like the others, with all the words and phrases under a hanging lamp.

But did *he* know *him?* Did he have a father's restless concern about every unsteady step he took in this world, where you had to protect yourself? He didn't know. He could read a lot in a picture, he had learned to do that, but not this. When he was a little boy, he had drawn his father. They had all shouted in astonishment. It was his mother!

Was it? He had quite obviously drawn his father. What about the cigar? Did his mother smoke cigars?

That was what was comical. What would the boy think of next. Uncle Martin had called it "Susanna in Hades." The smoke curled dreadfully around her head.

He stood in front of his father's portrait and moved his mouth as though praying. He had yielded to his mother now, had been friendly, had been gracious and friendly. He grimaced. And his father grimaced back. Not much. Slightly. Like all his mimicry: hints and irony.

He begged her pardon for that. Not for his attitude, for she had determined that. She had confused his world with a consciousness that didn't agree. As in mathematics, when two figures are supposed to be similar and aren't; they just played at being similar. They were wrong. One was wrong in relation to the other. So the other became wrong.

Could two figures like that rub themselves together to become alike? Pretend that they were alike until they did become alike? They couldn't coincide. They had to disagree, and that was much more painful than if they had never been alike. . . .

He begged pardon for that, stood there and begged *his* pardon, he who had left a ship that didn't sink, who had said to a world: go on, float, you can do it; I'm going to sink a little.

So it was good that the snow had stopped falling inside the egg. The shine had gone off it, no matter how much he shook it. There was an "S" scratched on the egg—a coincidence. It had been scratched with a diamond. An "S" that begins and ends the same, a figure to stand on its head. No one saw any difference. The strange thing was that when you played Bach, there was a point at which you couldn't say it would ever stop. You were ruled by the law of infinity, where one section gave birth to the next and only the state of the rhythm could make a section the last—unless you used force.

He must have scratched that "S" there absentmindedly, it was a sign of boredom. Susanna was a name. When he was little and amused himself by spelling it backwards, he'd called his mother Annasus. It had been so sweet. People laugh a long time at only children. But this "S" hadn't stood for Susanna, either forward or backward. It had stood for his mind's inconclusiveness, its fatal boundlessness. He knew him now.

And because he knew him, he had given in to his mother. She had no talent for practical things. But she got what she wanted! And to Uncle Martin, her brother. He had the talent. He didn't know it. They were going to travel together—a little journey disguised as a business trip, because if it wasn't successful. . . . Uncle Martin didn't know this, he did it in good faith. Taking his father's place.

He grimaced. But there was no answer now from the portrait. Once again it was severe with its short beard and stiff collar. So, he didn't like such thoughts.

That Uncle Martin took his place? He didn't give a damn, not a fat damn, as Uncle Martin said. No, but that he, Wilfred, made fun of it.

He wasn't making fun of it. He was fond of them in his own way. They meant well. He would do what they said. He had a world that they couldn't reach. There hadn't been any choice because they forced their way into everything of his from all sides and wanted to share what couldn't be shared. Love of the forbidden—and forbidden people. He wanted to be mute.

19

It was winter in Vienna. When they came out of the hotel on Ringstrasse, there was a thin covering of snow on the streets. Uncle Martin was disappointed and secretly bitter about it. He always over-estimated the earliness of spring's arrival in central Europe. In the sleeper on the way down, he had depicted the conditions with a lack of imagination that became more and more panic-stricken as he realized just how far out of his depth he was getting. His own sons—thank goodness—had never required him to intervene directly in any field, to the unceasing relief of the twins and Aunt Valborg.

The notion of being a guardian had never been so burdensome for him as on that morning when he went out into the city he knew so well with a ward he knew less about than what he might have guessed about the person shining shoes on the corner. At least with the stranger you knew he shined shoes and smoked the ends of small cigars that other people had started.

Out of sheer distraction, he almost took his nephew's hand as they were about to cross the street below the hotel. He stopped himself at the last moment, but he still had the feeling of being some kind of shepherd, and that the sheep might easily slip away among the streetcars with their ringing bells, or tumble into a fire department tank any time.

At the little restaurant in the nook by St. Stephan's Cathedral, where he loved to eat his hearty breakfast, there were music stands on a podium that was squeezed in between the serving counter and a group of plush chairs that had legs turned on lathes and imperial crowns on their backs, each carefully draped with a piece of crochet work with a hole in it, so that the crown and eagle could peek out in amazement at the golden morning.

Wilfred jumped when he noticed the music stands. He involuntarily grabbed for Uncle Martin's sleeve to hold him back, but Uncle Martin, thinking that this was the beginning of an attempt to escape, took a firmer grip on his nephew's hand and led him inside the restaurant mercilessly, where bland men with little moustaches were already entrenched behind enormous newspapers on racks and tiny cups they didn't drink from.

"Uncle—do you think they're going to play?" His lips formed the words.

A smile passed over Uncle Martin's face. "Not before twelve, my boy," he said reassuringly. And he was reassured himself. But he found this sensitivity to music quite unreasonable for someone who had such eminent musical talent. He wasn't particularly musical himself, but in any case he was sufficiently musical not to be embarrassed when music was played. To tell the truth, he didn't always notice it.

For the tenth time, he told Wilfred that there was no need to be nervous about the visit to this doctor they were going to see. He was a famous man in his profession, of course, but Uncle Martin had written to him personally and gotten a very favorable reply. Martin felt like a miracle worker himself, now that he had learned to read things from the boy's lips that were particularly important. He was beginning to think that maybe this particular art wasn't so mysterious, if you just applied yourself. Experience had shown him that this applied to almost all aspects of life. A wide-awake person could learn incredible things. It was just a matter of keeping your eyes open.

The moment they'd set out on this journey, Wilfred had begun to be fond of his uncle. It was agreed that his mother shouldn't come to see them off at the station, so they felt like a unit together, a strange, new feeling for both of them. Uncle Martin had made it his principle to let other people turn his sons into men of the world, the kind their careers would require them to be. Having his young ward in tow, therefore, was like conquering new territory. Besides, his way with languages made it a pleasure for him when he could help others.

Uncle Martin kept looking at the clock. The appointment was for ten o'clock, and the doctor's office was only a quarter of an hour's walk away. It seemed impossible to get the various watches and clocks on the wall appreciably past nine-thirty.

When they were finally walking through the streets on their way there, the snow was already melting and the city was beginning to take on the form he knew from so many previous visits, for business and for pleasure. Uncle Martin had reassured his nephew so incessantly that he'd made himself nervous. As a result, he continued to reassure him until Wilfred had to shut out the words to avoid becoming hysterical. He had no intention of starting to nod or shake his head when he was standing face to face with the miracle worker. He was going to make the most of his opportunities this time, if for no other reason than to give Uncle Martin the triumph of not having made the trip in vain. He had no fears for his personal integrity in such simple company.

The house was an ordinary one from the 1890s, with rather narrow stairs. The staircase was panelled in brown, and there was a yellow stripe that tried to keep up with you as you ascended, but it had to give up for considerable distances, the victim of washing and the teeth of time. Wilfred liked the staircase; it wasn't splendid at all. There was something anonymous about the neighborhood and the house that filled him with confidence from the very first. He had none of the plebian patients' feelings of being the center of other people's interests; but on the other hand he wasn't embarrassed or anxious. He was rather uninterested in the whole proceedings, except for his uncle's sake.

They were shown into a little passage by a friendly lady who didn't make much of their arrival. There was a modest name-plate on the door. Nothing miraculous about that. And the lady wasn't dressed like a nurse, nor did she have the professional, preoccupied look of having to protect her employer against intruders. She read Uncle Martin's card carefully and let it disappear into the pocket of her apron, then she asked the two gentlemen to be seated. There was no picture of Emperor Franz Josef on the wall. It was the first room Wilfred had been in where there wasn't such a portrait hanging there. There were two Frans Hals reproductions to which Wilfred drew his uncle's attention. He nodded energetically, as though to ward off any further outburst that might prove embarrassing. He wiped his forehead with his handkerchief several times in that cold room. As a healthy person, visiting a doctor made him feel uncomfortable and agitated.

Neither of them had noticed the door open until the doctor was standing in the room with them. The first thing Wilfred noticed was that he was very thin. The next was his handshake. It was firm and quick, and made no attempt to convey that confidence-inspiring assurance which he was so accustomed to receiving from doctors: Well now, my young friend, we'll soon get this over and done with, the two of us.

After that they sat in the big office, where there were no shiny instruments either lying out or in glass cabinets to show what the doctor could do if he liked. It was a brown room, also panelled, with dark leather armchairs and two narrow windows with starched curtains that looked like they'd been put up that day. The doctor pulled his chair a little in front of the table, so that he wouldn't be sitting behind fortifications; then he sat and listened calmly to Uncle Martin's stammering account of some of the superficial aspects of the illness. Wilfred sat the whole time looking at the doctor's rounded beard. It was mostly brown, slightly speckled with gray—he must have been in his early fifties . . . and at his hands; he'd thought that a miracle doctor must have transparent, restless hands, something like Uncle René's, hands that could make things vanish or appear in nervous agitation. But this doctor's hands were small and firm and calm, not striking at all. And there was no hypnotic glow in his eyes, which he could have used to control his patients. Wilfred was a little disappointed. His need for the sensational was always lurking nearby. For a moment he felt overcome by the desire to do unheard-of things. He was disappointed by this thin man, who listened so politely to his uncle's rather misleading account.

When Uncle Martin had finished, the doctor stood up and asked him to go. He wasn't discourteous, but a little peremptory. Uncle Martin gasped for air and protested: He had come this long way. . . .

Couldn't Wilfred find his own way back to the hotel? If not, he could send him in a taxi. The doctor was already standing with his hand out. Uncle Martin looked around desperately, but Wilfred nodded; he was silently amused. As he walked out of the room, Uncle Martin sent his nephew a look that revealed little hope of them ever seeing each other again in this life.

Had a smile flitted across the man's face? Perhaps a shadow of a smile, but all the same enough of a smile to say: He meant well, so let us two grown-ups come to an understanding. Wilfred wanted to thank him somehow and struggled with his lips; but the doctor stopped him with a gesture and walked to the window. Then he turned and said:

"Do you sing?"

Wilfred shook his head energetically. He acted like he was playing a piano. The doctor immediately countered with: "I know that. You are also very occupied with paintings. . . ." He reached up quickly to the bookcase, where volumes of all sizes and degrees of wear struggled for a place. He opened the big book that Wilfred guessed right away must have reproductions;

he opened it at random and held it out: "Austria has also had its great painters," he said. The picture showed a woman lying down, surrounded by trees, by a stream—it was from the Romantic school. The doctor drew up his chair alongside Wilfred's and they sat and looked through the picture book together. It was a cross section from all periods: Spanish cave paintings; Egyptian pharaohs, immobile and expressionless; Nordic rock carvings of potbellied reindeer marching in place. The doctor turned the pages randomly. There was no calculated casualness about his movements, no intended reassurance. You could see that the book was much used; notes written in pencil popped up here and there in the text. It seemed to Wilfred that the man was playing at being his uncle.

At that very instant, the doctor got to his feet and shut the book. He put it aside and walked back to the window, where he stood for a moment, looking out.

The soft sound of carriages with rubber wheels just barely reached them from the street. Then the doctor turned, took several steps toward him, and said:

"Sie sprechen ja deutsch?"

"Aber natürlich, Herr Professor!" Wilfred replied instantly.

Did a smile cross the doctor's face? Not this time. Not a smile. Not so much as that. A chill of understanding. Wilfred sat there, twitching his lips. These were the first words he had spoken in three months. He wasn't as surprised as he was embarrassed.

A great indifference had fallen off him, or was beginning to leave him. He began to talk; he wanted to explain to this stranger, this Austrian, that he hadn't been pretending all these months, that in a way he had been able to speak, but when he was supposed to. . . . He mixed everyday expressions with his exquisitely grammatical German, which satisfied even Aunt Klara; he assured him again and again that he had no great objection to cheating and lying about many things, but not this at all—!

Then the doctor did smile—a frank smile, not broad and genial, one that was more in his eyes than around his mouth, and yet not a doctor's omniscient smile that said: Save your breath, young man, we wise people know everything. . . . The smile was friendly rather than encouraging, wise rather than knowing.

Wilfred told him many things, the most surprising things. This man was a stranger. Besides, he had a lot that had been dammed up.

They sat talking together for a long time. Wilfred saw the sun cross the window. The telephone rang twice, and the doctor answered; both times he talked calmly and energetically, his eyes on Wilfred's the whole time. Wilfred thought then that he was like someone he knew—his father perhaps? Something about the eyes. No, he looked like Mrs. Frisaksen . . . someone free of all pretense, an honesty *behind* the disguise, *beneath* it, not put in front as a facade, like a new disguise marked "honest." The two times when the doctor talked on the telephone were almost the greatest moments of the consultation, for then *he* could study *him,* he could let himself be quite free; this man didn't try to tie you down, like Dr. Danielsen at the hospital or Dr. Monsen at home; he set you free; he didn't wear that mask of insistent interest that ultimately seemed to be an obligation, so that he felt obliged too.

"Why did you ask if I sang?" Wilfred said after a pause.

The other gave him a friendly look and shrugged his shoulders. "Why? One has to ask something. Your interest in music. . . ."

"Does it happen that the dumb suddenly sing?"

"It does—have you read Hans Christian Andersen's 'Nightingale'?"

"Nightin . . . ," Wilfred understood almost right away. And he read in the doctor's face the moment when *he* realized that he had understood.

"It's true," he said and looked down. "I have felt like that clockwork nightingale that was wound up." He could feel tears coming now.

"Or like the live one," the doctor said. "The real one that was banished by schemers."

Embarrassed, Wilfred said: "I was mute to my immediate family. I became mute because of them. They made me mute. They acted so badly that I made myself mute!"

He had shouted. He was very intense now; he simply had to defend himself against this man who knew "The Nightingale."

The doctor nodded once. Not one of those overly affirmative movements that says: I understand; I understand perfectly; I understand everything. Just one nod. It was just right.

"And don't you think that this would be rather inconsiderate toward your family to continue this act?" he asked.

He was unexpectedly severe now. Wilfred wanted to protest, but the doctor cut him short: "By acting, I don't mean something false, I'm referring to the dissimulation you've established in self-defense—do you understand that?"

Wilfred nodded; he nodded several times. He sat there and nodded and nodded.

"Well now, that's enough nodding!" the doctor said, smiling. "It's easy to keep doing that sort of thing. People imitate. They take after themselves."

Wilfred had never thought he would have been able to put it so accurately: "Are you a hypnotist?" he asked.

The other smiled. "Don't say anything against hypnosis, young man. It just doesn't belong here. You don't have to be afraid."

"I'm not afraid," Wilfred said firmly. The doctor stood up. He went toward the window again, and once more the room was filled with that calm that was almost physical.

"Do you mean that?" the doctor said, turning from the window.

"What? —Excuse me. . . ."

"That you're not afraid? You said you weren't afraid. . . ."

"I meant of hypnosis. . . ."

"Or shall we say that you meant it in general?"

Wilfred looked down bashfully. "Naturally I'm afraid," he said softly.

"Of course you're afraid. Everybody's afraid." The doctor fell silent for a while, walked over to the table, and sat down. "You're a very mature young man," he said. "You've lived in what people call a sheltered milieu. I'd like to ask you whether you would like to undergo treatment here with me."

Wilfred said: "But now I can talk. . . ." He realized at once how naive that sounded. But the other person stood and came toward him. Only then did Wilfred see that they were the same height; he was maybe even a hair taller!

"You're right," the doctor said. "And will you promise—no, you shouldn't feel obliged to me, a stranger. . . . But don't you think that it's best for you to speak from now on?"

Those tears, those damned tears. He didn't want to have anything to do with them now. He had used them as a means. He had made himself pathetic with them—as he had made himself cheerful by smiling. But they came; they were there, something hot and disgusting.

"Ah, yes," the doctor said, "if only we could cry—laugh and cry—!"

He said it as though it were something he lacked personally, as a person says when he realizes his own insignificance but can do nothing about it. Wilfred thought it was best to say good-bye. He had heard that the miracle man was very busy. He stood up. The doctor came toward him quickly.

"I'd like to hear you play!" he said.

Wilfred looked around the office. But the doctor went over to some drapes facing the desk, opened a sliding door, and a little living room came into view—a small room overfurnished in golden plush with a bay window onto the street and a shiny, brown piano in one corner; it reminded him of the buffet at Andreas' place.

"What do you prefer to play?" the doctor said and quickly walked over to a pile of sheet music on a tiny table with tassels.

"Beethoven," Wilfred replied automatically.

"Really?"

"Why not?" This man's brilliant guessing made him feel slightly defiant. "You probably prefer Debussy?" he said.

The doctor smiled. "I asked you what *you* preferred."

"For the time being Bach," Wilfred said casually. And again he had to wonder whether a faint smile didn't flit across that worn, little face; there was something nut-like and worried about it; it was healthy and ravaged at the same time; that was what reminded him of Mrs. Frisaksen.

He played one of the little preludes, then he played a fugue. He didn't notice when it began—but it was the first time he had heard himself play for several months. It was a good, clear instrument, rather slight in tone, but so pure—like the man himself.

Then his thoughts turned back. It was like that time when the "orchestra" was at Uncle René's: he wasn't leading and he didn't have the feeling of being led, but what happened was that he merged with some power that dwelt within him without being his and that he was giving an outlet to.

As his thoughts returned to that time, the sensation ebbed away. He brought the fugue to a close and got to his feet, embarrassed.

"Excuse me," he said. "And thanks."

"I thank you!" the doctor said and sprang to his feet. "Why are you apologizing?"

He stood there, just as helpless. "I don't know. I should probably go now."

The man hesitated for a moment, then followed him into the office again and closed the sliding doors. So strange: it was almost like being at home there—in that room. . . . He wanted to head for the door.

"Just a moment," the doctor said. "You know we agreed about your—what shall we call it?—course of action—with regard to speaking. . . ." He smiled: "Shouldn't you ring up your uncle and tell him you're coming?"

For an instant Wilfred felt himself stiffen, as if his lips wanted to tighten; his mouth quivered.

"We don't know where he is," he said rather thickly.

The doctor replied at once: "We could try the hotel—but wait a moment . . ." He thought. "I'd guess that at this moment your uncle is sitting in the Café Mozart having a glass of beer."

Wilfred stiffened at once: "Mozart—why Mozart?"

"Because it's a well known restaurant where tourists think they can experience Vienna. And they may very well be right: I don't know."

"Excuse me, *Herr Professor,*" Wilfred said—he felt that his own seriousness was slightly comical, but he let it be. "Is this something that you've arranged?"

The famous doctor laughed, this time a frank, open laugh, completely convincing.

"You're a shrewd young man," he said lightly. "It would have been a pleasure to have crossed swords with you sometime in the future—so, we're agreed that we try the Café Mozart?" He picked up the receiver.

20

Already while they were eating soup, there were two versions of Uncle Martin's experience at the Café Mozart. One, Aunt Valborg's, was that he'd almost fainted when he heard Wilfred's voice on the telephone. The other, Uncle Martin's, after he'd thought it over, was that he had basically not been so surprised. From the very first, he'd been completely confident about that miracle doctor, and when the result had been achieved, he had accepted it with composure and at once disposed of his most pressing business; at the same time he sent a telegram to his sister. Uncle Martin told the truth, as much of it as you could expect. He had been sitting in the Café Mozart, and when the telephone call came his mind had been occupied with other things and a glass of Austrian beer. He had been very worried about Wilfred and felt most of all that he wanted to snatch him from the clutches of that suspicious fellow they really didn't know anything about.

His thoughts had wandered, meanwhile, and there had been

plenty to look at. So, when Wilfred's "Hello, Uncle" came through the telephone, he hadn't been surprised at all. He'd momentarily forgotten the whole business. Afterwards, yes, afterwards he'd made up for lost time and arranged a proper faint. So, to that extent, both versions were correct.

They talked about the Austrian doctor as little as possible. It was something that the family had been through—and now it was all over. Martin, of course, had to tell them how the doctor in Vienna had suggested keeping the boy for further treatment. He had used words like trauma and neurosis. Uncle Martin had waved him off very wittily by pointing out that the boy had recovered his speech and that they had "new roses" in Norway, too. Aunt Valborg did not look pleased when he said those kinds of things.

It was over now, and it wasn't their custom to talk about what was over and done with. They stuck to the present. It had also been an unpleasant time. Susanna Sagen had recovered remarkably quickly. She had given up her wool shawl, and there was nothing about her elegant carriage or the welcome smile with which she had welcomed her guests that made her seem like an old woman.

Wilfred unfortunately wasn't there. He was looking forward to seeing them all, but he wasn't there. He had flung himself at his books and music again with all possible eagerness. He was at the Conservatory and would join them later.

Wilfred wasn't at the Conservatory. He had paid a quick visit to a restaurant on Stortingsgate and was now sitting on a bench in Frogner Park discussing music with Miriam. He said: "But don't you see that he sort of makes curls, Mozart does, all of his stuff is curling and boasting just to please. Can't you hear him actually primping in front of his proud father all his life? He was in love too, but it wasn't very happy. He permitted himself that. With him, everything was as it should be."

Miriam smiled.

She was surprised by his passion, by the obvious unfairness of almost everything he said. It was as though he were determined to be wrong, no matter what he talked about. The smiling was her way of contradicting him, he knew it; he knew it all beforehand, this boy who was so different from her own people.

"And all this talk about grace, harmony . . . ," Wilfred lit his tenth cigarette there on the bench and glared at the dark spring evening and the mist on the ponds. "Look at those swans; we people put them everywhere there's water, what do we want them for? Harmony, movement, they're put there to please us, more than that: to create an illusion of happiness—of the swans themselves being happy. But just look how they behave. Oh yes, they glide with majestic calm, there's something sublime about them; that's merely because they swim that way and they have such long necks that they have to hold their heads up. They have to do something with those necks. But you can see yourself how they chase each other; they torment each other. They have their eyes in the wrong place, too, no doubt to make them see too narrowly and intensify their suspiciousness."

She had to laugh. But it wasn't a happy laugh. She felt a warmth for this boy that she would only half admit.

"I don't understand," she said, "you people seem to be so busy finding fault and exposing everything."

"You people?" he asked.

"Yes, you people. Remember that I've lived almost only among my own people. We Jews don't go around finding fault with each other in our family, not first and foremost. We quarrel a bit, but we don't go around coddling what we think is wrong."

He suddenly became serious. "Your father—I know that he's had a bad time. . . ."

"Father? Yes of course Father has, why do you always ask about my father? The others, my uncles, my mother's brothers—they've all had a terrible time. All the Jews in Galicia did, all the people who didn't own anything."

"And the people who owned things?"

"They had a bad time in their own way. But many of them bought their freedom. Many others helped, too. We were helped. We're well off now."

He sat savoring that word. She used expressions like well, good, and said that people were good. That, no doubt, was their ability to smooth over and cover up—he knew that better than most, demonstrating the opposite of what one knew.

"What do you mean by saying that you're well off?"

She looked at him in amazement. "What do I mean? Economically—yes, that for example. But we also have a good time together. My brother is a well-known lawyer, you know that."

"I have a friend who takes evening classes," he said.

She sat for a while looking over at the swans. He was right; they looked malicious. Their movements, which were always "queen-like" to her, they didn't always possess majestic calm.

"I know what you mean," she said. "You can't see the advantage of striving so hard for things: evening classes, the Conservatory. . . . But it makes people happier!" she said, glad to have found a solution.

"Are they glad about that—becoming happier?"

He had spoken quietly. He hadn't been asking her. She said: "Why do you make yourself somber inside?"

"I don't know why everyone has to be so happy," he said moodily.

"No—your Mozart wasn't happy!"

"You don't think so? I think he made a big thing out of it."

"Like you!" she said passionately. "That's just what you do. You go around licking your wounds. That's what you do."

Defiantly he said: "I know that. But it doesn't make me any happier."

"Yes, but you don't want to be. No self-pitying person gets happier—They'd be squandering too much then. That's exactly what *you* say."

"Miriam," he said, "I believe I love you."

She sat completely still then. She had a way of sitting still that was more like a state between two movements. There was a thin edging of snow left on the dusty, graveled area. It seemed to hypnotize her.

"I'll never marry anyone but a Jew," she said. "I'll never let myself love anyone but the man I marry."

He thought, and there was a sort of cool fire inside him the whole time: It's right for her to be good. People should be like that. But it hurt him.

"Menkowitz in the violin class is a Jew all right."

"Yes," he said. And a little later: "He's a clever teacher too."

Well, what about it? he thought, irritably. Isn't she going to come out with it? We've been good friends. I've walked her home. I love her, perhaps. The northern lights.

"I'm fond of you when the northern lights are in the sky," she said and laughed a little. "On the wall by Uranienborg. I'm fond of you then."

That damned instinct. Had he said "northern lights?" She'd been sitting there, guessing, like his mother, like Erna, like Kristine. Was it always so easy to follow his thoughts?

"When you wouldn't see me, when you were—sick . . . ," she said.

He didn't help her. He looked at the swans. They swam according to a system, circling around each other. When *he* wanted, she didn't want. When *she* maybe wanted, a third one came. Then the first went for the third one, while *she* swam away calmly. Majestically.

"I stood outside for three quarters of an hour, before I dared to ring the bell."

Well, so what. . . . He'd rung Andreas' bell once and then gone and hidden on the stairs to fool an old servant. That's what he was like, that's what those who weren't good were like.

"Do you think it's any fun not being able to speak? To sit there fighting with your larynx when people are watching you?"

"I could have gotten you to talk, maybe," she said. "I believed I could."

She'd thought that she could have gotten him to do it! She'd believed that had she? So she'd presented herself humbly, like a temple servant.

"And why you precisely?"

She made a little gesture of surrender. "The hour's over now," she said.

The lesson was over. Her violin lesson was over. She'd been a truant too, in order to be with him—she'd lied, she who never lied. She missed a chance to see her Menkowitz. . . .

"I ought to be touched," he said. "We'd better go. Besides, I have a family at home too. They've killed a fatted calf."

"That's more than you deserve," she said and stood up.

He stood up too and looked angrily at the swans: "It was more than that rascal in the Bible story deserved, too. But they did it. They always kill a fatted calf."

They parted at the little wooden gate by Kirkeveien. He watched her walk away quickly toward Munthesgate. The deep ruts were full of water that looked golden because of the reflection from the red sky.

"Your fiddle!" he shouted suddenly. He was holding her violin case in his hand. At that instant a huge beer wagon came along, drawn by two violent horses. He had to jump to avoid their hooves. He stood there, spattered with water from the ruts.

"Did you notice that it was golden?" he said and laughed toward her. She was terrified. She had seen the wagon coming. The driver turned around on his box, furious, and asked if he was blind.

"Dumb!" he replied, pointing to his mouth; he made a circle on his forehead with his index finger. She laughed. "You *are* crazy," she said. "What did you mean—the water was golden?"

"The same water," he said, pointing to his trousers, "this dirty water that Lilly will have the pleasure of removing, was golden in the sunset, didn't you notice?"

They looked up Kirkeveien together, right up to where the birch trees began in earnest by Majorstuen. The salmon pink sky turned the ruts into two long, golden stripes.

"As with the swans?" she said and laughed softly. "But let it be golden. Let the swans hold their heads high. Let that be what you remember about them. Then you can clean your pants yourself and remember that the water was golden!"

Her eyes were golden too. Two suns that were setting, or rising. He didn't know which.

"For me, I suppose, they're setting," he said and handed her the violin.

"What's setting?" She didn't understand. He went quickly to her and kissed both eyes. "These two," he said.

He stood there waving. She turned and waved. Then he stopped waving, but he stood there. She turned again far down the street. She waved. He waved back. He ran forward a few steps and stopped. Then he walked back to the park. He threw a rock at the swans. It didn't hit them. A guard appeared and asked him angrily if he was throwing stones at the swans!

"Yes," Wilfred said, "do you want my name?"

The guard stepped back, terrified. He stood under a tree watching him. He didn't leave that spot until the young man was walking towards the exit.

"That look," he muttered.

But when he reached Drammensveien, he also stood outside the house, not daring to go in. He saw them sitting there, as he had always seen them and always guessed what they were going to say before they said it. They would be sitting there now waiting for his entrance. Oh—they would be so composed and unaffected; they wouldn't stop what they were doing for a moment: they would go on talking and Aunt Valborg and Aunt Klara would be glued to their game of Go-Bang—until someone happened to notice him: "Well, I declare, here's Wilfred. How was the music?"

And all that just because they wished him well, too well. He could give them something in return—love. But it wouldn't be from him, not his love. He could give them love, give his mother a son's love—some son's love.

Could he also beg to see Aunt Klara's brooch? In all decency he couldn't; they couldn't expect him to go back to his childhood again. But he *could* ask! He might get it in his head to be able to do it: ask to see the one inside, and the one inside that. He could bring it off, with luck.

He could show his gratitude toward Uncle Martin. Not directly. This wasn't Vienna. They'd been through all that; it was over. When you had gone through something, it no longer existed.

But if you didn't get through it—if it wasn't over? If every instant you experienced was a world of its own without premises based on anything that had taken place before and without anything subsequent as their result? If each moment was an organism, the beginning and end of all things—could one kill it? That would be using violence. But what did they do with the things they were *through with*—did they use a sort of eraser on them? The magical eraser that removes everything, hocus-pocus. . . .

Miriam had stood like that at the door, not daring to ring. So he should have been moved? Yes, he was. If she didn't see that, so much the better. She had her fiddle player, her brother was a lawyer.

Besides, he hadn't said anything about marrying. You waited until you were twenty-five for that. By that time, a person like Miriam ought to have been a mother for ten years. She ought to become one now. He ought to have thought of that.

No, he didn't dare go in. That is, he dared. . . . He could go through the veranda, then he would spare them having to pretend to be surprised. If he went that way, he would come on them from behind. On the other hand, he might really overhear someone saying something and that would be painful.

He went around to the side of the house facing Frognerkilen. Oscarshall lay white and shadowless, like a piece of chalk under the dead sky. A train thundered past. He ran up the steps during the noise and remained standing there.

She sat down on that step one time, Kristine did. No doubt she'd been crying about a life that hadn't amounted to more. Or perhaps it was something to do with her candy, for all he knew. She was sitting inside there now. He hadn't seen her since that brief visit of hers, when she hadn't said good-bye. That business was forgotten. Those "affairs" changed. One got through them. Hocus-pocus. . . .

He stood and listened. Uncle René was speaking. There would

be nothing to eavesdrop on there. It was better to go and hear what he was saying. He went in quickly through the little side door and said loudly, while he was still up on the low podium: "Hello, Mother. Hello to everyone!" And he went to them by turn, enthusiastic, restrained, cheerful . . . according to how they wanted him to be. Aunt Kristine had a touch of gray in her hair. That was the first thing he saw. He didn't let her see him looking at it, that would have hurt her. So she no longer has anyone to dye it for, he thought.

They were happy to see him. Why shouldn't he acknowledge them and be happy in return? He didn't ask to see Aunt Klara's brooch, but he made just enough of a fuss over it for her to know that he hadn't forgotten. He played with it quickly and said: "Your brooch—you know I managed the grammar just fine in Vienna. . . ."

So it was said. No one would have mentioned it otherwise. Now they didn't have to keep silent, so that it felt like they were mentioning it all the time. It was always like that with things that weren't said at all. It was best to say it first, not last—just a mention. Everyone has to be cheerful, then it will be all right. As it was at Miriam's house. They were good. She played her fiddle for the poor.

He had made the rounds. He had to go in now and get himself something to eat. He grimaced violently to himself when he eventually escaped. His mother followed him in, and he hid his face in his hands so she couldn't see it. Now that he could speak, he had to be allowed to make these faces. They couldn't take away everything from him. One day he would stop making them. Then he could do something else. And finally, he could just do nothing. His father had done that.

But his mother couldn't sit there with him. He could have had an attack of honesty to please her: he hadn't been at the Conservatory, he had been on a bench in a park with a girl. She would have been so glad, so happy at such irresponsibility—and that they shared a secret. That was why he couldn't have her there. He had to hurry up and eat. He would like to give her pleasure, but not with the little that he had left for himself. It was so little, it disintegrated. He drank a glass of red wine, and then another. He thought: more could come of this, these things that he had to himself—they could acquire dimensions!

He drank a few glasses of wine with his grouse. He also had a glass of sherry with his cheese, and a small glass of port. Just before he stood up, he looked around quickly and drank a couple of glasses of what was in front of him. He did that sometimes. It made things so much easier. Yes, things could acquire dimensions! He didn't really know what, but there must be a lot. Once he had amused himself with robbery and petty assault; he'd played with boys who did wrong. A lot could come of that kind of thing. He folded his napkin and drank a glass of port like lightning and went in to the others.

But he stopped in the doorway. A name had been mentioned, the name of a minister. It could have been a coincidence, but it reminded him of confirmation. He stood there, and it was too late to not have heard it. Stubb, that was the minister's name, or something like that. They were all crazy about him; they had their children confirmed at the Garrison Church just because Rev. Stubb was there. He was unique, so human, almost as if he wasn't a minister at all. That was the highest rank a clergyman could attain. They had spoken his name. Wilfred said: "He might as well baptize me at the same time!"

There was a deathly silence. Then Kristine laughed, a little bark of a laugh, and so did Uncle René, noiselessly. Then his mother laughed, and Aunt Valborg, too. Aunt Klara pretended to blow her nose.

"Something made me think about this business of confirmation," he said with abandon and went towards them. "Mother's not too Christian. It must have been Uncle Martin—dear Uncle, I have so much to thank you for. . . ."

It worked. So it *was* confirmation they'd been talking about. They weren't at all interested in that, not one of them. Actually it was Uncle Martin who had said that it was practical to have a baptismal certificate for when you wanted a passport—and in general. . . .

It worked. Was it possible to speak out about something and

get things to come out all right, instead of going around and sliding over and forgetting?

It seemed to be working. If you were just bold enough. If you'd just had a glass or two. But they didn't know that.

It worked. Thoughts were whirling in his head, but not in confusion, in real order. Perhaps that was what Miriam's family did: spoke out? It couldn't be true. It must be a nonrecurring phenomenon.

Uncle Martin said: "I almost think the boy's right, Susie—if you aren't so concerned about this—affirmation—?"

His mother laughed. Nothing was important to her, nothing was important if you were happy. Everything had seemed so unstable in her world. Now it was beginning to look like itself again. It wasn't very important to her. The matter was arranged, so to speak. He was as good as baptized.

He played for them. At their request. When Uncle René suggested Mozart, he played Mozart too. It didn't go very well, but Uncle René had wanted it. He thanked him once more for the reproductions. They could be taken out and hung up.

Uncle René looked horrified.

But he wasn't going to do that. You shouldn't see everything all the time.

Uncle René sighed with relief.

Uncle Martin had his whisky. Wilfred raised an imaginary glass to him across the table, thanked him for the last time, and winked. So it had been said again, one time too many really. He felt that he was beginning to overdo it. He wanted to overdo it. When Aunt Klara asked about school, he said that it was going well, disturbingly well, in fact there must be something wrong with the school. They laughed. They liked him to be cheerful. They had a share in it. It was their profit. It was the least he could do for them—to overdo it.

"The fact is that I'm quite gifted," he said. "We're a gifted family. Look at Uncle Martin's twins; they've almost become English."

Yes, he'd overdone it now. They weren't quite so placid anymore. At least two aunts had exchanged glances. He went into the dining room and drank a couple of glasses of what was there. It suited him just fine that things were like the way they were. He went back and sat quietly and made himself agreeable. Wasn't this a family gathering—then the least they could do for each other was to be cheerful, cheerful and respectable in a suitable order. And lay it on thick.

Yes, he would make everything good again, make it better and better. You couldn't overdo it, when you wanted to make everything all right. His decency became so enormous that it began to get the upper hand; his silence and reticence created an element of expectation around him. Wasn't this a family gathering, a reunion of all the people who had come through it? They had had a lot to go through—all of them perhaps. Each one of them had his little thing. He sat down by them in turn and looked at them. He distracted his aunts from their board game. He saw every move coming and thought it all out for them, so that they had a bewildered sense of moving their little pieces according to someone else's will. He stared at Uncle Martin's whisky glass and rushed over with the soda siphon. That made Uncle Martin nervous and he emptied a whole glass absentmindedly. He showed Uncle René a trick with two rings and a silk handkerchief. He did it three times; he'd learned it at school. Mother and Kristine were talking together quietly, they were speaking softly and earnestly about nothing, as people do when they want to mislead. He looked like he was listening to them and that made them stop. He stared at Kristine, undressed her in an instant with his eyes. He fetched Appolinaris for the ladies—totally unnecessary to bother Lilly for such a trifle. He made two trips for the bottles and each time had a little glass of something in the dining room as he passed by. He had forgotten the tumblers and went to get them. He had a little glassful then, and another. He had forgotten Aunt Klara and made another trip. . . .

His mother said, "Couldn't you sit down for a while now? You're making me nervous."

He sat down. He sat down so demonstratively, studying Aunt Klara's tiny solitaire cards, that there was almost a roar of silence around him. Yes, only good could be done here, so much good that there wouldn't be a sound out of sheer goodness. Wasn't he the family's youngest scion, who could serve as an example, even for his successful cousins who had made themselves English? Wasn't he an expert in the sport of pleasing—he would please them to death now. He sauntered out quietly and had a couple of glasses; no one was going to say that he fidgeted around and made people nervous. On the contrary, there was a magnetic calm about all his movements. He noticed his mother looking at him—discreetly, engaged in that everlasting conversation about nothing and nothing. Her gaze clung to him; she was hypnotized by the slowness with which he moved, at her request. He sat like a wall and let the many little glassfuls in him rise, as though they were going up tiny steps toward greater and greater heights.

The telephone rang in the hall. He didn't jump up; he got up slowly, deprecatingly—and so that no one would be bothered, he closed the door behind him. A deathly silence fell over the living room. He heard the silence behind him as he walked to the telephone and picked up the receiver.

"The boy's drunk," Uncle Martin said.

Mrs. Sagen got up and brought cigars for the men. "Nonsense," she said. "Does anyone feel like a game of croquet in the garden?"

"If we can see the balls," Aunt Charlotte said, agreeably. Wilfred was taking a long time on the telephone. They caught themselves listening. Kristine said: "We could put on coats. . . ."

She went toward the door but stopped. She didn't want to meet him alone there; besides, he was talking on the telephone. It was as though they were hypnotized by that telephone conversation, and by his absence. When he came in again, it was like a release. He fetched things for the ladies at once when he heard what it was for. They were going to play croquet, a peaceful game, a guarantee of harmony. He fetched everything he could find in the cloakroom and piled it up, capes and wraps; he helped them in every way. "But good God," Aunt Charlotte said, "we're not going to the North Pole!" His mother asked: "Who called?"

"Andreas," he said, "he'd forgotten his lessons again." Uncle Martin said: "Andreas—isn't he your friend with the glasses; he looks a little dumb?"

The ladies were fully outfitted now and filed out onto the veranda and down to the lawn for croquet, like a line of people being set free. Wilfred politely handed out mallets and then went indoors again. All the joy had gone out of him.

"Andreas is no fool," he said coldly.

Uncle Martin was taken aback: "I thought he was the one who—you said so yourself. . . ."

Wilfred felt the stirrings of temper: "Andreas is a very capable boy."

"Yes, yes," Uncle Martin said.

"Very capable," Wilfred repeated. "He's going to night school. He'll be somebody."

Uncle Martin carefully cut the tip off his cigar.

"His father's not well off," Wilfred said.

Uncle Martin lit it and blew out smoke.

"And his mother's ill!"

In order to put an end to it, Uncle Martin said: "How distressing. Really sad."

"And it's quite hopeless," Wilfred went on stubbornly. "He has two brothers, one stuffs birds—he uses arsenic."

Uncle Martin twirled his glass dejectedly. Something made him think about that letter from Wilfred's teacher his sister had shown him once. There was something about the ink. . . .

"Maybe you could hand me that ashtray," he said.

"He sells them to the museum—the birds. And I believe the father drinks."

It had never occurred to him that Andreas' father drank. All the joy had gone out of him. He wasn't Lucky Lillelord anymore. It had been the principal of his school on the telephone, he'd wanted to speak with his mother. He had said she was out. There had been some minor irregularities at school lately. He had been expecting a telephone call or a letter. He'd never get away from these petty things. . . .

"Not well off," he repeated stubbornly, "very badly off."

"Listen, my boy," Uncle Martin said quietly, "you must never get drunk at a family gathering."

Wilfred gaped at him.

"One can drink a little and one can attend family gatherings, but not at the same time. . . ."

Uncle René approached on his ceaseless rounds of inspecting things: "Crazy place for it!" he said about the icon over the entrance to the oriental salon.

The little things. They twisted themselves around you. That was just about what he'd wanted to tell the doctor in Vienna . . . about all the things that came again and again and tied themselves around him, like a net.

"Thanks for the warning," he said to Uncle Martin, when Uncle René had moved on again.

"That's all right," Uncle Martin said congenially. "You've started a bit early, as in everything, as far as I can see. . . ."

Wilfred looked at him lethargically. Uncle Martin was a man of the world; he knew what was what; he was moderately liberal-minded. He had two sons, but he escaped having to say difficult things to them. He was the man who knew about things and freed himself from them.

"And what if I have?" Wilfred said defiantly. Uncle Martin shrugged. Uncle René came over and suggested a walk before supper— "We three gentlemen?" Uncle Martin agreed. He wasn't one to prolong anything unpleasant. Mother's brother, Wilfred thought. He said: "Perhaps I had better go upstairs and lie down for a while."

He stuck his fingers down his throat and took two aspirin. Uncle Martin was right. One should not get drunk at a family gathering. One should not get drunk at all. That business at school—three of them had gone to the shop room and drunk during a break. Wilfred had brought the stuff. He had done it in all innocence, but one of the others had become rebellious during the religion lesson and said that Jesus was a socialist.

Principals like that one—why couldn't they maintain discipline in their schools? Why did they have to tell the students' parents? He was too old for this, too adult. He'd go to the principal in the morning and tell him a thing or two and put an end to it.

He lay down for a while. Yes, put an end to all these odds and ends. An end—that was the right word for it. Either to them—or to yourself. You could also leave this world, if that was what you had to do. If you didn't want to put an end to the little things. Or if there were more and more of them, and they got slightly bigger and wouldn't end.

He glanced quickly at the portrait of his father before he fell asleep. . . . One could put an end to it that way.

21

Ants were crawling over him; he was naked. There were evergreen needles in his wounds.

He rolled over onto his knees slowly and tried to crawl deeper into the forest. But his head was just broken glass. He lay down again and let it come. Ghosts with unknown shapes rode through his brain like heavy knights, leaving craters of light.

These wounds. . . . Cautiously touching with his fingertips, he felt along one arm, from the elbow down. His fingers drew back in horror at what someone else's hands felt. One hand felt around by his eyes. They were like someone else's eyes, or hands. Small, dark blue gusts of recollection came with his groans, leaving islands of open fire. *This* mustn't be true. . . . Or *that*. . . . Memory curled in blinding thrusts, like an angry sea. Then everything was mercilessly swept away, until something popped up again and he caught hold of one or two gentler memories.

Kypare! He had tried to pretend that he was Swedish somewhere. He had called *kypare,* or whatever the word for waiter was, and men in black had come running. That must be. . . . That must have been—where?

He had been talking about his father. Right! About his strict father, of all things—oh, if only they knew how strict he was. When he took off his shirt cuffs and put them on the desk and got his rattan cane from behind the mirror. . . . He had been thrown out—no, wait, he had been asked to leave. A manager with red hair, parted in the middle—but that wasn't there. . . . He prayed to God for gentle sleep without end and it came, but not gently—it came with flashes of red lightning, full of soundless visions: and not without end, it was interrupted by white seconds of a clarity that glowed with limitless pain.

For a moment he sat up and looked in surprise at the spruce trees around him, then a feeling of faintness passed through him, broken by evil shudders.

One of those little refreshment places with spotted tablecloths and waiters as white as potato shoots, with pimply skin—that was where he had called for the *kypare* in Swedish. There were several of them: cafés full of silent men with little bottles, and red-cheeked, dead-tired fat men behind large glasses in the booths. There had been several of them, these cafés like long caves, leading to houses inhabited by fathers. He had watched them with curiosity, greedy for discoveries. He had behaved well, drunk a few small glasses and kept quiet. Once he had a desire to shout a bit. . . . Where had that been? When? Yes, yes—Mother was in the country, he was in town; he'd come in with the boat, was going back, that was—well, perhaps yesterday, though it didn't sound probable.

The Masonic Lodge. That was it! He had investigated the secrets of fathers brooding behind glasses in the little refreshment places and had been very well behaved. Then he had gone to that restaurant at the Masonic Lodge. He was the well-dressed young man there. He ate things in the right order and drank an expensive white Bordeaux. He had spoken with a French accent and conferred with the wine waiter. He had taken great pleasure in his food and drink.

It was really only when he was drinking his coffee that things had begun to go wrong. The tables had filled with well-dressed people; he was well-dressed too and all was well; he ordered brandy.

The manager had come. He had bent over the table so you could see the straight part in his hair; he'd bent down discreetly and asked the young gentleman's age.

Age? Twenty-one. He was often taken for nineteen, so he could easily add a little. —Did he have anything to prove that? —He was sorry, but they had their regulations. —Some paper? What sort of paper? Well, a certificate. Were people supposed to carry certificates? Well, if not. . . . What sort of certificate, a certificate of baptism? Sorry—he was a Moslem, perhaps they didn't serve Moslems? It was his Moslem sabbath, had the manager heard of that? Then he turned towards Mecca and drank his brandy. . . . But he hadn't been thrown out. The man with the part in the middle had listened indulgently to his nonsense and then asked him to pay his bill. Then he'd stood by the exit commandingly and motioned with his eyes. He had left the restaurant stiffly, in an orderly manner, passing between tables occupied by people who smiled slightly and perhaps turned to watch.

Afterwards. Afterwards there was a full stop. A cellar in Vaterland? A cellar full of bogeymen, a cellar with beer. A walk along the waterfront. That was it! Guessing boats' names! He had walked along, crying quietly and seen the *King Ring*. Then he'd caught sight of the *Kongshavn* with her elegantly curved bow. He had gone aboard. Yes, yes—that was where he'd landed. The Kongshavn Baths Restaurant-Varietié. That's where it had begun.

He had a vague recollection of the little round tables under the crowns of the trees, and the stage with the eager performers, who stopped their song or dance for a moment or two while the train thundered past, yes, by God, roared right through the park between the leafy auditorium and the stage, while the singers stood with their mouths open, and the two violinists pointed their bows like spears, marking time until the last car had passed and everything could start up again where it had been before.

That was it—the strings of electric lights between the trees had gotten much more powerful as dusk fell, and above them was the dark velvet of the August night, with stars between the leaves. Oh, the degradation—he remembered it all now; he clung to this memory because it was good.

All the rest wasn't good. Two fellows had come. . . .

Yes, two fellows had come. He'd noticed them at once. They didn't sit together but at separate tables where there were other people sitting too. But they were together all the same. He knew that from the very first. He was still sitting alone. But as darkness fell, all the tables were filled. Those two fellows, first one came over—a young man his own age, his exaggerated age—eighteen, nineteen, he had a cap with a visor; he pushed it up a little, sat down, drank beer. After a while the other one came, he was older, dark—he had a straw hat with a blue band.

They had asked if he was beginning something. He didn't catch on at first, then the dark one pointed to his glass, he was drinking wine. Wilfred was also drinking dark wine. Then he'd understood: they wanted him to buy them drinks. They grinned at each other, these two guys, when they heard him say it, and the one with the cap stuck his thumb in the air and ordered a bottle. It wasn't a good wine, and he let them drink most of it, but they were friendly and wanted him to drink with them.

On the stage Isa Dahl was singing about lilacs, interrupted by the train from Bekkelaget; it was all very pleasant.

They were likable fellows. A little unfamiliar at first, but pleasant enough after a while. He gladly bought them a second bottle. They drank and had a nice time. He let them drink most of it; he had had enough.

But they were really likable. They wanted him to join in. Some acrobats from Malaya appeared on the stage; they formed a pyramid. The train came. They had another bottle; they talked about things—the one with the cap—he didn't really remember—they got him to talk about himself, and he told them about his strict father who took off his shirt cuffs before he beat him. They leaned over the table toward him.

Did he hit hard?

Hard? Wilfred demonstrated just one of his swings; the bottle fell on the ground, and they knocked the table over trying to save it. It was all very pleasant then.

Have you heard about my father?

Yes, yes. You've told us about your father. He beat you.

Have I told you about his revolver? He carried a whip.

Did he carry a whip?

Yes. He traveled to lots of countries. He rode. He had sixteen horses.

Jeez! The two guys looked at each other uncertainly. What did he want with them?

Sixteen horses. And ten wives.

Ten wives? They were winking now.

He had ten wives. He was actually a Moslem.

They nodded. A Turk?

Moslem. That's not the same as a Turk. He had a palace in Bengal and commanded an army.

Palace? Did he have a palace?

In Bengal. And a house in Hurum. His favorite wife's name was Annasus.

Annasus. Annasus. The two fellows savored the name. The dark one knew a girl named Lispet. He could easily get her to join them, if they wanted. The one with the cap wanted it. Wilfred did too.

Lispet must have been nearby. She had a sore by the corner of her mouth and deformed fingernails. She asked the dark one to get a bottle of wine. The dark one looked at Wilfred and urged him to do it. Wilfred looked at the fellow wearing the cap. He in turn looked at Wilfred, but he did more than urge with his eyes. Lispet got her wine.

Oh, he remembered a lot now. He had kept his end up very well. He drank in little sips. Then, all at once, the sips weren't so little. He wasn't keeping up so well anymore. The roof of leaves with the velvet and stars above it, fire-eaters on stage, the train tearing through, whistling by Bekkelaget. Lispet wanting to hear about his father. She had one pretty tooth in front and one not quite so pretty. She steered his hand towards her hip under the table. He sat there, his belly dancing, and bought them herring sandwiches. A caterpillar fell from a tree onto the food. Lispet removed it from the onion with all the elegance of a woman of the world. After that—?

Things had developed. He had called her his little Lucy; he'd praised with folk songs which he had recited. Dirty smut, she'd called it and sucked at her tooth.

Something had developed. He wanted to go.

But the gravelled garden seemed to be closed then. The stage was dark, the people must have left. There was the girl, Lispet or Lisbeth, she was somewhere. He'd wanted to go.

But they were there. The one with the cap, the dark one with the blue hatband. They and others—they were there. They were lurking by the exits. He'd wanted to go. But he tumbled into someone every time he moved.

Yes—that's how it was. The cap, the one with the cap. He'd asked him to sit down. Wilfred said that he would. They'd talked together, told each other things.

The pictures that were pleasant to remember began to give way to the ones that brought pain. One of them had said something about a creep, a freeloader. He'd told a story about Rodeløkka. He had known someone once who was a creep like that, a sly devil who slipped up to Rodeløkka now and then to get the boys there to do bad things. A guy just like Wilfred, he resembled him, but he was much shorter, a twerp from the west side of town. Once he had killed an old Jew. . . .

Killed—?

Killed. A Jew-hater. Upper-class creep . . . if he just had him there! German spy probably. Just a kid. Well, he knew that the Germans were speculating about war, didn't he. That Kaiser Wilhelm was contemplating war? The capitalists were pro-German, didn't he know that? He was a socialist. The one with the cap. Lisbeth wasn't there then. The dark one listened threateningly.

Killed? Killed?

Killed. A poor old Jew who had a cigar and tobacco shop. He hadn't died at once. Not right away. Later.

Killed?

The shock of it. Shock or something like it. Poor old Jew from Galicia or somewhere. The Turks had kicked him out. Or the Russians, he didn't know which. There'd been a big funeral. His niece, yeh, she must have been the daughter of the old guy's brother who was a Jew too—had done a lot for him, poor guy. She still came up there and played her fiddle for them, at the hall at Dærnenga. God's angel from Jew-land, Miriam, that was her name. . . . That's what it was like in Rodeløkka. . . .

But that was while things were still pleasant. While the one with the cap was talking; he'd drunk a lot. Sat there telling a story in an undertone. The dark one listened. Lispet! he'd said into the leaves. Lisbeth had appeared again with the sore by the corner of her mouth. She smelled of onions. He'd looked for the caterpillar, to see if it was coming out of her mouth.

No, no, no, no, no.

Lispet, he'd said. The dark one—he could say things without moving his mouth. Lisbeth had come out of the foliage. He wanted to go. He had gotten up. The stage was dark. Empty. He had spent a lot of money.

He wanted to go, but they were there. There was no one else on the coarse gravel under the trees, but they were there—by the exit. They were at the other exits too. The electric bulbs in the branches had been turned off. They were there, the dark one was. First by one exit, then by the other. The one with the cap talked and talked. A creep, just like him, but not so tall. Killed the poor old Jew. . . .

The dark one was there, at both exits. Lispet, he said out of the corner of his mouth, almost as if he were spitting.

And Lispet was there, she popped out of the leaves, everywhere.

He and Lispet were friends, weren't they? Lispet was willing.

Lisbeth stood there with her red arms, squeezing his hand. His belly was alive; he was dead everywhere else, but alive there.

He and Lispet could go to the Ekeberg Forest. . . .

He and Lisbeth—up a steep, dusty road and then onto paths. They were alone then. Or were they? Lisbeth hung on his arm. Heavy and slightly drunk, she slobbered, belched a little, it smelled of herring, they climbed. Yes, yes, now he remembered: get dirty, sink down really low. Down, down into deep pits. There was a rustling in the trees. The others? Had probably gone home. The fellow with the cap? Must have gone off somewhere. The dark one with the straw hat? Oh, *him*—! . . . Lisbeth was willing. Lisbeth smelled of onions. She knew about a place up in the woods. A little farther up. She played with him here and there. Touched him.

Killed? Killed—! What had he been saying, the one with the cap?

Oh, him, nothing. He was crazy. A socialist or something. She knew about a place up in the woods.

Who was this Jew he had talked about? Tobacco shop—?

He was weird. Nothing to bother about, not him, not for Wilfred to worry about. *He* was a gentleman. She, Lispet, only liked fine gentlemen; she couldn't stand such common people. They trudged upwards in the darkness. The path was slippery because of the dust.

He'd said something about a funeral—someone had played—?

Just some sort of demonstration. A Jewish girl who came and was charitable. She knew a place up in the woods. She touched him.

But there were eyes in the trees. Bushes with evil spirits behind them.

She was strong when he had tried to run away. She was as strong as a man when he tried to tear free. Footsteps in among the trees. They popped out. The one with the straw hat. They appeared on several sides. Faces like ovals in the night. Stars above—a great sighing. And then—a rain of sparks in the night. . . .

Ants were crawling over him. That's what had woken him. The wound under his eye was intensely painful, some needles had gotten into it. He heard church bells.

Sunday. It had been Saturday. He should have taken the 6:30 boat back. He had made the round of little cafés. He tried to raise himself up on his arm, but it gave under him. He lay on his back and held his arm up. There was bright sunshine now. The arm felt like it was broken. It was black and brown with blood from the wrist up.

His wristwatch—the watch from Berlin, the new Swiss watch to wear on your wrist. He lifted his painful arm with the one that was all right. It was gone. His body ached. He was naked. He was lying on a root. He heard children laughing; he turned painfully. They were in the trees—a little girl in a blue apron and three boys. One of them had a slingshot. He hit him. They laughed. He hit him again. Wilfred tried to get up, but he sank back down again. A shriek.

Stark naked!

Naked! P'lice!

Church bells all the time. It must be at least half past nine. He was lying naked on Ekebergsåsen at half past nine on a Sunday morning. The pieces of the mosaic fell painfully into place. Lisbeth—had she—? He looked down at himself. Couldn't remember. That sore by the corner of her mouth. Dr. Strønen on Youngsgate, the boys at school had talked about him. They read an advertisement for a skin specialist as pornography. They revelled in it. Dr. Strønen of Youngsgate. Open on Sunday. Used a hypodermic needle. Strønen the cobbler they called him.

Youngsgate? He was naked. Ants were crawling over his thighs. He picked needles out of the wound under his eye.

Police! the girl was screaming hysterically behind the trees. A man's voice. People everywhere. Eyes everywhere in the bushes.

He rolled over on his side and got up. The bushes were alive now, laughter behind the trees, sly boy's laughter, and one man's voice. —Police. The girl wailing. P'lice! P'lice!

He got to his feet, ran into the woods and through to the other side. He saw people on a road, out for a walk. He saw the fjord, Sunday blue, little boats floating deep in the blue. He ran the other way. Rustling in the bushes. He ran.

He ran, wailing. He held his broken arm with the other one.

A hammer was banging and banging under his eye. He was running for his life, he came to a clearing. There were tents there, a rifle range. . . . He ran in behind a tent flap, but he was met with a shriek. A swarthy woman was standing there, washing herself. He ran out, back out into the open, hid behind the tent by the rifle range. But there were people behind him, behind the trees. A guard quickly came out of the woods, a cord around his cap, a stick in his hand.

Shouts of P'lice! were coming from everywhere. The girl was screaming in the bushes farther down. Bushes and trees everywhere. The guard was approaching.

He ran from the tent across to the open space to the merry-go-round; he dove behind a green cow with a saddle; he hid behind the cow. The guard was coming. Police! someone shouted. P'lice! P'lice! Laughter and screaming behind the bushes everywhere.

The guard was coming closer again. He kept under cover and pulled the cow with him with his good arm. The cow came; the merry-go-round moved with him; it began to play: *Ach du lieber Augustin, Augustin.* He pulled the cow with him more and more quickly; he was still hidden by it. The guard jumped onto the merry-go-round and came towards him, moving from animal to animal. Now he was swinging around the white horse with wings. He let go of the cow and ran.

He ran from the fairgrounds down through the woods, through the barberry bushes, out onto a path. It was deserted. The church bells were ringing. He ran down the path and caught sight of the fjord, blue and twinkling through the pine trees. It hammered and hammered under his eye and everywhere. One arm dangled helplessly, but it no longer hurt.

P'lice! He heard the shouts far away, behind him and to the side. He stumbled over a root on the path and fell on his dead arm. Stabs of pain like lightning all over his body. They were after him now; he was in a closed world, a world he didn't control.

Was this his world?

Thoughts tumbled through his mind as he ran. They were

after him everywhere. Ahead of him were the slopes that led down to the fjord. He saw the roof of the black and brown tar refinery between Grønnlien and Kongshavn. He rushed down the slope. But there were people there, sitting on the benches and strolling.

Then a lady turned and screamed, a man turned, they were all turning around. The shouts were getting closer now, from behind and the side. He had stopped, frightened. He ran on again downhill, but to the other side, towards the yacht harbor at Grønnlien. He saw the red buoys in Bjørvika. He saw them from above; he had seen them once before—from above. He ran in that direction, slipped on the slope, rolled over, got up again, ran. A stretch of iron fence ahead of him, he swung himself over it on his one arm and fell, fell, and fell. . . .

It was a slope with some sparse grass. The sea below, behind him a wall with a hole in it. He crept into this cave; there were newspapers lying there; someone had been spending the night there, an empty bottle of Siemen's Punch with a paper cork; he crawled farther on his knees and one good arm. His back hurt from the fall. He couldn't hear any shouting behind him.

He lay on his stomach and groaned; he bit at a stone that was sticking up. Then a feeling of greatness came into him, a rush of power. Pain replaced his body and let it sail off toward the clouds; the pain remained and *was* him. Greenish visions rose and fell in him. He had lain in a cave once; he remembered that. He had been in a glass egg. The egg was broken open! It was no longer snowing inside. Sunshine snowed over everything; he was a singing star in boundless space; a buzzing, singing star in space. There were no voices around him now. Just the song of airless space against his skin that bled till it was blue.

Mrs. Frisaksen! He met her whizzing by; he was an incorporeal roar in space, going toward her. She was in her boat floating in the golden sun, and there was beauty around her; there were rays around the boat, a bright halo of sanctification. And the sun darkened around her wrinkled face, which was turned toward a certain land. He didn't see the land, but her face became fresh and smooth in the reflections of its coast with scattered skerries and with sunlight dripping onto the blue sea. Now she was pulling up a whiting. There was a flash of silver. There was a supernatural grace about the hand holding the fish.

A crazy place to put that icon.

One shouldn't get drunk at a family gathering. . . .

A grace that raised its light over everything and was gone.

"Mrs. Frisaksen!" he groaned, his lips mute. They were swollen from the beating; there was blood in his mouth. He couldn't speak. He was mute.

All the things the little Mozart had done for them, his father's pride and the apple of his eye. His little fingers had run like frightened animals over the keys. The applause of the court trickled like silver from the room.

A crazy place for it. . . .

A little girl stuck her head into the cave, and the opening got dark. Light came slanting in along her cheeks. She resembled Erna when she was small. Erna with the silk cord. Erna with her unused affection and plates of health food.

A scream. A shout. Police! Police!

Voices of angry men: "The water. He must be down by the water. . . ."

The egg was broken. It was snowing dark sunshine inside him. Miriam—she went and played for the poor; she was good. A tobacconist had died of shock. I'm a socialist, let me tell you. New times—change, his mother said. Uncle Martin: War. . . .

They were outside his cave now; they couldn't find the opening; they walked around searching. An arm. A long pole was thrust in. A boat hook to use on a wild animal. It groped in the dark, scraped against the wall of his cave. "No—." The boat hook vanished. A spider let itself down silently from the ceiling, spun a thread and then another, climbed like lightning up to the top and dropped again—a thread, a web.

The net. Soon it would be too late. He could still break through it. The spider climbed up, dropped down. It was taking shape before his eyes—a net over the opening. He crawled on his knees and one hand toward the opening. There were voices out there, voices screaming above and below. The spider was industrious. It had a cross on its back and evil eyes. It paused on its web and looked at him. They looked at each other; one was spinning the web and the other wanted to get out.

He half got up, bumped his head on the stone ceiling, felt faint, and sank to his knees again. The spider was industrious. It was spinning more quickly now. It was in a hurry.

There wasn't much time. He half got up and went forward; the web bent and broke; it felt sticky against his cheeks. He had the water below him. The light blinded him. The voices became a single shout now. They could see him; he was there, by the wall. "He's bleeding!"

He was bleeding from his eye, from his hand, from all the wounds he'd received. He ran. They were in a group now, a body of people that became one person.

He swung himself over the fence by the railway and lay on the cool rails. If a train came now—he wouldn't get up; it would surely be a relief to feel the first pressure of the wheels.

No train came. A wonderful weariness came over him—like lilacs in his blood; a tiredness that had to last his whole life through. No train came. His pursuers had been stopped by the fence. The roads—there were so many roads in the world; they forked; they were full of possibilities. But what then? You didn't choose your road; he had thought that, that he had chosen roads that led to a realm of possibilities. But you didn't really choose. A road came along—you were there. He lay bleeding to death on his road which was barred. He had made a wrong choice.

"Quick. The boat. . . ."

They were behind him and on the sides. He wriggled over the fence on the lower side of the railway line. They were beginning to climb over the fence behind him. There were people lower down. He veered to the right, ran horizontally, flung himself down a slope with bushes sticking up out of the dust. Right down by the water there was a group of men in their Sunday clothes, ready to catch him.

He swung off to the right again, toward the yacht harbor, toward the sewer that formed a green and black river running out into the blue. There was no one there. He ran through the voices. There was blood on everything now—blood in his mouth, he gurgled and fell, got up, ran diagonally above the yacht harbor and down the last slope. Then he jumped. Greasy slime from the sewer filled his mouth. "Father!" he gurgled.

There was dead silence on land. People were ready to run along the shore, but they stopped. A nimble man with a club foot had cast off a boat with an excessive push. Gulls rested on the heavy air that was saturated with the ringing of bells.

His head came up, covered with slime. He swam, one arm trailing behind. The shouts on land became a single shout. A bristling forest of arms pointing. Two boats appeared and formed a barrier.

"There!" the roar swelled from the crowd on the slope. The men in the boats rowed steadily. One had a dark blue work shirt and a moustache. His little eyes peered vigilantly at the glistening head in the stream of sewage.

"There!" the crowd roared.

The man in the blue shirt raised his arm to reassure him. Then he leaned out so far that the boat overturned.

"We've got him now," he said.